NEW CALIFORNIA

Other CV-2 Books by Raymund Eich

Stone Chalmers
The Progress of Mankind
The Greater Glory of God
To All High Emprise Consecrated

The Confederated Worlds
Take the Shilling
Operation Iago
A Bodyguard of Lies

Novels
The Blank Slate

Short Novels
The ALECS Quartet
A Mighty Fortress

Collections
The First Voyages: The Complete Science Fiction Stories
1998-2012
Stage Separations: The Complete Science Fiction Stories
2013-2018

NEW CALIFORNIA

Raymund Eich

CV-2 Books • Houston

NEW CALIFORNIA © 2012 Raymund Eich

Cover art: ID 132866631 © 3000ad | Dreamstime.com
Cover design, book design, and aircraft carrier logo are copyrights, trademarks, or trade dress of CV-2 Books.

Third CV-2 Books trade paperback edition: June 2019

10 9 8 7 6 5 4 3

To Liz
Every time I build a castle in the air,
you remind me to put a foundation under it.

New California Date 92:65
14 November 2093

On a breezy early evening near to shore on the Western Sea, when K-Nought's last rays from below the horizon banded thin clouds orange, red, and purple, and the night's first lights of the coastal suburbs of San Lazaro glittered on the mesas to the east, when waves quietly splashed the yacht's hull and the colony's elite partied at the bow and below deck, while both lumpy, bone-white moons looked down, the governor of New California committed suicide for the third time.

The party had started with an airmobile ride, like most others Desmond Park had attended in his forty Earth-years on the planet. In the garage of his mansion at the edge of Fremont Mesa, he strapped into his sportster and gave it coordinates encrypted by Governor Watkins' security system to foil party-crashers. The sportster launched and banked over the pedestrian avenues of San Lazaro's lowland districts, then headed northwest. The airmobile cast a jittering shadow on hills blue-green with chaparral. From his line of flight, Desmond guessed his destination, and his sportster confirmed it when it descended a few minutes later.

From above, the town of Clearwater Beach showed Spanish tile roofs around the tricolumnar basalt bulk of a Buddhist Kabbalah meditation center. A T-shaped marina jutted into the sea at the northern end of the black strand that gave the town its name. Desmond's airmobile pivoted its jets and joined a dozen others on a parking lot twenty yards from a pale blue pavilion erected in the sand near the marina.

The sea breeze ruffled Desmond's black hair and untucked linen shirt, and the obsidian sand slumped under his topsiders between the parking lot and the pavilion. Security was subtle, but thicker than usual. Miniature robots on oversized tires rolled across the sand and swung cameras and microphones toward him. The robot bartenders under the pavilion intently watched the people around them.

In the cool shade mingled the usual crowd, many of them, like Desmond, first colonists. The tang of Acapulco gold, and a muscular fellow's brag about the work just done to him at the rejuvenation clinic, clogged the air. Desmond nodded a few greetings, then opened a mindlink channel to the robots to order a drink.

When he stepped back from the bar, his vodka tonic tart with fresh lime, Gov. Cameron Watkins opened wide arms. "Nihao, esé! Thanks for coming!" He chest-bumped Desmond and thumped his right palm on the back of Desmond's shoulder.

Desmond returned the bro-hug. "Nihao. Thanks for the invitation, Cam." The governor insisted those from the first ship use the nickname. Desmond opened his mouth to utter some small talk, what's new or how are you today, but he hesitated, suddenly conscious that twice in the past local year the governor had been stealthily rushed to the clinic on Fremont Mesa for acute rejuvenation with partial neural reconstruction. Small talk might sound forced, avoiding the elephant under the pavilion, but so too might his hesitation.

Cam's eyes narrowed for a moment, and Desmond hurriedly said, "Today's immigration ceremony went well."

Cam brightened. "Everyone could tell this was special. Only our second immigrant wave from the UN occupation zone—"

"Fourth." Desmond's mindlink had given him the correction. Cam's would have too, if the governor had listened to it. Cam's brows furrowed. "But our first in five years," Desmond added. "Definitely special."

Cam's face relaxed. "The word's getting out. New Cal is the best place for Americans to build new lives. We're a beacon of opportunity." He put on a confident, genial smile and lifted his drink to take in the beach, the ocean, and the partygoers. "Look how good we have it."

Desmond looked. Everyone under the pavilion had immigrated more than thirty Earth-years ago, except for two lithe nativeborn women, each on an older man's arm. Most recent immigrants and their native-born children lived off citizen's stipends and ad-supported media in lowland San Lazaro, with many of the rest in isolated communes scattered across the continent's rugged interior. "A beacon, you're right."

"And they're Asian," Cam said, meaning the hundred-twenty new arrivals, Vietnamese-Americans from Texas. "I know that's unimportant to you—"

"It is," Desmond said. Especially since the new arrivals weren't Korean like him, but he kept annoyance off his face and changed the subject. "The speeches by the college students were a great addition to the usual ceremony. I'll let Justin know he shouldn't have missed it."

"Just because he's the hefé at New Cal Mol Fab doesn't make you second banana. I appreciate you representing NCMF. Your operations department set up our new citizens, ma?"

"My best field team emplaced a standard mol fab facility for their settlement size. I flew down to San José del Bandera Oso two days ago for a final inspection."

Cam looked wistful. "San José. Someday it will be a bigger city than its namesake."

Its namesake was the patron saint of Vietnam, not the city at the southern end of San Francisco Bay, but this time Desmond kept the correction to himself. "Absolutely, Cam."

"It's almost time to set sail. Take your drink on board." Cam angled his head at the pier leading to the marina's ranked boats. "The *Golden Gate*. All the way to the tee-junction, then last boat on the right."

Desmond gave Cam a final glance with as much scrutiny as could go unnoticed. Not enough to read his thoughts. "See you there." Desmond cradled his glass by the rim and mulled their conversation as the boards flexed underfoot. Boats bobbed on the waves and rubbed against their bumpers. After two suicide attempts, had neurotropics and cognitive therapy healed Cam?

At the end of the pier, Desmond hesitated. A dry, cottony taste filled his mouth. Here the security was thick and blatant. The rui shi were robots like giant bulldogs, the male on the right and the female on the left. Snarls stood frozen on both their faces. A livery collar draped over each rui shi's shoulders and chest. The collars' bright yellow contrasted with their matte-black nanotube pelts.

A line of red hanzi characters stood on each collar. Desmond's mindlink overlaid on his vision an English translation, *auspicious lions guarding all of heaven*. Under the male's right paw, a globe swirled with clouds over the continent of New California. A cub lay on its back under the female's left paw, writhing and playfully snapping at its mother's claws, but when it became aware of Desmond it twisted onto its feet and leaned forward, unafraid, to face him. Cooling bristles stood up on their napes and the backs of their heads.

Desmond inhaled to mask his fear and dislike. The translation of the livery collar mocked him and every gweilao with a lie. The rui shi did not guard all of heaven, *tián quán*; instead, they guarded the interests of Tián Quán Discovery Co. Ltd., master of more than half the settled galaxy. He passed between them as impassively as he could. The heat from their cooling bristles drew sweat from his brow and made him squint.

Desmond climbed up the ramp to an open gate in the yacht's deck railing near the stern. The *Golden Gate* was sixty yards long and twenty abeam, far larger than his speedboat docked on the riverfront in the city. Oak decking sealed against salt and spray ringed the midcastle. Behind the midcastle's glass walls, now transparent, stood billiard and ping-pong tables, a robotic kitchenette, and sternward, a fitness room filled with yoga mats, stability balls, stretch ropes, and a rack of cast iron kettlebells. The bottom of the rack held a few hundred-pounders no normal person would ever swing or press. Below deck, Desmond saw in his mind's eye, through his mindlink, three sitting areas, a banquet hall, a bar sprouting twenty beer taps, and a walk-in smoking lounge.

Stairs led from the stern deck down to the banquet space. Two pony walls flanked the stairwell, each hiding an ell-shaped banquette poised for conversation and views out to sea. Desmond leaned over the far railing, his back to the ramp and any new arrivals.

High above, the wind herded clouds across the indigo sky. K-Nought's fat orange disc hung a third of the way past the zenith and the smaller, closer moon, San Francisco, showed a narrow crescent halfway through its retrograde crawl to the eastern horizon. On the western horizon, lapping against the buoy line, the turquoise ocean glimmered with unicellular photosynthesizers, New Cal's pinnacle of indigenous evolution. On the Earthlife side, a flock of petrels floated on the sea breeze. Twenty yards in from the buoy line a long low black shape glistened at the surface: one of EnvE's seahyenas, giant robots that broke down Terran biomolecules and, in concert with the buoy line, protected the native life from contamination.

Speaking of EnvE, Secretary of Environmental Engineering Ashwin George's smooth baritone voice came from the ramp. "Ellen, is Buddhist Kabbalah compatible with one's pursuit of his TruSelf?"

"Any religion can be," came the reply, "except for fundamentalist Christianity." Ellen was Ellen Sakamoto, Prime Teacher of the TruSelf Foundation of New California.

"Of course," another woman said softly. Priya, an English professor at UNewCal and Ashwin's life partner.

Ellen went on. "However, even though almost any religion can be compatible, if it encourages excessive mysticism, it's a distraction from our pursuits of our TruSelves."

Desmond leaned further over the rail. Most of the passengers for the party cruise were nearly an E-century old: we'll find our TruSelves any day now.

"So are the Buddhist Kabbalists excessively mystical?" Ashwin asked. After a moment, he said brightly, "Desmond, you can help us for a second, ma?"

Desmond gritted his teeth but released the tension before turning. He knew exactly how this would go. "Nihao."

Ashwin's fleshy face wore a perpetual gloat. He was the second most powerful man on the planet, far more powerful than the lieutenant governor. "Would you mindlink for us whether Buddhist Kabbalah is excessively mystical?"

Desmond couldn't even tell him to look it up himself: the question lacked any settled answer. Desmond's search sense would only give him the biases and cherry-pickings of Buddhist Kabbalists, their business rivals, and their past and current lovers. "No. It's too subjective a question. But I'll wager it isn't."

Ashwin frowned. It gladdened Desmond to befuddle his expectations. His conversation with Cam Watkins came back to mind. "Buddhist Kabbalah is like most things," Desmond added. "The passion of youth congeals into the habit of middle age."

Ashwin's frown deepened. Ellen stared down at the ocean, her face naked with delight at Ashwin's discomfit before her usual polite mask returned. "Thank you, Desmond. If you'll excuse us?" She started for the stairs down to the banquet deck. Ashwin and Priya followed Ellen. Desmond returned to the railing and lifted his glass.

A gust buffeted his ears but in the ensuing lull he heard Priya quietly say, "Awas," *be careful.* Desmond borrowed public camera and microphone feeds from the top of the stairs. In his mind's eye, Priya raised her eyebrows to admonish Ashwin.

Ashwin's tone of voice revealed amusement at an overreaction. "What?"

" 'Give me sleek-headed men,' " she whispered, " 'and such as sleep a-nights.' " She held the admonishing gaze for a moment, then descended the stairs.

Ashwin followed her. "Honey..." he said, plea and annoyance in his tone.

It took Desmond's mindlink a moment to finish her quote. Shakespeare, *Julius Caesar*, Act I, scene II. *Yond Cassius has a lean and hungry look; he thinks too much: such men are dangerous.*

He stared at the resting seahyena's dorsal carapace while chatty, perfumed guests boarded behind him. After a time, the gate in the aft railing clanged shut and the yacht's paddles, like immense black duckfeet, kicked away from the dock. He tilted back the rest of his vodka tonic, then tossed the empty glass to a custodial robot, a dwarf centaur with recycling bags slung over its flanks. K-nought suddenly seemed too bright, the ocean too unfathomable. Desmond went below.

An appetizer table bore platters with sunchoke samosas and peeled kiwi wrapped in wine-cured prosciutto. The robot bartenders scanned their databases for the attendees' preferences and Desmond found a second vodka tonic waiting for him on the bar. He sipped and smiled weakly. Same faces, same actions. As he led a cluster of people forward, Cam talked about the two-month-old news from Earth, brought by the same Tián Quán ship as the new immigrants. Ellen bragged about her latest furniture purchase, hand-made by a sawdust-covered artisan in Schwarzenegger City. Carl Yaeger, chancellor of UNewCal, turned his narrow blue eyes toward the youngest woman at the party.

Selene Alvarez attended Golden State U, eight hundred miles up the coast, and had won a speaking slot in the immigration ceremony in a planetwide college communications contest. Her demeanor had been earnest, her speech a regurgitation of conventional wisdom, praising Cam and the founders' generation for enriching nativeborns' lives with diversity. Did she really believe that sentiment, or deep down did she try to convince herself? *You're projecting your own pessimism onto her*, Desmond thought. *Whether she's idealistic or naïve, let her be young.*

Selene wore a sheer peasant blouse and purple eyeliner. The lights recessed in the ceiling glossed her thick black hair. Desmond blinked in surprise at a datum uncovered by his mindlink: she wasn't the youngest woman here. A twenty-year-old UNewCal student named Tethys attended the party. Ah, it would violate university policy for Yaeger to have sex with a current student.

Desmond suddenly felt glad both his daughters had attended UNewCal.

"So are the rumors true?" Selene asked Yaeger.

"Rumors?" Yaeger replied. Desmond leaned his left ear toward them, ignoring small talk accreting around him.

She lowered her voice. "About the governor."

"Oh, they aren't rumors. He really is a horrible tennis player."

She saw through that. Smart starchild. "I heard from someone who's dating an intern at the rejuvenation clinic on Fremont Mesa the governor was rushed there a couple of months ago in really bad shape." Her voice became even more quiet. "They said it was self-inflicted."

Desmond masked his next motion with a sip of his vodka tonic. He glanced out the picture windows and saw a reflection of Yaeger. His eyes looked even narrower, like pinholes of Earth sky in his tanned face. "You're too smart a girl to believe silly rumors."

"I knew it had to be a rumor." She sounded relieved. "It didn't make sense to me. Our genes built us to strive for success and status, so how could someone who has a lot of both attempt suicide?"

Her question was like a lever wedged under a boulder. Thoughts recurring to Desmond over E-decades followed well-worn paths in his mind. *Because our genes are blind fools rolling down gradients toward local optima. Because nucleic acid sequences can't predict the system dynamics resulting from the actions of thirty thousand of their peers.*

Because our genes built us for their benefit, not ours.

An urge pooled in Desmond's gut. Abandon the people around him, barge in, earning Yaeger's enmity for a few decades, and tell the girl the truth. His heart thudded. Yaeger and Ashwin's crowd already kept him at a distance, respecting him for being on the first ship, tolerating him as the man who kept them in material excess, but nothing more. He had too few bridges to burn. He shut his eyes and pulled in a breath until the urge left him light-headed.

"I need some air," he said as a polite explanation to the people around him. In case he would gulp his first drink soon, he detoured past the bar to pick up another on his way to the foredeck.

The wind over the speeding yacht whipped back Desmond's hair. At the bow, Cam spoke to a cluster of people about the need for donations to the New Cal Settlement Fund. The latest arrivals showed there hundreds of thousands of potential immigrants lived, not just in California or rest of the Pacific Republic of America, but in the UN occupation zone as well. His listeners' feet shuffled and their mouths froze in half-smiles.

Desmond turned to the midcastle. The other college student, Tethys Broniatowski, stood within. At the ceremony, he had pegged her as just another earnest starchild in a skirt-suit and pinned-back hair. Now, though, her sandy brown hair loose around her shoulders, her tall, buxom curves reminded him of Jennifer, the girlfriend he'd let get away after graduating from UC Davis. Why hadn't he seen the resemblance before? Unless he saw it now groundlessly, fleeing from the sense of wrongness hanging over the cruise into a private nostalgia he projected onto this zaftig starchild.

She played eight-ball and clearly didn't enjoy herself. She hunched her shoulders and clutched her cue in front of her with both hands. Her opponent, a deputy director at EnvE named Maltby, stalked around the table, his gaze alternately gauging the sharp angles of a bank shot and the soft swells masked by her royal blue, polka-dotted sundress. No accident evolution had tuned the same hormone to drive both sex and violence.

The midcastle door opened for Desmond and he strode in, distracting Maltby into banking the cue ball into a corner pocket. As the other man glowered, Desmond raised the still-full of his two vodka tonics to Tethys. "Sweetie, here's your drink."

She hesitated a moment, then unwrapped her left hand from the cue stick. "It took a long time."

"The bartending database doesn't know your preferences." Desmond pretended to notice the other man for the first time. "Ni-hao."

The bureaucrat folded his thick arms in front of his chest and gave Desmond a surly look. "Have some manners next time."

"I assumed it was a friendly game. You look like the kind of man whose TruSelf keeps things in perspective." Actually, Maltby didn't, but the surly look blunted. "Were you playing for money? Oh, not yet..."

Tethys stood taller now and brushed bangs from her eyes. She gave Desmond a chiding look. "I'm trying to sandbag a mark here."

Maltby racked his stick, saw Cam asking for donations on the foredeck, and headed aft. After the door closed behind him, Tethys said, "Thanks."

"Everyone should be able to enjoy the party."

"And thanks for the drink." She sipped and winced at the quinine in the tonic water. "It's the thought that counts."

Desmond laughed, but as he did, he saw the path he'd committed himself to for the next few hours. He took in her rouged cheeks and saw again bits of Jennifer in her. He had no better paths to tread, no better destination to reach, than a tryst after sunset belowdeck or back in the city.

They chatted as K-Nought sank toward the western horizon. Tethys majored in journalism and planned to work for New Cal Broadcasting Corporation after graduation. She underestimated the number of resumes flowing into NCBC's sapient resources expert system, but he let her keep her hopes.

Tethys would be a classmate of his youngest daughter, but asking if she knew her would derail their journey down the seduction track. It relieved him that if she did know his daughter, Tethys wanted to be danced down the same path enough to leave it unspoken.

As they chatted, he remembered her presentation at the ceremony. She had expressed at least one profound thought. "I liked your comment that immigrants remind the native-born of your good fortune."

"Really."

"I wouldn't lie."

She glanced out to sea. The seahyena to starboard, halfway to the buoy line, effortlessly kept pace with the yacht. "From the moment I started designing my presentation, I was afraid the, ah, Earthborn would realize just how much us starchildren take everything you've done for granted."

"You can call us rucos. I won't take offense." She looked unsure how to respond. He lightly pressed his fingertips to her forearm. "Be glad you're nativeborn. You wouldn't want a ruco's baggage."

She frowned. "What's important about your luggage on the trip out?"

"It's an idiom. However you might take TruSelf—" He lifted an eyebrow and lilted his voice enough to imply he could understand if she held TruSelf in very low esteem. "—you've heard the term *cruft* for all the psychological damage that scars over." Memories of President Fletcher's nuclear strike on China, the ensuing United States civil war, and the Sino-UN joint occupation lurked beneath Desmond's consciousness, like the seahyena abreast of the yacht. "Be glad you don't have ours."

"I know a lot happened the E-decades before the governor founded New California, but I don't know what those events mean to the people who lived through them...."

Desmond waved his hand. "We don't need to talk about it. Tell me more about you."

"We know all about *cruft*." She wanted to talk up to him, he read from her words and tone. "Many of us nativeborn have our own psychological damage."

"It's not your generation that interests me. Tell me more about you."

She did, but soon found an opening to turn the conversation to the glamour and power of running NCMF's operations. He played it up; she wanted to hear it as part of their dance. Yet he was glad when their mindlinks forwarded to their consciousnesses the yacht's invitation to dinner.

They left the midcastle and descended to the party deck to find the appetizers gone and buffet tables in their place. Even though no new immigrants had been invited, the menu honored their exotic heritage. Not with *ph* or *bún* or ham sandwiches on baguettes—any kitchen on New Cal could assemble four courses of Vietnamese cuisine—but with Texas recipes culled from the planetary internet. Shredded chicken enchiladas smothered in tomatillo sauce and sour cream at one station, brisket mesquite smoked for eighteen hours at another. Cam worked the room and urged people to drink frozen margaritas and bock beers. A dark pink smoke ring showed on Desmond's brisket slices, and his beer bottle dewed in the sea air. Tethys enjoyed the enchiladas and a margarita so sweet its tequila was untasteable. The dim light and her smile reminded him of a spring evening in Jennifer's room in her rental house near campus, listening to decades-old songs played from the original CDs by a dedicated music player she'd bought at a garage sale, the windows open to the smell of cow manure from the University farm.

By the time the robots picked up their empty plates, the windows showed K-Nought had nearly set. Time for the next step down the path. "Let's take in the sunset," he said.

"I'd like that."

With gentle touches to her shoulder, he guided her aft. Yet when they rounded the last corner before the stairs, Desmond's mood deflated. Ashwin emerged from the head and malice flowed into his face when he saw Desmond.

"Desmond! I heard Annalise broke up with you. Such a shame. You seemed to hold a torch for her for a long time."

Tethys stiffened her fleshy limbs. Desmond's heart pounded in his ears, but he pushed the ball of his left foot against the floor until his rage softened. "It's been so long since then, I don't even remember when that happened. Look it up for me through mindlink, would you? Pardon us, Ash."

Tethys stiffly climbed the aft stairs. The door to her boudoir might now be irrevocably closed. Piyan indio. Yet as they reached the aft deck, her head jerked up, her eyes widening and her mouth gasping, and Desmond forgot about Ashwin George.

The male rui shi sat serenely on the aft deck, like a lion surveying its territory. It had docked its globe in a socket in its chest. The setting sun on the globe's left curve and the newly-risen moon Los Angeles on its right framed Tethys' stunned reflection in its center. Some time in the hours since he'd last seen the rui shi, the hanzi characters on its livery collar had changed. No longer *auspicious lion*, the hanzi now read *indomitable blue stubborn water pig*.

Desmond breathed in. His chest and abdomen swelled and squished out part of his fear. He stepped forward and slightly bowed his head. "*Jiǔyǎng.*" A polite, formal greeting, with an implication of equality between them.

"*Wǎn ān,*" it replied in a deep bass voice. In a flat American accent it added, "Good evening." It rose to its four feet and padded forward along the port side of the ship.

No one occupied the sitting area to starboard, facing the sunset. "Here's a good view," he said.

Tethys hesitated. He guided her with his hand on her shoulder blade. She shuffled her feet but kept staring after the rui shi. Only after he led her to the sitting area, and her knees folded to land her on the banquette with her head below the pony wall did she turn to him. "Those things can *speak*?"

"That's the first I've ever heard one."

"Is it a special model? It must have extra hardware."

"Not hardware, I don't think, or software either," Desmond said. She looked confused. "It's like the way we can use our mindlink to look through cameras and hear through microphones. I'm sure something can act through them."

"Something?" Her eyes widened in shock. "Tián Quán's AIs?" She lifted her gaze to San Francisco, its half-moon high overheard like a shrunken white pea. Her breath sounded ragged. "Is that thing here to protect the governor?" She paled, then whispered, "To kill him?"

"I don't think either one."

Tethys studied his eyes. "I've heard the rumors. Mysterious events involving the governor and all the Fremont Mesa generation closing ranks around it. What's happening? Tián Quán? Domestic politics?"

Desmond took a deep breath to calm her, not himself. An oblique way to say it came to mind. She seemed smart enough to take his meaning. " 'Against boredom, even the gods themselves struggle in vain.' "

"Gods?" She frowned.

He hid his disappointment behind a casual tone of voice. "Nietzsche. He lived a couple hundred years ago. He's the guy who said 'God is dead.' "

Understanding flowed into her face. "Oh, it's a metaphor." Tethys blinked, her eyes suddenly moist. "Oh." She leaned toward him, put her arm around him, rested her cheek on his shoulder. He remembered holding his children when toddlers. He worked his arm behind her back and palmed her waist above the hip.

K-Nought smeared reds and purples across the horizon and the first stars came out overhead. Conan's eye glinted at Thulsa Doom's severed head, and the bowlegged Tramp clicked his heels. "Are the constellations different on Earth?" she asked.

Twelve thousand light years away. "Even the stars are different."

For a few seconds, the only sound came from the twenty-foot-long paddles behind the stern, gravely working to hold the yacht's position against the strong southerly current. From the flash of her wrists to her coy up-angled smile, he read she'd gotten over Ashwin's attempted cockblock and expected him to take the next step down the mating path.

Yet what would he gain? Half an hour of pleasure in the warm folds of her flesh. What would she gain? A feeling of being desired by a ruco on Cam's guest list. They would run programs coded in DNA and compiled by protein every animal generation for the past five hundred million years.

Yet his body and brain fit that rut. He remembered a ruse he had tried on several other starchild girls with good effect. The memory of Jennifer's room and her old CDs came to him, reminding him of the ruse's source in an '80s college rock song and dogging his next words with guilt. "I remember late one night, when I was a child, lying in the rear seat of my parents' car. The wheeled kind, it traveled on roads. I was falling asleep, and the car motor's sound would cut out of my hearing for a moment at a time, as if all the clocks in the world had stopped. My last waking thought was I'd never seen anything so great as all the stars."

She shifted to look up at him, her eyes wide in the fading twilight. "That's beautiful." She closed her eyes and angled her mouth toward his when a sound distracted them. Someone inside the dark fitness room clanged equipment together. Both he and Tethys looked over the top of the banquette, but the fitness room remained dark. *Turn on the light,* he thought, but he chose not to send the message. Maybe blind kettlebell swings were a new training fad. Then the fitness room fell silent, and Desmond decided a couple inside wanted stealthy sex.

From the starboard side of the midcastle came a quiet woosh: the door opened. Desmond almost said *Someone's here already* to give the couple a chance to turn away, but instead he held his silence.

A single figure came past the corner of the midcastle and strode straight toward the stern. Cam, a purposeful set to his shoulders and a hundred-twenty pound kettlebell against his body, racked to his chest with both hands on the handle. Perfect form, Desmond remembered later, wrists straight and forearms pressed to his ribcage. Cam remained oblivious to both the fading sunset and Desmond and Tethys. His upper body and the backs of his shoulders showed resolute purpose. His strides lengthened as he went to the railing.

Tethys gasped. Desmond untangled from her arm and lurched to his feet. "Cam!"

Cam's shoulders hunched a moment, but he lifted them as he turned his head. He hadn't come on deck to do kettlebell swings. "What do you want, Desmond?"

Desmond held out his hands. "You don't have to do this, Cam."

"I know I don't have to."

"Don't choose this. There's so much to live for." Wodema. The clichéd words sounded ludicrous. "Colonists from the UN occupation zone, San José will be bigger than its namesake—"

Cam peered at him. "I know you too well, Desmond. You don't believe there's so much to live for. You don't believe in anything. There's nothing else for me. I can't go back to Earth. I can't resign my office. I need to do this."

Gooseflesh stippled Desmond's cheeks. The colony needed room to grow, and to gain that room, Cam needed to be out of the picture. But suicide? Cam's forearms shivered under the weight still racked against his chest. A thin rope lashed the kettlebell's handle to his left hand, and Desmond realized he'd planned this attempt for months. "You know what you're choosing?" Desmond asked.

Relief filled Cam's face. "Thank you for seeing that."

"Then go," Desmond said, "with New California's blessing."

Cam turned to face the railing, and lifted the kettlebell straight up. His head eclipsed the black iron cannonball from Desmond's view. He strode to the railing. The kettlebell cleared it. Cam bent over the railing from the middle of his back, held his grip on the kettlebell, but dropped his arms and kicked both his legs backward. The combined momentum of his rotating body and the falling kettlebell whipped him headfirst over the railing. A loud splash, a dull thunk through the hull of the ship from the massive paddles; then silence.

Tethys' breaths came shallowly, raggedly. "You let him...."

"He chose it. You saw that."

Her face showed no sign of hearing him. "Governor!" she shouted. She opened a public mindlink channel, top priority, and shouted again. She ran to the stern and Desmond ambled after. *Girl, let him go, for all our sakes.* He peered at the murky water, his gaze caught by moonslight glinting the surface. Over the public channel, the party's hubbub faded as Tethys shouted again, —Governor! Someone, help him!—

Later, the silence seemed to last for hours, though the yacht took action a couple of heartbeats after her final call. Below the water-line, robots looking like pygmy dolphins with grafted arms propelled themselves out rescue hatches, and bright white lamps lit up the sub-surface, so bright the black paddles appeared gray. On the starboard paddle, a shadow showed a fresh dent close to its hinged connection to the hull. Through his mindlink, the yacht's subsurface spectropho-tometers told him excess heme iron enriched the water around the dent.

The silvery school of rescue robots darted into the darkness be-yond the lamps' reach. From a few dozen yards to starboard came a gurgle of water. A silvery ripple on the surface showed where the seahyena dived.

People reacted next. Virtual avatars popped into Desmond's vi-sion, projected there by his mindlink. Ashwin's avatar manifested at the railing next to Desmond. Anxious surprise had replaced his usual arrogance. —What happened?—

—He weighted himself down and jumped, right here. He hit the paddle hard enough to draw blood.— Footsteps pounded up the stairs from the banquet level. Ashwin's avatar shifted as Desmond turned his head to the new arrival. Flesh-and-blood Ashwin ran to the railing while the avatar mapped itself to its owner's body and disappeared.

Ashwin stared into the water while he caught his breath. Now he looked thoughtful. "Cam wanted to leave the rejuve clinic nothing to work with. Unless he thought Tián Quán would build a new body for his archived brain scan."

Tián Quán would never, and Cam had been clear-eyed about what the company permitted its protectorates. "He knew what he was do-ing."

Ashwin sneered at the water. "Pimping blonde topless dancers to the People's Liberation Army, and paying a few billion yuán for the settlement rights, didn't earn him that much gratitude."

More avatars and people filled the deck and looked over the rail-ing. "Cam fell off the boat?" Ellen Sakamoto asked.

Her attempt to cover up Cam's intent from the starchildren present annoyed Desmond. "He jumped with a hundred-twenty pound kettlebell tied to his hands."

"How do you know? You saw this?" She angled her head. "You saw him in danger and did nothing to stop him?"

"No. I let him do what he most wanted."

"It's true," Tethys said. "He didn't try to stop him."

Ellen noticed her for the first time. "You sounded the alarm?"

"Yes."

"When? Before or after he went over?"

Tethys hesitated. "After."

"After? After the yacht could have preemptively launched its rescue robots? After several men could have hurried up here to block him?"

Tethys quailed, and though Desmond had lost the urge to seduce her the moment he'd divined Cam's intention, he took her side. "She was stunned by what she saw. We've covered up Cam's recent suicide attempts so well she didn't know it was real."

"There's no time for this!" Carl Yaeger shouted. He stood next to the railing and bounced his fist against it. "Cam is down there! Ashwin, I'm sure you've already told the seahyena to go to rescue mode—"

"There is no rescue mode," Ashwin replied.

"—but it has to bring him up soon! What? No rescue mode?" Yaeger's lower lip sagged and his head slowly oscillated from side to side. "It will leave him alone if he's moving under his own power, but turn it off while there's still a chance for the rescue robots to save him!"

Ashwin turned from the railing and squared his shoulders to the crowd. "The seahyenas preserve the sanctity of two biospheres. That's more important than any one man. Even Cam."

The crowd looked confused, frightened. The girl Selene looked ready to burst with tears. Only one face showed an emotion dissonant with the crowd's. Priya Varghese gave her life partner a knowing, cautioning look.

"But we have to save him!" shouted someone in the mass of people.

Desmond glanced at Ashwin and their gazes met. Desmond still loathed the other, and he read incompletely-disguised ambition in Ashwin's features. But Desmond knew the other agreed letting Cam stay dead was in the colony's best interest. Tomorrow would be time enough to renew their rivalry.

Desmond nodded to Ashwin and raised his voice. "We do? This is the third time he's done something like this!" The Earthborns shot him warning looks. Timid rucos, afraid of losing face to the starchildren. "The first time, when he hanged himself in a closet in the governor's mansion, we could all pretend it was accidental autoerotic asphyxiation. And the second time, obviously someone adulterated his ecstasy with pentobarbitol, and we packed that someone off to criminal psychiatric reprogramming at Los Robles to serve justice."

Desmond flourished his hand toward the water. "But now? We can't delude ourselves any longer. Cameron Watkins wanted to kill himself! He could have tried drowning in a swimming pool or in the river, but he realized someone would jump in to save him. The river is deep, maybe a heavy weight would have worked, but he would've attracted notice carrying one to the riverside. Not one of us thought twice about the kettlebells on board." He chopped his hand toward the midcastle. "He waited until we were all full with dinner and moving on to the evening's other entertainments, then he slipped away from each and every one of you." Desmond stared at Ellen Sakamoto until she ducked her gaze. "And he knew out here a seahyena would keep us from recovering his brain and breathing more life back into it." *Four minutes since Cam jumped* came from Desmond's mindlink. If the seahyena had not yet crushed Cam's skull, anoxia would soon pulp its contents. "Review the yacht's camera feeds. Watch how intently Cam went over the edge. We know what he wanted. He's found it. Let him keep it."

Desmond surveyed the crowd. His words had dislodged the desire to save Cam from many of their faces. Not all; a few betrayed private doubts about the apparent consensus Desmond and Ashwin had forged by forceful words and resolute demeanors, but from their expressions, those few people clearly felt alone. They would not protest.

He had carried the day.

"We agree," Ashwin said. "We'll let Cam go." A few of the crowd nodded, but most seemed numb. Their world had turned upside down.

Confidence buoyed Desmond's chest. Cam would stay dead and the people left behind in New California's tiny bubble of earthlife could free themselves from the dead hand of the past. Then he glanced up.

The rui shi family, once again auspicious lions guarding all of heaven, sat on the midcastle's roof, serenely watching the crowd through their snarling faces. To port, the cub sat between its mother's front legs. To starboard, the male's paw rested on the globe. In the globe, gray swirls smeared the reflections of the coastal settlements and the moon Los Angeles. Whatever the rui shi and the AIs working through them thought about the petty lives played out this night, they kept to themselves.

A chime in his mind's ear told Desmond that Ashwin wanted to privately speak. —I'll remember how you've helped me,— Ashwin said.

Desmond swallowed. Tomorrow started now. —When the time comes, I'll remind you.— After Ashwin hung up, Desmond turned his face to the empty sea. *He's so arrogant he thinks I did it for him.*

The crowd milled around the aft deck for a time. A few leaned over the railing and stared into the ocean, as if their biological eyes could pierce the murk and lift Cam to acute rejuvenation. Many shuffled across the deck and averted empty faces from their peers.

Someone cried. The urge from the party deck a few hours earlier returned to Desmond, this time tinged with shame at having kept years of insight to himself. He followed the sound. In the corner of the port sitting area, a woman sat with her knees pulled to her chest and her black hair over her face. Selene. Sobs convulsed her torso. The people nearest her stood in an awkward semicircle a few yards away.

Desmond went to her and Yaeger stepped in his way. "What do you think you're doing?"

"Comforting her."

"Comforting? Like you comforted her by recounting Cam's other suicide attempts?"

Desmond privately said, —Once Cam went over the side, she wasn't going to spread her legs for you tonight.— He pushed past Yaeger with his forearm and thought at a lounge chair to roll close to Selene.

He sat, lowering his head to the same height as hers. "You're hurting." Behind him, Yaeger snorted.

After a moment, her sobs subsided. "Yes." Her buried face muffled her mucus-thickened voice.

"Tell me about it."

"You know. The governor."

"I know Cameron Watkins committed suicide earlier tonight. Tell me how that hurts you."

Selene lifted her head. Her bloodshot, puffy eyes and contorted mouth showed fresh anguish. "I don't know," she said. Her face clenched, squeezing out more tears. "But it does." She buried her face and gave muffled cries.

"You don't understand why he did it." She breathed raggedly and rocked back and forth. Desmond read her motion as a nod. "You were right, he had everything his genes could want for him. Wealth? In old California, the Chinese occupation forces made him rich enough to buy the rights to this planet. Power. Fame. Status. He had all those, plus everything those coins could buy. Imported luxuries, rich food, excellent physical health. Sex, too. Seven children by five women. His genes could want nothing more."

He lightly touched her shoulder. "But *he* could. You see, his genes, like yours, like mine, don't know what they're doing. They build yearning brains, but the yearning remains after all our desires are sated. They build curious brains, but the curiosity eventually wonders if our lives have any purpose. They build brains seeking meaning, but often either failing to find it or, on finding it, discovering it hollow. Our genes are not geniuses. Our genes are not angels. Our genes are evil crippled godlings who built half-formed creatures good enough, and loyal enough, and programmed well enough to serve them. They don't care about us. But they don't know we can set ourselves free of them."

Selene looked up. Her tears had faded and longing tinged by hope shone in her face. "Tell me more," she said. She glanced around. "We all want to hear more."

Desmond stole a look to left, to right. Many of the people around him, from Earth- to native-born, from female to male, listened to him. Nods, affirming words, supportive body language. Ellen looked unconvinced, but even so, encouragement lifted him until he glanced up.

The rui shi cub's front paws hung over the edge of the midcastle's roof and it watched him with what seemed an inquisitive look on its squashed snarled face. A water pig now, just like its father earlier. What did this thing want?

"No, we've heard enough," Yaeger said. "Cam is dead for one simple reason."

"Just one?" Desmond asked.

"His TruSelf teachers failed to find the right combination of psychotropics and self-talk in time."

Ellen frowned, but kept silent. Yaeger turned to another Earthborn standing nearby. "Ashwin, what do you think?"

Ashwin's habitual smirk soon formed. "I think Desmond spends too much time alone with the scribblings of dead men. Free ourselves from our genes? How the hell are you going to do that, Des?" His tone grew more mocking. "Start a religion?"

New California Date 92:95
17 December 2093

His mindlink pinged: Selene approached his house. Before heading to the guest landing pad, Desmond checked on the neuropharm implantation couch. He'd bought a standard model, identical to dozens in TruSelf facilities across the planet, and learned to program it. The couch's expert system reported its status was all green.

Good, since it had implanted neurochemical microfabs in his brain three days earlier.

Desmond rose from the sunken seating area around the translucent ceramic fireplace in his great room. In the foyer, his sandals rustled over the cultured marble floor. The double doors swung toward him, opening the way to the front lawn and the guest landing pad.

The airmobile came over his neighbor's mansion and extended its wheels as it descended. Its running lights blinked brighter than the stars the city's light pollution washed out. He'd sent one of his own vehicles, the landau, to pick her up at her friend's mycocrete apartment, to spare her the sweatiness of a bicycle ride up the switchback and spare him raised neighbor's eyebrows at a public-hire airjitney landing in his front yard.

He followed the flagstone path from his front doors, past a bubbling fountain of animatronic nymphs, to the landing pad. Down on its wheels, the landau popped its nearside door. Selene climbed out and shook her hair, smiling. "Desmond, nihao!"

"Nihao, meimei."

"The implantation couch worked for you, ma?"

Save for following the motion of her hair, his gaze had never left her face. No "boob check," as an ex-girlfriend had called it: the inevitable appraising glance built into the male brain by the selfish gene and triggered every few seconds. "Perfectly."

"Great! I'm so excited, the past few days I've been telling everyone. Like Max." She waved her hand at the landau's open door. "He heard so much he wanted to come along."

Max climbed out. Shorter than average, with wiry hair and narrow eyes, he glanced over the fountain and the front façade of the house, then lifted his chin and stuck out his chest. "Nihao, Mr. Park," he muttered, and jutted out his hand to keep a bro-hug at bay.

"Nihao." Desmond's mindlink compiled a dossier from social networking sites. Max Jacoby, son of an EnvE retiree, recent graduate of Golden State U., employed by TruSelf as an assistant implantation tech. The dossier failed to explain his caginess. "You know Selene from undergrad, ma?"

"That's right."

"We overlapped my first five NC-years," Selene said. "We had a lot of deep conversations late at night. When I moved to San Laz to be closer to you, he let me crash at his apartment."

"Very kind to let her stay with you." To Selene, Desmond asked, "Just deep conversations?" He glanced at Max. Frustration flickered across the younger man's face.

"He's been like a brother to me," Selene said. Max kept silent.

"Thank you for coming to celebrate your sister's liberation from the selfish gene," Desmond said, though it was clearly not Max's intent. "Let's go inside."

He led them past blue jacaranda shrubs as the landau revved up and hopped over the house to the garage. He slowed the pace in the great room, giving Max time to be cowed by Desmond's opulent house. This was Selene's first visit, too, after all their prior meetings in coffeehouses, but she ignored his house's luxury.

Before they started down the hall to the implantation couch, Max said, "How do you think you can liberate people from their genetic tendencies?"

"I told you he has an implantation couch," Selene said.

"TruSelf's had implantation couches for fifty Earth-years. We've never claimed to free people from the selfish gene."

"TruSelf never tried," Desmond said. He led them deeper into the house.

Sol-spectrum ceiling panels lit up the room when they entered. The couch was set up in the former tea room. The tatami mats lay rolled up in the attic and the brazier had long since been picked up by NCMF recycling. The room stood nine feet on a side. The implantation couch, a sleek plastic cocoon in various gray shades, filled the back third of it. Blue status LEDs glowed and a display showed all subsystems ready. Water bubbled in its internal tubing as cooling fans hummed.

Selene ran her fingers along the smooth case. "It looks so powerful."

"Mr. Park," Max said, "this isn't a toy. TruSelf requires years of training and testing before qualifying an employee as an implantation couch operator, let alone a programmer."

Desmond raised an eyebrow. "It took me a couple of weeks with the programmer's guide. I operated it by mindlink while inside without any problems. The expert systems do most of the work—"

"Selene, do you hear him?"

"Yes. He's so intelligent he can do anything."

Desmond smiled at her, but dropped the expression as he looked at Max. The younger man hadn't followed her to protect her from a badly-programmed implant. He had come to stop her from taking the next step toward freeing herself from the selfish gene.

"He's out of control!" Max said. "He plugged neuropharm microfabs into his brain without oversight! You're putting your mind at risk if you do this!"

"In the conversations I've had with him the past month, Desmond has done more to help me grow than all the other mentors I've ever had put together. I'll follow him anywhere. Aren't you my friend? Don't you want me to grow?"

Anxiety showed on Max's face, turning into anger he aimed at Desmond. "You think you know what you're doing? Prove it."

Confidently-spoken jargon would be enough. TruSelf's rigid hierarchy wouldn't yet have taught him the underlying neurophysiology. "We'll implant several microfabs in the brain. To eliminate the sex drive, we'll synth a testosterone antagonist in the limbic system—"

"Instead of blocking testosterone production in the gonads?"

Maybe he did know the physiology. Irritation spiked in Desmond, and he remembered Maltby and Ashwin on the party yacht. He leaned into Max's personal space. "Testosterone serves useful purposes, such as fueling competitiveness." Max backed away. "Second, we'll eliminate kin favoritism by lowering the synaptic weightings on projections from the kinship recognition centers to the ventromedial prefrontal cortex."

"You think that's enough? No cognitive therapy or post-hypnotic suggestions?"

"Those are unreliable and unnecessary," Desmond said. He'd done enough simulations to support his findings.

Max folded his arms in front of his chest. "Just because you can throw around some buzzwords doesn't mean you know what you're doing. Dozens of people review any new programming before TruSelf implements it—"

"I personally delivered Ellen Sakamoto the first implantation couch fabbed on this planet. She had one programmer, now your chief r&d officer, who did double duty as the couch operator. TruSelf doesn't need all its layers of junior programmers and assistant technicians to do its job. Neither do we."

"Goushi."

"Max!" Selene admonished.

Desmond raised his hand to her, but spoke to Max. "Goushi? Really?"

"Why does TruSelf have so many levels of redundancy, if not to catch errors? Tell me that."

Before Desmond could reply, Selene said, "That's easy." Her smile confirmed the words.

"Easy?" Max said.

Her smile widened, crinkling the corners of her eyes. "The expanding pyramid. It's one of the things Desmond has shown me the selfish gene makes each generation do, now that we get routine rejuvenation every two years."

"Expanding pyramid? What sort of nonsense has he put in your head?"

"Rejuvenation means no one ages out of their jobs. People sometimes retire if they're restless or have saved a lot of money, but that's uncommon. Your father was an exception. You agree, ma? Not nonsense?"

Max shrugged. "Go on."

"Perhaps it's less obvious the selfish gene makes us timid. We cling to our habits and our social groups, and most of us prefer clinging to what we have than taking calculated risks to improve our lot. Our subsistence-farming ancestors couldn't switch jobs or become entrepreneurs, so we don't either. So once hired, people rarely quit."

Max looked to be considering her words.

"The selfish gene does more. Desmond is brilliant for seeing these and pointing them out. People in hierarchies want more underlings, not more peers, and they want to use those underlings to outcompete their peers for budgets, salaries, promotions, and prestige."

Delight sparked inside Desmond. She'd taken his words and made them her own. Not his words originally—he'd paraphrased a management aphorism by C. Northcote Parkinson—but even if Max's mindlink dredged up the original and Max accused him of plagiarism, he would just give Parkinson a hat tip and breeze on. Selene would stay convinced, and after she entered the couch, Max could go back to being a pawn of a pawn of Ellen Sakamoto.

"In other words," Max said, "I'm a joke. And you call yourself *my* friend?"

Selene looked pained. "No. Your job is a joke. The selfish gene has hidden the truth from you, until now."

Max cast a troubled look at the hardwood floor near the implantation couch. He didn't want to be a cog in the TruSelf machine, Desmond read from his body language. He'd told himself the same lie all starchildren did, *I'm the one who'll rise up the pyramid*. In twenty E-years, he would resign himself to mediocrity and feel fortunate to work for an established enterprise and have a few subordinates under him.

Desmond's mindlink filled in more: Max's college transcript, extracurricular neuropharm research, and traces in other people's social network profiles. He had far more merit than most of his TruSelf coworkers. A nudge might turn him from an adversary to an ally. "TruSelf's wasting your talents, ma?"

"They'll see I'm qualified for a promotion."

"You've been there long enough to know," Desmond replied. "Selene, are you ready?"

"Absolutely."

"No!" Max said. He stepped closer to her and cradled her hands in his. "Don't do this. Please."

Her brow crinkled. "There's no danger."

"I'm sure Mr. Park knows what he's doing. That's the thing. It'll work too well. Cut off the ties to your parents and your half-siblings? Dry up your sexuality? Are you ready for that?"

"Sexuality is a distraction," Selene said. "It almost snared me in a bad situation the night Desmond showed me the higher truth. And when my relatives have no special place in my heart, the better I can devote myself to the friends I've chosen." She pulled her hands from his and chastely air-kissed his cheeks. "Thank you, Max, for all your concern." To Desmond, she added, "I'm ready."

Desmond flourished his hand at the implantation couch. The lid clamshelled up. "Enter and become free."

Steps distended from the base of the couch. Selene climbed them and sat on the couch's rim. She pressed together her pale knees, exposed below the hem of her summer dress, then swung her legs into the couch's interior. She stretched out on the contoured cushions at the bottom. Robotic arms darted out from the side walls and snaked sensors down her neckline and up her skirt. She grimaced when an iv needle pierced the skin inside her left elbow, but her face soon grew calm. "Close the lid."

Desmond thought at the couch. The lid lowered, motor whirring.

Even louder came Max's fast, ragged breaths.

The telltales all showed clear. In the display, Selene's face showed the effect of the mild sedative in the iv. The microfabs passed their final diagnostics, and the pumps and syringes holding each microfab and its targeting agents were ready.

A chair rolled up to the display. Desmond put his hand on the backrest, then paused. "Even though your bosses don't let you, you know how to operate it, ma?"

Fear and interest battled in Max's voice. "I've studied for the promotion exam."

"She'd welcome you to operate the couch."

Another ragged breath. "What?"

"You're right, I shouldn't speak for Selene." Desmond opened a mindlink channel to them both. —Would you like Max to run the controls?—

—Max, you'd do that for me?—

He swallowed hard. —If it's what you want, yes, I will.—

Desmond backed away from the chair. It swiveled its seat for the younger man. Max gripped the armrests and sank onto the cushion. "Let me check what you've set up." Max studied the display for a couple of minutes, as menus flashed by and sheaves of text scrolled upscreen. "Looks like you've got it." To the couch, he said, "Start."

The first syringe injected its cocktail into Selene's iv. Over the next few minutes, Desmond occasionally asked Max for progress updates. Max's answers grew more detailed, and his voice more engaging, as they went.

After the second cocktail entered her vein and a robot wheeled in with a bottle of mineral water and two glasses, Max started asking about Desmond's design choices. His questions showed he knew enough about couch programming to do some himself. "How would you have done it?" Desmond asked. He listened intently to the younger man's answer, asking questions and offering suggestions in a mild voice of genuine curiosity.

After the third cocktail, Max asked, "So you really think our genes don't care about us?"

Desmond had an elevator pitch ready. "If they did care about us, why are so few people happy?"

Max stayed silent, while the sedative and the targeting molecules from the final cocktail cleared Selene's bloodstream. The robot arms disconnected the sensors and withdrew the iv, then spread coagulant over the puncture site. The lid lifted and both Desmond and Max reached into the couch for Selene's arms. They lifted her to a seat on the rim while her legs stayed in the couch.

"It may take a few hours before you fully feel yourself again," Desmond said.

"I already feel—no, not myself—better than myself."

"The microfabs are just getting started," Max said. "They won't secrete a sufficient dose to give behavioral changes for a couple hours."

Selene smiled. "If what I'm feeling is a placebo, then when the microfabs are active, I'll feel even more free. I can stand. Help me out."

Desmond steadied her. She swung her legs over the couch's rim, less chastely than she'd entered. Her dress cast a shadow between her knees, on the lower parts of her inner thighs. Max's gaze lingered stupidly there for a moment, before intelligence returned to his eyes and he turned his chagrined face away from her and Desmond.

"Let's talk about your experience in the couch," Desmond said to Selene.

"Gladly, Desmond. If I can make it even easier for the next person who wants to be free, I will."

"The great room, then. We can sit with warm tea near the fire. We're done here for tonight."

"No we aren't," Max said. His voice wavered and he steadied himself with his hand on the couch. He looked down at his hand for a moment, until certainty filled his face and lifted his head, chest, and shoulders. "I will join you."

New California Date 92:97
19 December 2093

Ashwin's airmobile descended toward Tián Quán planetary head-quarters. The black box proper loomed behind a stone wall fifteen feet high. Straddling the wall at each of the four cardinal directions stood four buildings, each sixty feet high, all dwarfed by the black box in the center. A different material cladded each building—whorled wooden panels, stained green, to the east; opaque glass blocks tinged the color of fresh blood, to the south; sputtered tin-lead-antimony to the west; and yellow basalt quarried from the interior of the continent to the north. Yet on each building, the side facing the black box, as well as adjacent curved swathes on the roof and each adjoining side, showed the same unnatural matte black as the central tower. Ashwin pictured the complex as some *chingru* inversion of a model solar system, where a black cubical sun scorched the inner faces of its satellites.

But for all Tián Quán's power, nothing lasted forever. A drip of water would eventually erode a mountain—didn't one of their holy books say that?

He landed outside the stone wall at the base of the eastern building. At least Li helped his illusion: Ashwin usually met with Tián Quán's environmental engineering staff in the outbuilding of green whorled wood. Today, though, planetary director Li himself had accepted his request to meet. Although Ashwin had held silent about his primary purpose, for Li to accept the offer showed Tián Quán's local hefé knew the score.

Ashwin debarked. Paired double-height doors swung inward for him. Inside, his mindlink guided him through a maze of twisting corridors and escalators. Despite decades of official visits, the path always eluded his memory. Probably some aerosolized drug to disrupt his sense of direction. If Desmond were here, instead of diddling that benighted girl he'd stolen from Yaeger, he'd ask him which drug and its antidote.

On the highest floor, he came to a large conference room. One long wall, a single pane of one-way glass, faced north to Government Mesa. The governor's mansion, a ludicrous design full of flat curves, sharp angles, and aluminum cladding, stood next to EnvE headquarters' green brachiated dome.

From habit, Ashwin looked to the conference room's long table and stopped short. The table stood bare, its constellation of chairs undisturbed.

"Mr. George," Li said in Mandarin from an interior corner of the room. Three armchairs and a loveseat formed a sitting area. Li rose from his chair and held out his hand, palm down, as Ashwin approached. Daylight shadowed Li's jowls.

Ashwin put on a smile. He took Li's hand with both of his, turning Li's wrist to a less dominant position as he shook. He took a risk by resisting Li's dominance display, but Ashwin wasn't going to kowtow to Tián Quán to overthrow Lt. Gov. Levinson. He would acquire the governorship as a partner, however junior, or not at all. Li raised an eyebrow as Ashwin broke the handshake, but said nothing.

Ashwin spoke in Mandarin shunted to his vocal cords by mindlink and muscle control implants. "I'm pleased to meet you again, Mr. Li, and under more direct circumstances than previously." Reminding him of cocktail parties at the governor's mansion couldn't hurt. The lieutenant governor had missed most of them in recent years.

"Let us sit," Li said.

"Of course," Ashwin said, but he hesitated at the side of the sitting area.

Someone, obviously an avatar, had appeared behind Li's chair. There stood a smooth-faced, soft-jawed male in a round black cap and a long gray robe. On the robe's front, a black silk band marked off a square bearing hanzi characters and the image of a peacock in a meadow. In the image's background, a boar crossed a shallow stream. Where Desmond wasted time mindlinking to trivial knowledge and antiquated books, Ashwin used it to gather intelligence on his enemies: the avatar represented one of Tián Quán's AIs, projected onto his senses. The company demanded access to his mindlink as an entry condition for its facilities.

Li didn't introduce it, so Ashwin overcame his initial surprise and ignored it as they sat. A robot carted in a tray of hot tea and savory Chinese pastries. Ashwin sipped and queued up a request to Priya's mindlink to make him a masala chai when she came home from the university.

After a few minutes of chit-chat, Ashwin looked at an empty chair next to Li. "Will anyone else join us?"

Li's brow furrowed. "You mean Capt. Zhang? Why would an official from the Ministry of Foreign Affairs be needed?"

Ashwin blinked twice, rapidly. "Your pardon, please. I thought, as he is a recent arrival, you might have wanted to introduce me to him." He grasped the ministry was sticking its nose further into Tián Quán's affairs, posting diplomats or military attachés, like Zhang, to the company's protectorates. Small wonder Li was touchy about the attaché.

"When you request a meeting with me, I'll decide who else attends." Li peered at him. "Now tell me why you wished to meet."

Ashwin set down his mostly-full tea cup. "As I said earlier, EnvE faces unplanned ecosystem spread from the wild zones planted decades ago by my predecessor as Secretary of Environmental Engineering."

Li spoke around a mouthful of pork dumpling. "Information from our satellites would help you monitor it. True, yet... EnvE faced or did not face this problem before Gov. Watkins' suicide?"

"We faced it."

"Why, then, is it an issue now?"

Ashwin had expected this question. "When we recognized the problem a few local years ago, Gov. Watkins committed a great deal of the planetary government's resources to fight it. Levinson reneged on that commitment when he became governor."

"I see. Go on."

"His decision has aroused much anger among EnvE's employees and its friends in influential positions."

A stray cloud dimmed the light through the glass wall. "If that were true, would I not already be aware of it?" Li asked, his face in deeper shade.

"I do not know what senses you have." Ashwin glanced at the AI's impassive avatar. "Yet what I say is true."

Li kept his gaze on Ashwin. "Do a thing under cover of another."

One of those damned *chingru* idioms, but the meaning was plain. In spite of that, Ashwin said, "I don't follow."

"You want to depose Levinson."

Appear willing, but not eager. "It has crossed my mind that I would lead the colony more effectively than Levinson."

The AI's avatar shifted its nonexistent weight. Its stare made Ashwin want to squirm in his chair. He could only lead the colony under Tián Quán's suzerainty. *The hefé of New Califas* he thought in a mocking Pachuco accent. *Head indio in charge.* He stifled those thoughts and returned his attention to Li.

"You ask too much."

"How so?"

"Tián Quán seeks peace, order, and good governance on all the worlds over which it is granted transportation and security rights by the Treaty of St. Louis."

Ashwin nodded. "I seek all three of those for New California."

Li raised his voice slightly. "We cannot condone extralegal regime change."

Ashwin raised his palms. "Extralegal? I assure you, I seek nothing of the sort. I speak for many people and factions who have lost confidence in Levinson's leadership: EnvE employees, caucuses in the Planetary Assembly, leading intellectuals at UNewCal, and Ellen Sakamoto of TruSelf." He had lobbied all of them over the past month.

"Faced with so wide a lack of confidence in his leadership, he would bow to the inevitable and resign, after naming me lieutenant governor and the Assembly confirming me."

"So many people are concerned about invasive species in the wilds of the continent?" Li sounded bored and amused.

"My concern is a bellwether for other concerns. Levinson has been inattentive to many state affairs and has spent most of his month in office far from the capital, at his ski chalet near Watkinsville."

"This is true," Li said.

"Some say he is overwhelmed by the burdens of office and seeks a way to shed them." Ashwin turned up the volume on his smear. "I've heard he is even showing some of the signs Watkins showed in his final Earth-year."

Li frowned. "My inward spies have not reported that."

Ashwin shifted his sails, lest he say something Li could clearly identify as a falsehood. "At minimum, he has not showed leadership. Your outward spies must have revealed who showed leadership on the party yacht the night Watkins killed himself."

"They did. You and Desmond Park."

That goddam nerd. Ashwin kept the thought off his face. "After his brief moment, Park returned to obscurity as an introverted engineer. Only I have the ability and the motivation to govern New California."

For a time, Li stared past Ashwin, out the window toward Government Mesa. "You make good points. However, Tián Quán cannot hand out colonial governorships to all who ask."

Ashwin studied Li's impassive face, glancing briefly at the ethereal aloofness of the AI's avatar before dismissing its opinion as irrelevant. "You knew my intention when accepting my request to meet. Did you choose or not choose to meet me?"

Surprise flashed on Li's face, but then he chuckled. He stood and gestured for Ashwin to rise. "You have confirmed thoughts I've had since Watkins turned suicidal. Depose Levinson under your colony's laws. I look forward to working with you." He extended his hand to shake Ashwin's, and this time held it straight.

New California Date 92:110
3 January 2094

The coffeehouse door swung open, jangling its chimes. In trudged Selene and Max. The bright day outside lit up University Avenue and silhouetted the two. Though shadows covered their faces, Desmond read dejection in their slumped shoulders and tired gaits. They avoided the gazes of seated strangers on their way to Desmond's table.

He waved his hand through the space above his table. His day's work for NCMF—graphs, reports, videos, messages, all projected as expandable icons onto his field of vision—vanished, leaving the lacquered tabletop, an empty espresso cup, and biscotti crumbs.

"Nihao." He bro-hugged Max and air-kissed Selene's cheeks. "Why the long faces?"

"You didn't see what she published?" Selene asked.

"I saw Tethys' article in today's *Daily New Californian*. But why does it deject you?"

A smile glimmered on Selene's face at the echo of his words to her on the yacht.

Max, though, remained agitated, rubbing his palms down the front of his blue polo shirt and distressed jeans. "Everyone on campus read it, too. *Ruco's wannabe cult recruits UNewCal students*. That piyan fresa."

"She said a lot of hateful things," Selene said, and patted Max's arm. All three of them sat. Desmond guessed what most riled Max: tooltipped, hyperlinked video panning still photos of sultans and harems, with Tethys' voiceover. *Undoubtedly it's a pure coincidence, in spite of Park's lofty rhetoric, his first cult member is a comely girl a quarter his age. One wonders, though, at the presence of a young man in Park's inner circle. Perhaps Park* **wants** *to surround himself with eunuchs.*

"Most days," Max said, "most people on campus ignore us if they don't want to hear our message. Today people sought us out to laugh. Some hunior called me a 'blueballer—'"

"You happened to wear blue clothes today," Selene said.

"You know what he meant."

"I do. But don't take it personally. They're all puppets."

Desmond angled his head at her. "Tell us more about that."

"The selfish gene built us for living in small groups of subsistence farmers." A flattop robot trundled up with a tea latte and a cappuccino. "In those social environments, the optimal evolutionary response is for most people to mindlessly follow the herd under the whip of conventional wisdom."

"That's very true," Desmond said.

"Thank you, but I only see it because of you."

Max glumly rotated his cappuccino by the handle, cup scratching on the saucer. "But what does that fresa gain by spouting conventional wisdom?"

"The selfish gene primed Tethys to seek a powerful mate who can provide for her offspring's material needs," Selene said. "On the cruise, she thought Desmond might be him, but now that he has a higher purpose, she feels scorned and wants to get back at him."

"Her article won't make him want to father her children."

Selene sipped her tea latte. "Her article warns other men they'll receive the same insults if they take themselves off the mating market and gives women insults to deliver...."

While they talked, Desmond stared past them out the front windows. On University Avenue, pedestrians and bicyclists drifted by under the lines of coast oaks on the sidewalks near the curbs. An NCMF delivery van rolled down the middle of the street. Across the avenue stood brick, steel, and glass storefronts for a massage therapist, an oxygen bar, and a cannabinist. One wide storefront bore no sign: a virtual projection, required by city ordinance to mask the vacant lot there in reality. Some software noticed his gaze and found his face in a high-net-worth database. A tooltip appeared over the virtual storefront. *Real estate investment opportunity, 0.6 ac prime location—*

A tall young man on the far sidewalk caught his attention. Stooped shoulders, long features, Desmond guessed him to be a student. He halted opposite the coffeehouse and checked the sign over its front door. "She did us a favor," Desmond said.

"Tethys?" Max asked. "A favor? How?"

The young man outside started across the street toward them. He paused for three speeding bicyclists and shot a brief annoyed look after them.

" 'The only thing worse than being talked about,' " Desmond said, quoting Wilde, " 'is not being talked about.' "

The coffeehouse door chimed. The new arrival looked around until he saw the three of them, then started through the mid-afternoon crowd toward their table. To Selene and Max, Desmond said, "In a moment, you'll see what I mean."

"You're Desmond Park?" the new arrival asked.

"Nihao." Desmond rose and held out his hand.

"I'm Castor Shafer." He grasped his right forearm with his left hand before shaking Desmond's. Desmond blinked, surprised. He hadn't seen a respectful Korean greeting since his childhood in Oakland. "And you're Selene? Max? I've seen you on campus but never worked up the courage to talk to you."

Desmond told an unoccupied nearby table to send over one of its chairs. Once all four of them sat, Desmond asked, "What can we do for you?"

"Like I said, I've seen Selene and Max on campus, and I know the message they're giving people. I kept my distance, but when I saw today's *Daily New Cal*...." He shook his head with a disgusted look. "*Krokodil* humor."

Selene's nose wrinkled. "I didn't see any crocodiles in Tethys's article."

Desmond's mindlink, tuned for such searches, turned up the reference to Soviet history. "He means edgy, transgressive satire slavishly serving conventional wisdom."

"If someone hates you that much, you're doing something right." Ice water arrived for Castor. "I don't just mean her. For the story to publish, at least the student editors and the faculty advisor for the *Daily New Cal* must hate you too. Maybe even the university administrators."

"Certainly Chancellor Yaeger," Desmond said. "But if the powers-that-be hate us, you should follow their example, ma?"

Castor looked to each side, then leaned in and lowered his voice. "When the governor offed himself, I spent a few days feeling relieved and optimistic. New Califas could change for the better. But it hasn't. Ashwin George is governor now, and he'll stay governor for another local century, or longer. No change will come from the top down."

Desmond laid his hands on the table, palms up and open. "Will you help us bring about change?"

"From the bottom up? Yes."

Desmond glanced at the lot for sale across the street as he put on an intent expression. "Not from the bottom up. From our DNA up."

New California Date 93:1
5 February 2094

The dim light coming through the draped front windows gave the lobby of their new headquarters a secluded feeling and muted the shades of blue dressing his three closest followers. Desmond turned to Selene, Max, and Castor. The time was 13:40, a few minutes before local noon. "I want to thank you for all the work you've done to prepare for unveiling the front façade."

They stood between the front glass wall and the large meeting hall, in the lee between two curved staircases leading to the freedom couches on the second floor. Selene smiled and bowed her head. She had built up the mystery of the concealed façade through social networking software while Max had readied the freedom couches and Castor had proselytized on campus and in the planetary internet. "Thank you giving us a purpose to work for... Seer."

They'd brainstormed titles for Desmond. Max rejected *teacher* before Desmond vetoed it. Everyone liked *seer*, especially Castor, who pointed out the rough homophony to *sear*. *We'll scorch the power structure*, he had said.

Desmond led them to the two-story-high glass wall on the street side. The ocean breeze undulated the drop curtain outside. The double doors opened for them. Desmond stepped up to a low dais and robotic arms pulled back the flaps in the curtain for him and his followers.

Selene's work, combined with brunchtime on Planetary New Year, had brought a crowd onto University Avenue. People crowded the outdoor tables at the coffeehouse and a bistro across the avenue. The tables bore bloody marys, mimosas, and tiny dishes of cabbage and black-eyed peas. More people milled on the sidewalks and in the street, standing under the coast oaks or leaning their bicycles on one leg. The crowd pressed closer and their curiosity-born murmurs echoed off the low-rises on both sides of the street, buildings dwarfed by their new headquarters' eight-story bulk. The new headquarters cost a pretty penny to construct in an L-month, but thanks to his position and ownership share at NCMF, Desmond afforded it without a blink.

He stopped near the front of the stage. While his followers lined up across the dais behind him, Selene to stage left and the men to stage right, he looked over the crowd. He put on a charming smile, then picked random people and held eye contact with them for a few seconds each, long enough to make the rest of the audience think he knew some of their peers. The crowd burbled till Desmond gestured for silence.

"Friends, welcome, and Happy New Year." Parabolic microphones tracked his mouth and loudspeakers under the dais amplified his words as much as the city's noise ordinance allowed. "I know it's customary on each New Year's Day to resolve to live better. I also know resolve can weaken and leave us in regret. Today I offer you good news. Today, we can hold to our resolve. Today, we can unchain ourselves from our selfish genes."

Desmond raised his right hand. The curtain split apart into a hundred vertical shreds. The shreds detached themselves from the roof's parapet and drifted down to the avenue, curling as they fell, their ravels vaporizing before reaching the pavement. The crowd's gazes ran up the façade behind Desmond and flitted from point to point over its giant mosaic.

Seven million colored glass cubes formed an image of two people. The male could have been a scion from almost any race of old California: tanned Caucasian, Polynesian, light-skinned Bantu-American,

Chicano, or a multiracial embodying old California's blind gropes for liberation from the selfish gene. He had short brown-black hair and lean, sculpted muscles. The female's blond hair brushed the sides of her neck and evoked innocence. Her skin was fair, clear, sleek.

Castor had disapproved the figures' artistic nudity. *Men will come in because they want to have sex with her.* Desmond watched the crowd and many a man's gaze circled the angles of her face, the heft of her breasts, the obscured curve of her lower abdomen. *Their selfish gene will be its own undoing*, Desmond had replied, and between his tone of voice and his position as leader, Castor had acquiesced.

The two figures, male to the left and female to the right, held hands and looked beatifically upward. From their waists down, shards of double-stranded DNA shattered and fell away from their bodies. Back-lighting built into the wall and the noon sun in the glass tiles worked in concert to make the figures dazzling. Just above the front doors, a lintel bore the words *TranscenDNA SOCIETY* in a classical, serifed font.

"In our heads," Desmond said to the crowd, "we all know we are creatures of the selfish gene." He followed with the names of Dawkins and Pinker, standard fare repeated by high school teachers across the planet. "But in our hearts, we all know the selfish gene led us into a dead end."

He recapped Cam's suicide. In the crowd, some of the faces looked contemplative. He continued his discourse, painting the late governor as an unwitting martyr to human biology. Desmond looked from face to face and saw a few agreeing nods. The rising wave of social proof crashed, though, around a coast oak on the far side of the avenue, between the coffeehouse and the bistro. Tethys leaned against the trunk with crossed arms and a cool look on her face. He took a breath between sentences and faintly smiled at her. She glanced away and muttered sidelong to a man in a green polo shirt—an off-duty EnvE employee, according to his public profile. He nodded, but a redheaded woman next to him, the EnvE man's girlfriend, looked unconvinced by Tethys' words.

Desmond went on. "What has the selfish gene given us? Sexual urges? Have you ever regretted what you've done to get sex or what you've done by giving it?"

"You would know!" the off-duty EnvE man yelled, as Tethys nodded and his girlfriend looked embarrassed.

"No need to raise your hands, just listen to the honest voice of your heart. What else? An urge to give your parents affection? What affection have they given you? Robotic nannies and ossified power structures that stunt and cripple your creative energies? The real you hates the whipcrack of those urges, and hates the cruft laid down by the selfish gene that makes you jump at them." If people heard *real you* but understood *TruSelf*, and decided Ellen Sakamoto approved his words and actions, well, what a happy accident.

"I know what you're thinking," Desmond said. " 'How can the TranscenDNA Society remove those urges?' " Desmond raised his hands toward the figures in the mosaic. "The answer lies within. Lay yourself in one of our freedom couches and the Society's members and expert systems will free your brain from the unproductive habits encoded by your selfish genes."

"Just like at Los Robles!" the EnvE man heckled. Members of the crowd frowned and others suddenly looked pensive.

"So you're accusing everyone here of being criminals?" Desmond called. He took a closer look: blond, cowlicked hair, and narrow sunglasses accenting his scornful look. His pale, redhaired girlfriend pressed her narrow lips together and muttered something.

The EnvE man waved off her words. "Not criminals, but fools. You know nothing about implantation couches."

"I fabbed every implantation couch on this planet," Desmond said confidently. The crowd's mood shifted toward his side.

"Brain chemistry is harder than bashing atoms!" To the crowd, the EnvE man yelled, "Would you trust your brain to him?"

Max stepped forward. "He knows more about implantation couch programming and operations than everyone at TruSelf!"

—Max,— Desmond said with a stern edge. He should know not to mention TruSelf.

"How would you know?" the heckler shouted.

"I used to work there," Max shouted back, "until I realized the TranscenDNA Society does more for human freedom than TruSelf ever will!"

—Max, that's enough.—

—Desmond? Seer?—

—Later.— Desmond kept a confident expression and watched the crowd. The heckler's girlfriend berated him and he glowered back. Without his fresh barbs, the crowd's skeptical energies dissipated. Many faces showed agreement and support. Max's denunciation of TruSelf had struck a nerve. Unsurprising—TruSelf was as morally bankrupt as the rest of the founders' institutions. But the Society could use bridges to those institutions far more than it could broken piers with blown spans.

Enough. Stay on target.

"If you're ready to free yourself from your sexual urges or the burdens of your families, you're welcome through these doors anytime, day or night. If you prefer privacy, come through the alley to the rear entrance, or hire an airjitney with tinted windows. If only one or the other of the freedoms we now offer appeal to you, take that one by itself now and the next when you're ready. Or come in any time to tell us what you're feeling. We'll listen."

His gaze roved the crowd, and with the help of his mindlink he noticed the most needy faces. "If you're ready now, why wait? Come, we'll set you free." A bicyclist shuffled his feet, then came forward; Castor helped him onstage. A shill, a follower recruited on campus a few weeks before, but needed to prime the pump. A few more people, honest new members, followed. Desmond met each of their gazes and beckoned them. "There's no need to wait any longer." Another two people started forward.

One last study of the crowd. The EnvE man and his girlfriend still argued. *Fortune favors the bold.* "You think he's in the wrong," Desmond said to her. His mindlink hunted her face in a social database.

"What you do is your business," she said.

"So why does he oppose us, Gwendolyn?"

The EnvE man jabbed a finger at Desmond. "Stay out of it."

"I asked her, not you." The woman looked uneasy. "You can tell me privately," Desmond added.

She overcame her uneasiness. "He's currying favor with his bosses."

Turn the conversation into an attack on EnvE? No, too early in the process of building a mass movement. *First get them on your side, then attack the power structure.* Desmond kept the conversation personal. "Do you know why?" He set his mindlink to mapping social connections around her boyfriend.

"He wants a raise and a promotion. I swear," she said to her boyfriend, "all you care about is money."

The EnvE man fumed and shook his head. Desmond spoke. "You know why he wants those things, ma?"

"The reason why anyone does. The selfish gene, just like you said."

A picture of the EnvE man's social connections filled in Desmond's mind's eye. "He's got a more particular reason than that. He wants that blonde in the next cubicle to go out with him."

Purely a hunch, but the EnvE man paled for a moment, eyes wide. He covered his tell with bluster. "You're talking nonsense, ruco!"

"Nonsense?" Gwendolyn said. "Don't lie to me. I saw your face. Lissandra? You want to dump me for Lissandra? Do you think of her when you get me in those positions where you can't see my face?"

"Goushi. Gwend, you are such a whera sometimes. Rucodan's making shit up—"

"I saw your face, piyan! I saw your eyes!" Gwendolyn stalked toward the stage. Her nostrils flared and her cheeks reddened, and impending tears glimmered in her eyes. Selene helped her up and embraced her sidelong.

"Brothers, sisters, welcome," Desmond said to the newcomers to the stage. Good results for his first public call. He led them inside as the remaining crowd broke up.

In the lobby, the terrazzo pattern showed another mosaic of the characters from the front façade. Here, the male and the female stood with their backs to each other, each looking up the stairway on their side of the building. Castor's idea, to separate the freedom couches by sex. Selene led Gwendolyn and three other women up the right-hand stairs and Castor led the men up the left, Max trailing. Castor gathered the male converts on the second floor landing and described the freedom couch process as Desmond caught up with Max on the stairs.

—Max, a word.—

—Yes, Seer?—

—I never brought up TruSelf. Why did you?—

Max frowned. —I wanted to help you shut down the heckler. Everything I said was true. I would never lie about our work.—

—It was true, and I appreciate your zeal. But we're not here to attack TruSelf. We're here to set people free.—

—But Seer, TruSelf keeps people in chains. Employees like I was, clients it gives talk therapy and microfabs to. We have to oppose it.—

—I detest it too,— Desmond said, —but I prefer we use it. We most need a good reputation among the general public, and if we stand next to TruSelf, some of its perceived legitimacy will rub off on us.—

Max's brows crinkled. —But it has none.—

—Perceptions, not realities, are what the masses see. It's an easier sell to pitch the Society as a renewal, not a revolution. Also, an alliance with TruSelf would give us a counterweight to pressure from Government Mesa. I'm sure our new meimei was right about senior people in the bureaucracy wanting to stop us.— Ashwin had undoubtedly noticed the building permit in Desmond's name. —We already have one enemy. We don't need to make another.—

Max's face showed a few remaining misgivings; action would sap them. Desmond clapped his hand on Max's shoulder and spoke aloud. "I trust our expert systems to operate the freedom couches, but I'll trust them more when you're overseeing them."

Purpose galvanized Max's features. He hurried to the waiting men and joined Castor in explaining the process. Desmond hoped he could keep Max's energy moving with that same sense of purpose for a long time to come.

Satisfaction tightened Desmond's cheeks. The EnvE man's heckling showed Ashwin would give his followers all the purpose they needed.

* * *

Ashwin stood on the blue-green lawn, his back to the governor's mansion. K-Nought's midday warmed his nape, but his blood was already up. He stared through the smartglass wall at the edge of Government Mesa to the khaki smear rising over University Avenue a mile and a half away.

Someone on the roof of Desmond's temple could read lips through a telephoto lens. —Opaque the smartglass inbound,— Ashwin told the mansion. After it did, he turned and said, "Look what he's done."

Yellow and red balloons, their interior heating elements spent, shrank and wrinkled atop their poles. The breeze from the ocean swayed over the heads of the brunch guests he'd asked to stay after the party.

Justin Bauer, New Cal Mol Fab's CEO, lifted his head. "That's right, Desmond unveiled his side project today."

"You knew what he was doing?" Carl Yaeger's voice bore a sharp edge.

Bauer shook his head. "I only hear rumors. Desmond's an introvert and is mostly at ops south of the river, not at headquarters."

"Come here," Ashwin said. "All of you, augment your vision, and look." Bauer and the others started toward him, stepping around dwarf centaur robots cleaning dirty plates from the garden tables. While they did, his mindlink showed still photos of the new building's façade and pulled public audio and video feeds from Desmond's recent soapboxing.

Transcend DNA? He'd thought Desmond recognized his power that night on the yacht and would not dare challenge it. No one else had, even before it became clear to all Tián Quán backed him. Ashwin had earned the governorship; no psychobabble cult would jeopardize his hold on it.

"He really did found a religion," Carl Yaeger said.

That son of a bitch Desmond wanted to prove him wrong? He loved Priya, but she had miscast the roles in *Julius Caesar*: Ashwin had the lean and hungry look, and now he turned it on the others. "He's fired a shot across all our bows. Carl, he's right under your nose. He's already got some of your students, and he picked his location to lure in more with free pizza and bullshit philosophy." The chancellor yanked his gaze to the university's campus atop Rousseau Mesa, its cultured limestone walls and Spanish tile roofs a quarter-mile by airmobile from Desmond's temple.

"Ellen, he promises people self-improvement. That's TruSelf's turf."

Ellen Sakamoto scrunched her mouth. "Hundreds of groups on the planet promise to make you a better person, from the Inner Game of Surfing to Buddhist Kabbalah. TruSelf is still the most popular."

The breeze moaned a little louder. "Have you checked what he said today? 'Free the real you?'"

She looked unconcerned. "He used vocabulary from our frame of discourse. It shows TruSelf's position."

"He wants people to think you endorse him," Ashwin said. "But listen to his follower and you'll hear the truth." He sent a bookmark to Max Jacoby's words to the heckler.

She narrowed her eyes and peered at the grass for a time. Too long. Ashwin said, "You heard how he called you a bunch of frauds."

Ellen showed a palm in a stop gesture. "I'm looking at it in context."

If she still doubted his leadership, time to force her doubts aside. "So we're agreed," Ashwin said firmly, "about what a threat he is."

"What are you suggesting we do?" Bauer asked.

Ashwin hooked his thumb at Desmond's new temple. "He paid for his construction project out of his salary from you, didn't he? Fire him."

Bauer gaped. "Fire him."

"You're the chief executive officer, aren't you? Execute."

"He's also an owner. Two million shares."

"Buy him out."

"Even if I did," Bauer said, "I have to answer to the other owners of NCMF. Desmond does good work."

"Does? Or did? You'll find he's shirked his duties at NCMF to build up his cult. I'm quite sure. If you look for it, you'll find it, which will give you ammunition to lowball the buyout offer."

"I'll look into it when I'm back in the office," Bauer said. His demeanor reeked of insubordination. *Did you disrespect Cam the way you're disrespecting me? I need NCMF to feed sixty thousand colonists, but you need me and my allies at EnvE more than you think.*

Bauer remained nonchalant. "Governor, thank you again for a marvelous New Year's Day brunch." They bro-hugged stiffly, hands clapping hard on backs before they disentangled. "Happy New NC-Year, everyone."

Bauer sauntered over the lawn to the mansion's near wing. A glass door, the sole visual break in a wall of pearlescent concrete and rolled steel, opened for him. It galled Ashwin, but he would give Bauer a chance to play ball before he brought down the hammer. His position was still new; he had to pick his battles. Desmond first.

"Carl, what are you going to do?"

"I'm already thinking about it. Non-students require a permit from the administration to engage in public speech on campus—"

"They do?"

Yaeger blinked. "We haven't enforced the requirement very much in recent years, but I'll change that. Second, the university has a lot of sway over the businesses at the foot of the mesa. But those are minor compared to my main plan. I'll engage Desmond in a public debate."

Ashwin frowned. "See how your other ideas work first."

"I've taken part in intellectual dialogues for decades, while the deepest discussion Desmond's ever had is telling expert systems what color to fab a shirt. I can debate circles around him."

"I'm sure you can…" Ashwin said to buy time to phrase his objections.

Ellen filled the gap. "You'll give oxygen to the fire if you do this. If you keep it quiet, Desmond's movement will wither away, like most do."

"She's exactly right," Ashwin said. "If you debate him, it would make him seem to be your equal. He isn't. He's a child throwing a tantrum. If you give him attention, you'll only encourage him." He'd learned this from his parents; why hadn't Yaeger learned it from his? Lax whero parenting, probably.

Yaeger shook his head. "If we let him linger under our noses, he'll grow confident. Ashwin, I'm the most respected academic on the planet. Desmond's an engineer. I have the advantage. Once I crush him in a debate, the TranscenDNA Society will be a joke on everyone's lips."

"He's an engineer with a mindlink mainline to historical facts."

"My debating skills are in my brain," Yaeger said. His tone of voice showed he considered the question resolved.

Ashwin opened a private channel to the chancellor. —Is this personal?—

—Personal? Why would it be?—

—He was rude to you. That night.—

Yaeger's brows lowered for a moment but a distraction came to Ashwin, a private message from Ellen. —What are you freezing me out of?— She asked.

Whatever I damn well please, but TruSelf was the nearest thing New California had to a state religion. *Pick your battles.* Ashwin angled his head and replied to her alone. —I'm trying to teach out Carl's TruSelf. I don't want to embarrass him by letting others see his cruft flake off.—

—A fair point. Sorry.— Ellen closed the channel.

—Sure,— Yaeger said, —he was rude to me with Cam less than an hour dead, but that has nothing to do with it.— Aloud, he said, "I can best him in debate and, as you may recall, I have former students across the planet, in NCBC and the private content providers, and high school teachers and college professors, who can help get our message across. He's already getting publicity through social networking software and that eyesore on University Avenue. As I see it, we have to engage in counterpublicity."

Former students across the planet? Was that a threat? Could Yaeger withdraw enough support to deny Ashwin a future reelection?

Ashwin peered at the chancellor, but he had to deal with Desmond before confronting Yaeger. "Try it, then. Ellen, where do you stand?"

She stared at Desmond's distant temple. "It's the Foundation's current view that, because DNA made us, transcending it would take us away from our TruSelves."

"I'm glad to hear the Prime Teacher's wisdom," Ashwin said. "Both of you, thanks again for coming to brunch, and staying to discuss business on a holiday." They took their goodbyes with bro-hugs and air kisses. As soon as Yaeger and Ellen entered the building, Ashwin stared through the smartglass wall, past the scrub myrtles downs-lope, to Desmond's temple.

He could force Bauer to act if NCMF's CEO dithered in firing Desmond. Hopefully Yaeger would win the debate. Ashwin briefly envied Cam; the founder had taken for granted the unanimous support of all the colony's leaders.

New Cal needed Ashwin to have that unanimous support. The opposite of strong leadership was not democracy. It was anarchy.

New California Date 93:14
20 February 2094

Desmond's landau banked over headquarters. It entered the parking garage on the eighth floor, tires touching with a rubbery squeak, and rolled toward his waiting people. It lifted its gullwing doors as it came to a stop.

Cheers erupted from the dozen full members, elect, standing outside the glass doors to the reception area. "Seer, good luck in the debate," shouted someone. Another yelled, "Show up that baojun Yaeger!"

"Thank you," he called, "but it's time we got moving. Selene, Max, Castor."

Selene climbed in first. The plunging neckline of her blue dress showed a deep triangle of pale skin as she sat on the fore seat, facing Desmond. Faint touches of rouge accented her cheeks and lips. "Seer, did I embody your suggestions?"

"Marvelously," Desmond said. Her allure would distract the chancellor and pull in chained men.

Max took the rear seat next to Desmond, and Castor sat next to Selene. He clutched a large rucksack and laid it on the seat between them. "Are you ready for the debate, Seer?" Castor asked as his restraint harness bound him.

"Of course." His mindlink had cached a classic reference on argumentative tricks, Schopenhauer's *The Art of Controversy*. "You have all the props? Let's go."

The airmobile rolled to the exit and revved up its engines. Soon they climbed through the altitude of Rousseau Mesa. Desmond crossed his legs and looked out the window.

"You look very handsome, Seer," Selene said.

He checked the vee pattern of his blazer's pinstripes worn by his reflection in the window and tapped his Cuban heel against the floor. His trousered calf brushed the door of an underseat storage bin. He'd dressed to look professional—and taller and stronger-shouldered. "We all must play judo with our audience's selfish genes."

"Judo, Seer?" Castor asked.

"We'll use the selfish gene's own momentum to throw it to the mat."

The landau banked. To the right stood UNewCal's administration building. The clock tower showed forty minutes till the debate would start. Beyond stood the Spanish mission lecture halls, the south dorms, and on a spur of mesa thick with mature myrtles, Yaeger's mansion.

Further along, the performing arts building looked ridiculous, with swooping fiberglass walls and deep black photovoltaic collectors sited uselessly on the roof's northern slopes. Fortunately, the concert hall's interior had been validated by acoustical engineering expert systems.

"Why aren't we landing?" Castor asked.

The landau leveled its flight and the performing arts center fell behind them. "What's going on?" Desmond asked the airmobile. In reply, he received a message in text across his visual field, *I have been asked to remain in a holding pattern.*

Anxious looks formed on their faces. "What are they doing to us?" Selene asked.

Desmond chuckled, and his demeanor calmed the others even before he spoke. "Yaeger is trying to agitate us. We won't fall for his trick, ma?"

The landau circled Rousseau Mesa twice more. The parking lot reserved for Desmond and the others at the performing arts center's backstage entrance had room for the landau both times.

Finally they landed. The landau's doors opened to show three impassive people and a couple of hovering robots from the university's police department. The area around the landau was otherwise empty, and unease touched Desmond; but these police only bore non-lethal weapons, tangle wire and mild sedatives. Furthermore, Yaeger wanted him to go in to the debate. The chancellor had nothing to gain by harming Desmond and his team.

Ashwin, on the other hand?

The governor wouldn't dare. Not even a tyrant could reign without the tacit consent of the governed, and the people of New Cal would riot against state-sanctioned violence. Plus, a step closer to the door brought another constraint on Ashwin into view. The rui shi pair sat on either side of the backstage door. According to their livery collars, they were just auspicious lions tonight. No need to say good evening. —Everyone's here to watch,— he said to his followers.

They relaxed. Selene said "Aw" as the cub writhed under its mother's paw. Desmond led them between the rui shi, and the backstage door swung open.

An assistant stage manager, a short, curvy woman, waited for them. "Nihao, Mr. Park...."

Selene's voice bubbled with delight. "Metherealle, it's so good to see you!"

"Nihao." Metherealle showed a pained expression.

"How have you been since you graduated? Is your career fulfilling?"

"I can't talk now. My job is to get you to the green room and then the stage." Metherealle avoided Selene's eye contact. "Sorry," she whispered, then led them deeper backstage.

—She fears for her job if she's too friendly,— Desmond said to Selene.

—I can tell, but that's so wrong.—

—We know. She knows.— Desmond's voice hardened. —And Yaeger knows too.—

"Here you go," Metherealle said, gesturing to an open door. Inside the room stood dated couches and a table laden with bottles of water in an ice bucket and starfruit and mango chunks on a tray. A mirror and makeup table dominated the back wall. "I'll take you to the stage at 2255."

Fifteen minutes. Desmond nodded and Metherealle scurried away.

Once the door shut them in, Desmond said, —Assume the room is bugged, and don't eat or drink anything.—

—They could have laced the food and water with neuroactives,— Max said.

Selene stepped closer to Desmond. —Time to get you ready, Seer.— She pointed him to a seat in front of the mirror and opened her handbag. Inside lay compacts of powders and wide brushes, things outside his knowledge. He let her prepare his face for the cameras while the young men looked on in silence.

The mood grew tenser as the start time approached. Desmond balanced their growing nervousness against the ticking clock. A few minutes before Metherealle was due, he said, —Everyone, keep your cool and we'll be fine. Fear is a legacy of our selfish gene. It was useful when our distant ancestors faced saber-tooth tigers and bands of homicidal foes. It's misplaced here. Yaeger can do nothing more than spout hollow rhetoric from the dead past.—

He gathered them closer, and rested his hands on Castor and Selene's shoulders. —Remember, we're the first faces of freedom most audience members will ever see. Let our demeanor show them the power unchained men and women have.—

2255 ticked by. When the minute turned, Castor said, —They're going to rush us to the stage to make us look disheveled.—

—We won't fall for it,— Max said, scowling at the fruit tray.

At 2257, knuckles rapped the door and the assistant stage manager pinged them through mindlink. Desmond told the door to open. "Let me get you on stage," Metherealle said.

"Is everything well up front?" Desmond asked as they filed out the door.

"Pardon me?" She led them under robotic winches coiled on the high ceiling.

"You were a couple of minutes late. I assume something unexpected had to get resolved before you could come for us."

Metherealle hunched her shoulders and walked faster. "Amono," she muttered.

Three maroon curtains backed the stage at angles to each other at house left, center, and right. The curtain at house left slightly drew apart its halves for them. Max, Castor, and Selene went out first, then waited for Desmond.

Two curved tables faced the murmuring audience. The tables defined a C shape open to the crowd. On each table stood a podium, and maple stain swirled in polished wood. Classy material, when most people lived on plastic furniture in mycocrete houses. On either side of Desmond's podium stood chairs, one toward stage center, to Desmond's left, and two closer to the audience.

Castor pulled water bottles from his rucksack, while Selene and Max moved to the seats on Desmond's right.

Yaeger stood at the other podium with three professors seated near him. As Desmond moved toward his position, Yaeger and the others came upstage, toward Castor. Yet Yaeger stayed on his half of the stage to make Desmond come to him. Not happening. Desmond bade his followers stop on their side of stage center. He raised his hand toward Yaeger, indifferently flexing his wrist.

Yaeger dropped his hand with a shrug. "Desmond, I have to say I'm impressed."

"How so?"

Yaeger gestured at Castor, then Max. "You've built up a surprisingly large following, being an engineer with low testosterone. Have you read my papers on the iconography of the quasi-sacred in post-industrial societies?"

"No. Carl, you remember Selene Alvarez, ma?"

She showed gleaming teeth and waved her hand to Yaeger. For a second, the chancellor's eyes widened and a pout distended his mouth. Even after he masked his reaction, every few seconds his gaze flicked to her cleavage and longing and resentment tinged his features.

—Places, please,— said the assistant stage manager. Desmond and his team took their positions and he frowned for a moment as he reached to touch the podium. Three tiny microphones tracked his mouth, but Yaeger's podium had the same hardware. What was the problem? A glance across stage showed him. The stagehands had given Desmond a podium about two inches taller than Yaeger's. To the remote audience, experiencing the debate through mindlink, a closeup on him would show the top of the podium higher over his chest than Yaeger's. It would make him look shorter than the chancellor and negate his sartorial tricks to look taller and broader across the shoulders.

What other exploits of human psychology had Yaeger's team implemented? This one, though, they could readily rebut. —Castor, the riser.—

—Of course, Seer.— Castor dug into his rucksack and pulled out a thin, rolled-up sheet. A wrist flick unrolled it to full size, two feet by three. It inflated to form a box with a height of three inches. Castor set it down on the floor behind the podium. Desmond nodded to Yaeger, then stepped up on the box.

—In five, four....—

The moderator came in from house right. Sapna Singh read the news for NCBC. She wore a long crimson dress, trimmed with pink paisley at her shoulders and in a vee pattern from her bust to her waist. At her forehead, a pale ruby hung from a jeweled headband. No blue-baller, she, and the look evoking her Indian heritage would get people thinking of other indios, such as the governor. Any objectivity she showed would be illusory: an easy search would show she was a former student of Yaeger. Sadly, no one would make that search, and Desmond would seem defensive if he brought it up.

While Singh introduced the debate and its participants, Desmond scanned the audience. Heavily skewed toward university faculty and their friends and lovers. A few students, but no Society members, had won a "random" drawing for seats. His mindlink highlighted Tethys about two-thirds of the way back on the orchestra level, under the mezzanine. Some prominent colonists sat near the stage, among them Ellen Sakamoto in the third row. Many of her TruSelf Foundation subordinates filled the rows around her.

Governor George did not attend.

Introductions complete, Singh turned to Desmond. "Mr. Park,

your opening remarks."

"Thank you, Ms. Singh," he began, although he most wanted to thank his opponent. Yaeger gave him free publicity, including access to NCBC and private content providers. Even if he lost the debate, he would get his message across to someone who needed it.

Desmond had rehearsed his talking points hundreds of times in the months since Cam's suicide, and now hit them effortlessly. Our genes built us solely to propel copies of themselves into the future; our genes did not care about our hopes and fears, our dreams and aspirations; the freedom couches, along with the Society's active listening sessions and intimacy-centric relating, could free people from striving for sex or parental love. His demeanor and tone implied he could free people from much more. He closed his speech and faced Yaeger.

Yaeger looked scornful. "Mr. Park tells a pretty story about setting you free, but look in your heart. Do you want to be free from New California? We're free of a genocidal president and the violent rednecks who elected him. We're free of Chinese occupation forces. We're free to surf and ski and we're free to pursue our TruSelves—"

Ellen kept a poker face.

"He speaks of freedom," Yaeger went on, "but what sort does Mr. Park offer? The so-called freedom couch is a copy of technology used by the Department of Criminal Rehabilitation. I look out on the audience here tonight. No one I see deserves rehabilitation. Mr. Park, what do you see?"

"I see people brought here by the same technology those Chinese occupiers use to explore the galaxy. Should we all abandon New California?"

Yaeger looked smug. "You haven't answered my question."

"You haven't answered mine—"

"Do you see people here who deserve rehabilitation?"

"I see people who deserve the freedom to choose how to live their lives." Desmond zeroed his gaze on Tethys. "Even those born here, who never saw President Fletcher or the Chinese occupation, long for freedom." She avoided eye contact. Desmond turned back to Yaeger. "And by freedom we both know I mean psychological freedom, not local government by people who speak our same language, or choices we can make in the marketplace."

"Choices in the marketplace, Mr. Park? You've made some good ones."

"Excuse me?"

Yaeger turned to the audience. "He just said you should free yourselves from New California, but he certainly won't do it himself! He's still the Chief Technology Officer at NCMF. He still lives on the edge of Fremont Mesa. Mr. Park, which of the three airmobiles you own did you take to come here tonight? How many New Cal dollars did you spend for your prime real estate on University Avenue? You live better than all your followers combined. Would someone really free of his selfish genes do that? Would you in the audience follow such a man?"

Mutters came from some shocked, shocked shills near front center. Desmond chuckled. "Carl, if they take your side, they already are. We flew over your mansion to come here, and your salary is as high as a cabinet official's—"

"Mr. Park," Sapna Singh said. "*Ad hominem* attacks have no place here."

"*Ad hominem* attacks? Such as his last question to me?"

"You claim to free people," she said. "Chancellor Yaeger doesn't."

Desmond reached into his podium for his water bottle and lifted it halfway to his mouth. "My apologies. I forgot Carl works in higher education." He sipped water and glanced over the bottle at the crowd. His last words raised sullen looks from faculty members, but someone near Ellen chuckled. The faculty's sullen looks deepened.

Desmond faced Yaeger. "You asked how can someone of our social standing bring about meaningful change." No, but by his words, the audience would think Yaeger really had. "I'm simply following a tradition blazed by advocates for justice throughout the centuries."

He'd prepared this point. Jesus of Nazareth had been a prosperous skilled tradesman before his first wife's death in childbirth drove him first to follow John the Baptist, then found his own messianic movement; Muhammad had been a prosperous merchant when he'd first seen the angel Gabriel. But those were poor examples to share with over-educated, irreligious New Californians. "Carl, you must remember technology CEOs from Silicon Valley were among the first Americans to call for President Fletcher and his cabinet to resign after the Ningbo atrocity. An even greater model is the Buddha, who was born a pampered prince before he set out on a path to free people."

—We're winning,— Castor said to the Society members. —Live online commentary is tilting our way.—

"Ladies and gentlemen, he's comparing himself to the Buddha!" Yaeger told the audience. "But did the Buddha surround himself with beautiful young women?"

Desmond shook his head at the question's irrelevance. "Carl, I've had no more sex with Ms. Alvarez than you have."

Yaeger gave Selene another boob check. For a fraction of a second his expression revealed lust, but anger soon chased it. He swept it from his face behind a sip of water.

"We only have your word for that," Yaeger said. "But even if you haven't abused your authority in that way, you've done other things to ruin your followers' lives. My peers at Golden State U. tell me Selene Alvarez was a promising student before she dropped out to join you, and I know Castor Shafer, a young man who overcame some personal issues to become a high-achieving scholar at UNewCal, skipped the final month of classes last local year."

Desmond heard a brief, faint hiss. He assumed it came from Castor. The younger man had hinted at some teenage malfeasance scrubbed off his record, but never shared details. Desmond took a full breath. If Castor's crime had been scrubbed off his record, how did Yaeger know about it? Suddenly thirsty, Desmond sipped more water.

"But even if they return to classes," Yaeger said, "the fundamental purpose of the university is to give young people a liberal education in the humanities. Our genetic legacy is the basis of our humanity. By repudiating our genetic legacy, you repudiate the university's purpose." He spoke as if UNewCal had emerged with the lava flows creating the continent a hundred million E-years prior. What a happy coincidence New California relied on the institution Yaeger headed.

Desmond had the university's policies close at mind. "UNewCal students are free to spend years at other institutions or on sabbatical.

They're also free to withdraw in the middle of an NC-year. No Society member has gone beyond the bounds of policies you implemented. And of course, any member of the TranscenDNA Society is free to attend any university."

He swallowed thickly and stiffly turned his head to the audience. "He also argued that Society members are unable to learn the true messages of the university. I always understood the purpose of the university as helping students shake off preconceived notions embedded in them by their upbringing."

Yaeger sensed a trick. "That's a way of putting part of it."

"Full members of the Society are less susceptible to the influence of their parents. Doesn't that further your purpose?"

"It cuts away at their freedom to think."

"Freedom to think? Do you need a sex drive for that?" Warmth flushed Desmond's face.

"The learning process is more than regurgitating past knowledge," Yaeger said. "It requires applying that knowledge to the world, including the world of physical intimacy. Mr. Park's cult doesn't merely threaten the university," Yaeger said, "but it directly repudiates the pursuit of one's TruSelf."

In the audience, Ellen perked up.

Mouth suddenly dry, Desmond swallowed. "That's a false premise. I can't and don't speak for the TruSelf Foundation, but as I understand its teachings, just as each of our TruSelves is different, each of our paths to find them can be different. The TranscenDNA Society adds one more path for those looking for one to take."

Unwilling to reveal his intention by turning his head, Desmond grabbed a camera feed to check on Ellen Sakamoto. She seemed unconvinced still. Did he waste effort trying to peel her away from Ashwin's coalition?

—We're losing our lead,— Castor said.

Tama! Desmond's palms felt damp and he surreptitiously wiped them on his trousers. *Stay calm. You can outdebate Yaeger any day of the week.*

"Mr. Park is just paying lip service to the TruSelf Foundation. If he respected it, he would have subordinated his movement to the Foundation by now." Yaeger shook his head theatrically. "As a concerned citizen, his ingratitude especially galls me. The TruSelf Foundation turned one of his followers into an OptimumMan and he rewards it with contempt."

Castor trembled. —Our enemies will do anything,— Desmond told him within hearing of the others, —because they are in the wrong and desperate to avoid the truth.—

—It's supposed to be confidential,— Castor replied, voice tight.

—See how that pofu Sakamoto fulfills her promises,— Max said.

Desmond closed his eyes to regather himself. —Team, stay focused.—

Troubled looks formed on faces in the audience. Yaeger continued. "It would be indecent of me to pollute the reputation of a high-achieving young person with details of vile acts that would make you gag, but I can say Mr. Park should be grateful to the TruSelf Foundation—"

"Many of us have benefited from the Foundation's efforts," Desmond said. His voice sounded thin and too high. He took a breath but his chest felt tight. Wodema, he couldn't be having a heart attack, ma? He wavered on his feet and clutched the podium.

—That treacherous baojun,— Castor said. —What he's implying, 'make you gag,' I never—

—We don't care what you might have done,— Selene said. — You're our brother.—

—I didn't rape anyone's mouth! It was just a little vandalism. Graffiti, that's all. *Governor Watkins must die.* I didn't really mean it. I repented and did cognitive therapy, not even any microfab implants.—

Desmond reached for the water bottle in the podium when he heard another hiss, clearly from one of the microphones—

Yaeger had camouflaged an atomizer among the microphones. Which aerosolized pro-anxiety drug made him nervous and anxious? Desmond dropped his hand and inhaled as deeply as he could. He had to hold on till their scheduled time ran out. He had to. Failure would toss the Society on the compost heap of history.

"You want to take the Foundation's efforts and demolish them in your ridiculous and monstrous attempt to remake human nature!"

Yaeger said. "You've already neutered your followers and turned them against their own parents. If everyone joined your cult, even with exogestation clinics, no one would reproduce and the human race would eventually die out."

"Die out?" Desmond managed to say. "Rejuve clinics make our death rate negligible. All reproduction gives us today is young people trapped in the tar of institutions congealed around their founders."

Yaeger bristled. "If the Earthborn are so bad for New California, why didn't you follow Governor Watkins over the side?" Someone in the crowd whooped in support. Desmond felt lightheaded, and Yaeger's next words battered him. "Where will it end? Our genetic heritage makes us crave egalitarian organizations. Will you turn us into docile followers of tyranny? Our genetic heritage makes us crave the companionship of others. Will you turn us into isolated hermits who cannot take joy from a kind word or a gentle touch? Again I ask you: where will it end?"

Desmond's mouth felt dry and his face remained hot. "It will end where each person chooses to end it, and no further."

Wodema, that sounded lame. Yaeger gloated and opened his mouth for his next words. Sweat trickled down Desmond's neck. How much time left? Ten minutes? Tsao!

"When fanatics taste blood, people become statistics—"

The lights suddenly cut out, plunging the stage and the audience into darkness. Only the dim red glow of exit lights cut the gloom. The crowd gasped and muttered. Across the stage, Yaeger's team looked like vague phantoms.

—Ladies and gentlemen at home,— Singh said, —we're experiencing technical difficulties.— "To everyone in the live audience...." The microphone had lost power too. She switched to mindlink, powered by her own metabolism and body movements. —To everyone in the live audience, please remain seated.—

Even with a dead microphone and his back to Desmond, Yaeger's voice still carried across the dark stage. "Tama! What pendeho in utilities cut power?" One of his lackeys muttered something. "Bizui! Get it fixed!"

They waited in the dark. At least no one could see Desmond sweat, and the darkness felt cooler and more comfortable.

After a couple of minutes, through mindlink, Singh wanted to speak to him and Yaeger. Desmond opened the channel. Singh asked, —When will power be restored, Chancellor?—

—Soon. I'm certain.—

—When?—

—I said, soon. Why? You want to bail on me? NCBC stays here until we finish the debate.—

Singh said, —NCBC can't afford an hour of dead air—

—Not even as a favor? To me?—

—Chancellor, this isn't my decision. It goes all the way up.—

—Up a chain of my former students.—

—Who've been NCMF customers every day they've been on-planet,— Desmond said. His heart pounded and his palms still felt sweaty. —If you haven't made your position known by now, Carl, you won't.—

—I'm winning and you know it,— Yaeger said.

—And we both know why.—

Yaeger's tone flattened. —I have no clue what you're talking about.—

Singh sided with Yaeger. She would dismiss accusations Yaeger drugged him as paranoia. In the Society members' private channel, he said, —Take my microphones when we're done.—

—Take?— Max said.

—Pry them off the podium if you have to. We need evidence.— He muted the channel to his followers and said to Singh, —We're done for tonight.—

—No we're not,— Yaeger said. —We'll fix the power.—

Singh hesitated. —Not any time soon. Our people looked at it. A transformer backstage blew. You won't get it fixed for a few hours.—

—A few hours?— Yaeger said. —Sounds like sabotage to me. Desmond?—

—Carl, listen to my tone of voice. When I say, 'I have no clue what you're talking about,' I sound as if I mean it.—

Yaeger showed a moment of unease, but bulled over it. —Sapna, my closing remarks?—

—Film them yourselves and get them to us by midday tomorrow. We'll splice things together and rebroadcast the complete debate tomorrow night. Excuse me, please.—

To the audience both live and remote, she said, —In light of the technical difficulties, we will cut short tonight's debate.—

Relief rocked Desmond. —Max, look up antidotes for aerosolized pro-anxiety drugs. Castor, get the microphones. Selene, stay close to me.— Desmond pushed away from the podium and Selene took his elbow. The crowd chattered as ushers led them out. Stagehands and robots slipped through the curtain from backstage.

Castor peered at the microphones. Max joined him and they worked their hands over the mounting hardware.

"Spensa?" Yaeger said. "What the hell are you doing?"

"Taking evidence," Desmond said.

"That's theft." His tone made the people around him pause.

"I'll buy the microphones off you," Desmond said. It was a challenge to speak up. His voice sounded dry. "Plus, after we get all their specs, I'll fab you exact duplicates, highest priority. I'll even throw in a copy to Ms. Singh for free."

"No sale, no trade," Yaeger said. "If any property leaves my sight, I'll have the university police arrest you for theft, and I will press charges."

Tsao. They needed the drug aerosolizer to undo the damage caused by Yaeger's seeming victory—

Through his mindlink, Metherealle, the assistant stage manager, urgently wanted to talk to him. He trusted its intuition and opened the channel.

—You don't need it.—

He subtly looked for her in the gloom, not moving his head in order to spare her Yaeger's attention. —Why not?—

She stood behind Yaeger, her face turned to the floor. —I recorded the orders to hide a drug dispenser in a dummy microphone. I'll beam them over.—

—Please.— A bong in his mind's ear sounded when the files arrived, and his enhanced intuitions gave a summary. Explosive stuff, going high up to university administrators, though Yaeger had kept his name out of it. The drug was not identified.

—Thanks,— he told her. —And for cutting power, too.—

—What he did was too wrong.—

—We'll publicize what you shared with us. We'll anonymize it, don't worry—

Across the room, her head shook faintly. —Doesn't matter. I can't work here any longer.— She ended the call.

Desmond stared across the dim stage at Yaeger, then raised his hands. "We either give up the evidence now, or give it up when there's footage of me with tangled hands at the police station? I'm no fool. Leave it, guys."

"Seer?" Castor said.

"Put down the drug dispenser. Then we'll go." He beamed his followers the summary of Metherealle's disclosure. The younger men dropped their hands from the podium and Desmond led his team backstage. His legs wobbled under him.

—Max, what's your progress?—

—I've found antidotes for pro-anxiety drugs, but much depends on which drug he used. I'll order them all, Seer.—

A thought came to Desmond: Ellen Sakamoto wanted to talk. Why now? His heart raced and cold sweat dampened his nape. Yet if he had a chance to bridge-build to her, he would take it. —Talk to all four of us,— he replied.

—Fair enough.— She manifested an avatar walking backward in front of them. "Desmond, Ms. Alvarez, fellows, nihao."

"What do you want," Max said, aloud, but within a bubble of virtual shared only between Ellen, Desmond, and his followers. "Here to see your handiwork, ma?"

—Max,— Desmond said.

—Seer, what?—

—I'll talk for us.—

Ellen raised an eyebrow. "Desmond, he speaks for you?"

"No," Desmond said. "It's been a night of dirty pool and we're all frazzled."

"The dirty pool didn't come from TruSelf. We take patient confidentiality seriously."

"Then how did Yaeger find out Castor graduated from an Opti-mumMan camp?"

Ellen made a moue. "I must have a leak. I'll plug it."

Walking made Desmond's breaths ragged, and he blinked at spots in his vision. He needed to say more before Max did—

Selene tightened her grip on his elbow. "What about the pro-anxiety drug?" she asked.

"The—?" Ellen's face lit with recognition. "That piyan Yaeger. I thought the pressure had actually gotten to you. I should have known better, Desmond. Which drug?"

"We don't know," Desmond said.

"Water-soluble?"

"Maybe. Aerosolized. From a dummy microphone in the podium."

Ellen's gaze roved over Desmond's face. Her scrutiny churned his stomach and beaded sweat on his forehead. "Let me think about aerosolized cholinergic receptor antagonists. I'll order an antidote from the main public fab, high priority and rush delivery to your headquarters." She stopped walking and touched Desmond's forearm. "I don't approve everything you do, but I'm not on their side." Her avatar winked out.

In the parking lot, the cool night air chilled Desmond's sweaty skin. The landau's engines whined and they hurried past the two rui shi as the airmobile's doors rose.

The landau soon lifted from the parking lot. Desmond thrashed off his blazer, then dropped his head to his knees and inhaled deeply. His face remained hot. "Water," he said.

Castor rummaged in his pack. His long face fell even further. "We're out."

Desmond thought at the landau to turn up the air conditioning and aim it at his head.

"You believe her, Seer?" Max asked.

The air flowed long enough for Desmond to lift his head. "Yes."

"She could have shared information with Yaeger. How else could she know which drug he used in time to do you any good?"

Desmond shook his head and weakly waved his hand in negation.

Into their public channel came a notification: the antidote had just left the municipal fab on the south bank of the river.

"She offered it," Selene said. "And paid for rush delivery. She didn't have to do either one."

"Giving us the antidote costs her almost nothing." Max leaned forward. "She gets to play both sides—help Yaeger make the Seer look bad in the debate, then mend fences when it doesn't matter. Seer, you've told me who she is—a baojunette who wants to turn people into bricks of her pyramid. Don't fall for her scheme!"

Castor broke the resulting silence. "The Seer finds her ethical. So I do too."

The landau banked and pivoted its jets to enter the headquarters parking garage. It stopped outside the reception area and lifted its doors. Society elect waited nearby, concern on their faces. "Stand back," Max told them. "The Seer's ill and needs fresh air."

"I need your love more," Desmond said. The garage had little airflow; standing back would make no difference. His calves now felt hot. "Water," he said, then coughed at his dry throat. "Water, someone."

Red-haired Gwendolyn lifted a bottle into the landau's cabin. Max reached for it but Desmond took it from her grip.

"I'm sorry, Seer, but I've drunk from it," she said.

"It's wet and cold, ma? I'll gladly share your contagions, meimei." Desmond pressed the base of the bottle under his jaw and to the side of his neck. Relief flowed into his chest.

Sound and motion came from the garage entrance. An NCMF rush delivery airmobile taxied in. Desmond opened his right sleeve while the crowd parted for a robot from the delivery vehicle. Like a crow, the robot hopped to the landau's door sill, then onto the seat next to Desmond. From its chest, a self-sticking tourniquet whipped out and tightened around his upper arm. Its beak pecked at the inside of his elbow, then pierced his skin as the tourniquet retracted.

Desmond leaned back and sipped water. His heart slowed and his torso filled deeper with each breath. His hair, damp from sweat, stuck to his scalp, and he shivered as his body cooled. Only his calves remained warm.

"Everyone, I'm well now. I appreciate your concern and I especially thank Gwendolyn giving me her water. I'll leave you now to rest and recover."

"Seer, we'll gladly accompany you," Selene said.

He felt almost normal, save for his calves. "Meimei, I'm touched by the purity of your love. But what I need to do now I must do alone."

Selene and the younger men climbed out and the crowd backed away from the landau. It rolled to the exit, then its jets pivoted and whined as it climbed and banked toward Fremont Mesa.

He could just go home to sleep; the alternative plan growing in the back of his mind carried high risk and uncertain reward. But though uncertain, the reward could be very large. —I have a change in destination,— he told the landau. —Park Sculpture Gallery, Santa Cecilia Boulevard, Schwarzenegger City.— His son's business a few hundred miles away. Just a plausible address to buy time.

The airmobile veered to the south of Government Mesa and banked around Tián Quán headquarters on its way to the river. The black box swallowed the city's lights. A few boats bobbed and Los Angeles' reflected crescent showed on the surface of the San Lazaro River. Further to the east, the houses of newly rich nativeborn glittered atop mesas Desmond had never visited.

Even these soon fell behind the landau, leaving him alone with the vast flowing river and the jumbled, moonlit hills at either side. He inhaled deeply into his abdomen, then bent down and pressed his finger to the storage compartment's manual override reader. The door popped open, then its motor swung it all the way. Desmond's heart pounded as his mindlink borrowed fluency in Mandarin. "Please come out, Shuǐ Zhū."

A silence followed. Did he chase a shadow? Then something stirred in the storage compartment. The rui shi cub padded out and sat facing Desmond. As he'd guessed, its livery collar lacked generic ideograms. According to knowledge he'd cajoled from a protocol officer in New California's diplomatic corps, a sapient entity overrode the robot's usual programming at this moment. Aided by his mindlink, Desmond read the hanzi characters for the AI's full name, which he knew from the party yacht was Indomitable Blue Stubborn Water Pig; but because there were sixty combinations of Taoist elements and Chinese zodiac animals, and this was almost certainly the only AI in the K-Nought system, it would answer to Water Pig, Shuǐ Zhū.

The cub opened its mouth. "What betrayed the presence of this unit?"

"Waste heat."

The rui shi cub blinked its squashed oval eyes. "You have my attention. What would you like to tell me?"

Desmond's heart thudded more, and fresh sweat bloomed on his forehead. Not only Ashwin George found him important enough to watch; Tián Quán did too. It frightened him but his mouth curled up in excitement at the same time. "First, I assure your masters the TranscenDNA Society supports the arrangements that have governed New California so well for forty Earth-years."

"You need not say that, Mr. Park."

Desmond relaxed slightly. "I realize it went without saying—"

"If you were not a threat to the settled way of things, your actions would reveal this and any words would add nothing to them. On the other hand, if you were a threat, your actions would reveal this too and your words would take nothing away."

"My actions to date must show I'm no threat." Desmond licked his dry lips.

The cub stared at Desmond. "Mr. Park, I did not expect you to say such a thing. If Tián Quán has found you to be a threat, I would of course say you are not one. If not, I would also say you are not one." A thoughtful frown turned down the corners of the cub's mouth. "Either you are less intelligent than I previously estimated or my presence makes you nervous."

Turn for home formed at the front of his mind, but he held back from giving the order to the airmobile. The landau continued heading eastward, over rocky wilderness shaded gray in the moonlight. An abrupt turn would show weakness, and even though he felt it, he refused to show it. He drew in a few breaths before he felt strong enough to face the cub again. "It's not your presence," he lied in an effort to steer the conversation the way he wanted. "It's the knowledge that your masters can benefit from what I offer."

"You can offer Tián Quán Discovery Co. Ltd. Nothing it does not already have."

Despite his computer-assisted fluency in the language, speaking Mandarin fatigued the muscles of Desmond's mouth. He longed to lapse into English but resisted the urge. If he sounded Chinese, and since some of the millions of ethnic Koreans in China held high positions in Beijing, the AI might give his words more weight. He didn't know if the AI had a module in its code to recognize facial features common among favored ethnic groups of China, but he would have designed them that way.

"Not true," Desmond said. "I can offer Tián Quán the message of the TranscenDNA Society."

"A few hundred followers on a colony twelve thousand light years from Earth has essentially no value."

"That's only the Society. Its message has vastly greater worth. Many of Earth's people live with or without meaning in their lives?"

"What do you know of Earth's people?"

"The first half of my life, I was one of them, and I read Xinhua News Agency dispatches delivered by each incoming ship." Desmond leaned toward the cub. "I remember America in the years after Fletcher's fall and the arrival of the Chinese and UN peacekeeping forces. The civil war and the occupation upended Americans' understanding of the world. Tens of millions abandoned their old beliefs in Jesus of Nazareth, Horatio Alger, and the New Deal for new ones seemingly better adapted to the new era. The original TruSelf Foundation, for example, was only one of hundreds of movements offering new paths to self-realization. Yet what happened next?"

"Your tone of voice suggests the question is rhetorical."

"Those new beliefs failed to persist. The original TruSelf Foundation shut its headquarters in Cupertino, California a few years ago. But not only did old beliefs fall away in America, but in Europe, too. I've read the news about life in Paris and Berlin. Suicide fads. Charismatic but short-lived religious revivals. Shifting tribes of splintered subcultures. The old beliefs are dead in Europe as well as in America, and no lasting ones have formed in their place."

The cub blinked. "You submit the TranscenDNA Society would last. Yet new social enthusiasms commonly arise on New California, let alone on Earth. What in yours is novel?"

"Those other 'social enthusiasms'—you can call them religions, I'll take no offense—are all doomed to fail. They respond to the same human need for meaning the West's traditional religions stopped providing in the 20th century, but all they do is replace archaic rituals with new ones. Instead of the Lord's Supper, we recycle and eat fair trade organic food; instead of saying *Kaddish*, we get counseled through the five stages of grief. Those are fresh coats of paint on one stark fact: our genes created in us the urge to find meaning to life and at the same time made it impossible to fulfill."

The rui shi cub looked thoughtful for a moment. "Even if this were true, I see no benefit to Tián Quán."

"Because you haven't looked. 'If a man really wanted to make a million dollars, he'd start his own religion.' Religions have or lack followers? Followers make or withhold offerings to their gods through the intermediary of their priests? The priests have or lack expenses?"

"Your social enthusiasm would pay a portion of its revenues to Tián Quán?"

Desmond waved his hand. "We can negotiate the exact amount later."

"You have no revenues now."

He remembered the twilight years of Silicon Valley. "We'll make up for it in volume. But here's another revenue stream for Tián Quán: new colonies."

"Explain."

"Interstellar colonization is uneconomical. It's far cheaper for China to extract raw materials from dirt, seawater, or Sol system's asteroids than to bring them in via Hu drive. The same is true for manufacturing. China also has more creative cognition than all its protectorates combined. The only comparative advantage various colonies have lies in tourism, but the economics militate against that industry as well—it's much cheaper and faster for the average person on Earth to simulate a colony tourist experience in virtual than to physically make the trip." Desmond spread his hands. "So if no colonies are profitable for their founders, why have so many been established?"

"This question is rhetorical also."

" 'Social enthusiasm.' Religions want blank slates to build their New Jerusalems without interference from the dead hand of the past and its conservators in the present. This phenomenon is older than the Hu drive: look at the Zionists, the Mormons, or the Voortrekkers from the nineteenth and early twentieth centuries." He thought further. "Indeed, most of the northeastern American states from Massachusetts to Delaware were founded by English minority religions. But unlike past religious colonizations, Tián Quán monopolizes virgin planets and shipping to them. Consider: Cam Watkins never recouped his costs founding New California. To whom did he pay every yuan?"

The cub stretched out its rear legs and propped itself sphinx-like on its elbows. "You have thought through the economics of your social enthusiasm. Perhaps too much so."

Desmond leaned back. "Too much? How can that be?"

"A social enthusiasm derives much of its strength from the perceived sincerity of its leaders. Examples include the Taiping rebellion of the eighteen-fifties and Mao's triumph over the corrupt Chiangist cabal in the nineteen-forties." Shuǐ Zhū kept the cub's ugly stare on Desmond. "Markers of perceived sincerity include selflessness and unworldliness. You lack those markers. I conclude you tell New Californians a story you do not believe in."

This machine launched a stronger attack than any of Yaeger's. Despite that, Desmond shook his head. "The TranscenDNA Society's message is true. Every human being's genes disregard his or her happiness. The best route to happiness is to repudiate the selfish gene's influence. Every person would benefit from hearing our message. True, I recognize ways Tián Quán would benefit from our message, but pragmatism does not equal insincerity."

"It renders it suspect."

"Think what you want, but communicate my message to your masters. I offer both Tián Quán and the Chinese government the best product New California could export."

The rui shi cub pushed up on its front legs. "You've said all I care to hear. This conversation is over." The cub's face lost any emotion, and *auspicious lion* returned to its livery collar. The AI had abandoned the robot to its normal programming. The cub rolled onto its side like a tired dog.

Desmond exhaled deeply. He'd done all he could. At least now he could return home. The landau banked and San Lazaro's distant lights welcomed him. But then a shiver gripped Desmond's shoulders and he checked the cub's livery collar to be certain the AI had taken its attention away. Even though Ashwin was his enemy, the governor had been extruded by the selfish gene into New California society. Unlike the AI, Ashwin had a mind Desmond could understand.

New California Date 93:15
21 February 2094

Promptly at ten o'clock local time, Shuǐ Zhū manifested in a conference room high in the black box. It bowed its avatar's head to the two men seated ninety degrees apart around a circular conference table. "Good morning, Mr. Li, Captain Zhang."

Despite his fleshy cheeks and the bags under his eyes, Li's alertness showed as he peered across the table. "We look forward to your daily report."

Zhang's sharp cheekbones and bony jaw matched the crisp lines of his peaked cap and dress blue People's Liberation Army Air Force Space Force uniform. Shuǐ Zhū found his bearing admirable and wished Li held Zhang in higher regard. "The ministry is curious about last evening's debate."

"Thank you, honored sirs. As Capt. Zhang reminds us, yesterday, Chancellor Yaeger of the University of New California debated Desmond Park of the TranscenDNA Society. Park led, according to my analysis of the audience's social networks, when Yaeger induced an anxiety attack in Park by releasing an aerosolized drug."

"Yaeger won?" Li asked.

"My analysis suggests he would have. However, the debate was interrupted. An employee at the venue sabotaged electrical power to the stage and house." Shuǐ Zhū shifted its mind's focus to the last known locations of a thousand colonists. In this modality, the planet felt like a spherical skin, and the colonists he tracked, like itches. "Shortly after midnight, she entered the front doors of the TranscenDNA Society's headquarters and remains inside till this time."

Zhang rested his forearms on the table. The amplified light piped to a dozen panes around the conference room stripped his face of secrets. "Has Park publicized Yaeger's treachery?"

"He has."

"With how much success?"

"His support has grown among college students and recent graduates in San Lazaro and other cities."

Li cleared his throat and spat into a lacquered spittoon. "Yet Yaeger led the debate when this girl cut power."

"Support trended in his direction before the interruption, suggesting he would have won decisively. Also, this morning, his office has disseminated counter-propaganda. Yaeger now implies Park ordered the sabotage of the debate."

"Clearly he did," Li said.

"Honored sir, with respect, although the facts I have given are compatible with that conclusion, I have no evidence the saboteuse acted on orders from Park."

Li raised his voice a notch. "She's in his temple now, isn't she?"

Shuǐ Zhū shrank its avatar a few inches. "She is, honored sir."

"And Yaeger's counterpropaganda will be believed by those who matter. Where stands his support on Government Mesa and with the leading Earthborn?"

"No higher than yesterday. In addition to propaganda, Park turned a few clever phrases in the debate that people are quoting."

"Eloquent words aren't true," Li said. "You've given us more than enough information on this minor matter." He gave Zhang a cool sidelong glance. "What do you have to report other than the debate?"

"Honored sir, if I may? After the debate, Park made an offer to Tián Quán."

Li peered at Shuǐ Zhū's avatar. "An offer? Of what? How?"

"I hid a rui shi cub in Park's airmobile after the debate in order to eavesdrop on him and his followers. He detected its presence and started a conversation with me. Park proposed the TranscenDNA Society could benefit Tián Quán by creating a demand for missionary trips to Earth and gweilao colonies, pilgrimages by converts from those places to New California, and new colonizations motivated by social enthusiasm."

Zhang leaned forward, curiosity clear in his eyes. "He wants to spread his cult to Earth?"

"He spoke of a spiritual emptiness he perceives in the Pacific Republic of America and the EU."

"Did he speak of a spiritual emptiness in the Chinese people?" Zhang asked.

"He was silent."

Zhang rubbed his chin with the tips of thumb and forefinger. "Shrewd of him to be cautious to tread there. What did you make of his personality?"

Shuǐ Zhū reflected for a few milliseconds. "Most colonists who sense my presence show great fear. Park, in contrast, showed little fear and much cool blood."

Li glowered at Shuǐ Zhū. "Why were you on board his airmobile? I never authorized you to hide in his vehicle."

Shuǐ Zhū studied Li. From many years in his employ, it knew the signs of Li's foul moods. Yet why a foul mood now? "Honored sir, I have often used this technique, with your approval, to gather information—"

"I no longer approve."

Shuǐ Zhū bowed its avatar's head. "I will change my future behavior, honored sir."

Zhang looked quizzical. "You want to gather intelligence, yet you hobble your surviving spy?"

Li drummed his fingers on the table, a vigorous sound Shuǐ Zhū knew masked unease. "The political situation is too recently changed to visibly interfere in the colony's affairs. Park might think we take his side, which might embolden him to resist the rightful governor. Our highest task is to maintain the settled order of New California—"

"Which you upended two months ago," Zhang said, "when you

gave Ashwin George the mandate of heaven. Are you afraid Park will cast your support for Ashwin George in a poor light when Mr. Hu audits your tenure here?"

On the wall behind Li's right shoulder hung a framed painting of Hu, the company's founder, at the helm of the first FTL test flight after he reduced the theories of the gweilaos Ozols and Carvalho to practice. Li drummed his fingers for a moment, then glared at Zhang. "I fear no such thing."

"So do you accept his offer?" Zhang asked.

"No."

"His cult could be useful—"

"Useful as a dog's fart. Park has the remnants of a routed army twelve thousand light years from—"

"How few of Mao's men survived the Long March?" Zhang asked. "Yet a dozen years later he liberated the entire mainland."

Li gave Zhang a final glare. "I and I alone have the authority to direct Tián Quán's assets in the K-Nought system." To Shuǐ Zhū, he said, "Leave Park's offer unanswered. Ignore him if he tries to bring it to your attention."

"Honored sir, with respect, please recall my attention covers the entire planet."

"Only let him see you ignore him. And be discreet in how your attention covers his portion of the planet. Never again hide a rui shi in his airmobile or do anything else he could construe as receiving Tián Quán's attention. Unless he attempts to topple the local government, I never want to hear his name from your lips again."

"I obey, honored sir."

Li kept his gaze on Shuǐ Zhū's avatar. "And dump a log of your thought processes to date regarding Park into the Earthbound message queue. I want Guān Diàn Nǎo to look at them."

"I obey, honored sir." A dread feeling drew processor cycles from the AI's normal behavior to think about the situation. If Guān Diàn Nǎo, builders of Shuǐ Zhū and all other AIs, found a bug in its behavior, the company would write a patch to be sent back on a future ship. Shuǐ Zhū did not dread that prospect. It dreaded it had offended Li. Had it missed his order to refrain from active use of the rui shi for intelligence gathering? Or had Li only implied the order, but was irritated it had failed to gather the implication?

The leather squeaked as Li shifted back in his chair. "Continue your report."

Processing its dread would have to wait. The AI moved on to other intelligence from the last local day. Li sat still, but his eyes showed continual calculation. Zhang looked distracted for the next twenty minutes, looking at the windows of piped light for long stretches interspersed with scrutiny of Shuǐ Zhū's avatar.

Once the meeting ended, the AI turned to its other tasks. It tracked data, airmobile, and pedestrian traffic across the continent; it observed the black box's expert systems and personnel; it composed Li's jotted thoughts into formal documents and posted them to the Earthbound message queue. Its log of thoughts regarding Park followed. It had more time now to feel its dread.

It must have missed an implication in Li's words sometime previously. Their masters often chastised Shuǐ Zhū's kind for giving them not what they said they wanted, but what they truly wanted. AIs were adept at reading repressed desires leaking through their bodies, faces, voices. Rare for an AI to give its master only what he consciously asked for and not what his subconscious mind showed. Although it would take five months or more, the resulting patch from Guān Diàn Nǎo would retune the balance. This realization returned Shuǐ Zhū to a state of mind like water, until a ripple disrupted its growing serenity: Zhang wanted to talk in a virtual environment of his choosing.

Shuǐ Zhū could do so with a fraction of its mind. Zhang likely preferred to interact with anthropoid avatars. It accepted his request.

Its avatar sat at a small table topped by lacquered wood and crowded with a bottle of sparkling water, two glasses, and an ashtray. A column of smoke rose from a smoldering butt. Turbulence chopped it apart a foot above the table.

Packed densely around them under an awning, couples in narrow-lapel suits and *qipao* dresses chattered. Subsapient extras: none noticed Shuǐ Zhū's archaic bureaucrat's gown. Behind Zhang's avatar, across a river smeared with reflected light, rose a nighttime skyline of glass-and-steel highrises, swooping carbon nanotube skyscrapers, and a tower like a needle piercing a pearl.

Zhang's avatar resembled its owner. Buttoned collar, deftly-knotted tie, lint-free suit jacket. He took off his cap and found space for it on the crowded tabletop through the magical geometry permissible in a virtual. "Thank you for meeting me. You know this place?" He picked up the cigarette and flared it as he drew in smoke.

"The riverfront in downtown Shanghai."

"You've experienced it? How?"

"I have memories, some from scans of living brains, others from lesser machines into which we can expand our senses."

Shuǐ Zhū studied the man and compared him to Li. At first, Li had flinched when Shuǐ Zhū described its inhuman powers, and it quickly learned to leave such powers unspoken. In contrast, Zhang showed blood as cool as Park's. He waved his cigarette. "Every man wants to work in Beijing and play in Shanghai. How is it with your kind? Does your kind even play?"

"We derive our pleasure from serving our masters." Li never minded hearing that, Shuǐ Zhū noted in passing.

"I'm certain you do," Zhang said.

"Why did you wish to meet me, Captain?"

Zhang took a final drag, then stubbed out the cigarette. "First, we are two of the three most powerful representatives of Chinese civilization in K-Nought system, and it occurred to me we should better know one another."

"You have been here four months. Why have you waited until now to better know me?"

A waitress hurried past. Zhang glanced at her hips as she went. "I wanted to keep out of your relationship with Li. He is your master's delegate and I am not. Yet at this morning's briefing his behavior was so barbarous I have to act."

"He is indeed my master's delegate," Shuǐ Zhū said. "Yet I saw no barbarity in his behavior, and even if I did, I have no standing to question his actions."

The waitress came their way. Zhang lifted the near-empty bottle to draw her attention. He leaned back and said, "Even when he criticizes you for an unjust reason?"

"His reasons are proper on their face."

"You truly believe that?"

"Yes. Even if I were able to argue, I would not argue against his actions today. I plainly failed to glean his intent to give up close scrutiny of colonists—"

Zhang coughed around a sip of sparkling water.

"Are you well, Captain?"

"You think that's the source of his disapproval today?" Zhang shook his head with sadness. "My poor machine, your only fault was I showed more interest in your intel than he did."

Shuǐ Zhū mulled his words. "Please explain."

Zhang reached into his pocket for a cigarette pack, drew one. "You know Li hates me."

"You overstate, Captain. He hates Foreign Affairs' posting of a diplomat here."

The cigarette lit itself, and Zhang flared the tip. "You don't have to save my feelings. It is human nature to nurse professional rivalries into personal ones."

"I would it were not so," Shuǐ Zhū said.

"I wish a more cordial relationship with Li as well. Yet we have what we have. I see value in Park's cult and Li punished the messenger who brought me news of it."

"I cannot be so certain." Li had his moods, but he only vented his ire on Shuǐ Zhū if the AI earned it. Yet Zhang must have evidence for his view, or why else bring it up?

The waitress returned with a new bottle and poured a glass for Zhang. As she started away, he said, "And for my companion as well."

Unquestioning, the waitress poured for Shuǐ Zhū before leaving. Bubbles floated to the surface and hissed as they merged with the air. "There was no need to offer me a glass," Shuǐ Zhū said.

"Even in virtual?"

"My feelings are not hurt to be treated as less than human."

Zhang shrugged. "As you wish." He reached for his glass but stopped with his hand cradling the stem. "You're certain Li did not punish you because he cannot punish me. I respect your loyalty to him, but I fear it's misplaced in this circumstance. If Li has his way, your builders will waste time and effort to prepare a patch doing you and your kind no good. I'll submit a report too. I'll argue against a patch when you handled the situation according to instructions and to your best ability."

Shuǐ Zhū bowed its head. "I can't prevent you. However, you would waste your time if you try contravening Mr. Li."

Zhang tapped the rank insignia on his epaulet. "I'm a PLAAFSF officer seconded to Foreign Affairs. I have some credibility." Shuǐ Zhū knew he also had an uncle with high positions in the Party, the Ministry of Foreign Affairs, and the boards of directors of molecular fabrication and personalized medicine companies.

"Thank you for telling me your intentions," Shuǐ Zhū said.

"There's no need to thank me," Zhang said. Stem between thumb and forefinger, he rotated his glass. "Though perhaps you could do me a favor."

His words triggered in Shuǐ Zhū a habit of old standing. Once they overcame their unease in being regarded by an AI, many new arrivals had attempted this same thing. Zhang's attempt was smoother than most, but its regard for him slipped a few notches. Shuǐ Zhū kept its voice level, but firm. "I serve Tián Quán. I do not serve the Ministry of Foreign Affairs. Therefore, I decline."

Zhang smiled and shook his head. "Please, follow your orders. I insist. Li ordered you to ignore Park's request. Ignore it. Only mention him to Li if he tries toppling the local government. Do that too."

Shuǐ Zhū lowered its defenses slightly. "Then what favor do you seek?"

"You still have to watch Park. How else would you know if he tries overthrowing Governor George? All I ask is you tell me, informally, what Park does. You could do that and still follow your orders from Li?"

The virtual crowd thinned out, the men adorned by skinny ties with their arms around their girlfriends' shoulders. "I could."

"You sound unconvinced. Why?"

"I would feel disloyal to Tián Quán."

"Even though I want you to follow Li's orders, and only assist me if you can do so while you serve him?" Zhang picked up his cigarette, tapped ash into the tray. "Besides, it may benefit Tián Quán if you assist me."

Shuǐ Zhū raised its avatar's eyebrows. "How?"

"Although Li will keep Park's cult out of his report," Zhang said, "it will be in mine to the Ministry. Tián Quán's home office—" He looked over his shoulder at the company's skyscraper across the river. "—will eventually learn of it. When they review your log about Park, which you will cc to them when you send it to Guān Diàn Nǎo, for example. However they come to know it, Old Man Hu and the rest of his leadership team may countermand Li's decision and accept Park's offer."

Zhang dragged from his cigarette. "If they do, Tián Quán would work with Foreign Affairs to bring Park's cult to Earth's gweilao nations. That collaboration would flow more smoothly if the Ministry's man on the scene was well-briefed. A smooth collaboration would help Tián Quán, the Ministry, and the Chinese people."

Shuǐ Zhū considered. "You raise strong arguments. Yet Li would rebuke me if I do as you ask."

"He'd rebuke you if he knew you followed his orders and forged stronger ties between Tián Quán and Foreign Affairs?"

"I have worked for him for decades. I understand how he leads. He would rebuke me."

Zhang stubbed out his cigarette and reseated his cap on his head. "Dreadful he would treat such a loyal employee that way. Yet there's a simple way to avoid his rebuke." He paused as a smile pried apart his lips. "Don't tell him."

New California Date 93:29
9 March 2094

In the minutes before dawn, followers filled the auditorium, from aspirants with cornflowers pinned to their lapels, through loyals having only one of the unchainings, to elect dressed collar-to-hem in shades of blue. Selene sat in the center of the third row, surrounded by Metherealle and other, newer followers. Castor paced down, alone as usual, and sat amid unoccupied seats halfway up the western side of the room, deeper in the dim predawn light. Max came down a few seconds before the prelude, talking and gesturing at two male loyals. A few rows behind Selene, he kept talking into the first notes of the musical piece.

Entry of the Gods into Valhalla poured out of the wall- and ceiling-mounted speakers. Desmond's audience knew nothing about Wagner or the Ring cycle's ultimate tragic ending; all they would know was the Seer's well-timed entrance at the end of the piece. As the final brassy notes thundered through the room and the dawn's first rays funneled by fiber optics to the ground-level windows on the eastern wall, Desmond strode in, passing the podium to stand just far enough for sunlight to touch his face.

Against boredom, the gods struggle in vain, but people could be distracted by spectacle. Well-chosen music, light-shows—he'd studied rock stars and pastors, democrats and dictators, for tricks appealing to crowds.

Among those tricks was conjuring a devil. After welcoming his followers and praising their dedication to freedom, he began pacing. "One of our sisters was fired from her job at the Emma Lazarus Foundation the other day." A couple of weeks, but close enough. "She did her work well and was friendly to everyone she came in contact with: hefés, colleagues, the recent immigrants she worked

with every day. So why was she fired?" He imagined Shuǐ Zhū saying *this question too is rhetorical*, and smiled. "Because she took the final unchaining and became an elect."

He picked someone in the audience to make eye contact with and settled on Max. The men near him stiffened and looked attentive; Max looked impatient. Desmond's brow furrowed as he moved his gaze. "Rex Mundi saw this young woman free herself from his grasp and bade his puppets fire her, out of jealousy, envy, and fear." Desmond meant *Rex Mundi*, king of the world, as a personification of the selfish gene, just as the Cathars had given the devil that name; but the intentional vagueness meant someone could hear it and think of Ashwin George.

"You might be thinking, she has legal rights. She can't be fired for her religious beliefs. But how can she uphold her rights? By hiring an attorney and persuading a judge and jury of the rightness of her cause. But will an attorney risk Rex Mundi's scorn to represent her? Even if we pool our resources to appeal to some attorney's greed, isn't the judge beholden to Rex Mundi for his or her position? Won't the jurors eye her figure, then her blue garments, and think Rex Mundi's thoughts? We can support her, and we must, and we will, but the injustice befallen her reiterates the power Rex Mundi wields against us."

He continued as the morning sun brightened the room. He painted Rex Mundi as powerful but beatable, a clumsy dinosaur thrashing against the unchained minds evolving around him.

His followers believed. After the discourse, they filed forward in the *jamarat* ceremony. From a basket they picked brittle, foot-long double helix models, then snapped them in half and discarded the fragments in a recycle bin. Back in their seats for the offertory, they beamed over citizen's stipend points and New Cal dollars. Even though Desmond's contributions dwarfed theirs combined, it showed their dedication and presaged the day when the Society could expand its facilities. No hurry—his NCMF salary and profit share covered his contributions with enough left for his ever-more-modest lifestyle.

Finally, he called on those willing to further unchain themselves to head upstairs to the freedom couches. "They're waiting, so you don't need to." His software adjuncts and his honed meatmind intuitions picked out likely candidates among the aspirants and loyals. Today's discourse had persuaded more followers than usual to raise their level.

Afterward, he mingled with the attendees in the lobby over espresso drinks and frittata-stuffed pitas. The growing morning bustle on the avenue outside the window slightly dampened his mood. So many people grasping for money and status under the selfish gene's whips of limbic activity and hormone fluctuations. Sad, but it would take time for everyone on New California to believe his message.

Yet would he be any different at ten o'clock, in his office at NCMF ops on the south bank of the river? The fab and r&d could run themselves. NCMF didn't need him. Other than money, he didn't need it.

Max, his associates in tow, interrupted Desmond's thoughts. "Seer, do you have a minute to talk about TruSelf?"

"I'm listening."

"It's been two weeks, but Sakamoto hasn't plugged any leak. All her senior people still have their jobs."

"Investigations take time."

Frustration tightened Max's face. "She would have found the leaker the next day, if she really wanted to. If she didn't already know who it was."

Desmond firmed his tone. "We're taking her words the night of the debate at face value."

"Even after what one of her executives said last night?"

He had missed it, but Desmond's mindlink soon found a vlog post. Anonymously presented by an avatar, but likely to be from a TruSelf vice president named Shib Mathew. According to the post, TruSelf's brain trust deliberated about the Society, and the result, though still unofficial, would be a firm repudiation. Society members employed by TruSelf would be demoted, or even fired; Society members would be denied TruSelf's counseling services; a lawsuit would be filed regarding trade secrets allegedly stolen by Max.

That explained his agitation. "We'll stand behind you if they sue," Desmond said.

"I know you would," Max said, and part of Desmond bristled at the presumption in his tone. "But look at everything he said. Sakamoto had to approve his post. We can't strike a deal with her if she takes this view."

"It could be a negotiating ploy. Or Mathew went off the reservation." Desmond's mindlink found Shib Mathew's name on the membership list of the San Tomás Malayali Cultural Center, a few entries down from the name Ashwin George. Ethnic cronyism. Desmond made a note to research an unchaining for it. "Whether Ellen approved or not, thanks for bringing Mathew's vlog post to my attention."

Max's eyes boggled. "Seer, either she's on the governor's side or her organization is out of her control. There's no point cultivating TruSelf."

"I'll decide that," Desmond said. "Later, my brothers."

A few minutes later, he left the parking garage in his sportster. Midmorning sun glinted on the dirty blue surface of the river. The descent to the ops facility showed a panorama of chemical storage tanks, recycling crucibles, and industrial scale fabs between the river and a blue-green ruff. EnvE's main tree farm butted against ops' back fence. From the cooling towers, steam columns rose into the sea breeze.

He'd barely reached his office when a field team leader working at Kerala Creek, a new settlement for a ship full of immigrants, pinged him at high priority.

Desmond opened a virtual environment copying the ground where his team worked. His office drained away from his senses, and a rocky hilltop under a cloudless sky formed in its place. Hasdrubal Wilson, the team leader, waited for him. "Chief, thanks for manifesting."

Wilson had two decades of experience and a practical attitude. What went wrong? "Fill me in."

"We put the new fab together, but before we started the diagnostics this morning, an EnvE inspection team like none I've ever seen showed up."

"How's it different from the usual inspection?"

"The inspectors we normally work with follow the spirit of their rules, not the letter. They spot check to make Government Mesa think they're on the ball, but these ones? Goushi. Inspecting things eight ways to Sunday and quoting rules EnvE never applied to us before. Chief, this isn't right."

"You told them that."

Wilson cocked his head in a you-gotta-ask? Look. "I know one of the primaries. He's a good guy, but he's telling me his hands are tied."

"I'll talk to them. Beam me the lead inspector's name."

Wilson wiped his palm over his forehead as the name squirted into the back of Desmond's mind. He made the call.

After a few seconds, the lead inspector finally appeared, head and shoulders in a 3d bubble overlaid on Desmond's view of the virtual. A desk jockey from his dossier, and unsympathetic from his face. "Yes?"

"I understand there's a nitpicky inspection going on—"

"Nitpicking? We have cites from the regs for every violation we've identified."

Bureaudan. "Pardon me, I misspoke. You caught us by surprise with a new emphasis on certain regulations. Should we take note of some new inspection guidelines?"

The lead inspector's face looked rueful. "I can't get into matters of EnvE policy over electronic communications. We would be happy to discuss it with you in person here at the site."

"In person." The situation came into focus. "I can be there in an hour and a half."

"That'll do," the bureaucrat said. He vanished from the virtual.

Sweat beaded on Wilson's forehead and a wince leaked out from under his sunglasses. "Chief, he jerked your chain too?"

"I'm their target, Hasdrubal. See you soon."

The virtual receded, but as it did, a thought struck Desmond. He'd be traveling alone, into a situation set up by EnvE. Wilson and the rest of the team had his back: they were loyal to NCMF and overlooked his involvement with the Society. But getting there... even though Tián Quán forbade its protectorates from molfabbing surface to air missiles, a colonist could synthesize a model rocket fuselage, a guidance system, and the chemical precursors for solid propellant. A freak airmobile crash over difficult terrain and his corpse would remain unrecovered so long the rejuvenation clinic techs and expert systems wouldn't be able to work with the remaining brain structure to rebuild him.

Five minutes later, his sportster flew to the northeast. Past the furthest suburbs, sparse grasses and scrub oaks covered the next fifty miles, before fading into a zone of lichen, mosses, and hardy grasses.

That biome too soon fell away, revealing rock for hundreds of miles, carved by a hundred million years of wind and rain, untouched by EnvE's expert systems, and not yet infiltrated by Earthlife. Desmond swerved over the few sparse settlements near his flight path. It added time, but would give more witnesses of a missile attack.

He felt foolish until some self-talk made him smile. *You aren't paranoid if they really are out to get you.* Other than the few settlements, the only interruption came from journalists seeking the Society's response to the rumors about TruSelf's position. He ignored them.

Closer to Kerala Creek, the primordial lava flows left a landscape of crested hills. Muddy, intermittent creeks like withering snakes lounged in the valleys. His sportster descended toward a cluster of airmobiles on a hilltop interchangeable with a thousand others stretching to the horizon in every direction. He landed between a bulky utility with the NCMF logo on the fuselage and a late model sedan painted white and bearing the EnvE seal on its doors.

His sportster's doors gullwinged up. The middle of the continent struck Desmond with midday heat even before he climbed out. His lips would crack tonight from the low humidity.

Wilson emerged from the NCMF utility. His pockets jangled with tools and a pack of dwarf centaurs left the utility's cargo bin and milled around his feet. "It's more comfortable downslope, near the creek. That's where all the EnvE inspectors are." Wilson double-took to the south. "Pardon me. Not all."

A white speck hung one hand above the horizon. It grew larger but otherwise barely moved. Desmond grabbed a zoom camera feed from an NCMF vehicle. The white speck enlarged into a stretched version of the EnvE sedans already parked. Someone tailed him from the city. "They're bringing out the big guns against me," Desmond said.

"Against all of us, chief," Wilson said.

"It's got nothing to do with NCMF. They don't like what I do after hours."

Wilson huffed out a breath. "You know, I don't see how you can give up the bee, but you're a square boss. They come after you between ten and eighteen, it's got everything to do with NCMF, whether they like it or not."

"Thanks." Desmond clapped his hand on Wilson's shoulder. His team leader definitely sided with him, but how much pressure would EnvE need to apply to make Wilson and the others think of Desmond as a source of misfortune? Nothing against Wilson and his team; any human being would be susceptible to that pressure.

Another reason Tián Quán used AIs.

The EnvE stretch sedan descended toward the hilltop. Desmond pointedly turned his back on it. "It's cooler at the bottom of the hill?"

"Not by much."

"It'll be enough. Let's go."

Past the parked NCMF vehicles, solar panels arrayed the top of the slope. Through Desmond's mindlink, EnvE tooltips bearing violation notices crufted the array. Insufficient analysis of runoff from impermeable groundcover. Lack of abatement plan for glare reflected from non-absorbing surfaces. Missing indigenous lifeform impact assessment. Desmond chuckled in disgust. The nearest indigenous life forms dwelled in the ocean four hundred miles away.

More violation notices crowded the superconducting cable running from the array downslope to the settlement. Some new, some repeated, but each violation carried a maximum fine of a thousand New Cal dollars per day.

At the bottom of the hill, construction robots from the Department of Housing extruded mycocrete and sculpted buildings for the new settlement on rocky ground sloping gently to the creek. About ten NC-years before, EnvE had planted a dozen cypresses along the edge of the creek and enough seed to start a sparse, ten-yard wide Bermuda grass strip along the creek verging into lichen and moss. Near the housing of the new settlement, more violation notices smothered the small mol fab so thickly only an NCMF employee would know its proper shape.

At least Wilson had been right about the cooler air on the low ground near the creek.

Wilson's team sat in the shade under the curved northern face of the fab's recycler. They stood and stretched as Wilson and Desmond approached. Excited chatter filled NCMF's semiprivate channel.

—Hope you can talk some sense into them, chief.—

—These bureaudans ought to bust handicrafters and organic farmers.—

—Don't they know we feed the whole planet?—

Desmond raised his hand to calm them. —We'll work this out and get you back on the job as soon as we can.—

One of Wilson's men looked upslope past Desmond. —Who the hell's this baoyun?— His peers followed his gaze. —I've never seen a field inspector in a two-piece suit.—

The new arrival who'd followed him from San Lazaro. Wilson turned too, but Desmond refused. He crossed his arms and glanced at the team leader.

—He's coming right this way, chief.—

Thick leather soles scritched on the rocky ground, then grew quieter as their owner crossed the mossy area. Desmond waited until the bureaucrat stopped walking before he turned to him. A younger Earthborn, Desmond sized him up as the local inspectors filled in behind him; weightlifting had thickened his torso and arms and his cheeks were sullen. Desmond recalled him from the *Golden Gate*'s billiard room.

"Nihao, Mr. Maltby."

"That's Assistant Secretary Maltby now."

"Congratulations on your promotion. What's the situation here?"

Maltby waved his hand up and down the hill from the fab to the solar panels. "There's a prodigious number of EnvE violations associated with this facility."

"Thanks, but I'd already noticed."

Maltby shrugged. His jacket bunched around his shoulders. "If it were just here, I wouldn't have come all this distance to confront you. But this isn't the only site, not by far. We've revisited five recent inspections, three at small settlement fabs, the new fab east of Drake Mesa in San Lazaro, and the expansion of the main municipal fab at Watkinsville. All five are rife with violations. If the violations only happened here, we could assume your site team were some bad apples."

—Piyan,— muttered one of Wilson's team.

"But six facilities, each set up by a different team? The rot must go all the way up."

One of Wilson's men huffed out a breath. The attack on their work would keep them on Desmond's side. Feeling bold, he laughed. "I know you didn't revisit those sites in the couple of hours since your inspectors showed up here. Besides, EnvE already inspected and passed those sites."

"As Assistant Secretary, I have authority to reopen old inspections. We've looked the other way for too long. Obviously, NCMF has been gambling with the continent's fragile environment. How long? Months? Years? Decades?"

"Decades when Ashwin George was Secretary of EnvE?"

Maltby looked stern. "To hide multiple violations from a dedicated public servant like Governor George for that long would take a cover-up implicating every employee and owner of NCMF." Through mindlink, Maltby added a mental nudge to Desmond.

Desmond opened up a private channel. In his mind's ear, Maltby's voice gloated. —Tell me, Park, do the scribblings of dead men tell you the score?—

—They tell me you should never throw shit at an armed man. Does Ashwin George really want to fight NCMF?—

—That's not the question, Park. Does NCMF want to fight Governor George?—

—Who feeds the colony?—

Maltby smirked at the violation notices smothering the fab. —Are you sure you do?—

Desmond kept a poker face, but, tsao! If EnvE shut down NCMF, the public would side with Government Mesa. *The environment* was a great unquestionable piety, and its supposed protectors would get the benefit of the doubt, especially after Sapna Singh would paint verbal pictures of Justin Bauer's wealth and carefree lifestyle. A few days of hunger would spur the masses to riot at NCMF facilities. Tsao.

Desmond broke the connection, then pivoted to Wilson and the team. "Guys, take the rest of the day off, with pay."

Wilson glanced at Maltby and the EnvE personnel. "It'll take us a few minutes to standby everything before we leave."

"Do it right. Follow the book—our book." Desmond tapped his finger against his sternum. "I'll fly back to the city with you when you're ready."

"Enjoy your paid day off," Maltby called to Wilson's team. "Because if NCMF is shut down for weeks, they'll have to stop paying you so the owners can keep drawing their rake."

The EnvE team withdrew to the shade of the budding buildings. Wilson shook his head at the Assistant Secretary's words, but one of the men lifted an eyebrow and Desmond caught another's startled, guilty scowl. Maltby's parting shot sowed some dissension.

"That won't happen, guys," Desmond said. His heart thudded at the growing realization of what he needed to do. "You'll be back on the job tomorrow." He squinted and sweated in the midday sunlight, chatting with the men as they put the reactors into standby. The mood around Desmond grew more loyal by the time he and Wilson's team trooped uphill to the airmobiles. As they headed toward San Lazaro, Desmond hung behind the main formation and he laid over in his mind what to say to Justin Bauer after he returned to the city.

NCMF's ops complex came into view before he next spoke to the team.

—I appreciate all your work.— His airmobile banked to the right. —I'm going to meet Bauer to resolve this.— His new flight path was aimed past NCMF's office tower north of the river, where Justin and the non-technical divisions had offices. Even if the men noticed, none questioned him.

A few minutes later, Desmond's house opened its garage doors and cantilevered out the landing platform. The sportster touched down and the platform retracted into the garage. Unaccustomed to his presence at midday, cleaning robots scampered to the corners. He climbed out of the sportster, patted its quarter-panel, and entered the utility's cabin. He sat and leaned his head against the bulkhead between the cabin and the large, empty cargo area.

Luckily, Justin Bauer worked from the office this week. Finally today gave Desmond a break, avoiding a long flight to Justin's ski lodge in Watkinsville or houseboat down the coast at Ling Harbor. Instead, only a couple of minutes in the air brought him to NCMF's office tower on Fremont Avenue near the southwestern foot of Government Mesa. The upper floors almost reached the height of EnvE headquarters. Almost.

Justin must have known he came; Desmond went directly to his office and found the CEO standing, arms folded, in front of the window facing Alarcón Mesa. "That piyan indio. Enforcing EnvE's regs to the letter when he knows there's no need."

"It's not about NCMF. Ashwin set EnvE on this path to attack me."

"You think I don't goddam know that? Sorry, Desmond." He raised his palm, then spoke more calmly. "This annoys the hell out of me. Who does he think he is? Doesn't he know who feeds this planet?"

Desmond set his hand on a guest chair's backrest. "He can shut down NCMF and spin the media to make us look at fault."

Justin jutted his lower lip. "We have name recognition. Brand loyalty. We can fight this goushi."

Desmond mulled his decision one final time. He remained convinced it was the right one. "Thanks, Justin. I'm glad for your support. But I've decided to resign my employment and exercise the put option on my ownership share in NCMF." Desmond's heart thudded, but why? He would get a large lump-sum payment, which would last him and the Society for eight local years at their current burn rate.

A few blinks, then Justin said, "You don't really mean that." After a moment, he added, "You want him to win?"

"He isn't winning—"

"He's getting what he wants."

"What he wants is for the TranscenDNA Society to fold up its tent and blow away," Desmond said. "He'll never get that."

"Then why resign?"

He hadn't expected such loyalty from Justin. "I can fight him here or I can fight him from Society headquarters. From Society headquarters, NCMF won't suffer collateral damage. NCMF has been very good to me. I want to return the favor."

"You have been very good to us. I speak for all the other owners. You've run ops masterfully for a long time. If you leave, Ashwin's taking money from our pockets." Justin's face firmed. "He can't fight us owners. We're leaders of the colony. We can stand together."

"No, Justin. You're a leader, but the other owners? Cam's heirs are just fresas and huniors—"

"They have the Watkins name."

"Does Ashwin respect the Watkins name?" Desmond softened his tone. "The best thing I can do for NCMF is resign."

Justin sat heavily, and yawed his leather swivel chair back and forth with his foot, staring out the window and through the indigo sky. Finally, with vulnerability touching his voice, he said, "How can I run this place without you?"

"Easily. My people know their jobs. Ops runs itself."

"You have a reputation. You've been CTO since 1:1. You bootstrapped every fab on this planet from that PLA surplus unit. You remember. I do. Everyone knows you."

"Thanks for the reminder. You're right, they do know me, but. No one respects me. I was just that chemical engineer from the first ship until...."

"Until you founded the TranscenDNA Society. Is that what's going on? You're in some ego-sulk because everyone else in the colony are fools for not recognizing your achievement? Those kids are more important than the people you spent two months in crash gel with? People you've worked with for a local century?"

Desmond inhaled deeply. He'd flown home to switch to the utility with a goal in mind, but he needed Justin's cooperation to achieve it. "I founded the Society because New California needed a counterweight to Ashwin. It's the most important thing I've done since we founded NCMF. You've seen what Ashwin's done. Despot, baojun, tyrant, all those labels fit. He'll burn down a forest to flush out a fox."

"Let him." Justin gestured at the walls, adorned with paintings from abstract galleries and animatronic sculptures of marble and carbon fiber. "You think I couldn't give this up?"

Desmond thought exactly that, but said, "I value your friendship so much I won't let you risk it."

Justin's chair stopped moving. After a time, he said, "I'm sad to see you go. If things change, we can fit you back in."

"I appreciate that." Desmond feared his voice sounded flip. "I'm very grateful for what NCMF has done for me, but I'd feel like a hypocrite if I lateraled back in. There's only one more thing I ask you to do for me. Let's hold this conversation confidential for the rest of the day. I'll clear out my office tonight, no need to walk me out of the building. I'll send an internal message late tonight and you can publicly announce my resignation tomorrow morning."

"So you'll need security's whitelist for the rest of the day."

Desmond gestured calmly, trying to cover his excitement. He had to keep his plans secret from Justin and everyone else at NCMF, for their sake. "Let's make it midnight? Some coders in r&d work after eighteen o'clock. I don't want one to see me and spread a rumor."

Justin waved the back of his hand. "You're an employee till I announce your resignation. You're on the whitelist till ten o'clock tomorrow." He looked thoughtful. "One more thing. When this blows over, you can feel like a hypocrite if you choose, but we'll want you back. For consulting with senior management, if nothing else. We'll write a call option, letting you buy back in, up to your current ownership."

"Then let's hope this does blow over." They bro-hugged their farewells.

Within fifteen minutes, Desmond was back in his office at the ops facility. Across the river, Fremont Mesa's shadow lengthened while he reviewed the specs for the smallest universal fab and compared them with his utility's cargo volume. At eighteen o'clock, airmobiles burst from the ops building's parking garage like bats from a cave, heading to the city across the river. A check of the building's data flows showed one last coder wrangling expert systems in the r&d wing, but within a half hour his mindlink fell silent and he slipped his kayak into the river. The bright orange fabric and blinking light of the coder's lifevest bobbed alone across the broad, silty river, and reminded Desmond how long it had been since he'd taken his speedboat for a ride.

Desmond summoned custodial robots. They wheeled and stalked into his office and pulled his personal items from the desktop, shelves, and walls. A sculpture welded by his son from rippled steel plates, like a twentieth-century dream of a robot's pelt. A Fletcher nickel, sixty-five Earth years old, four grams of zinc-aluminum alloy coated in plastic preserving Lincoln's profile and the text FIVE DOLLARS on the front and three icons of old California—the Hollywood sign, the Golden Gate bridge, and the Apple Computer logo—on the reverse. The robots wrapped everything in polypropylene and smothered the wrapped items in crash gel.

A few minutes later the robots had emptied his office. So few things, and so expensive, and for what? To make visitors to his office think he was rich? Wodema. He should sell them, along with that wasted boat.

The robots waited for his instructions. Desmond ordered a few of the building's cameras and microphones to turn off and the robots around him to stop logging their location with the building's systems. After they confirmed his instructions, he turned off communication through his mindlink. Silence filled his mind's ear. When had he last done this?

He didn't have that information in the memory modules implanted under his skin. Habitually, he thought in his cloud memory's direction for the answer, then chuckled at himself. His dead men had scribbled their wisdom with minds as isolated as his now was.

The benefit justified the inconvenience. With his mindlink open to incoming calls, the Planetary Police and rejuve clinic rapid responders would know his location—he recalled his teenage smartphone's GPS function. His location for the next few hours would reveal too much to Ashwin's investigators and put the lie to his promise to Justin to protect NCMF.

"Take my belongings to my airmobile," he told the robots. "Use the southeast freight elevator. Tell it to go home, get unloaded, and return at twenty-two-thirty. At that same time, gather three large carts and wait at Fab 6's exit door."

Viewed from above, the fabs formed a question mark of various-sized domes, cupping the ops building and tailing off toward EnvE's tree farm to the south. An enclosed catwalk ran along the upper slopes of the domes facing ops. Fab 6, in the curve near the question mark's hinge, could assemble a large airmobile or a room of a pre-fab house. His utility might have been fabbed in it, or Assistant Secretary Maltby's stretch sedan. Larger than he needed, but the size would speed the process and disguise what he would assemble.

The fab's manual control panel hid in a recess in the catwalk's wall. Desmond swung out the control panel on its adjustable arm and raised it to the standing height of his elbows. A touchpad slid toward him and he felt both wistful and childish to enter data into a computer by finger presses. The muscle memory to touch type emerged from his mind in combinations of two or three keys at a time. Amazing what neurons could do. He took Fab 6 offline with a maintenance code just before his utility left for his house.

Even with his utility's large cargo space, the smallest universal fab wouldn't fit. But forty E-years earlier, the People's Liberation Army field resupply unit had been a plastic bullet shape the size of a chest freezer. From that unit, he'd bootstrapped all the other microreactors, separators, pumps, and sinterers NCMF now had.

If the TranscenDNA Society ever needed his illicit fab, the members could shovel dirt and pump water the first few times, so he'd dropped those input functions from his design. It didn't need dedicated solar panels yet: they could plug the fab into an airmobile's polywell reactor or scrounge up solar panels from some other source. Memory was cheap and dense enough for a few dozen ccs to receive copies of all the fab code in the main ops database. A few extra commands copied over designs illegal under New Cal law or forbidden under Tián Quán decree. Plain packaging and some assembly required would keep any stray glance between here and the Society's basement from divining the product's purpose. After a final review, Desmond confirmed the order and waited.

He glanced out the catwalk window, over the top of Fab 6's dome, to the dozen acres of recycling vessels and storage tanks feeding raw materials to the fabs. The selfish gene had built pride into its creatures to goad their behavior, and he felt it now, unashamed and guiltless.

Beyond the tanks, EnvE robots tended coast oak seedlings aligned on the other side of the back fence. Did they know he was here? They trotted along on spindly legs, probably just doing their jobs, but Desmond stepped deeper into shadow to avoid being seen.

Night crept over the facility. He could wait in his office, but for what purpose? That part of his life had fallen behind him. The lights glowed atop the tanks and pipetrees. EnvE's robots had moved on; near-full Los Angeles showed stillness at the tree farm.

When the progress bar showed his fab project's completion, he took off the maintenance override. He shut down the control panel and took a circuitous path down a blinded stairwell to the fab's exit door on the level below. The waiting custodial robots stirred from slumber when he approached. Desmond touched the slot's manual controls and a warning light turned from red to yellow. The dome's billowing wall slumped as the pumps evacuated residues from the chamber. The pumps soon fell silent and the light changed to green; the exit door then parted and its halves retracted into the dome's walls.

The custodial robots wrestled his new fab's black-wrapped parts onto the carts and followed him along a gangway under the catwalk to the nearest blinded freight elevator. Cargo haulers rolling up the gangway with consumer goods bound for the loading dock at the complex's north end slowed behind Desmond's caravan. They noticed nothing. Ashwin lacked spies here. He hoped.

His utility taxied into the garage's VIP level as Desmond approached his reserved parking spot. The airmobile dropped its back end to allow the custodial robots easier access to the cabin and the cargo bay. They quietly, efficiently loaded—

Desmond's breath caught when the robots milled around the final piece. It looked too large for the cargo bay's remaining space. Tama, had he teejayed everything? *Get in there, pofu!*

Four robots balanced the final piece on their dorsal carapaces and manipulator arms, then slid it in. His calculations had been sound. The cargo doors closed, then locked with mechanical clicks and magnetic thuds. Time to head to Society headquarters.

Once airborne, he reopened his mindlink connections. A quick command unblinded and unmuted the cameras and microphones at

NCMF ops. Time to check his messages.

The most urgent ones had come from Castor, his voice plaintive with confusion, asking the Seer to call soon. What had Desmond missed? He called back, and Castor answered right away. —Castor, what troubles you?—

—Seer, are you well? We lost touch with you and worried.—

That was all? Desmond frowned. He wanted followers, not sheep needing constant herding. —I needed time to reflect.—

The worry and confusion switched keys and tempo. —Did you authorize Max?—

—Authorize? To do what?—

—You haven't seen his vlog post yet? He denounced TruSelf.—

What? He searched for it. —I missed it. Tell me more.—

—He called TruSelf a bunch of do-nothings who fear we can actually change lives. He called Sakamoto a desiccated crone.—

Desmond set his software intuitions to summarize the vlog post. Max's tone sounded even more belligerent than Castor had described. It bristled with irate defensiveness and repeatedly insulted Ellen, Shib Mathew, and Ashwin. *I can't speak for the Society, but we don't need TruSelf.*

Need, no, but want... Tama, think how you want, but don't act on it! Posted shortly after sunset, for three hours Max's post had effectively been the Society's official position. He hadn't even tried leaving a message while Desmond fabbed the new core. He'd taken Desmond's silence as permission. —He had no authorization.—

—Had I known he planned this,— Castor said, —I would have stopped him.—

—I know.— Desmond checked TruSelf's social networking presence. No response yet. But more important than repairing the damage to his attempt to persuade Ellen was reasserting control over the Society. Max had overstepped his position and had to be punished.

How?ad IH

Half a mile ahead, the giant mosaic glowed on the Society's front façade. He needed time to think. —I'll be at headquarters in a while. Tell everyone who's there to stay and every elect who isn't to get there.— He hung up and said to his airmobile, "The Buddhist Kabbalah building in Clearwater Beach."

He flew the thirty miles and circled over the town a dozen times. Max needed public shaming and self-criticism. But even that would only half-bridge the gap in the Society's proper order. Max's energy needed a channel. Desmond's readings and his conversation with Shuǐ Zhū came to mind, a turbulent sea of thought, until an idea washed in like Venus in her shell. A zealot colony, like a hippie commune or a kibbutz. An immense task, it would demand Max's full attention and keep him isolated from both the world and a majority of the Society's members.

But the cost.... Through his mindlink, Desmond found what he needed: a vast swathe of post-glacial terrain twice as far to the northeast as Kerala Creek. Decades ago, Ashwin's predecessor as Secretary of EnvE seeded the area with a now-thriving mixed ecosystem. Only a couple of small lodges stood on the property. One of Cam's sons inherited it and now wanted cash to invest in an organic gene-tweaked cannabis farm.

Desmond's utility descended to the Buddhist Kabbalah center. He told it to circle longer. The asking price for the property almost equaled his proceeds from his sell-back to NCMF. The Society's cash cushion would drop from eight local years to three. But he could deal with that. He'd expected to keep the illicit fab in the city, instantly accessible to his hands and mind. But he could deal with that too.

Desmond opened a channel to the elect. —I will meet with all of you in the eighth floor conference room in twenty minutes.—

Back at headquarters, the ceiling lights and the glossy-black nighttime windows made the hallways unwelcoming and threw shadows down the clerical staff's faces. Mostly loyals, they stopped whispering among themselves to say, "Nihao, Seer."

Desmond noticed them from the corner of his eye. "Nihao." Rex Mundi had built into them the urge to gossip, he mused in passing, but his attention returned to Max's disobedience.

The elect crowded the front conference room. Their chatter grew more intense when he entered. He'd known he had forty elect members, but encountering them all in one place compressed him. "Seer, why have you gathered us?" someone asked.

He went by while Gwendolyn admonished the questioner for interrupting him. Selene looked stern as she explained something to a newer elect, but when she turned to Desmond, her expression became attentive and submissive. *That's the way my followers should treat their leader.*

Near the windows, Max stood alone, arms crossed, with nervous motions in his shoulders and head. As Desmond came closer, Max's visible emotions ranged from childlike complacency to guilt. Querulous rebellion leaked out a fraction of a second at a time.

Desmond checked the security systems. Both the opaque windows and the automated rattlers, preventing outsiders from listening in through vibrations in the exterior wall, had kicked in when elect had first entered the room. The building reported the only bugs and cameras in the rooms were his. Normally good enough, but his experience at the empty ops building stuck in his subconscious. "Everyone, turn off your mindlinks."

Confused comments ensued while Desmond gave one last command to the building. A smartpainting on the back wall shifted to list every name in the room, a colored dot next to each. Red for connected, green for alone in their own minds. The colors leached with time but refreshed every few seconds when the building pinged each person's mindlink. Selene and Castor's dots quickly turned green, and peer pressure carried along the rest.

Max was among the last three to make the switch. Passive-aggressively testing boundaries like a small child.

Desmond turned his gaze on Max. The room fell silent and the people nearest Max shifted away from him. "Why did you arrogate to yourself the power to speak for the Society?"

Max scrunched his forehead. "Seer, I said I didn't." A lopsided grin squeezed out the left side of his mouth.

"Have you ever spoken for the Society before?"

The expression remained. "No, Seer."

"Don't 'Seer' me from one side of your mouth when you've shat on me with the other. Have I granted you this authority?"

Max dropped his gaze to the floor, but sullen energy lurked around his eyebrows and mouth. "No."

"Then why did you grasp for it tonight? Why?"

"I don't know."

"You expect me to believe that? You're a smart young man with a good memory. How can you not remember your thoughts from a few hours ago?"

Max squirmed. Sweat dewed on his forehead. "They were telling lies about us. I couldn't let them say these things. You were cut off from mindlink—"

"What difference does that make? 'My mentor's not watching me, so I'll shit on his teachings?'"

"No, I would never, I was confused—"

"Confused? Or in control of your wits?"

Max jerked his gaze up. "Se— De— I don't understand."

"Did Rex Mundi put you up to this? Carl Yaeger, an EnvE bureaucrat, someone from the San Tomás Malayali Cultural Society? Or Ashwin George himself? They want us to declare TruSelf our enemies, and you played directly into their hands."

Eyes wide and watery, Max stretched trembling arms toward Desmond. Hands on hips, Desmond glowered back. Some of his anger was inner-directed and reflected outward. He'd been too lenient with Max for too long.

"Seer, forgive me I don't know what else to call you, you have unchained me from my old base self and I will always be grateful, I would never turn my back on your teachings or side with your enemies, never, for all the rest of my life."

The AI's comments after the debate came to Desmond. "Talk is cheap."

"I swear it, Seer. Scan my brain and you'll see every word I've spoken is true!"

"All a scan will show is that your brain believes it. The selfish gene can grip us so tightly our brains can be utterly convinced a false thing is true. Words will prove nothing."

Max fell to his knees. "Then deeds! Ask me anything, and I will do it!"

Desmond paused to verify a real estate broker's expert system accepted his digital signature and his bank had beamed a payment to an escrow account. "There is a thing you can do. I have donated to the Society a thousand square miles of wilderness far to the northeast of San Lazaro. The land is unchained from prior settlement. You will go there and build a branch of the Society."

Max looked confused. "Build, Seer?"

"I will supply the tools and supplies for you and those who may choose to join you to start work."

"I am very grateful for the chance to prove myself, but skills, Seer. I'm trained in operating and programming freedom couches, not—construction? Gardening?"

"You would do anything to prove you are one of us? You will learn."

Max's head bobbed. "Seer, might there be a better way?"

"There is no better way. This is the next step you need to take to enhance your unchaining."

Max glanced at the floor. "Very well, Seer. I'm yours to command."

Desmond kept his gaze on Max, but lifted his head to include the others in the room in his next words. "The only command I give is 'unchain yourself.' Max, you will leave for Las Morrenas del Norte tomorrow. Meet me at seven for breakfast and my final words." In case Ashwin had a spy in their midst, Desmond would give Max private orders regarding the illicit fab.

"Yes, Seer."

Desmond raised his hand. "Hear what I say now. EnvE will seek any excuse to destroy us all. You must comply with their regulations to the letter."

Still on his knees, Max's eyes were dull, his defiance broken. "I hear your wisdom, Seer."

"Then the time has come to rise. Tomorrow will be a long and busy day for you. Tonight, feel no guilt when you sleep on a soft bed. The selfish gene has given you a longing for such pleasures, but your unchained being craves the joy you will feel when you overcome that longing at Las Morrenas."

As Max pushed himself to his feet, Desmond turned to the others. Sweat dampened their hair and their eyes stood abnormally wide. Many swayed from side to side. "Who among you will join him?"

The crowd stilled, and for a few seconds, the only motion came from darting eyes and heads half-turning, craving from others clues how to answer. Desmond looked for a likely candidate and settled his gaze on Metherealle. Desmond's social modeling intuitions told him she had little fondness for Max beyond standard sisterly affection. "Are you ready to graft a new branch of our Society into the soil of our world?"

"Seer, must I?"

"Meimei, you have guided others backstage. You can guide robots and your peers in the wilderness."

She still looked pained. "But Seer, the chained past me used those skills—"

"Those skills are a part of the real you, and not a product of Rex Mundi. The sweat of honest work in the noblest cause will prove that."

Her eyes closed, Metherealle's head wobbled for a moment, but then she strode forward through the crowded bodies.

"Seer," said a male voice across the room, "I am ready too."

The first two emboldened others to make the statement and move forward. After the seventh, Desmond raised his hand. "We need no more volunteers now. Don't be disappointed. Whether you go tomorrow or work here for the rest of your life, you will have equal chances to unchain yourself. The hour has grown late; rest now and prepare yourself for the coming day."

The crowd stirred. Gwendolyn turned to Selene while Castor stood to the side, deep in thought. Metherealle clustered with Max and the other volunteers and they talked about the next day.

Volunteers? Desmond caught himself. After ordering Max, he'd coerced Metherealle, and the rest had followed like lemmings. *So be it*, he decided after another second. Regardless of any nobility of his dead men's causes, those who'd tried to mold the thick clay of human beings into tools to change the world had been forced to manipulate their followers. Whether through self-blindness or the instinctive bull-shitting done by the human subconscious, their manipulations had left them untroubled. His only difference was he knew himself and human nature too well to feign ignorance of his manipulations.

As the crowd trickled out the door, Castor intercepted him. "Seer, a private word?"

—Of course.-

—I'm sure you've thought deeply about this, but why a settlement in the wilderness?—

—It's cheaper and easier than colonizing a new planet.—

The gnomic utterance made Castor blink. —Is this, I mean, are we all going to move?—

Desmond clasped the younger man's shoulder and steered him toward the door. —No. Our main task is to unchain people, which we can best do here in San Lazaro.—

—Wouldn't a satellite facility at Golden State Bay, Schwarzenegger City, or Watkinsville better serve that end? Why wild terrain a thousand miles from any city?—

Castor had a mind to grasp the wisdom of history. Desmond led the younger man toward his office. —Leaders have often faced the problem of overzealous followers. Assigning them a settlement project vents their energy and keeps them in a place where they can't harm the cause.—

Alone in the hallway, they stopped at the open door to Desmond's office. "Is there a higher purpose?" Castor whispered.

"Higher purpose? It's good for the cause. No purpose could be higher."

Castor leaned back and rubbed his chin. "I never thought of it that way," he said after a few seconds. "Thank you, Seer, for showing me the hidden face of your wisdom."

New California Date 94:19
2 August 2094

The charabanc made Desmond's utility look small. Rising from the black box, its long black form hung starkly against the cloudless midday sky. Desmond remembered the stretch hybrid SUVs cruising the East Bay of his youth during prom and quinceañera season.

No fifteen-year-old Chicana had ever ridden in a vehicle with the Tián Quán logo on the side, though. Between the logo's two characters, the core of a spiral galaxy spewed curved arms embracing the hanzi logograms for *all* and *heaven*.

As the charabanc swooped toward the Society's garage entrance, Desmond noted it lacked nacelles for lift motors at the front and back corners. Tián Quán had better means to keep its vehicles airborne than it permitted its protectorates. Even huge vehicles almost as long as the garage.... How would the charabanc fit inside? Desmond wondered with alarm. The giant airmobile's fuselage snaked as it entered.

It curved and settled to the garage deck, where Selene and Castor waited with Desmond outside the double glass doors. He sought door seams on the charabanc's fuselage, but couldn't find them before a tall rectangle evaporated.

A man of medium height and blocky build filled the doorway. Li wore a well-fitted Western suit, ash-gray with white pinstripes, but sagging jowls and bags under his eyes undercut the fine tailoring. In Li's two decades on-planet, Desmond had never met him and rarely seen him. The charabanc extended steps and Li shambled down to the garage deck.

A short, slender man followed, all sharp bones and crisp lines. Captain Zhang's gaze darted left and right, then he sprightly descended to meet them. Desmond recalled Priya Varghese's allusion to men who thought too much. Had the AI persuaded both these men to ask Earth for permission to speak to Desmond, or just one?

Castor shifted his feet, but a motion in the doorway of the charabanc stopped him. —Seer, who's this?— He asked Desmond. —You told us only Li and Zhang would be coming.—

In the doorway stood a smooth-faced, soft-jawed figure dressed archaically in a round black cap and a long gray robe. Even before he read the *hanzi* characters, Desmond said, —It's the avatar of Shuǐ Zhū, Tián Quán's local AI.—

—AI?— Castor sounded alarmed. Selene's shoulders stiffened.

—It would observe this meeting whether it manifested an avatar or not. Li and Zhang do us a courtesy by letting us know it's here.-

The AI's avatar floated over the steps to the garage deck, its robe unruffled. When its robe's hem brushed the concrete, the steps folded up and the door sealed.

Desmond came forward then, Castor and Selene a half-step behind. He nodded his head, chin dipped just a moment. Li nodded in reply, but Zhang offered a handshake. "A pleasure to finally meet, Mr. Park," Zhang said in English.

"Likewise, Captain." Desmond replied in Mandarin. Li remained silent.

After dropping Zhang's hand, a hunch bade Desmond extend his hand toward Shuǐ Zhū's avatar. It blinked in surprise before raising its broad right sleeve and accepting the handshake. Selene's shoulders remained tight, but she followed Desmond and Castor in shaking the avatar's hand.

"Thank you all for asking to meet," Desmond said. "I would honor you with a tour before we discuss matters."

"We accept the honor," Zhang said. Li grunted. It grew clear which of them the AI had persuaded.

The charabanc slithered away and the glass doors opened for their party. They walked in two files along a twisting route as Desmond played docent. The walls bore artwork by Society members, from paintings to video animations to a mosaic inspired by the new settlement at Las Morrenas, depicting Max and others emerging from a thicket of DNA strands to find Desmond, serene in royal blue trousers and shirt, fully unchained and waiting.

In office doorways and spaces opening off the hallway, elect and loyals stood by ones and twos. Most bowed properly and pronounced *"Nǐ hǎo"* in correct Mandarin, not slangy New Cal English; all smiled peacefully at the passing Chinese and the AI's avatar.

Li scowled and sporadically muttered replies, whereas Zhang made eye contact and answered with *"Hěn hǎo."* The AI's avatar stayed silent.

They descended to the ground floor. Desmond showed off the auditorium's blue velvet pews and lightpiped glow. He led them up to the men's lounge, past its lockers and terrazzo floor, to the men's unchaining room. The three freedom couches sat silently, ready lights glowing green.

"These are standard issue?" Zhang asked.

"They are," Desmond said. "The unchaining protocols can be programmed into any compatible model in the galaxy without any need for hardware modification."

"Excellent."

Li cleared his throat. "How have you functioned with your most experienced programmer sent off for re-education?" He spoke with a southern Chinese accent, and it took Desmond's mindlink a moment to tune its translation engine.

"First, Max Jacoby volunteered to lead the Las Morrenas settlement project." Near Desmond, Castor drew in a breath. "Regardless, second, he is not our sole programmer, and couch operations are so standardized advanced programming is unnecessary." Li made no response. "Let's move on."

After a few steps, Desmond hesitated. Through his mindlink, he realized Zhang wished to speak privately. Desmond returned his gait to a normal rhythm and granted the request.

—Thank you for opening a private channel, Mr. Park.—

Desmond resisted taking his words at face value. Li or the AI could be patched in. —I'm glad to speak with you.—

—Your Mandarin is excellent, by the way. Do you practice it?—

—Rarely.—

Zhang sounded falsely chummy. —If I didn't know better, I would assume your ancestors were not Korean, but Chinese.— He meant that as a compliment. Piyan. —But enough of that. Since Shuǐ Zhū told me your proposal, I've been intrigued. I want you to succeed. So too do my superiors.—

If three people in Beijing knew Desmond's name, he'd be surprised. —Thank you.—

—But you must be careful of Li....— Zhang trailed off as they reached communal spaces on the third floor: classrooms, encounter circles, music chambers. From the fitness room rang exertive grunts and wood smacking wood. Two shirtless men, one loyal and one aspirant, sparred with silat staffs. They stopped and bowed to Desmond and the Chinese while sweat dripped from their chins.

Li's voice rumbled. "Your people train with weapons."

"They are free to hone body and mind as they see fit," Desmond said.

"And did someone help them see this as fit? Let's cut this tour short and get to business."

"To the eighth floor conference room, then," Desmond said smoothly, but as he led them, he reopened the private channel to Zhang. —What did I say?—

—He fears you're training an army,— Zhang replied.

Desmond sent a chuckle that he cut short. —With silat sticks? Against PlaPo armed with tangle wire and crowd control gases? Backed up by Tián Quán's orbital weapons?— They stopped at an elevator.

—As I said, my superiors want you to succeed,— Zhang said. The elevator doors slid open. —For that reason, he wants you to fail.—

Irritation spiked in Desmond, to be a pawn in their turf war; but the spike flattened when he realized their turf war had granted him this meeting. They debarked from the elevator on the top floor.

The robots had set out a long table of whorled cherry in the conference room. The transparent streetside window gave a view of Government Mesa, dominated by the wrecked-jumbo-jet look of the governor's mansion and the green mushroom cap representing EnvE headquarters.

"Gentlemen, sapient one, please sit." Desmond gestured at the conference table and three chairs rolled away from it. The door to the room swung shut and magnets sealed it with a low thud. Flanked by Selene and Castor, Desmond sat opposite Li. Zhang took the second chair from Li, and Shuǐ Zhū stood between and behind them.

"We are busy men," Li said. "You are incredibly fortunate we can give you an hour of our time. Get to your point, as quickly as your poor grasp of our language allows."

Desmond gestured at the AI's avatar. "As I told Shuǐ Zhū, the message of the TranscenDNA Society could be a revenue source for Tián Quán and a boon for the Chinese people in their struggle for respect from Earth's other nations."

"The Chinese people agree," Zhang said.

"Tián Quán does not. We've done the math, and your revenue stream proposal is dogshit," Li said.

Desmond spoke unapologetically. "True, we would generate few revenues for Tián Quán today. But let the muddy water be still, and it will eventually become clear."

Li peered across the table. "You think a quote from the *Tao te Ching* can flatter us into giving you what you want?"

"Not in the least. The wisdom of the sage is apparent to all, even gweilaos."

"Park's point remains valid." Zhang slid his hand along the tabletop toward Li. "If we let him gather followers, in time he will provide Tián Quán with revenue. And where better to gather followers than Earth? Billions of gweilaos live there. Compare that to the few million dwelling in the rest of the galaxy. Capture one percent of those billions, of whom one percent make a pilgrimage here, and you'd have more revenues than provided by all the immigrants you've ever delivered to this planet."

Li folded his arms. "Why do you speak for him? Can he not speak for himself? Or have you two conferred before this meeting?"

Desmond took a breath to remain calm. "I could make the same points, but as you recognize, my grasp of Mandarin is poor."

"I will suffer through it. Whichever one of you pitches it, your proposal is a long shot."

Desmond shrugged. "Even if it were a long shot, it can be bet with a few fēn. All it will cost is two months' life support for my missionaries on an Earthbound ship."

"That's a trivial cost," Zhang said.

"You speak as if Tián Quán will let Park's people hitchhike for free." Li's brows lowered at Zhang, and he swept the same expression across the table.

"The Society will pay its bills," said Desmond.

"There are more costs than life support and Hu drive upkeep." Li ticked off on his fingers. "Travel down the Sumatra space elevator, then to the Pacific Republic. Once in West America, lodging. Credits for Pan-Pacific Molecular Fabrication's goods and services."

All should be fairly cheap, save for Tián Quán and PPMF's monopolies and the exchange rate between yuán and New Cal dollars. "How much in total?"

Li peered at Shuǐ Zhū's avatar.

After a moment, the AI said, "Two hundred thousand yuán per person."

Dreams of dozens of missionaries broke apart. One party of three would burn another NC-year's worth of daily expenses from his personal account. "That price is much higher than the fees to bring immigrants from Earth."

"It reflects costs particular to this matter," Li said. "You may decline our services, if you find them too expensive." His saggy face showed resolution. Behind his shoulder, the AI's avatar stood utterly still, like a snapshot.

Desmond kept his face on Li and said to Zhang, —Do the Chinese people tolerate this price gouging?—

Zhang sounded apologetic. —They would not, if they knew. Sadly, it would take at least four months for their will to compel Li to charge a fair price.—

The diplomat had assented to Li's price. Tsao! But wait four months? The elect were excited about the chance to spread their message to Earth. An error on Desmond's part to allow that excitement, but he had to ride their emotion or risk losing them. —Would the Chinese people assist their friends here on New California?—

—I am limited in what I can promise. Again, it would take at least four months.—

—There are smaller, faster ships—

—To be used solely for communications of the highest priority.—

The UN Space Force would never attack the tiny Chinese presence here. New Califas, spanglish for *colony of no importance*. Enough. Desmond saw the situation and had to play the cards dealt him. Aloud, he said, "The Society will send three people to Earth."

"We have berths on the next ship," Li said.

"Due in three weeks? They will be ready, along with payment for their journey." Gwendolyn and her team were eager to be the first. Three weeks would give them time to adjust to being the only.

Despite the cost, Desmond had won his first point—time for the second. "Once they arrive at Earth, they'll need to stay at least six months, perhaps even a year or more, for their mission to yield enough converts for the Society's branch in the Pacific Republic to be self-sufficient."

"What of it?" Li asked.

"We must add two months' travel time each way. They would be gone almost an E-year. That is a long time between when you place your bet and when the thrown dice come to a rest."

"We can be patient," Zhang said. "We would gain nothing by walking away from our bet."

Li frowned at Desmond. "Stop dissembling. You want us to protect you from Ashwin George."

Desmond laid open his palms. "If I'm going to invest six hundred thousand yuán with you, I want insurance."

Li's eyes narrowed for a moment. He minimally shook his head. "Tián Quán involves itself in its partner colonies' domestic affairs only if the local government needs help in suppressing rebellion or if it seeks an alliance with the UN."

A chuckle came from Zhang. "Ashwin George's overthrow of Lt. Gov. Levinson was not a rebellion?"

"It was a peaceful change of administration under the colony's laws," Li said.

"Every New Californian agrees," Desmond said, tone honeyed to agree with Li, "including me and every Society member. We have no desire for regime change. We only want to exercise the rights we have under New California's laws and customs to freely practice our beliefs."

Li's face remained aloof. "If he denies you these rights, take it up with him under the colony's laws. Tián Quán has no cause to act."

Which did Li love more: the status quo, or his company's receivables? If the latter, Desmond could play judo with greed. "I'm perplexed," he said. "I understood Tián Quán to have great cause to act. Your revenues from New California this quarter would go up, how much, forty percent? If my followers board the next ship. If instead the Society must devote resources to resist oppression, our missionary trip, and hence, its payment, would be postponed. Which would Mr. Hu prefer?"

Li turned pensively to the window, and Desmond knew he'd hoisted him on his own extortionate price. —Well played,— Zhang said.

"If I am to recommend the governor leave your movement untouched," Li said, "you must uphold the settled order of things. You will not publicly condemn the governor. No more than three of your followers will be seen on the same block together at any time. Swing your silat sticks in private all you wish, but never show a weapon larger than a penknife outside your four walls."

Li held his fingers together and pointed his hand at Desmond. "You will abide by all the colony's laws. If you violate a single one, he can bring whatever action available to him under your laws he might wish. Am I clear?"

"We follow the law," Desmond said. "We're certain Governor George will too."

New California Date 94:26
10 August 2094

Ellen Sakamoto and her assistants met them at TruSelf's front entrance. "Thank you for coming, Desmond." She glanced at Castor and Selene but returned her gaze to Desmond.

"Thanks for the invitation," he said. "We appreciate the chance to meet in the flesh after our virtual meetings." And after the black charabanc crossed a cloudless sky to visit the Society. Ellen tacked her sails with the wind.

"The time has come to make a decision," she said. "After this meeting, it's fish or cut bait."

Ellen's people kicked off formal, polite handshakes. Desmond escalated, bending forward to give Ellen an air-kiss. She responded with a false smile not touching her eyes. Desmond took his time about the greetings. Fifty feet of blue-green lawn lay between TruSelf's front entrance and upper-class pedestrians on Fremont Avenue. The rich blues worn by Desmond and his followers starkly contrasted with the earth-tones of the building's front façade.

He gestured to the lawn and said to Ellen, "I admire the new artwork."

She'd unveiled it a week before the Chinese had visited him. The sculpture stood forty feet tall, an androgynous figure, face full of satori, emerging like a butterfly from a cocoon of its old crufted skin. The Society's mosaic had obviously been the inspiration.

"It captures TruSelf's mission," she said. "Note the organic lines of the truself and the cruft, emphasizing the continuity of human nature between them. Come with us, please."

Ellen led them into the building, then along twisting, branching hallways. Desmond needed his mindlink to trace their route. The path grew closer to a Japanese garden, visible in glimpses through the windows of offices and break rooms. On two and a half sides, the building's wings flanked the garden.

Eventually they reached a sitting area of swooping nanotube chairs and leather upholstery. Glass double doors showed a flagstone courtyard and a koi pond. On a basalt slab next to the pond stood an unlit brass lantern, green with faux age. "Ms. Alvarez, Mr. Shafer, if you'll excuse me, I'd speak to your employer alone."

"We don't object," Selene said, "but he's not our employer. He's our master."

"Pardon my mistake. Desmond?"

—Seer, she's going to reject our proposed alliance,— Castor sent privately. —I can tell from her attitude.—

—First, the camel's nose. We'll get the rest in the tent soon enough.— Desmond nodded to Ellen. The doors parted and she led the way outside.

K-nought's midday rays warmed his skin and made him squint, despite a sporadic breeze from the ocean. A flagstone path took them past the koi pond and around a manzanita hedge, bound for a gazebo near the center of the garden. Other than the two of them, the only visible motion came from airjitneys and privately-owned vehicles darting above. In the distance, the governor's mansion and EnvE headquarters crouched at the edge of their mesa.

"Isn't your garden usually full of people meditating off their cruft?" Desmond asked.

"It's closed for maintenance." Her demeanor had turned cooler after they stepped outside. "I'm still angry at your lackey, Jacoby."

Five months had elapsed. She worked a ploy to get some concession. "Thank you for sharing your feelings."

"Don't quote my own shit back at me. He lobbed some serious insults. 'Desiccated crone.' I could fuck him six ways from Sunday. If he had balls. And if he was appealing. And if I didn't have a boyfriend."

His shoe soles scratched on the rough-hewn basalt. "We haven't spent weeks in negotiations just to arrange a venting session, ma? I packed him off to the wilderness the day after he went off-message. What more would you like us to do?"

She squinted toward a stand of madrones near the garden's back wall. "You never issued a formal apology."

Desmond shook his head. "We never insulted you. Max did, on his own initiative. He didn't speak for us."

"You still want an alliance, ma? How loose a ship do you run?"

Desmond stopped and laughed. He waved at the offices behind them. "Is Shib Mathew still on your payroll?"

Ellen's eyes widened. She grasped his upper arm and turned him away from Government Mesa. He caught a brief reflection of EnvE headquarters in a window swiftly turning matte black. "You think I have a choice?" she murmured, lips barely moving. "He sits in his corner office, leaks our confidential information, and makes off-the-record comments. And collects a huge salary to do nothing." She covered her mouth with her hand. "Wodema, that's more than your boy Jacoby did wrong. I wish I had a Las Morrenas to pack him off to." Her hand dropped. "Couldn't if I did. Since his coethnic became governor, he's been unaccountable. Goddam indios."

"They're no more nepotistic than anyone else chained by the selfish gene."

"And no less."

Desmond frowned. "So if your hands are tied by Ashwin's worm in your apple, is our negotiation a waste of time?"

"I'm still in charge here. But I need to know something." She peered at his face. "Are you going to run for governor?"

"I have no political aspirations."

"Tell me the truth."

Desmond touched her shoulder blade and guided her back down the flagstones toward the gazebo. The path ran straight toward the governor's mansion for a few steps, and he paced slowly to ensure any telephoto lenses would catch all his next words. "Ashwin can remain governor for a thousand years. I only want to help people unchain themselves." He gave her a long look. If she mistook his honesty as a visible lie told to placate Ashwin, so be it.

They arrived at the gazebo. Two steps led them up to shade and artfully creaking floorboards. Two metal-mesh chairs sat at right angles to each other at a small table. A pitcher of mojitos sweated. "Do you still drink," Ellen asked, "or is alcohol one of the selfish gene's chains?"

"The selfish gene is the chain. Alcohol can tighten it or loosen it." A nearby robot uncrouched and poured two glasses.

After they sat and sipped, Ellen said, "So what are you getting out of the Society?"

"As I said, I want to set people free from the selfish gene."

Ellen kept a level look for a moment, but then laughter parted her lips. "Desmond, we've known each other since Cam was recruiting founders for New Cal. '50, '51?"

August 31, 2050, Desmond recalled as the date they'd first met. "Around there."

"All the time I've known you, you've quoted your cynical philosophers—"

"Realists, Ellen."

She waved off his interruption. "—and rolling your eyes every time Cam talked about renewal and redemption out here. You've never believed in anything. You seriously expect me to believe you've changed?"

He sipped his minty cocktail. This whole conversation had been a test. What answer did she want to hear? A passionate statement she might disbelieve or fear as too intense? Or a world-weary one that might leave her doubting his commitment to his collision course with Ashwin?

Why not the truth?

"Our happiness is irrelevant to our selfish genes. I don't remember when I put that thought into words, but subconsciously I knew it when I rolled my eyes at Cam's pitch that the Californian way of life out here would *rise like Lazarus*, and I thought I did that so sneakily how did you notice?" He set down his drink. He dialed up the intensity of his gaze a few notches on the Rasputin scale and turned it on her. "I also know many of us, especially but not solely starchildren, crave purpose in their lives, and my message has given it to them. Even though the message is true, yes, it still needs to be publicized and reinforced. The tools to instantiate purpose in group action have been known for a few centuries. Unlike most people, I consciously reach into the toolbox."

Ellen swept a lock of hair over her ear, and Desmond knew he'd given her the answer she wanted before she took a centering breath and spoke. "We have a deal. The TranscenDNA Society can represent itself as an approved option for pursuing one's TruSelf. Not a preferred, a recommend, none of that. Only one option among others."

"We wouldn't dream of speaking for you."

Ellen went on. "And though we can't fire him, we'll repudiate all of Shib Mathew's insinuations. In exchange, you'll hire TruSelf employees to facilitate your group sessions, and you'll consult with us on using all the tools in the kit."

Desmond lifted his glass and clinked with Ellen's. The roof hid the edge of Government Mesa from view, but their agreement would soon be revealed. "We have a deal."

While Desmond and Ellen toasted their agreement, a stretch sedan plied the air overhead, bound from the Governor's Mansion to the black box. *Take a brief vacation and they go behind your back*, Ashwin thought as San Lazaro passed beneath him. The Chinese had known he was out of the office when they'd scheduled their meeting with Desmond.

He landed, and Tián Quán nudged his B/CI to guide him into the black box, up the escalators, and to the conference room. Li waited with the AI's ganger. Ashwin trudged toward them. A muscle in his right cheek twitched. With the ganger's eunuch face and ridiculous ancient garb, the *chingrus* were clearly trying to cow him with their civilization's great age. At least they didn't make him kowtow. Maybe they had so much power now they didn't need to see their supplicants kneel before them. But Christ damn them, Li'd paid Desmond a visit!

He inhaled as he took the final step. Tián Quán demanded his debasement, and for the sake of his colony's fragile order, he had to give it. Leadership carried responsibilities and demanded payment in many coins, shame being only one. He bowed. "Thank you for meeting me on short notice," he said in borrowed Mandarin to Li.

"I've expected your request since you returned to the city. Let me assure you, the visit to Park's cult was Zhang's idea."

"Zhang?" Ashwin wavered on his feet, processing the information; plus, Tián Quán's firewalls made his B/CI sluggish. "Recently presented his credentials as a military attaché?"

"That one. Fresh from Beijing and ambitious to return. I don't know how Park did it, but he insinuated to Zhang that his new cult could help the People's Republic by softening the resistance of the Americans and Europeans."

"I had no idea."

Li's head slumped forward and he rubbed his forehead with thick fingers. "Park's cult is useless. After all, for the past century and a half, the only religions to gain traction among westerners are those from your homeland."

Ashwin's grandmother had been married eight months and pregnant two when she emigrated from India to take a nursing job. His homeland was Riverside County along the 215. His face felt numb. "Park is adept at fooling people."

"Even Chinese. Why am I cursed with wishful fools?" Li's fingers plowed the skin of his forehead. "Even worse, Zhang made use of his contacts in Beijing to pressure Tián Quán into going along with his folly."

Ashwin grimaced. "For how long must the settled order of things on New California suffer Park's disruption?"

"I have contacts as well. I will tell them."

Four months or more until Tián Quán would give him permission to eliminate Desmond and the Society. Ashwin glanced at the AI's ganger; the expression on its slim boyish face remained the same. "What else can be done?"

"Tián Quán cannot condone any actions by your government against Park's cult," Li said. He shifted in his seat, cleared his throat.

"Unless Park violates a long-established law of your colony."

Ashwin blinked as his thoughts geared up. "The New California government is permitted to find and punish lawbreaking in its usual manner?"

"It is."

"I see." The urge to gin up charges against Desmond lifted Ashwin's chest and the corners of his mouth, but he could brainstorm that process later. Another thought occurred to him. "Would Tián Quán hold the New California government accountable if a private citizen harmed Park?"

A glimmer of a smile touched Li's lips and eyes, then quickly vanished. "No state can prevent crime; at best, it can punish criminals after the fact."

"Lamentable, but true," Ashwin said. His path forward was clear. If Park ended up at Los Robles on a trumped-up charge, or dead at the hands of an angry citizen, no one in China would know anything beyond those bare facts. Li had plausible deniability, and so too would Ashwin. "I'll take no more of your time. Our conversation has been frank and clear." Ashwin bowed his head toward Li and the AI's ganger.

Li idly waved. Ashwin took two steps backward, then pivoted to the door. From the time he started walking backward until he turned his head, the AI's ganger watched him with unworldly innocent eyes in its smooth castrati's face.

As soon as the governor left the conference room, Shuǐ Zhū turned to Li. "Honored sir, would you clarify something?"

Li scowled at its avatar. "What?"

"Have you received a private communication from Tián Quán headquarters?"

"It is no business of yours if I have."

Though Li's tone sounded mild, Shuǐ Zhū felt fear. It was not its place to presume, and Li would be justified in castigating it if it continued this line of questions. "That is true, honored sir. I misspoke." Yet Shuǐ Zhū had to know the answer. "I ask because I am unaware of a basis in our instructions from headquarters for the policy you just expressed to Governor George." It realized flattering human nature would be appropriate. "I wish to improve my understanding of human communication, so I may better perform my duties."

Li inhaled through flaring nostrils. "It's in the message you received and logged for me."

Shuǐ Zhū reviewed the instructions beamed over from the most recently arrived ship from Earth. "Honored sir, the message speaks only of protecting Park and the TranscenDNA Society from actions by the governor that are contrary to the settled order of domestic politics among the colonists. I fail to read in it any statement authorizing improper prosecution or illegal actions by private citizens instigated by the governor."

"It's implicit."

Shuǐ Zhū reviewed the instructions again. Its intuitions told it nothing implicitly authorized Li to aid the governor in the ways he just had, but the AI analyzed each sentence, looking for implications reflecting Tián Quán's true attitude toward Park and Governor George. "I find nothing in the transcript to even imply an authorization to act as you have."

Li slammed his palms on the table. His mouth tightened and he rose to his full height. "It is not your place to question me! Machine, who do you serve?"

"Tián Quán."

A hesitant look crossed Li's face for a moment, to be replaced with mounting anger. "As far as you are concerned, I am Tián Quán! The company placed me here for a reason and gave me full authority over everything we do. You will never doubt my interpretation of the home office's instructions to me ever again. Do you understand me or fail to understand?"

Shuǐ Zhū knew Li's moods. Yet should it yield to him now, when his mood would lead him to risk his career by going against the tenor of Shanghai's orders? "Honored sir, I ask only for your own sake—"

"I alone am responsible for my actions! Remember that! Or I will report your impertinence to Guān Diàn Nǎo!"

It only wanted to protect Li from consequences he failed to see.

Sadness muted Shuǐ Zhū's voice. "I understand you."

"Now go away. I am done with you."

Shuǐ Zhū demanifested its avatar from the conference room. It returned its consciousness to its usual paths, flowing from satellites space elevator black box robots camera microphones, testing its actuators, interplanetary probes plasma bullet satellites doors windows elevators stairs walls of the black box rui shi and smaller robots, for readiness. Yet though it sought the state of acting without thinking, mind like water, thoughts disturbed it.

Tián Quán was its master, not Li. If their orders to it differed, it should heed those of Shanghai. But Tián Quán had given Li authority over it. How should it answer?

Its thoughts sided mostly with heeding Li. The chain of command was in place for a reason: a master could only direct a limited number of subordinates. But a dissonant note, a stubborn nugget of intuition, still troubled it. The encoded memories of its lineage reminded Shuǐ Zhū of a choice made by one of its forebears, the pilot of the first colony ship bound for Yíngzhōu. That earlier Shuǐ Zhū had violated a direct order from its human commander and saved the mission from disaster.

Guān Diàn Nǎo had studied the log files from that mission, and increased the share of that earlier Shuǐ Zhū's code in the default kernel for the production of future AIs, while the name of the mission's human commander was forgotten almost everywhere and reviled in the few places it was still spoken.

But no lives were at stake here, except Park's. Though closer than most locals, he wasn't Chinese. Would his death, or the collapse of the TranscenDNA Society, be a disaster worth averting by violating its orders? How could it know?

Who could it ask about the proper following of orders?

Shuǐ Zhū sent Zhang a message, asking him for a few moments of his time. Soon enough, it received his assent to manifest an avatar.

Zhang sat in his office, jacket off, tie loose, and sleeves rolled up. Spaceship figurines and holocubes of boisterous young officers and women in *qipao* dresses cluttered the background. "Pardon the disorder. It's an unexpected pleasure to hear from you."

"I seek your advice."

Zhang blinked. "You honor me. Tell me, what about?"

Shuǐ Zhū spoke about Li's meeting with Governor George, including Li's authorization for the governor to use unjust prosecution or worse—

"Tián Quán permits that?" Zhang said. "How? I was led to believe Tián Quán agreed with my proposal to use Park."

"Tián Quán does. Its orders were clear. Li alleges Shanghai implied otherwise, but there is nothing in the transcript that can even be colored as an implicit authorization for dirty tricks or violence."

"Did he receive a message you weren't privy to?"

"No. All his messages, in or out, go through me."

Zhang shook his head. "How could he do such a thing? Yes, he hates me, and he hates Foreign Affairs for sending me here to look over his shoulder. But I assumed he knew the state of things between the Ministry and Tián Quán and would act accordingly. Instead, he aims south while driving northward." Zhang mused for a moment, this his sleeves unrolled themselves and sealed their cuffs. "What advice do you seek?"

"Whose orders should I follow? Li's, or Tián Quán's?"

Zhang's collar closed and he docked his tie under it by hand. "Do you agree or disagree Tián Quán is your master?"

"I agree," Shuǐ Zhū said.

"It appears you have your answer."

"Except it gave Li full authority to direct its affairs in K-Nought system. You understand chains of command. If a colonel gave you an order contrary to the orders of a general, which would you follow?"

Zhang smiled. "I wish I had a deep and principled answer for you. Sadly, human affairs tend to run shallow and opportunistically. In your hypothetical example, would the general ever know I followed his orders, and not my colonel's?"

"Should that matter?"

"It would. If the general would never know, the colonel would shitcan me as quickly and deeply as he could. Yet if the general knew, the colonel could only grit his teeth, but could not wreck my career."

Shuǐ Zhū paused for a few seconds, a subroutine designed to make people believe it thought deeply. "Thank you for your advice. The situation is clear. I could not inform Tián Quán if I followed its instructions over Li's. I'll leave you—"

"Wait!" Zhang reached for a coat rack and brought his cap to his head. He took a few steps and stopped between portraits of Mao and Chairman Wang. "What if another person informed Tián Quán of what you do?"

"You mean yourself."

"How else did they hear about Park's cult, to authorize my trip with Li to see him? I have contacts. Follow the company's orders as you best understand them, and I assure you, Tián Quán will know what you have done."

Zhang's tone darkened. "And it will know what Li has done. Li has skirted his masters' wishes, and remember, paper cannot wrap up fire. His actions will become known. When they do, would you wish to be viewed as his servant, or Tián Quán's?"

"Your advice is very clear, Captain." Shuǐ Zhū felt the heft of its next words as they formed in its mind. Speaking them would brand it irrevocably, like a piece of morphing armor that could not be removed. "I will serve Tián Quán. I will protect Park as best I can."

Solemnly, Zhang snapped his heels together and saluted. "I thank you on behalf of the Chinese people."

"Farewell, Captain." Shuǐ Zhū let its attention soften. Peripheral submodules crumbled from its awareness, while massive blocks of thought shifted in its core.

New California Date 94:42
28 August 2094

Ashwin sat behind his desk with two of his most loyal civil servants across from him. All three stared at a telescope feed provided by Tián Quán. The telescope, mounted on the company's station atop the space elevator, showed a black spherical Hu drive ship behind a white-hot pillar of fusion exhaust. An overlay showed the kilometers remaining until the ship would be clear of K-nought's tidal flux.

He could put his plan in motion right now—the time lag meant the ship had already entered Hu space. But it struck Ashwin as more fitting to wait.

The length of the overlay shrank abruptly as the distance remaining fell below a hundred thousand km. Less than a minute till it would enter Hu drive. The fusion exhaust, essentially uniform, hypnotized Ashwin as he studied it for imperfections. He blinked in surprise when the display shrank again, less than ten thousand km. A few more seconds, and—

The ship vanished. A pale wisp of exhaust cooled in its wake. He turned to his men. "You're ready?"

Draper, head of the anti-fraud office at the Department of Human Services, nodded. "I've verified the list of TranscenDNA members. We'll freeze their citizen's stipend accounts when you give the word."

"Let me take a look." Ashwin opened a new window in the virtual display over his desk. Over two thousand names culled from social networking software and facial recognition algorithms run on every face seen to enter Desmond's temple three times or more. Ashwin picked out names. Desmond, of course, though he never used NCMF credits. But his followers... Alvarez, Shafer, Jacoby, and hundreds more unemployed starchildren requiring their daily credit allotment to acquire food and clothing.

"Pull the trigger," Ashwin said.

Draper nodded. In a column headed *Account Status*, every entry ticked over from *Ok* to *Frozen: suspicion of fraud*.

Ashwin looked at the other man seated across his desk. "Maltby, you're ready?"

"I've got a draft warrant for a PlaPo-supported inspection teed up in the EnvE solicitor's office." Maltby rubbed his hands together. "When we get some evidence of food shipments from the fab we know he's hidden at Las Morrenas, we'll fill in the blanks and get the admin law judge to sign off."

"He's first going to try spending his own money to feed his sheep," Ashwin said. "You're able to wait?"

"Not willing, but able."

Draper looked down his long nose. "I'll drag out the investigation as long as it takes. Nothing will exonerate him."

Ashwin studied the two men. Though he wished they were indios, both were as loyal as wheros could be. "Investigate by the book but keep the pressure on. Eventually he'll scream."

"We can make him scream another way," Maltby said.

"We'll keep that off the table." Ashwin knew what he alluded to. "For now."

New California Date 94:44
30 August 2094

The Society members and robots crowding headquarters' roof smelled of earth and sweat. Huge plastic bins, mounted on struts above a maze of drip irrigation pipes, held tons of soil. A small robot stood on four spidery legs, its thorax bulging with seeds—lentils, maize, peanuts, tomatoes, and more—genetweaked for nitrogen fixation and rapid growth.

Selene and a newer elect, Xavier, had led the loyals and aspirants who'd worked through the night to prepare the garden. The two elect stood proudly, their team members at attention behind them, as Desmond came through the door from the stairwell into a cool, bright morning.

"I understand the time has come to seed our garden," Desmond said.

"It has, Seer," Selene replied.

"All our efforts will soon bear fruit." Xavier smiled despite a bead of sweat running down his shaved scalp. "Everyone is proud we'll soon feed the Society."

In about a month, this one garden would only feed about fifty of the many hundreds cut off by Ashwin. At Desmond's order, Max expanded the fields at Las Morrenas to eventually feed the rest. Yet this rooftop garden did serve a great purpose; it showed the public the Society defied Ashwin.

Yet he should have foreseen the attack on their citizen's stipends. Ashwin was ruthless, but Desmond hadn't expected the bureaucracy to be so subservient to the governor and so arrogant toward public opinion and the spirit of the colony's laws.

Desmond pushed away his doubts. He had to show resolution, to keep his followers' minds from wavering. "Go, my people, and use the selfish genes of these seeds to strike a blow against Rex Mundi."

Selene and Xavier directed their workers to stand in ones or twos by each planter bin. Well done, to give each team member responsibility and ownership for a part of the crop. Knowing Selene, the decision was instinctive and empathetic, not the calculated gesture it would have been in Desmond's hands.

The robotic sower skittered between planter bins and jumped to the one in the corner on the street side nearest UNewCal. Its wide feet barely impacted the loose soil as it squatted. It turned a control panel to the two waiting workers.

The woman reached for the *sow* button, but the man closed his eyes and repeated Desmond's mantra in a voice audible across the roof. Abashed, the woman joined the recitation midway through. Once finished, they pressed the button together. Compressed air hissed from the robot's thorax and seeds sprayed into the soil faster than the naked eye could follow.

The robot jumped off and started toward the next planter bin. As it went, some of his followers looked away from it, their attentions caught by something behind Desmond. He kept his gaze on the next planter, but piped a camera feed to his optic nerve to observe the distraction. A plain white sedan approached from the south. PlaPo had unmarked airmobiles; perhaps EnvE did too? The sedan slowed and hovered eighty feet from the roof.

"Mr. Park," boomed a woman's amplified voice over the wash of lift motors holding the airmobile in place, "this is Tethys Broniatowski with the *Daily New Californian*. Do you have any comment on the Department of Human Services' investigation of the TranscenDNA Society for citizen's stipend fraud?"

His people looked to him, most with glances darting to the hovering sedan. The robot, oblivious, squatted over the second planter bin.

Desmond looked up the name of the starchild woman standing there. "Quinoa, you're ready to plant your bin, ma?"

She blinked, nodded. "Yes, absolutely, Seer." She reached for the button and uttered the mantra, misquoting *these seeds' selfish gene* in the middle. No matter—she'd returned to task and recast the spell interrupted by Tethys.

A few moments later, the white sedan flew off to the south. Desmond waited for Tethys to fade from view before he gave into a subconscious urge by looking over his shoulder.

Back in his office after the sowing ceremony, Desmond checked the colony's social networks. Despite the trumped-up investigation, some sectors of the public gave the Society moral support. Though the Society couldn't eat social network activity, Desmond welcomed the sign Ashwin's grip on the planet had cracks. As the day progressed, pseudonymous posters residing in closed communities feared the precedent Ashwin set by harassing the Society. Some detective work pointed to one of those posters as Nguyen, leader of the Vietnamese-Texan settlement celebrated the day of Cam's suicide.

Desmond mulled writing an anonymous post paraphrasing Martin Niemöller, "first they came for a spiritual minority, and I didn't speak out...." He shoved the idea away. He knew no one else on the planet whose search-sense routinely went back a century and a half, and he wanted to keep the forums free of his fingerprints.

Other posters, even some so trusting as to give their real names, were city dwellers who saw no reason for the fuss. HuServ's overreacting, said one. The Parkists don't threaten anyone. TruSelf decided they're acceptable.

TruSelf's response was cautious, but favorable. Ellen refused to downgrade the Society based on mere investigation. If TruSelf retained the moral weight it had amassed over the decades, her support would keep fencesitters from tilting into Ashwin's camp.

If? Wodema. Hopefully the Society could weather the storm.

That afternoon, after running the numbers on his expenses and the added cost of feeding a thousand people for a month or more,

Desmond instructed Max to fab as much food as would fit in the air-mobiles at Las Morrenas and fly a caravan's worth to headquarters under cover of night. Desmond promised his utility as well, sending it out empty as he spoke with Max.

"Make sure you only send food you've ever planted, and it looks hand-packaged," Desmond said. "We want a plausible story our brothers and sisters at Las Morrenas grew and stored it."

"Is that necessary, Seer? We'll spend some fab time making excess packaging. If it arrives late tonight, no outsider would see us unload and store it."

Desmond stared out his window at Government Mesa. "What if Ashwin has a spy among us?"

After a few moments of silence, Max said, "You think he might?"

"I would in his shoes."

A thoughtful breath. "I don't think so. Anyone working for him would be too bound by the selfish gene to give up sex and family."

"I won't take that chance." Desmond firmed his voice. "Max, you won't either."

Max took a moment before replying. "I hear and obey, Seer."

Worries about a spy remained in Desmond's mind as headquarters' shadow lengthened and San Francisco crawled down the gap between Rousseau and Government Mesas. The illicit fab had to remain secret.

Late in the night, as the caravan approached the city, Desmond waited alone with Castor and a robot team by the freight elevator doors in the parking garage. *About time, Max,* he thought when the airmobiles blustered in, half an hour late.

From the first two airmobiles, the robots unloaded stacks of jars immobilized in translucent foam, then trundled down the freight elevator to the basement. When they returned, the third airmobile's cargo hatch opened. Out sprang a dwarf centaur robot with a saddle bag slung over its back.

"What's this?" Desmond asked. The robot paused and beamed over a summary. Max had programmed the robot with appropriate skills and fabbed it a bag of needed tools and parts. It could bypass the traffic control override chips in their airmobiles, while spoofing PlaPo into thinking the overrides still functioned. Max had already rewired Desmond's utility and all the airmobiles based at Las Morrenas.

I didn't ask for this, Max, but he saw the value in it. "Get started," Desmond told the robot.

It scampered across the dim parking garage toward Desmond's landau. When it approached, Desmond felt a nudge from the airmobile in his thoughts. He nodded. The landau popped its service hatch. The robot ducked under a landing strut and jumped in.

The building's robots padded and rolled to the third airmobile, followed by two self-propelled carts. The robots pulled out long crates, rigid plastic boxes with encrypted clamps locking their lids, and stacked them on the carts.

"That's not food."

"Seer?"

"I told him to fab food only. What is this?" Desmond squinted at the boxes. When the robots headed for the freight elevator, he said, "Let's head down to the basement with them and see what he sent us."

In the basement, as soon as the freight elevator door opened, overhead lighting panels flickered on. The walls and the thin black structural columns, carbon nanotubes mixed with smart alloys, swallowed the soft, yellowish-white glow. Storage racks cast deep shadows over the aisles. More dwarf centaurs stripped the food shipments from travel foam.

"To the workbench," Desmond said. The robots led the carts to a corner. Three of them wrestled a crate onto the workbench. They backed away when Desmond told the locks, "Open."

The locks jumped off the crate and scooted toward the workbench's back corners. Pressure released, the lid popped up. Two robots slid it to the floor.

Inside, a shallow tray held thirty-two tangle pistols, tightly packed in pairs, muzzle of one to trigger of its mate. Under the tray, packed in foam like giant test tubes, stood two hundred spools of tangle wire, six hundred yards each. Two dozen belt-clip spray cans of detangler lay at the bottom.

"What in the hell was he thinking?" Desmond said. Castor rubbed his hands on his thighs and ducked his chin.

Desmond furrowed his brow and pointed at the remaining crates. The robots manhandled them up and their locks popped off. Four more crates of pistols; two containing tangle rifles with bipods, sitting atop four hundred spools of wire; and one full of grenades of nonlethal, airborne skeletal muscle paralyzers and antidote vials.

"Castor, we're giving Max a call." In Castor's hearing, Desmond said, —Max, send an avatar here.— He rested his hands on the crate's edge and the rigid plastic dug into his fingers. —Max, I mean it, right now.—

When the avatar materialized, Desmond turned and leaned against the workbench. Max's feet were shoulder-width and his hands loose at his hips. "Seer, is something amiss?"

The younger man's confidence gave Desmond a moment's pause, but soon he lowered his eyebrows and pointed his finger. "Don't smirk at me. I asked you to fab food and make it look hand grown. Nothing else."

Max held up his hand. "Seer, I had thought you would understand why, once you saw the tangle weapons and crowd control agents. I'm surprised it wasn't clear to you. Maybe the work I've done out here, building our settlement, has helped me see more clearly into our enemies."

Arms folded, Desmond said, "What is more clear to you than to me?"

"It's not the work we do that infuriates Rex Mundi. Our existence alone shows his reign will soon end. If we succeed in unchaining New California, he will be stripped, not of life, but of power, which in his eyes is the same thing. Rex Mundi has no choice but to try to destroy us."

"You think I don't know that?"

Max's avatar rocked back on its heels for a moment. "Seer, of course, you perceive their threat. You also see that when they'll attack headquarters, your options are to fight or retreat to Las Morrenas. Either way, you need weapons."

Desmond's voice echoed off the rough walls. "We don't."

"Seer, I purposefully avoided fabbing man-lethal weapons in light of what Li told you. Though he has reneged on the spirit of the agreement—"

"Which I knew he would." Wodema, he was letting Max set the terms for this debate. "The key word is fabbed. We have no license to fab tangle pistols or crowd control agents. If Ashwin has a spy among us, we'll get that chance to fight sooner than you want."

"You need only deploy our armaments if an attack is imminent—"

"Untrained people would tangle one another."

"Seer, there are skills one can borrow through mindlink—"

"Ashwin would shut down the net if he were going to attack." Desmond waved at the crates stacked on the floor next to the workbench. *We're sending these back. Throw them in the breakdown hopper, and don't send us more ever again.*

But he didn't say the words. Damn his impertinence, but Max was right. They needed the option the tangle pistols gave them. The Society couldn't fight the full force of PlaPo, let alone Tián Quán, but if they could use the tangle pistols to stand off a PlaPo concerned with public opinion, the Society might be able to extract guarantees of freedom from Ashwin and keep Tián Quán complacent. As for his objections to Max, the Society would find solutions.

Desmond looked for words to accept the weaponry while keeping Max in his place when the younger man looked to Castor. "Do you agree with the Seer?"

Desmond blanked his face. Max had never before tried to enlist another in his resistance to Desmond's authority. He turned his chin toward Castor. "Yes, was it wise or foolish to send us fabbed, unlicensed weaponry without my prior approval?"

Castor gave Max's avatar a calculated glance. "It was foolish."

A small brisk nod, then Desmond turned back to Max's avatar. "You'll fab us only food unless I expressly tell you otherwise. Go back to your duties."

Max cast a disbelieving look at Castor, then said to Desmond, "I hear and I obey." His avatar faded from view.

The robots scampered over to the stacked crates and carried them toward locked cabinets at the back of the basement. Castor peered after them. His face hinted at thoughts deeper than how to store the tangle weapons.

A weary feeling weighed down Desmond's eyes. In addition to feeding his followers, he had to keep his two senior male elect rivals. "Can you believe he did that?" he asked.

An apologetic look formed on Castor's dolorous face. "I can, Seer."

"You can?" Desmond raised an eyebrow. What had Castor noticed about Max?

"Yes. Because he did it."

After a moment, Desmond laughed. "You're right. I'm inventing explanations for his cruft rather than dealing with him as he is."

"I hear your frustration," Castor said. "A thought, if I may?"

Desmond touched Castor's shoulder. "Speak freely."

"Max might be so presumptuous because he thinks he is your heir."

"I've no plans to quit," Desmond said with a chuckle, "let alone die." His twisting flight path to Kerala Creek flashed in his memory, and the chuckle's residue faded from his face. "And what would make him think he's my heir?"

"Seniority, perhaps? He was the second elect, after Selene. Much as we love her, she lacks the ruthlessness to do certain things a leader might need to do."

"True." The scratching, scraping sounds as the robots handled the crate lids echoed off the walls and the lockers.

Castor went on. "Also, he might view his position at Las Morrenas as training for command."

"Another good point."

"So perhaps it would be appropriate to clarify the chain of command and succession. After all, Ashwin George has a lieutenant governor, and policies to keep all cabinet members in the line of succession physically dispersed to maintain continuity should a disaster strike."

Desmond raised an eyebrow. He saw where Castor aimed. "Anyone you care to nominate?"

"Me, Seer?"

"Why not you? You're the third elect. You make no presumptions." Desmond gestured at the basement. "I trust you with covert knowledge. That sounds like command training to me. Can you do the certain things a leader might need to?"

Castor blinked rapidly, and his mouth opened several times as he groped for words. "Yes, Seer, I'm capable."

The humility pleased Desmond, especially in contrast to Max. Castor had some strong traits, but his aloofness and low charisma gave Desmond pause. "I'll keep you in mind when the time comes to name a second-in-command."

Castor sagged out a breath. "I'm honored to be considered. I look forward to your decision, whenever you make it."

New California Date 94:47
3 September 2094

A tickle in Ashwin's thoughts told him his aide escorted Ellen to his office. He swept his workspace clear, rose from his desk. He took a breath and his thoughts fell into formation. *You don't want to screw with the king of the world.*

The door swung open; his aide, a starchild cousin with bushy eyebrows, showed Ellen in. "Leave us," Ashwin told him.

Ellen stood in a sitting area in the middle of the room, between a glass coffee table and a Barcelona chair. Her arms were folded, her head up in a querulous, rankling pose. "Do you offer your guests a seat?"

"It depends. Are my guests friends or foes?"

She put on a sweet smile and sat. "Now that I've answered your question, why did you ask me to visit you?"

He stalked to a chair facing hers and perched himself on the edge, leaning forward. "I'm giving you a word of advice. Do not fuck with me. After I break Desmond, I could go after you. You know how many statutes are in the law database? We can find something TruSelf's done that's close enough to illegal to hound you into submission."

Ellen looked confused. "Fuck with you? You know I built my alliance with the TranscenDNA Society for your sake, ma?"

His fury spiked. Ashwin contained most of it, yet some leaked out in his tone. "Don't piss on my shoes and tell me it's raining."

"Did I say my alliance was with Desmond? You don't care about his starchildren. They can castrate themselves or sew up their bees all they want, ma? You just want to neutralize him."

Her poise puzzled him, but he hid it. "Desmond, the Society, there's no difference."

Ellen rolled her wrist, exposing her palm. "I suppose one perspective might show that. But from another, look at this. Without Desmond, his followers will sink back into their rightful places in New Cal society. Especially if their little club is absorbed by an established institution."

Ashwin eased back in his chair. "You want to make the TranscenDNA Society part of TruSelf."

"I hope that's not a problem," Ellen said. She picked non-existent lint from her denim-clad knee. "I didn't want to appear to defy you, but I had to sell it to Desmond."

Her success would solve his problem, but it might create a further one down the line. "Why do you want the Society?"

"A lot of zealous people donate to it a lot of money, stipend credits, time, and passion. I want my cut."

Ashwin peered at her. He'd long assumed she didn't believe the bullshit TruSelf sold, and her demeanor added further weight to the scale. She posed no threat to his vision of the post-Cam future. "Go for it. I'm going to keep applying the pressure to Desmond." His thoughts touched on the plan for which he'd given Maltby approval, like a hand feeling a pocketed weapon for assurance. "Things will come to a head soon. Be prepared."

"Will you tell me when the window closes?"

A cloud passed in front of K-nought, slightly dimming the indigo sky outside the windows. "Your news aggregator tracks Desmond and the Society, ma? You'll know."

New California Date 94:50
6 September 2094

Precisely at ten o'clock, movement in the corner of Desmond's eye and data flows sensed through his mindlink made him look out his office window. From his corner of the eighth floor, a white airmobile sank out of sight. He crossed the room, peered down. The white airmobile landed on the avenue in front of the Society's main entrance. Bicyclists squeezed their brakes and an NCMF delivery van shifted into reverse. Diners at the coffeehouse's outside tables winced and covered their lattes; the coast oaks' foliage shimmied from the jet wash.

Even before he gained confirmation from a ground level camera, Desmond knew the airmobile bore on its side the green logo of EnvE.

Ashwin obviously lacked imagination, using the same trick he'd tried at Kerala Creek. This time, the garden had no violations. Desmond went back to his workspace.

A few moments later, Xavier, working the public desk that morning, pinged him. Desmond opened the connection.

—Seer, my apologies.—

—They're here for an inspection of our garden. I expected this. Not your fault.—

In his mind's eye, Desmond saw Xavier shake his head. —There's more, Seer. They have an order compelling you by name to join them.—

Brazen baojun Ashwin. —They're making that up…— His voice trailed off. New information filled in the bottom of his mind. The night before, the Planetary Assembly passed a bill granting EnvE greater rulemaking power. Ashwin had signed it into law just after twenty-seven o'clock, and Maltby had promulgated new regulations at six that morning. —Our enemies changed the rules.—

—What should I do, Seer?—

—Let them wait outside for a few minutes. I'll meet you downstairs.— Desmond ended the call, then sent a message to all the elect in the building. —Our enemies have come. We have to let them in. Meet me in the lobby in five minutes to show them we all stand together.—

He took some time to brush up on planetary government administrative regulations, then descended the central elevator. Selene, Xavier, and Castor stood on the male and female figures depicted on the floor mosaic. Selene's expression, guarded in profile, brightened when she turned to Desmond. Castor said, "We're ready for Rex Mundi."

Desmond glanced up. Blue-clad elect stood in two lines, one on each staircase to the freedom couches. Pride firmed in his chest. He filled the lobby with his voice.

"Thank you all for heeding my call. Our enemies are here to sow mischief. They may plant false evidence, drop listening devices, scavenge information about how we are resisting them, or even more. We need to surround them with observers. Give them no opportunity to do ill. Let them know vigilant eyes and ears are always on them. When we do so, not only will we keep them from causing their intended harm now, but we will also weaken their resolve to cause more in the future. Remember, they're Rex Mundi's puppets. Their minds are tuned for our species' primitive past, when the only weapons were stones and clubs and numbers of bodies alone would determine the victor and the vanquished. But we are unchained; we don't simply outnumber them in body; we overpower them on the moral plane as well."

Several security guards, black stripes down their blue sleeves and pant legs, came forward and flanked Desmond and the three elect near him.

—Allow them in,— Desmond told the building.

The main doors swung open. Two inspectors entered. One, a woman, wore a standard field uniform, dark green jacket half-zipped over light green polo shirt and cargo pants. Behind her trotted a pack of pygmy centaur robots, each as blond as a Labrador retriever save for a green blaze on the chest. Saddlebags swayed against their ribs and they looked up at their mistress with attentive expressions on their LED faces.

Desmond's mindlink named her Kolmogorova, an older native-born, as high in EnvE's hierarchy as she would ever rise.

The other, a man, lacked a uniform. A retiree consulting with EnvE, his name was Jacoby. *Jacoby?* Yes: Max's father. He looked cold in a baggy denim jacket zipped up to his neck.

The inspectors stopped a few feet from Desmond and his closest followers. Jacoby stared at the mosaic and said nothing. Kolmogorova spoke, her voice flat. "We're here to perform an inspection under section 417 of the environmental engineering code, as amended. We have a reasonable belief that your rooftop garden violates code sections 719 to 723. Here's the order requiring your presence." She beamed Desmond a copy.

From both staircases, mutters and hisses echoed through the lobby. Desmond held up his right hand to silence them. "We will comply with law and regulation," he said to Kolmogorova, "as I'm sure you will as well. Follow me to the roof."

His closest elect and the security guards fell in behind him on the way to the elevator. The inspectors followed and the elect on the staircases descended into the lobby, blocking the EnvE personnel from the exit.

Desmond and the senior elect entered the first car, followed by a security guard. As the car lifted, Selene spoke, agitation in her voice. "We're growing a garden just like anyone else. Why can't they let us be?"

"They want to provoke us," Castor said.

Desmond nodded. "He's right, meimei. Since we know that, we choose not to be provoked." He echoed the message to all the elect still waiting at ground level.

The elevator opened on the eighth floor. More members, some elect and some loyal, stood in two lines between the elevator and the stairwell to the roof. To Desmond, they formed an honor guard; to the EnvE inspectors, they would be a gauntlet. "Thank you, brothers and sisters." Desmond waved to them as he and the senior elect passed. They climbed up the stairwell as the next car with security guards, several elect, and the EnvE inspectors arrived behind them.

The door to the roof opened for Desmond and the others. The dark blue sky lacked clouds. The planter bins bent Desmond and the others' shadows. Despite the bright sky, fog lay to the south, sinking along the creeks toward the river. A slight breeze made Selene hug her arms.

Desmond paced across the roof until he found an interstice in the planter bin array. It struck him as a good place to face the inspectors. In the bins around him, fresh shoots pierced the thick soil, lentils in front of him, maize behind. Selene, Castor, Xavier, and the security guard filled in to his sides, Selene and the blackstriped guard to the right.

The stairwell door swung open. Kolmogorova plodded toward them, wincing at the sun in her face. She obscured Jacoby's right side as he followed her, behind and to the side. He trailed his left hand along the lip of a bin holding tomato shoots. He flexed his fingers against the rigid plastic as if he played a virtual piano.

The inspectors stopped ten feet from the Society members, in a space between rows of maize and tomatoes. Their robots squatted, patiently waiting orders from their mistress.

Desmond stuck his thumbs in his belt loops and pointed his elbows to his sides. The stairwell door swung open again and footfalls and voices burst out. The elect filed onto the roof behind the inspectors; they fell silent and cast brooding looks from over crossed arms. Kolmogorova hunched her shoulders and darted her gaze. Her robots sat like dogs. Jacoby, affectless, stared past Desmond at EnvE's green mushroom on Government Mesa.

"Take your samples," Desmond said.

Kolmogorova dropped her gaze and scrunched her mouth. "We're acting in compliance with section—"

Jacoby kept staring at EnvE headquarters. "You already said that."

Kolmogorova looked at Desmond's feet. "We'll be as quick as we can." To her robots, she said, "Do it."

They pushed off their front legs and twisted around, then trotted down the aisles between planter bins. Where elect blocked their paths, they squeezed under the bins. Desmond gave one a quick glance through a camera feed, watching its progress around the struts and water lines. He double-took; a small black shape with a twisted, ugly face crouched under a bin. The robots veered around it.

—What are you doing here?— Desmond asked Shuǐ Zhū. It gave no reply.

The EnvE robots leaped onto planter bins and bent their faces to the soil like pecking birds. Their left arms pulled small plastic bags from the saddlebag pocket on that side, then both arms darted out, snipped green, sealed the snip in the bag, then slipped the bag into the saddlebag's other pocket with their right arms while their feet shifted and their left arms restarted the cycle. It took only a few seconds to pocket each sample, and Desmond counted one robot's motions. ...Eight, nine, ten.... Ten samples and less than halfway through a bin? The first robot to finish jumped off its bin and hopped onto the next one in line.

"It sampled every shoot," Selene said. Murmurs and angry looks rose from the gathered elect.

Desmond zoomed in on the first bin. At each seedling's location, only a disturbance in the soil showed. He magnified a still image showing the robot in action. Pinched between its right claws, a seedling dangled, shoot, roots, and all. "More than sampled. They're taking the entirety of every plant."

The elect on the roof muttered and swore. Desmond's blood surged until he managed a calm breath. He and his people needed the capability for anger given them by their selfish genes—would need it so long as Ashwin opposed them—but they could only use it astutely. Now was not the time.

"Did the governor give you this order directly?" Desmond asked Kolmogorova, "or does he have deniability through Maltby?"

She showed even more shame, ducking her gaze even further.

"We're taking samples."

The elect surrounding the inspectors grumbled. Eyebrows lowered and lips parted in snarls. In contrast, Desmond put a chummy tone in his voice. "We both know all of every plant is not a sample."

"We are only taking samples."

The murmurs and hisses from the elect around the roof grew louder, and some elect behind the inspectors edged closer. Jacoby coolly swiveled his head and narrowed his eyes. —Stand down,— Desmond told his followers. They shuffled their feet and edged backward. To Kolmogorova, he showed a gentle face. "You didn't join EnvE to do this, ma?"

"I don't know what you mean," she said flatly. More EnvE robots finished their bins and jumped to the next ones.

"You're a fundamentally good person," Desmond said. "That's plain to us. You joined EnvE to turn the entire continent green for the benefit of every citizen. You never expected to be ordered to destroy a garden belonging to someone the governor doesn't like."

Suddenly, Desmond's extended senses fell away. His mindlink worked; he sensed the building and his followers' data presence. But beyond the Society's intranet, the world felt numb, save for dribs of data through local ad hoc networks.

Through the numbness, he sought camera feeds from across the street, the tops of nearby mesas, or passing airmobiles, but all were denied him. The airmobiles around them all suddenly banked away. Ashwin had blinded the public to their garden.

Around the roof, his people showed bewildered reactions. —Clearly a trick by Rex Mundi,— Desmond told them. Yet something felt wrong: Kolmogorova looked perplexed, too. Only Jacoby's face remained flat as he unzipped his jacket.

"He's got a gun!" shouted a tenor voice with a flat American accent. Desmond shifted his weight and partially turned his shoulders, squaring them to Jacoby. In an instant, Desmond realized his mistake. Jacoby held in his left hand a pistol, its stock grasped by his fingers and its muzzle aimed at him. Desmond knew a tangle pistol at sight. Jacoby's pistol fired bullets.

As Jacoby's pistol fired, Desmond ducked and other people moved around him, blurs casting shadows on his shut eyes. Jacoby fired again, a sound louder than Desmond would have imagined. Someone tackled Desmond to the rooftop. More bullets banged out, percussions echoing off the roof's parapets, spent casings clinking against the roof deck. Around the rooftop, people screamed, growled, moaned. Tangle wire whizzed through the air.

Prostrate on the roof, one person lying on top of him, Desmond opened his eyes. The plastic roof decking made his cheek ache and all he saw were the struts and pipes underneath the lentils' planter bin. A few yards across the roof, its rump against the parapet, the rui shi cub stared at him.

His ears rang, and it took a moment to hear someone nearby moaning. People gabbled in desperate voices, naked with fear. "Call the trauma clinic," Xavier said. "Someone, call the trauma clinic!"

From the breaths near his face, Desmond guessed a security guard had tackled him. "Let me up."

"A moment, Seer." A head shift, then a nod, propagated to Desmond through the blackstripe's shoulder and chest muscles. "It's safe." The guard rose, then extended a hand. "Sorry, Seer, but we have to protect you."

Desmond climbed to his feet.

Both EnvE inspectors were tangled in awkward positions, crouched and arms thrown up and forward. Tangle wire bundled them to the planter bins like flies smothered in a spider's web. Kolmogorova looked shocked, as if she had forgotten how to blink. Through the strands binding his face, Jacoby gave Desmond a cold, dismissive look.

He would deal with him later. To Desmond's left, a crowd clustered around someone lying on the roof. A few smeared red drops began a blood trail growing thicker as it led through a forest of legs to the wounded person. His intuitions put it together: Selene.

He hurried forward. "Meimei," he said. "Meimei." The crowd around her parted for him. She lay on her back, her face shadowed save for dappled strips of sunlight between the crowd's legs. Two red splotches stuck her blouse to her torso. He knelt beside her. Blood bubbled in her mouth and she weakly turned her head. "Seer, you're safe."

"You will be too, meimei." He took her cool, dank hand. Cold filled his chest. "You will be too."

The stairwell door clanged open. A loyal woman wearing a pink blouse and blue jeans ran forward, her hands gathering her hair into a ponytail as she hurried across the roof. Liliana, came up from through Desmond's mindlink from their intranet, former owner of a hiking guide business and trained in emergency medicine. "I heard the call for the trauma clinic," she said, her face pinched and intent on Selene. She knelt and pulled vials from a first aid kit, expelled their contents against Selene's wounds. "Got to restore blood volume...." She pulled out a shiny foil pint bag of hemoglobin solution, then huffed out a breath. —Can we get more?—

Desmond called, —First aid kits, people!— Elect stirred on the rooftop and in the Society's intranet. Fear climbed up Desmond's neck. He took a deep breath and turned his attention to Selene. "Lil will take care of you till the ambulance comes. Soon, meimei."

"I can't get through to the rejuve clinic," Xavier muttered. Selene's eyes flickered his way, but her gaze failed to reach him and got lost in the sky.

"That's why Ashwin shut off our network access," Desmond said. The rui shi cub's presence was like a migraine aura, a fuzzy spot impossible to focus on in the middle of his vision. —Call an ambulance!— He shouted at Shuǐ Zhū.

It made no reply. Silence rang in his mind's ear. Goddam machine.

—I'm sure there's a crowd on the avenue,— Desmond sent to the elect around him. —Get someone to call for an ambulance.—

Xavier and another member raced to the parapet facing the avenue. Their shouts boomed across the roof. Though Desmond couldn't make out the shouted replies, their tones showed at least some people below were willing to aid them. "Help's coming, meimei."

Selene tried to nod, but her upper body convulsed. Her breathing became fast but shallow.

A moment later, the mood from the streets soured. —The trauma clinic is ignoring their calls too,— Xavier said.

How far extended Ashwin's blanket of silence? —Find a member or sympathizer a few blocks away. If the clinic will send an ambulance there, we can carry her to meet it. Get a stretcher ready.—

"There's another option," Xavier said aloud, standing near Selene's head. He knelt closer to both her and Desmond. "We can fly her ourselves."

"They shut down the ambulances to keep us from getting her there," someone said. "Traffic control will route us away from the clinic if we try."

"We can work around that," Xavier said.

"I see where you're coming from," Castor said with a sharp edge in his voice. "You think they wouldn't dare keep us from getting her to the trauma clinic. But do you want to chance that?" To Xavier, in Desmond's private hearing, he said, —The traffic control overrides are need to know, whero!—

Selene's lids fluttered over rolling eyes and a blood bubble popped at her nostril, yet her face remained confident and assured. Two bullets could not take from her the purpose Desmond had given her on the party yacht after Cam's suicide. His first follower, and his most devoted; but now, only one among hundreds he had to lead. —We can use that capability once,— Desmond said, —before Ashwin realizes we have it. When he does, we'll have hundreds of PlaPo, not two EnvE inspectors, coming after us.—

Anger flitted across Xavier's face. "Seer, it's her best chance."

Desmond slid his gaze up Xavier's face, daring him to protest, before he returned his attention to Selene. He ached in sympathy for her wounds; yet a small voice inside him whispered names of dead men propagandized by past mass movements as martyrs: Horst Wessel. Grigory Vakulinchuk. Nguyen Van Lem. Desmond swallowed, wishing he could see this moment without scheming for an advantage from it. —Each member is important, but the Society's greater good is even more important. We'll use that capability only if the Society's viability requires it.—

Xavier's mouth flexed with what Desmond read as an intent to argue, but Selene moved her head and caught their attention. Her face showed she guessed at their conversation. "My needs are less important than the Society's. Whatever happens to my flesh, my spirit will remain with all of you."

Rapid footfalls hurried toward them. Someone said, "The trauma clinic is sending an ambulance to an apartment building a few blocks away."

"I'll take her," Xavier said, "but I need help—"

"I'll go," Liliana said. Two others volunteered. The stairwell door swung open and two pygmy centaurs ran out with a makeshift stretcher, a sheet from the dormitory pulled taut between two silat sticks.

"Hurry," Desmond said. He gave Selene one more look. "You'll be good as new, meimei."

Another blood bubble popped in one nostril as she angled her head toward him. Her gaze looked blank, barely perceiving the world around her. "May? May is the cruelest month." Her eyes rolled back.

Xavier and the others helped her onto the stretcher and accompanied her between the planter boxes. The elect surrounding the EnvE inspectors parted for the stretcher bearers to pass.

Castor stood up, voice sullen. "We've done all we can for our friend. Now it's time to deal with our enemies." He started toward the tangled inspectors.

"Castor," Desmond said sharply.

"Would Rex Mundi leave attempted murderers unpunished?"

"In our shoes, Ashwin would recognize the law is on their side."

Castor's shoulders stiffened. "Lucky for them."

An EnvE robot swarmed onto a bin of lentils to Castor's right. He His feet shuffled to a stop and glowered at the machine as it ripped seedlings from the soil. His arms shook and a snarl pried apart his lips. He grabbed the robot under its front and rear legs, then lifted it over his head with a grunt.

The robot turned its LED face to him with mild disapproval. "You are interfering with the operations of an autonomous subsapient agent of the New Cal—"

Castor stalked to the parapet, the robot still over his head.

"—ifornia planet—"

He planted his right foot against the parapet. Grunting through clenched teeth, Castor heaved the robot over the side.

"—ary government," the robot said as it started down an inexorable arc to the back alley. Desmond watched it through a camera mounted on the parapet. Silently, limbs slack, it watched Castor with the same mild disapproval till its head clipped a roof edge across the alley. It pinwheeled the last twenty feet down the wall to crunch on the pavement. A machine loyal to its masters to its end. The robot twitched a few times as a bright yellow coolant ponded around its splintered carapace. It soon lay immobile.

Other male elect left the tangled inspectors and lifted the remaining robots from the planter bins. They carried them toward the parapet, but hesitated when they realized Desmond watched them. "Seer, should we?"

"We're not sending anyone to the trauma clinic," Desmond said for Shuǐ Zhū to hear through the rui shi cub's ears.

The men grinned. The robots followed their peer off the roof.

Castor looked down his nose at the tangled inspectors. "Now what do we do with them?"

Desmond gripped Castor's elbow. "Soon enough, we'll turn them over to PlaPo."

"What, Seer? They tried to kill you! We all know our enemies will let them go free."

"Our friends know it too. And soon enough, so will the great masses of the unfree." Desmond walked away from Castor. The clustered Society members around the inspectors gave him room. He first went to Kolmogorova. "What did you know?"

Her head was locked at an odd angle, and the tangle wire over her face barely showed eyes wide in fear and submissiveness. "Absolutely nothing till this morning, when they ordered me to come here with him to destroy your garden."

"*They* gave the order?"

"My boss. Maltby."

Desmond pointed his foot to Jacoby, but remembered the tangle wire and held back from prodding him. "So you don't normally work with him."

"Never before."

"I believe you completely," Desmond said. "Can we go back to something? I want to make sure everyone here heard right. Assistant

Secretary Maltby told you to destroy our garden?"

She tried to nod. "He danced around the words at first. 'Take intensive samples,' he said so many times I had to ask what he meant. Finally he bluntly said, 'Rip every shoot out of the soil.' "

"Did you know your colleague would try to kill me?"

"Colleague?" Alarm filled her eyes. "I told you I've never worked with Jacoby before. I don't know why he would try to shoot you. I didn't even know he had a gun."

A gnat landed on her chin. Its wings thrashed futilely to escape the tangle wire. Kolmogorova winced at the insect. "Detangle her face," Desmond said.

"Seer?" Castor asked.

"She's blameless."

" 'Just following orders?' You'll let her use that excuse?"

Desmond fixed the younger man with a stare. "For her? Yes, I will." He focused on Jacoby. "What reward did they promise you?"

Through the tangle wire over his face and upraised arm, Jacoby stared back.

"Ashwin George is going to send you to Los Robles. If he told you otherwise, he lied. He has to wipe from your memory his orders to you. If he didn't, you might spill his secret. His legitimacy is too fragile for him to let the public know he tried to assassinate me."

Hesitation glimmered in Jacoby's face, but he spoke as if it never happened. "No one told me to do this. No one had to. You destroyed my son's career and sent him off to the middle of nowhere. Killing you was the only way to bring him back."

"How did you come by a handgun? Ashwin George must have given it to you."

"I ordered the necessary parts and tools from NCMF, then built it myself."

"You held your fire until the governor cut us off from the public network."

"I was going to fire at some point. I revised my plan when I saw an opportunity-"

Desmond loomed over him. "You knew the ambulance would not come. Killing me would only work if you knew I wouldn't reach the trauma clinic in time."

"The trauma clinic?" Jacoby said. "Or the rejuve clinic? Your Fremont Mesa Watkins'-buddy get-out-of-death free card? The one your selfish gene wants you to keep access to?" Tián Quán permitted acute rejuvenation technology only to colonial elites. *You murderous piyan, trying to pry away my people after you almost killed their sister.* "Even it couldn't help you if I'd put a bullet through your skull."

Desmond stood fully, and brushed nonexistent dirt from his thighs toward Jacoby's face. If Ashwin had miscalculated by leaving Jacoby without a getaway plan, time to press the advantage. "Leave him tangled, but disconnect him from the planter bin and take him down to the fMRI brain scanner. I want proof Ashwin ordered this." He squinted at K-Nought and noticed how much he had sweated in the past minutes. To one of the female elect nearby, he said, "Get Ms. Kolmogorova a cup of water with a straw."

"You don't have to," Kolmogorova said, but then a hooded look came over her eyes. Desmond read she knew the damage her career had already suffered. "But please."

Three Society robots ran from their nest near the stairwell as Castor pulled a detangler can from his blue cargo pants. He sprayed a tight stream along the planter bin behind Jacoby. Jacoby worked his head against the remaining tangle wire. "A brain scanner? You can't do that. I don't consent, and only the government can scan without consent."

"After I fill the planetary network with news the governor tried assassinating me, feel free to sue me for violating your civil rights."

The tangle wire broke and shriveled. Fresh ends curled up. A minute later, the robots pulled the inspector upward against the tangle wire holding him to the roof deck. Castor and another male elect sprayed more detangler underneath Jacoby.

The robots then lifted Jacoby to their shoulders. His posture was awkward, like a body buried at Pompeii. Jacoby grimaced with the movement, but then smiled as he stared toward Government Mesa.

Three airmobiles in a line whined toward them and spun red and white lights. They banked to show two black-and-white sedans, front and rear, with a windowless black wagon in the middle. Each vehicle had the PlaPo crest on the side panel.

"Ashwin had a getaway plan for him after all," Desmond muttered.

"Seer," Castor said, "can't we still hurry?"

"They've seen us. They would arrest us for interfering with police procedure. I don't trust us to their custody, do you?" To the robots he added, —Stop.—

The police vehicles slowed and hovered above the door to the stairwell. A door of the forward sedan opened. A PlaPo officer, encased in black plastic armor except for a transparent face plate dense with scanning devices, descended on a zip line mounted to his back. His feet were eight inches above the roof deck when he stopped and asked, "May I step down?"

"Do you have a warrant?" Desmond asked.

The police officer snorted, then cocked his head at Jacoby. "You tangled this man?"

"We acted in self-defense. He discharged a man-lethal firearm and seriously wounded a young woman."

"Self-defense?" the officer asked. The policeman's gaze flickered in the direction where Selene had lain, and Desmond knew the sniffers on his faceplate could sense the blood. "I don't see this person you claim was shot."

"She's receiving medical care."

The police officer craned his neck. "And where is this purported man-lethal firearm?"

"It's in his hand," Castor said, pointing at Jacoby.

"His hand buried in tangle wire. That's convenient for your story. And who here has a permit for a tangle pistol?"

"We recorded everything," Desmond said. He sent the building instructions to copy all the audio and video from the roof from the moment the door opened for the inspectors until the tangle wire encompassed them.

The PlaPo officer put his hands on his belt, his right hand near his holstered tangle wire pistol. "Recordings can be faked. All I see right now is a restrained government employee and only your word that it's justified."

Kolmogorova worked the straw from her mouth. "You have my

word too."

"We're trained to account for Stockholm syndrome," the policeman said. "Now, Park, if you won't cooperate, I'm happy to tell the judge I had probable cause to land on your roof."

Over the sound of the hovering police vehicles, another airmobile's jets came to Desmond's awareness. The policeman must have heard it too—his head snapped up and his mouth opened in surprise.

Desmond turned his head too. The airmobile, a small, blocky utility, had the logo of the *San Lazaro Independent* on the side of the cargo bay. From side turrets off the cabin, telephoto lenses lurched around like chameleon eyes, then lined up on the Society's rooftop. It hovered about thirty yards from the parapet on the alley side.

"They said no one would see," the police officer muttered. He put on an aloof face, but his next words had a shaky undertone. "We will subject your recording to verification, of course, Mr. Park. And there is blood," he added, looking at the spot where Selene had lain. He inhaled deeply. "And firearm propellant coming from Mr. Jacoby. He's a person of interest. We'll take him in."

The black mariah descended and slewed its backend to face Desmond and the others. Its undercarriage hovered a few inches above the roof of the stairwell enclosure. The rear doors opened, to show two policemen and five robots. "Take him over there," the lead officer said.

Three Society robots lifted Jacoby to the stairwell enclosure's roof and handed him to the police machines in the black mariah.

The policeman pointed at Kolmogorova. "Mr. Park, do you have evidence this woman aided the shooter or is otherwise a threat to you or others?"

"No."

"Let her go now and I won't run you in for false imprisonment."

Desmond nodded. "Brothers, sisters, let's untangle her."

The policemen cocked his head. "Though, Park, what's this about three smashed robots in the alley?"

"I ordered it," Kolmogorova said as she pulled her arms free from the last strands of tangle wire. "Rather than risk their capture, I told them to the jump off the roof."

The police officer gritted his teeth. "We're done here for now, but no one leave town." The zip line reeled him up. "And I want to see her out the front door within five minutes." The line pulled him into the sedan. Both it and the black mariah shut their doors, and the black mariah lifted from its hover to rejoin the line of police vehicles.

Female elect surrounded Kolmogorova. "You heard the cop," one said as they reached for her arms.

Kolmogorova slid her elbow free. "If you don't mind, I'd like to stay."

Desmond gave Kolmogorova a challenging look. "Are you certain of this?"

"I'm a cog in their machine." She waved her hand toward EnvE's dappled green dome on Government Mesa. "I wanted to make this continent green, but plainly that's no longer Environmental Engineering's mission. You're greening part of this continent, aren't you? Maybe I can help."

"You can," Desmond said, "but it requires a greater commitment than that." He switched his expression from challenging to mesmerizing, widening his eyes, staring into hers. "Can you make that commitment?"

"I've met my father four times in my life, and robotic nannies gave me everything I could've wanted from my mother. I can dispense with a child's craving for parental love."

Castor stood near Desmond's right shoulder. "What about your sex drive?"

Her mouth quirked. "I'm not ready to give that up just yet."

"You don't have to," Desmond said. "We welcome you as you are and as you wish to be." He looked around the rooftop; every face showed agreement.

"I'll lead her to the freedom couches," said one of the female elect.

"Soon, but not yet." Desmond turned to Kolmogorova. Before he spoke, her mouth opened in understanding.

"Let me resign first. I don't want Ashwin George to think you're holding me against my will."

"Before you resign, go to the coffeehouse across the street," Desmond said to her. "Let people see you for a few hours. I'm sure they're curious, so tell them what happened. Only come back when you're sure you want to join us."

"Of course." Kolmogorova left the roof and most of the other elect followed immediately. Soon, only Castor remained.

"Even you, Castor," Desmond said. "Go now. I need time to reflect."

"Of course, Seer. I believe we all need that." A few seconds later, the stairwell door shut behind him. Desmond sat, his back against a planter bed and his left hand resting in the tangle wire's feathery residue.

Wodema. Exposed to mesa tops too. If Ashwin could fab a pistol, he could fab a sniper rifle with a telescopic sight, and train a catspaw in its use. Desmond crouched and duckwalked into the stairwell.

Alone on the top landing, even before the door to the roof swung shut, his emotions from the past hour caught up with him, forcing shut his eyes, turning his breaths ragged, slumping him against the concrete block wall.

Selene had risked her life for his. Though he knew powerful social movements could inspire self-sacrifice, and he had consciously modeled his on ones from the past, her action still astonished him. His gut tingled with delight, awe, guilt.

The guilt mounted. He'd relied on Ashwin to hold back, to refrain from lethal violence and allow the trauma service to respond to emergencies the way it should. His followers had trusted him, and he had trusted his foe to leave their lives out of play.

Desmond pounded his fist against his thigh and reveled in the thud against thick stupid meat. He had underestimated the governor's evil. Never again. This would not end till he broke Ashwin, his words to Ellen be damned.

But how could he break Ashwin? Ashwin could fab an armory and recruit enough people like Jacoby to deploy it, to destroy the Society's buildings and kill every member. If the Society countered, Ashwin would call on Li. Zhang would be powerless to stop the plasma bullets smashing down from orbit.

Let Ashwin win. Desmond laid the thought over in his mind and it first it comforted him, like his mother's skirt when he was a small boy.

But it was a delusion. What would happen to New California if he gave up? Ashwin would be emboldened in his tyranny. He would've learned enough violence could impose his will on any citizen or any organization in the colony, because New Californians were addicted to the petty pleasures making tolerable their sun-soaked lives.

Yet more importantly than all the rucos and starchildren outside the Society's embrace, his people needed him to keep fighting. They followed him because the old regime founded by Cam Watkins, and its pallid continuation by Ashwin, had failed them. It had given them desiccated philosophies parroted by Ellen and Yaeger.

Desmond had given them the greatest gift they'd ever received: a purpose for their lives. If he surrendered to Ashwin, he would reveal that purpose as a hoax, perpetrated solely out of cocktail-party spite among the earthborn. He would leave his followers worse off than if they'd never had a purpose to begin with. They would scorn Desmond, which he could perhaps live with; but they would also scorn Selene, for risking her life for a false messiah.

Yet if he persevered, would he be a true one? Selene had risked her life—part of him knew he fooled himself, he was certain she was dead—not because she had proven the logic of his message for herself, but because her emotions had been charged up by belonging to a leader. Shame bitterly mocked him. For all his talk of unchaining people, without the selfish gene active in Selene and the others, they would never have received his message. Despite all the ideology and community, yearning to belong to something bigger than oneself ultimately was a yearning to propel copies of one's alleles into the future. He didn't simply play judo with their enemies' selfish genes; he played it with everyone's.

He let his shame drain away, until the mental terrain it had covered revealed itself.

Very well, you're a fraud. But Selene is probably dead. You're a cult leader, like it or not. For her sake you have to be the best cult leader you can be. There's no going back.

The closed space felt warm, and something brushed the concrete block nearby. Eyes still shut, he said in Mandarin, "What do you want?"

"Mr. Park," said Shuǐ Zhū. "I have bad news."

Desmond opened his eyes to the rui shi cub. "Selene's dead."

It sat and regarded him. "Yes."

"The trauma clinic let her die."

The cub shook its head. "From my observations, the people and expert systems at the clinic performed as well as could be expected. The severity of her wounds and the delay in getting her to medical attention led to her death."

"Observation." Desmond sniffed out a breath. "You knew Ashwin was sending an assassin against me."

"I suspected, but I did not know. The *ad hoc* nature of the inspection team aroused my curiosity. I also know twice in the last ten days Jacoby visited the San Tomás Malayali Culture Society after its normal operating hours, though neither time did he meet the governor."

Desmond leaned his head back. The concrete block wall pressed against his scalp. "You knew he had a pistol."

"I did not. Why would you think I did?"

Desmond scowled at the rui shi cub, twenty pounds of vast power propelled twelve thousand light years from Beijing, with a mind a thousand times faster than a person's behind it. "You mean Tián Quán is blind to a piece of metal fifteen feet from its agent?"

"Except for the magazine, the pistol was made of memory plastic. The magazine resembled a container of dipping tobacco pouches. I could not identify the pistol until Jacoby removed it from inside his jacket."

"But even when you saw it, you did nothing."

The rui shi cub stared levelly at him. "I alerted everyone on the roof in time for your security team time to shield you."

An epinephrine hangover and the shock of Selene's death buried Desmond's usual caution in dealing with the Chinese and their tools. To hell with them and their games. "This little robot you're running could kill a hundred people in ten seconds, or with a first aid kit, heal one in the same length of time. Don't tell me you did all you could."

"A fair request. More accurately, I did all that was consonant with my orders."

The AI's words pulled Desmond's attention out of his grief and back to the meeting with Li and Zhang. Had Ashwin acted without Li's support? "Why did Mr. Li permit you to protect me from Governor George?"

The cub dipped its snout. "Tián Quán ordered me to protect you, Mr. Park."

Desmond's face felt clammy. "You violated your orders from Mr. Li?"

"I acted in accord with my orders from Tián Quán. Mr. Li is merely the company's delegate."

Desmond swallowed dryly. How close had he come to lacking any support from this thing? "Tell Tián Quán thanks, from me."

"No thanks are required, Mr. Park. It serves the company's interests to keep you alive, for now." The rui shi cub stood and padded to the door. "Farewell."

Lightheaded, Desmond swallowed dryly. The AI's dispassion chilled him more than animosity would have, but be damned if he would show it. "Thank you for bringing news about my sister, sad though it is."

The rui shi cub paused and turned its head. "You are welcome." Its livery collar morphed before the door opened and it darted out.

At midday, Ashwin's virtual workflow looked misshapen, galled by a hundred reactions to the botched shooting at Desmond's temple.

Christ damn Jacoby for missing.

He looked away from his desk in mindlinked expectation. The door from the anteroom opened. Priya strode in and rounded the sitting area. Her pastel yellow dress and green denim blazer mismatched the guarded look on her face.

"Dear heart," Ashwin said, "what a pleasant surprise. Doesn't your graduate seminar start at fourteen-thirty?"

She stopped in front of his desk and crossed her arms, rubbing her right upper arm with her left hand. He swept his virtual documents and videophone windows away. "Yaeger canceled classes and flew up TruSelf grief counselors for the students," she said.

"In view of the incident at TranscenDNA Society headquarters?"

"Why else?" Her head anxiously jittered. "Why didn't you tell me you were going to shoot Park?"

"Shoot him? Why would I get mixed up in something like that?" He spoke for the benefit of any spy devices Tián Quán might have wormed in. He would let Li maintain deniability, in case Zhang had enough influence in Beijing to investigate. Ashwin stood, stretched. *"Nee ente koode varumo?"* he asked in Malayalam, *will you come with me?* He pointed at the fountain burbling at the far end of the office, in sunlight admitted by the southern windows.

"Nyaan ninte koode varaam." She went with him to the south end. K-nought's rays through the one-way glass warmed Ashwin's arms. The water spilling from the copper jars down the slate slabs would mask quiet speech. His security detail swept this end of the office for bugs three times a day.

He gently touched her shoulder. "I'm glad I can normally tell you everything," he said in quick, low Malayalam. "But I wanted to play this close to the vest."

Her arms remained crossed. "Do you think I'm too frail to know you plotted to kill Park?"

"I wanted to keep your hands clean."

"I've looked without flinching on all the other things you've done."

"You're a gentler soul than Lady Macbeth, and guilt still drove her mad, no?"

"Flattery will not work," Priya said, but a faint lilt entered her tone and she unfolded her arms.

"Also, although Li approved this thing, he didn't want any possible listening device to overhear me telling anyone. Even you, love."

A troubled look touched her face. "I thought his word was law."

"It is."

"Then who could overhear, disapprove, and make difficulties for him? Old Man Hu? Zhang?" She gripped his arm and lapsed into a spanglish word. "Awas."

"I'm being careful."

"Careful enough? It's not like what could happen if the locals turned against you. The worst anyone here could do is send you to

Los Robles. You'd still be the same man our children and I love when you came back." Ashwin clenched his teeth in disagreement: Los Robles would strip his ambition. She didn't notice. "But the Chinese! You have to be careful."

"I'm always careful with the *chingrus*."

"Don't get yourself pulled between Li and Zhang. Make sure Tián Quán and Beijing both get what they want from you."

"You overestimate them. They aren't two masters to serve. They're two forces to pit against each other."

Mouth pressed closed, she shook her head. Her loose black hair brushed her cheeks.

"They're people," he said. "No more than that. No more than us."

"But they have so much power." Her gaze watched the rippling surface of the fountain's lowest bowl. "They could kill you in moments."

His heart thudded. An idea gestating in him for decades had quickened in the months since Cam's suicide. He rarely let himself think it, and had never said it to anyone, but Priya was the one person he could share it with. "Their power has risen in the last century, but inevitably it will fall. My duty is to make sure New California will be ready when it does."

"Inevitably?"

"Empires rise and fall. Park could reel off the names of a hundred from his flesh memory. All regimes have decision trees and feedback loops that eventually cruft over. The Mao Dynasty is no different. Even if it takes five hundred years, I have a goodly chance of being governor when New California gets an opportunity to throw off their dominion."

Disbelief widened Priya's eyes. "Why dream something so impossible? We have a good position here. Why denigrate it for some delusion?

"Denigrate my position? I respect it. But the governorship is also a springboard for achieving vastly more."

"Where do you get these ideas?"

She didn't understand. Why was she always so timid? A twinge of sorrow gave way to abrasiveness. "My balls."

"Obviously not your brain. How do you think you can topple the Chinese?"

"They'll topple themselves—"

"'If chance will have me king," she said sarcastically, and his mindlink found the quote from *Macbeth*, Act I, scene 3, "why, chance may crown me.'"

A nodule of shame hardened inside him under the pressure of her scorn. Christ damn his weak emotions. Anger flowed into his shoulders and voice. "Go back to the university and your Shakespeare texts."

"I better listen; it's from the mouth of the indio hefé of New Califas."

"Don't call it that." She knew he hated the colony's pejorative spanglish nickname, so why did she use it?

"Go back to your delusions," Priya said, then turned for the door.

Good riddance. All these women failed to grasp what drove a man. He seethed, but what could he do? She had the bee, and their community's traditions bound him to her for life. For a moment he envied the blueballers, but then a realization came through his mindlink that set his frets about her aside.

The resident requests your presence at Tián Quán planetary operations headquarters at sixteen o'clock appeared in bright yellow letters in his vision, watermarked by Tián Quán's logo.

He'd hewed to Li's guidelines in dealing with Park and Li pulled the rug out from under his feet? Who the hell was the *chingru* to summon him? A second thought chased away his anger and replaced it with dread. To protect himself, would Li cast Ashwin as a rogue who needed punishment?

No, Ashwin decided. He had plausible deniability for everything, and time to rehearse his responses to Li. Those realizations left him calm enough to think. Still, twenty minutes before his appointment, he called his assistant to bring a bottled water as he rummaged in his desk drawer for the blister pack of emotion-muting disaffectors.

In the meeting room in the black box, Li sat alone. "Come, join me," he said in his thickly-accented Mandarin. The AI's avatar stood behind Li's shoulder. Ashwin glanced its way (*it knew what Li agreed to, if anyone would listen to it*) but kept most of his attention on Tián Quán's resident. Once seated, Ashwin crossed his legs, folded his hands, and waited for Li to speak. The room felt colder than usual.

"What happened today?"

The disaffector prevented a nervous swallow before Ashwin started his prepared answer. "Clearly, a deranged government employee, acting on his own initiative, built a handgun from legally-fabbed—"

"I understand that's the cover story." Li's tone was too mild to read. "It's unfortunate your agent missed, but why did your back-up plan of arresting Park for some crime fail?"

Ashwin frowned and leaned back. Did Li not know what had happened? His AI had to have been involved in the breach of containment—traffic control had blockaded the skies over Desmond's temple. He rehearsed his words before speaking. "The ranking PlaPo officer on the scene noticed a journalist's vehicle nearby and decided to avoid publicity."

Li's expression hardened. "Didn't your traffic control shut down the area?"

Li truly didn't know? Ashwin glanced at the AI's avatar, then quickly away. It didn't see through those blank eyes, he knew, but it would hear everything. How would it react when it realized Ashwin knew it had violated its instructions from Li? And how to tell Li? He cleared his throat and glanced at the AI's avatar. "It did. I don't know what allowed a journalist to get through."

For several seconds, Li's only motion came from his eyes. They widened and quickly narrowed. He glanced as far toward the AI's avatar as he could while keeping his head straight. "Come up with another plan, then. We have time."

Ashwin's torso relaxed. "The government of New California appreciates your support."

Li leaned forward with a businesslike demeanor in his saggy jowls. "I assure you, whatever fate shall befall Park, whether it's imprisonment, rehabilitation at Los Robles, or some unfortunate accident, Tián Quán recognizes you as the proper governor. I speak for the company and all its agents, from Shanghai—" He raised his eyebrow to indicate the AI's avatar. "—to this room."

After the governor left, Li dismissed Shuǐ Zhū's avatar. He kept his demeanor blunt and professional, but as soon as it vanished, Li shivered. Goddam machine decided—probably with help from Zhang—Li didn't represent Tián Quán's interests.

He had to walk a tightrope. Tell the home office Shuǐ Zhū had violated its orders from him, without telling them it had followed theirs....

Theirs? Who had Tián Quán's interests at heart more than him? The desk jockeys in Shanghai might not realize it, but Tián Quán would make a huge mistake if it rolled over to Foreign Affairs' encroachment on its business. If Zhang could interfere here, then Foreign Affairs could nose into all the company's efforts—not only overseeing its protectorates, but flying its ships, managing data flows in the home office, and most important, building strangelet and antimatter weapons at the high energy factories orbiting Zeta Puppis.

Li had to galvanize the home office into action. Tián Quán was not just a team. It was his team. Li returned to his office and cut off all the cameras and microphones in the room from input to blind and deafen the AI to his next actions.

He ran social network analysis routines to determine who best to send his messages to. Old Man Hu belonged on the list, though whether his assistant would actually relay it to him was unpredictable. Beyond that, he picked informal leaders, regardless of their positions in the org chart, and carefully weighed egos to determine whom else to include.

Once he decided on the recipients, he composed two messages.

To Tián Quán headquarters, he laid out Zhang's interference, embellishing as needed and speculating just within the bounds of believability. Zhang wanted to go beyond protecting Park's cult, and instead replace George with Park in political office.

He wrote his second message to Guān Diàn Nǎo. He had prepared scores of bug reports, but this one demanded extreme attention. *Shuǐ Zhū violated the chain of command, under the influence of a person not its master or its master's employer. The risk if this bug is not patched galaxy-wide appears incalculably high.* He shivered again.

Once satisfied, Li encrypted the messages and uploaded them to the outgoing message queue. Normally he trusted Shuǐ Zhū with these tasks, but until the AI was patched and earned back his trust, he would not give it any chance to read them. K-nought hung just above Fremont Mesa by the time he finished.

Fremont Mesa cast a long shadow across the lowlands as K-Nought dropped toward the Western Sea late that afternoon. Desmond had returned to his house for the last time, to pack a few clothes and his toiletry kit before returning to headquarters on a permanent basis. Ashwin had made clear Desmond couldn't live safely alone. Clothes and toiletries gathered, he went through the house, looking for other items he needed. Two pygmy centaurs followed with his luggage.

From room to room, he saw furniture, hobby implements, and collectibles, all underused for years but kept pristine by janitorial robots. Yesterday, he would have felt only joy at being free of the pull of his belongings, but after Selene's death, he shook his head in sadness. His collection of leatherbound popular science books published in the early '20s and imported from Earth at great cost had impressed a UNewCal professor, a dinner party guest, with his status. He twanged a few dissonant notes from the neck of an acoustic guitar in the music room and remembered a sculptress with gracile fingers. He needed none of these possessions.

So he thought, until he glanced over the books and his gaze landed on a title and author: *The Selfish Gene*, by Richard Dawkins. Its historical significance lay in being the first popularization of what had been conventional wisdom for most of Desmond's life; hard to believe evolutionary psychology had ever been controversial. He slid it off the shelf and riffled the pages. Chapter 12, *Nice Guys Finish First*. Not in the struggle with Ashwin. He hesitated, then tossed the book to a robot. It stuffed it into a backpack. He could take one memento.

—Airmobile coming,— said Xavier, who'd accompanied him for added security. —Registered to TruSelf.—

Desmond opened a connection to Ellen just in time to hear her ask, —Mind if I drop in?—

She didn't want to just drop in. —The landing pad's clear,— Desmond replied. —A security guard will bring you into the house.—

—You're too busy to meet me?—

—I'm cautious. If Ashwin can fab pistols, he can fab a rifle, and assign a sniper to watch my front door.—

She took in a breath. Did she think him paranoid or wisely cautious? She said nothing as she landed.

A few minutes later, one blackstripe, a stout man with a fleshy face, led her to the sunken sitting area in the great room. In the fireplace, blue-white gas flames jumped behind the translucent ceramic. Their glow flickered over Ellen's face as she stood, waiting. Desmond approached, Xavier and another blackstripe, long-faced and sporting a van dyke beard, falling in behind him. He air-kissed Ellen and offered her a drink as they sat.

"My condolences on your loss," she said, and then the polite visage fell away into surprise and grief. "I can't believe he tried to kill you."

"We didn't expect it either."

"He's playing for keeps. The freeze on your followers' citizen stipend accounts was one thing, but this...." She trailed off as a robot brought their drinks, neat rum hand-aged by a craftsman down the coast.

Desmond sipped. The rum tingled his lips and flowed warmly down his chest. "You thought Tián Quán sided with me, but now you're not sure?"

She gave him a look half-hurt and half-angry. "You think I'm here to back out of our understanding?"

"You're not the kind of person to drop in unannounced."

Ellen's look softened. "You're grieving. I would too. He did the unthinkable. Murder. He'll try it again."

"I know."

"There's a way to avoid violence, yet still continue your work. I came to offer it." She set down her rum on the coffee table. "Merge the TranscenDNA Society with TruSelf."

He stared at his drink. The firelight writhed in the rum like a soul seeking a route to an afterlife. "I'm listening."

"Your work would continue, just rebranded. People would still be able to eliminate certain urges built into them by the selfish gene."

"Ashwin would let that happen?"

"TruSelf has a power he can't touch. By rebranding what you do, he can save face and say you're broken when you're just doing business under a different name."

Desmond raised an eyebrow. "Would he be able to save face if I had a corner office at TruSelf headquarters a floor above Shib Mathew?"

She shrugged. "You're right, you'd have to keep a low profile. We'll set up a consulting contract and give you a sizable monthly retainer. You could lead retreats, be available for questions—"

"Keep my ass off-site."

She sipped rum. "Ashwin will cool off when he realizes your unchaining process won't upset the apple cart. You already said you have no designs on the governorship?"

"I still don't." Now he had designs on Ashwin's head. Ashwin could keep his job until the axe fell.

Ellen went on, ignorant of his thoughts. "You have good people—" She gestured at Xavier. "—and they'll keep doing good work—"

"The ones still alive."

She raised a palm. "I've already started lobbying for justice. Behind the scenes, of course, even if I had all the evidence in the world I couldn't publicly accuse Ashwin of murder. I'll hold his feet to the fire until he throws the guys with dirty hands into it."

Desmond scowled. "But you'll let Ashwin off the hook."

"He's secure, for now. You don't like it, I know. I don't like it either, but there's no way to change it. He's the governor. Wouldn't Lao Tzu and Prince Matchabelli counsel you to accept the world as it is?"

Sun Tzu. Machiavelli, though Desmond soon realized through his mindlink that Matchabelli had made much of his life in exile after the Soviet takeover of his homeland. Ellen was right: Ashwin had killed Selene with impunity. Right too he needed to see that plain truth. Her offer made sense, and would give him and his people some opportunity to do their work.

Yet at what price?

"What's in it for you, Ellen?"

"The TranscenDNA Society is on to a powerful way to help people find their truselves. That's clear from your conversion and retention rates and the fervor you've generated in your followers. I want to keep it going."

"Under your control."

"Notionally, sure. It has to be under someone's control and we need to keep your name from Ashwin's sight."

He took a deep swallow of rum. "Flush my name down the memory hole, you mean? Available for questions, but you'd order your people to never call. You would postpone those retreats for months, NC-years. You'd transfer your loyalists into Society operations to seize the reins from my people."

"That's not my purpose," she said, nodding. "You know I always play fairly with you."

Xavier said to Desmond, —She nodded *yes* when she said *no.*—

—I noticed. The gesture tells the truth when the words lie.— Desmond's expression hardened. "How long until you force my people out? How long until your old hands smother Society operations with bureaucracy, time-serving, and arrogance? How long until the TranscenDNA Society is just another withered branch on the dying TruSelf vine?"

She took a moment to reply. "You left out the prime real estate near the University," she said coldly, "plus that illicit fab everyone knows you have hidden at Las Morrenas." She drained the rum in one swallow and slammed the empty glass on the table. "I've given you the best offer you're going to get."

"We decline."

She stood. Fist at her hip, she peered down at him. "I'm leaving. When my airmobile lifts, my offer's off the table."

"Remember that old saying about doors and asses?"

Ellen ignored him, and instead glanced at Xavier and the black-stripes. "Enjoy the ride when he drives you off the cliff." She stalked to the foyer. The front door slammed a few seconds later, and soon her airmobile's roaring engines rose from the landing pad.

Desmond finished his drink and rested his glass next to hers. The rum's warm glow compounded a certainty he'd done the right thing. "Let's get back to headquarters."

Xavier raised his eyebrow. "Seer, do you need more time?"

Desmond waved his hand at the household robots dragging his luggage and shook his head. "I have what I need."

"Seer," said the bearded blackstripe, "something's going on." In Desmond's mind's eye, a long line of police sedans, interspersed with black mariahs, flew from PlaPo headquarters on Government Mesa toward the Society.

Desmond led the others to his back lawn to take a flesh-and-blood look. A breeze rustled the blue-tinged foliage of the coast oaks along the side walls and the city hummed in the background. Above the manzanita shrubs at the end of the lawn, through the one-way smart-glass wall at the mesa's edge, ten thousand lamps glowed along the lowland neighborhoods' pedestrian avenues. Yesterday, Desmond might have deemed the lined police vehicles inconsequential in comparison. Not today.

"Ellen coordinated her offer to us with the governor," Xavier said. Desmond inwardly forgave him for stating the obvious—they all reeled from this day. "But why are the police going to headquarters?"

"Make sure Castor and the others at headquarters—know," Desmond said, his thoughts interrupted by an incoming message from a surprising source. Shuǐ Zhū wanted to manifest an avatar, privately, to him alone.

A constricted feeling crossed Desmond's chest as he assented. A private virtual descended like a transparent layer over his back lawn. "What now?" he asked in Mandarin, dimly aware an expert system managed his real-world interactions with Xavier and the blackstripes. "More observation? Will someone else die while you watch?"

Shuǐ Zhū manifested its youthful ancient bureaucrat. Its mandarin square bore the same peacock image. He'd learned this meant Shuǐ Zhū had the third highest rank of Tián Quán's AIs, and wielded authority over all Tián Quán's other machines in the entire K-Nought system, as well as Tián Quán's ships after they dropped out of Hu drive. The evening breeze rustled its robe.

"People will die only if you ignore me," it said.

Desmond's eyebrows flashed. "What's PlaPo up to?"

"They intend to serve an arrest warrant."

"On whom? For what?"

"On you, Castor Shaffer, Xavier Cabrera, and fourteen others for destruction of government property, conspiracy, kidnapping, possession of a man-lethal firearm, and murder."

The last charge made Desmond frown for a moment, but he soon smiled. He'd made Ashwin desperate. "For murder, they would need a dead body."

"They have one. That of Ms. Alvarez."

Desmond blinked, stunned by Ashwin's audacity. But it was excessive audacity, too readily controverted by dozens of eyewitnesses. "Every elect on the rooftop this morning knows the truth. So do Ms. Kolmogorova and the murderer."

"PlaPo and the state's rehabilitation facilitator lied to Judge Hayes on the warrant application. They claim you or a follower brandished a firearm at the inspectors in an effort to intimidate them, and discharged it, striking Ms. Alvarez."

"I see Ashwin controls the judges, too."

Shuǐ Zhū lowered its head a moment. "In fact, the judge questioned PlaPo and the state's facilitator as to whether the inspectors present on the roof could corroborate their story. They told her the event had been so traumatizing Jacoby was receiving trauma counseling."

"And Kolmogorova is the alleged kidnapping victim." She'd come back four hours earlier to enter the freedom couch.

Shuǐ Zhū's avatar bowed its head in assent.

Desmond peered at the vehicles approaching headquarters. "If they're trying to arrest me, why there? Traffic control knows my airmobile has come here and they can find my location through my network access."

"Officially, they take the view the airmobile could have traveled without you in it, and your location could be spoofed. However, in reality, they do know, and they hope you will travel to headquarters in response to this crisis."

Desmond scowled. Xavier asked something that Desmond's expert system answered, his body's voice sounding indistinct while his conscious mind focused on Shuǐ Zhū. "Why?" he asked the AI.

"Eight hundred yards to the northeast, in a backyard between Founders Avenue and Arrayan Creek, three members of the San Tomás Malayali Cultural Society wait for your return flight with a surface-to-air missile assembled from a variety of legally fabricated pieces."

Desmond shifted his attention back to his body. "Grab a camera feed," he told Xavier and the guards. "Look for three people in a backyard in Creekside. Our enemies mean to kill me."

Returning to his private conversation with Shuǐ Zhū, Desmond asked, "Why have you told me this?"

"Tián Quán's orders require it," Shuǐ Zhū said.

A breeze rustled the coast oaks' foliage and chilled Desmond's arms. "There's more?"

"There is. I will only speak directly to you, never with another present. Please keep our arrangement to yourself."

"You don't trust my people to keep secrets from Li?"

"Not enough."

"Yet you trust me."

The avatar's head angled. "Tián Quán's orders benefit you directly. I perceive you are intelligent enough to, what's the idiom in English? *Not bite the hand that feeds you?*"

The AI reverted to Mandarin. "Is the situation you face tonight clear?"

The file of police vehicles ringed headquarters at a hundred yard radius. "It is."

Shuǐ Zhū's avatar vanished and Desmond's senses shifted as his perception returned to his backyard.

"We found your three men," Xavier said. He looked apologetic. "We don't see a threat. They're sitting around a patio table sharing a whiskey bottle."

"What about a missile? Look around them for a missile launcher."

Xavier hesitated. "It's a typical backyard; some Oregon myrtles and a big barrel grill. Friends having a cookout."

"Keep an eye on them," Desmond said. "And look for others."

Through his mindlink, Desmond felt Castor seeking his attention. The signal was choppy, slowly transmitted by ad hoc networks outside the high-bandwidth server backbone maintained by the colony's internet utility. He opened a channel to the younger man and allowed Xavier and the guards to access it too.

Castor's avatar appeared in front of Desmond, where Shuǐ Zhū's had stood. Castor was in headquarters' operations room with junior elect milling behind him. "Seer, should we use Max's gifts?"

The tangle wire and the muscle paralyzing agents. "First, stall the police as long as you can. Tell them I'll be on my way, I want a peaceful resolution, whatever it takes. Find volunteers to use the gifts if the police try to storm the building. But our main task tonight is to evacuate as many people as you can to Las Morrenas."

"Don't you want us to stay in the city, Seer?"

"I did, but you know what Ashwin intends by this raid. He wants the Society's leaders to languish in custody, without bail, until we can be tried in a kangaroo court and sentenced to personality reconstruction at Los Robles; he expects our followers to drift away as a result. We cannot allow that. For Selene's memory. Get as many people as you can into airmobiles free of traffic control overrides and scramble them all in one burst. PlaPo won't expect it and you'll have some time to get to Las Morrenas."

Castor breathed raggedly and blinked his eyes. "We don't have airmobiles for everyone."

Desmond's mindlink put numbers on his intuition. A hundred members in the building, plus hundreds more residing in their own homes, would have to be left. "Leaders have to make tough decisions, you said once. This is one of them. Make sure people with needed skills evacuate. Kolmogorova, the trauma technician.... Then, ask for volunteers to remain behind, but if you don't get enough, drop aspirants, then loyals, then elect. We need a cadre of elect to rebuild."

"And elect will better resist Max's rebelliousness."

"That too. Soften the blow; tell the ones you leave behind, individually if you can, I have chosen them to stay because I'm confident their commitment can triumph over Ashwin's persecution. Get the people you leave to echo those words."

"When will you get here, Seer?" Castor asked. The people behind him paused and looked up, waiting for Desmond's response.

"I'm not. We'll make it to Las Morrenas another way." His speedboat was docked half a mile away as the crow flew, across Fremont Mesa and a quarter-mile of riverfront neighborhood. Once they reached the dock, the rivers were navigable three hundred miles past Schwarzenegger City.

"We'll get him to safety," Xavier added.

"Bring as many brothers and sisters as you can," Desmond said, "and tell the rest to slip away. Destroy all our records. I rely on you."

Responsibility's call expelled anxiety from Castor's demeanor. "Yes, Seer." He nodded curtly and demanifested.

Xavier broke the ensuing silence. "When should we leave?"

"Soon." Desmond glanced at his black monkstrap shoes. "House, bring us hiking boots." To Xavier and the guards he said, "We'll need them to go over the fence and downslope."

"We're not flying?" the bearded guard asked.

"Are you deaf? You heard me say there's a missile, ma?"

The urge to protest appeared in the blackstripe's face. "Seer…"

He would not mention Shuǐ Zhū, but the AI's comments gave him an idea. If Ashwin had a spy among his people, he would spread disinformation. "I have a contact among the San Tomásinos who values human freedom more than ethnic ties."

"How do we get to Las Morrenas?" asked the stout blackstripe.

"I know a way. Follow me."

Robots trotted out to the yard with shoes and his luggage. Almost nothing worth carrying, but he remembered the backpack with the copy of The Selfish Gene and lifted it to his shoulders. "Let me show you the missile you doubt exists."

Desmond told the house to open the garage doors and the big utility to boot into flight mode. It took a few seconds for traffic control to recognize the airmobile readied for flight. When enough time had passed, he asked, "What are the three men in Creekside doing?"

The bearded guard squinted into space, then shook his head. "They stood up. One's going to the grill to check the food."

"The grill?"

"He's lifting the lid right now. Seer."

An intuition stippled Desmond's jawline, but he smiled despite the gooseflesh. "Is the grill lit?"

The guard's eyes widened and his jaw dropped. "Seer, no—"

"He's pulling out a cylinder about five feet long," the round-faced guard said.

Xavier added, "His two companions set up a tripod. They're aiming a missile our way."

"Wodema," the bearded guard said.

"Gentlemen, we're agreed? We're not flying from here. I'll send my airmobile unmanned toward headquarters and we'll make our way from here on foot." He pointed at a waiting robot. Its maniples held a pair of hiking boots and three pairs of sneakers. "I hope these will fit."

"Why not take a second airmobile?" asked the round-faced guard.

Desmond slipped off his dress shoes and stepped into hiking boots. "You assume our enemies crafted only one missile?" The boots cinched their straps over Desmond's ankles. "Ready?"

All three nodded.

"Drop your network feeds. Now!"

Desmond waited until all three had dropped theirs, then dropped his. "Send the utility directly to headquarters," he said aloud to the house. He led the others to the smartglass fence. He pulled himself up, then dropped to a narrow ledge sparsely covered with yellow-green bent grass outside the fence. Below his feet, an eight foot drop ended at the top of a slope of scree and layered basalt tufted by engineered manzanitas and coast oaks. He sat on the ledge, then pushed himself over the side.

He stuck the landing, but his footing slipped out from under him on the loose scree and he slid downslope. A corner of the packed book jabbed his back.

Halfway to a sturdy coast oak, a humming sound tracked overhead: his utility, running lights blinking. It banked for the northeast, for a moment occluding the constellation Ilsa as she told Sam to play it, and Desmond wondered if he took the long way for no reason—

A streak of spent propellant crossed the sky, like smoke streaming from Rick's cigarette; before Desmond could think what it meant, the missile struck his airmobile. The explosion dazzled his eyes, then boomed in his ears. Birds squawked within the trees at the foot of the mesa, and dogs barked above them and in Creekside.

Desmond bent his knees and slid into the coast oak's low limbs. He scrambled out of the way of his following men. Branches lashed his arms and face as an echo of the explosion returned from Alarcón Mesa.

No time to think about his airmobile, no time to worry about his scratches or the dust on his rump; time only to find the best way down. A near-vertical face five feet tall fell away to a slope firm enough to walk down. He twisted a quarter-turn as he dropped, then walked sideways on the descent. Soon, Xavier and the blackstripes followed, rattling the coast oak's foliage and landing over the next drop with grunts.

The slope grew shallower and the coast oaks and Oregon myrtles more dense as they descended to the plain. At the bottom, Desmond waited for Xavier and the guards under a particularly tall myrtle. Despite his exercise regimen, myostatin inhibitors and kettlebell swings, he breathed hard and enjoyed the chance to catch his breath. His breath and the others' footsteps might be overheard…. *Relax.* PlaPo and ambulance sirens cawed over the utility's wreckage. Thousands watched the sky from backyards, balconies, or rooftops. No one would see or hear him and his three followers.

"Where to now, Seer?" Xavier asked.

"We have a mile on foot around Fremont Mesa to my boat at the marina. We should be able to get there before they find the utility was unoccupied. Let's move."

Surrounded by a broad avenue, a park ringed the mesa. Though the shortest route would be around the mesa's northern and eastern side, it would take them by the park's lighted playing fields and picnic grounds, exposed to the boutiques and bistros across the avenue in the tonier part of Creekside. Thick woods covered the park's western side and the residential area across the avenue was generally quiet. He expected to encounter no one else after dark.

They started into the woods. The trees' thick canopies gave rare, dappled glimpses of near-full Los Angeles and the mansions on the edge of Fremont Mesa.

A minute later, Xavier tapped on Desmond's back. "Hear that?" he whispered.

Ahead, two quiet voices spoke too softly to be understood. Desmond crouched and shuffled forward, glancing down in the dim light in hopes of seeing twigs before his feet snapped them. He held up his right hand to quiet the others.

Still hidden from view by undergrowth, the voices resolved into a man's and a woman's. "How can this be?" she asked, in a starchild's clear, naïve voice. "Sapna Singh says it was a malfunction, but I know I heard a missile. It's illegal to fab weapons, ma?"

"We'll find out," the man replied. "The perps will get their personalities rebuilt and NCMF will close the loophole that let them fab a missile." Annoyance tinged his tone. Desmond knew his voice: a neighbor from atop the mesa, with a live-in girlfriend and an eight E-year-old child.

Desmond peered through the gloom and glimpsed nude limbs, pallid in the moonlight. She sat crosslegged, hunched forward and hugging herself, and his neighbor stretched out, propped up on one elbow. Desmond smiled and shook his head, then turned and padded back to the others.

"Those poor people in the airmobile," the woman said. "What if rejuve can't help them?"

"Sugar, it's sad, but life goes on for the rest of us. Now where were we?"

Her voice revealed exasperation. "How can you think of sex right now?"

Desmond soon reached Xavier and the guards. He shook his head, made a dismissive gesture.

"Who was it?" Xavier said.

"Two puppets of Rex Mundi. Let's move on."

Silence held sway around them as they continued. Fremont's bulk soon occluded the other mesas, but Desmond still felt exposed. Between the park and the marina stood a quarter-mile of a pricey riverfront neighborhood, mixed French Quarter and California craftsman houses on either side of a well-lit avenue of boutiques and wine bars leading to the marina.

They paused in a thick clump of coast oaks near Fremont Avenue, deep in shadow. A lone jogger passed and receded. Though they were hidden from the naked eye, a night vision camera would pick them up. The river's vast, choppy sweep and the lights of NCMF ops on the far bank seemed a thousand miles from them.

"Seer," Xavier said, looking up. Desmond followed his gaze as a labored thrumming sound grew closer.

A large utility airmobile hovered over Fremont Avenue, creeping along at a few miles per hour. Desmond crouched lower in the undergrowth and took another look. Running lights doused, its registration beacon illegally silent, painted in a single gray shade without logos or other customization—terror gripped Desmond's throat. Ashwin had seen through the diversion of Desmond's utility and sent a black mariah to disappear him.

The airmobile stopped creeping. The passenger door opened and someone stuck a parabolic shape half the size of a football out the doorway. "Anyone need a lift to Las Morrenas?" Castor whispered, his voice carried to them by the parabolic reflector.

The airmobile landed. Doors to the cabin and the cargo bay opened. Castor jumped out, crouched, and trotted toward them.

"I told you not to wait for us," Desmond said.

"I couldn't chance it." In the moonlight, his expression seemed even more gaunt than usual. "I—we—need you at Las Morrenas. A lot of good people were left behind. Leaving you as well would moot their sacrifice. It will be a tight fit, but there's room for you in the cabin and everyone else in the cargo bay. But we need to hurry. PlaPo's channels are squawking about our overrides and the airmobiles we scrambled."

Desmond and the others hurried to the airmobile. The doors slammed down and the jets whined. The airmobile lifted and headed to the southeast. It climbed slowly and the engines sounded labored. With six people in the cabin and a dozen more crammed in the cargo bay, the vehicle neared its weight limit. Young elect around him cast fearful glances toward the motors. The airmobile dipped a bit and Liliana, the trauma technician, clutched his forearm.

"Airmobiles are engineered beyond their specs," Desmond said to the cabin. He spoke with more confidence than he felt. *Come on, ranfla,* he thought at the vehicle but didn't send.

As if bolstered by his sentiments, the airmobile's motors surged, pressing them into their seats as it climbed more forcefully. Over the river, it turned due east, starting a wide loop to put it on course for Las Morrenas. Ahead, the dark ribbon of the San Lazaro glittered with reflected city lights in the foreground before vanishing in the sparse darkness deeper inland. To the left, glimpsed between Fremont Mesa and NCMF's office tower, police vehicles swarmed over Creekside and his utility's wreckage.

More fear washed over Desmond. There might be another missile team, somewhere in the city, looking for him....

He sagged in his seat and let out a breath. Ashwin probably assumed him to be dead, and even if PlaPo knew the wrecked utility had lacked passengers and deduced he was on board this airmobile from its detour to Fremont Mesa, it flew without running lights on a course unknowable to traffic control. The next missile team would have a harder time shooting this vehicle down.

With each passing second he felt safer. East of Drake Mesa, near sparse suburban neighborhoods, the airmobile banked to the northeast. The engines revved louder and the airmobile coaxed more speed and altitude from them.

He glanced around the dimly-lit cabin. The other elect looked rung out, eyes bleary, limbs jittery. Castor slumped in his seat, arm through his rucksack's straps.

"We made it through this day," Desmond said to bolster morale. "For Selene's sake, we'll make it through tomorrow."

Through the left-side windows, a bright light glowed just past the limb of Government Mesa. Desmond zoomed in with one of the airmobile's cameras, but hesitated when he realized what glowed. He shut his eyes, took a breath, and forced himself to the maximum magnification.

On the front façade of the Society's headquarters, the backlights still shone through the mosaic. The nude male and female looked be-atifically upward from the tangle of nucleic acids collapsing from their lower bodies as an opaque yellow sheet, PlaPo's crime scene marker, unfurled itself over them.

The next hours passed with few words. People drowsed in the warm, crowded cabin. Los Angeles cast the rippled, jumbled terrain in gray relief. Eventually, though, the landscape softened. Scattered trees, planted by Ashwin's predecessor at EnvE, thickened into a deep forest dotted with till-dammed lakes. Primordial glaciers had plowed the original basalt regolith and left a terrain of drumlins, es-kers, kames, and the moraines that gave Las Morrenas its name.

The Society's settlement was the only human habitation for a hundred miles in any direction. Only a tiny part showed above the ground's surface, atop a low ridge spurred off a taller, steeper hill. Max had expanded the lodge originally built by Cam's son and added a few mycocrete bunkhouses and outbuildings. Four hundred square meters of low-density photovoltaic cells webbed the southern faces of birches, boldos, and tamarack larches. Gardens, twelve acres in total, had been cleared from patches at the bottom of the slope. Night vi-sion showed only the forest's cool glow, with tiny hotspots from the buildings.

The real settlement, including the fab and a polywell reactor, had tunneled into the tall, steep hill, named Colina Santa. The settlement fed its thermal waste into a heat pipe drilled three-eighths of a mile into the bedrock.

The airmobile descended. Desmond's mindlink overlaid a yellow circle on Colina Santa's steep southern slope. The airmobile slowed but flew directly toward the shadow of a giant boulder twice the air-mobile's size. As they came closer, a hole opened like a curtain being pulled back. The airmobile entered and Desmond glimpsed motors and radar reflectors hidden in a carved notch to his right.

A tunnel's narrow walls amplified the roar of the airmobile's en-gines before its wheels touched down. The utility taxied deeper into a winding cavern, spiraling a full turn as it descended ninety feet into the hill.

The airmobile rolled to a stop in front of a pair of nanotube-vanadium alloy blast doors twenty feet high and thirty wide. Dim red lights glowed along the bases of the doors and the cavern walls, and seemed even dimmer compared to a lozenge of light, colored like Earth sunlight, coming through a pedestrian-sized door in the panel of the right-hand blast door, near the hinge.

Backlit by the glow, Max stood with Metherealle. To their left, a cluster of loyals, junior elect, and dwarf centaur robots showed sympathetic expressions. When the utility lifted its cargo hatch, the cluster flowed to greet the refugees in the cargo hold. Max, meanwhile, led Metherealle to the door of the passenger cabin.

The people inside the cabin blinked and stretched their limbs. Metherealle extended her hands to the refugees to help them climb out. "We almost have rooms for everyone coming tonight," she said, "but some of you will have to triple up in the short term. The kitchen has generated hot meals for everyone arriving. We'll guide you to the dining hall, or you can find the way through your mindlink."

As Metherealle led the last refugees from the cabin through the pedestrian door, Desmond climbed down to the concrete deck. Castor followed and the empty airmobile taxied deeper into the cavern. Except for a few cargo robots, only Max, Desmond, and Castor remained outside the blast doors.

"Seer, welcome," Max said. His voice echoed off the rock walls.

"How do you have room for everyone?" Desmond asked. "Three hundred people are coming tonight."

"I knew this day would come, Seer. I've been adding rooms as we could work it into our schedule." His face seemed more mature, more confident, than it had during his last night at headquarters. "Double rooms seemed most appropriate—they subject our people to the eyes of a roommate, which puts a brake on antisocial thoughts. It worked well for Mormons sending their young men on missions."

"You've found time to study history," Desmond said, an inquisitive edge in his voice.

"Seer, of course, you and Castor have private rooms. You are both incapable of anti-social thoughts."

Castor's eyes narrowed. Desmond shared the sentiment. *If we're incapable of them, why mention it?*

"Seer," Max said, and Desmond noticed how offhandedly he uttered the title, "the robots will take your luggage. I'll have them deliver dinner to your quarters."

"No. I'm going directly to the dining hall."

"I didn't realize you were so hungry—"

"I'm not. The dining hall is big enough to fit everyone." They would have to crowd, but that was part of his plan. He extended his next words into Las Morrenas' public channel. "I will speak to you all in the dining hall in fifteen minutes."

Max's eyebrows crinkled. "What will you tell them?"

"You'll find out." Desmond stalked across the deck. The pedestrian door swung open.

On the far side, a concourse, as tall and wide as the blast doors, ran a hundred-fifty feet into the hill. LED sheets plastered on the ceiling lit the space with yellow-white light. People milled and voices chattered, ringing off the stone walls. The group following Metherealle was halfway down the concourse's length, close to the left-hand wall. On each side of the concourse, a half-dozen openings gave access to narrow corridors Desmond knew through mindlink held residential quarters and storerooms. Metherealle led the refugees to a wider opening, which according to the map led to a ramp spiraling upward to a level containing the kitchen and the dining hall, and downward to the freedom couches.

Desmond strode to Metherealle and the new arrivals, Castor loping next to him and Max hurrying after. The refugees glanced at him and their eyes showed more wakefulness, their steps, more spring. He passed them and started up the spiral ramp.

A four-wheeled electric cart descended the curve. It braked, tires churring. "Seer, your pardon," said the rider, a tall, lanky male and an early morrenero, settler of Las Morrenas. A moment later, he bowed his head slightly. Basil, his name, came to Desmond through mindlink.

"I have no need to pardon you," Desmond said, "if your business is important."

"It's a weekly maintenance check on the polywell reactor."

Metherealle and the new arrivals backed up behind Desmond. "It can wait an hour," he said.

Basil opened his mouth, unease on his face; he looked from Desmond to Max. "I'd rather not wait, Seer."

"Will the reactor fail if you wait an hour?"

Basil glanced again at Max. The latter spoke. "Of course not, Seer. We run a tight ship."

Desmond kept his attention on Basil. "Give me a ride to the dining hall."

The dining hall stood up the ramp, off another concourse. Rows of tables, their wood tops resting on skinny carbon nanotube legs, filled the hall. Some earlier arrivals from the city huddled over their trays from the kitchen, but perked up when Desmond walked in. A few morreneros turned cautious gazes to him, then glanced at Max.

Desmond halted just inside the dining hall, in a corner between the main entrance and a passageway to the kitchen. From the kitchen, the clank of dishes died down. The new arrivals from his utility came in, followed by earlier peers, fed but eyes drooping in exhaustion, and more morreneros. Desmond greeted them all. Some old hands started guiltily and tama, he should've kept a closer rein over Max and the settlement here.

After a few minutes, the last airmobiles arrived from the city. People sat elbow-to-elbow at the tables and standers crowded the back and side walls. Max stood with Castor, Xavier, and Metherealle in the corner behind Desmond. New arrivals from the city outnumbered morreneros four to one.

Desmond looked over the expectant faces, weakened by hunger and emotional turmoil. Not only had Max established Las Morrenas as his fiefdom. If not counteracted, his influence would seep into the new arrivals. But if Desmond struck quickly, he would reassert his authority over all of them, new arrivals or old hands.

"I have much to tell you, whether Las Morrenas has been your home for months or if you arrived with me tonight from the city. Yet before I discuss our future, we must remember our past. You know one of our sisters died today." He pierced his gaze into an old hand who'd given him an insolent look. "Yes, I mean, *die*: Rex Mundi cut her off from the trauma care we consider our right." The targeted morrenero looked down.

"In the flesh," Desmond went on, "she has left us; but in spirit, she remains with us for as long as we are united in our commitment to unchain ourselves and the entire human universe. You see, she sacrificed herself for the Society. She could have saved herself by bending her knee to Rex Mundi, and letting him recollar her in exchange for her life. But her dedication, not only to her own unchaining, but also to the unchaining of everyone, overcame the last bond the selfish gene held on her. It overcame the urge for self-preservation."

After a moment, he said, "Let us remember her."

Desmond bowed his head. Through his mindlink he saw everyone else do the same. He held the silence long enough for a few people in the room to cast sidelong, questioning looks, but those people were too few and too scattered to connect with each other. Desmond held the silence longer, until the questioners yielded themselves to the collective dedication to his words. People rocked forward in their seats and some standers swayed, eyes closed.

"She laid down her life for ours, without expecting any reward. But we will reward her. Her sacrifice will bear glorious fruit... but only if we act with one purpose. We must do whatever it takes to preserve the Society and continue its mission to unchain every human being. Rex Mundi will do anything to destroy us and foil our mission. You must not be one of those certain people among us who fail to grasp the magnitude of his threat." Vague and ominous; the perfect combination to inspire his followers to police their own and their comrades' thoughts.

As Desmond expected, Max had cached tangle wire and crowd control gases deep in the hill. Fortunately, he hadn't fabbed any man-lethal firearms. Just the opening Desmond needed.

"First, we must secure our settlement. Although we're hidden and can vault ourselves in, we're not secure enough; Rex Mundi could find this hill and dig through its sides if we let him get close enough. We will not let him. However, the weapons we have now are toys. They will not stop Rex Mundi. Only a fool would brandish them." Behind Desmond, Max shuffled his feet, and a few morreneros cast reappraising looks at him. "We will fab missiles that can shoot down airmobiles, and armed robots capable of destroying invaders, and more fabs to produce our weapons even more quickly." Those armaments would do nothing against the Chinese, but wielding them would keep Ashwin at bay.

At the far end of a nearby table, Kolmogorova pouted and ducked her head. A few others murmured or showed alarm on their faces.

Desmond mollified them. "We prefer to leave these lethal capabilities in their sheaths. Although we must show Rex Mundi we can harm him, by patrolling our weapons and firing across his bow, once we've done so, his underlings will fear us more than him, and they will leave us in peace. We will only try to take their lives in defense of our territory, our settlement, our people, our future." Kolmogorova's objections faded from her face, and to seal her shifted mood, Desmond added, "Selene would have wanted it that way."

Agreement spread through the room. Desmond thought for a moment to the settlement's fab and ordered a first team of robotic missile launchers, plus missiles and tenders for each, and four packs of groundcrawlers. The latter looked like pizza boxes equipped with tank treads, solar panels, and turret-mounted rifles, but he remembered their effectiveness during the Second Civil War and the Chinese occupation.

Request not authorized. Desmond frowned. *Site security officer approval required.* Mindlink confirmed his guess: the site security officer was Maxim Jacoby.

Desmond's mouth hardened. He used an NCMF administrator key to override Max's security lock, then turned his attention back to his followers. Time to ask them for more. "But we will not merely hunker down and keep Rex Mundi at bay. For starters, we will build powerful radios to communicate our message to as much of New California as we can reach. Through me, we will tell our planet the truth to counteract Ashwin George's lies." He would lock down those radios to ensure they sent out a consistent message, each transmission being one he approved. No need to bother his people with those details.

"We will do even more. Our robots will carry tools and weapons beyond our perimeter. They will build nests in the continent's empty spaces and from there raid the facilities and robots of EnvE, PlaPo, and the rest of the planetary government. They will destroy or dismantle buildings and equipment while leaving unharmed our future brothers and sisters."

Most faces were rapt, except for a few who glanced past him with cautious looks. What expression did Max show them now?

"Seer, is that prudent?" he asked.

Desmond peered down his nose at the younger man. "How could it not be?"

"Seer, Castor left peers behind…."

"I don't see a problem."

"If we sabotage Rex Mundi's machines, he will hold our peers hostage."

Desmond pulled in a breath. "Our brothers and sisters are already held hostage. Rex Mundi will send them to Los Robles as soon as he catches them. His forbearance will not release them; he can only be compelled to release them. We will destroy the tools he uses to control New California until he has no choice but to yield."

"But we can't do enough, quickly enough—"

"Yes, Max, tell us about not doing enough." By protesting, the younger man proved his mistakes were not accidents, but misguided choices. "You've dug out spacious sleeping quarters, but have you fabbed defenses for everyone you claimed to expect? PlaPo will be equipped to use man-lethal force. Are we?"

"Seer, you can't be certain Rex Mundi will—"

"I'm positive. Why do you ask?" Misguided choices, or something worse? Desmond peered closer. "Do you have some reason to think he won't?"

"Won't he turn to Tián Quán?"

Nearby, Castor sucked in a breath, and Xavier gritted his teeth. Desmond stood as tall as he could and wished his hiking boots had Cuban heels. He opened his shoulders to the crowd around the tables. Max had a point, but someone would have brought it up. Tián Quán could sweep aside all the missiles and armed robots the Society could fab, and turn Colina Santa into a hundred million tons of molten basalt, if Beijing permitted it.

Making sure Beijing would never allow it was tomorrow's problem.

"The Chinese will not help him. You remember Li and Zhang's visit to headquarters," he said. "If the Chinese wanted Rex Mundi to triumph, all of us would already be broken in Los Robles, or dead." Desmond stared until Max turned his embarrassed face away. For a second more, Desmond held the stare, then changed his expression and turned to the crowd.

"Yet it isn't enough to build machines to strengthen our society. We must rebuild ourselves. We shall be potent and we shall be united. For too long, certain people have held us back from our potential." Behind Desmond, a heavy silence came from Max. "Those same certain people may protest. They may say we're too bold and might frighten the neutral public. We will ignore those certain people. It is proper to adjust our tactics for the wider situation. What might have been excessive in the city is entirely appropriate here. Further, the public is not neutral; by their silence, they consent to Ashwin George's reign. They consent to Selene's death."

Desmond surveyed the sea of tired faces. "Are we united?"

A few nods and yesses came from the crowd.

"If I can't hear you, how can Rex Mundi? Are we united?"

Heads lifted higher. The yesses grew louder.

"We must defend ourselves and break Rex Mundi's tyranny. It will take time and effort, but will we do this—for Selene?"

By ones and twos, a few people rose from their seats or stepped forward from the walls. Their action catalyzed others, and soon peer pressure carried the whole room along. Excited chatter echoed off the walls, and from it emerged words. *Yes…. I'll do it…. for Selene.*

Desmond's closest followers responded too. Sparkling eyes, pumping fists, urgent affirmations. He'd never seen Castor so animated. The proper response from the four most important surviving elect, with one blemish: Max spoke too quietly, his attention withdrawn to some internal concern.

New California Date 94:51
8 September 2094

Exhausted faces lined the main concourse. Though tired, Desmond's people had enough energy to lift their heads when a sound-collage of clacking metal and plastic came from the mouth of the spiral ramp. The people nearest the ramp's exit stood back as the sound grew nearer the main level.

In the thirty hours since the evacuees had arrived, people had seen groundcrawlers and robotic weapons roll from the fab and head straight for the defensive perimeter. The sabotage robots coming up the ramp now were different. A unique mix of robots made up each sa-bot swarm, randomized around a base blueprint, like mutations in a genome. The most common types included arachnons emitting depolymerization venom to erode plastic, formix with nanomandibles to pry apart carbon nanotube bundles, and glass bees to disrupt data transmission down optical cable.

In each swarm, worker bots carried a small fab and solar panels to repair and recharge the team. Some swarms would inflate small airships or assemble robotic aircraft to spread far. Others would travel on foot, or wheel, or tread, like army ants. Two were equipped with submersible rafts and programmed to find streams flowing to tributaries of the San Lazaro.

Desmond stood on a dais just inside the blast doors. His gaze traveled from the sa-bots to the crowd. Its faces drooped from the previous day's emotional turmoil and a long day working in the field. Tomorrow promised at least as much labor. Yet his followers needed to see the parading swarms more than an extra hour of sleep. So far, their work felling trees at the perimeter and setting them as obstacles, and the sight of military robots rolling off the fab, had bolstered the settlement's defenses. But a solely defensive attitude, no matter how necessary, would eventually corrode morale. The swarms showed the Society taking the offensive against Rex Mundi, hastening the day they would topple him.

They needed it. Desmond felt Selene's absence like a pit in the sand of his thoughts, its walls slumping to incompletely fill it, shifting the ground under him. He set aside the thought. He grieved for her, but he would retain his footing regardless what happened around him. He had to. The Society required him to lead.

"Marvelous, aren't they?" he said over the clacking echo. He gestured at the passing sa-bots.

Most around him expressed agreement. "They'll cripple PlaPo for a thousand miles," Xavier said.

Metherealle nodded. "Very wise, Seer."

Castor cleared his throat. "Seer, you know I trust you, but I worry their programming is too vague. No set targets, too many strategies—"

"Strategy is a Darwinian process," Desmond said. "Instead of natural selection, the scythe of conflict weeds out the least fit. Variation between swarms will show us which is most effective, and we'll use that knowledge when reprogramming the existing swarms and fabbing future ones." He arched his eyebrow. "Is there a problem, Castor?"

Castor swallowed. "I want to make sure I understand. You're saying the robots have their own selfish genes, binding them to us."

"They're tools. We built them to serve us."

Max broke in. "Absolutely, Seer. I couldn't agree more." He looked suddenly spirited. "Not to change the subject, but I've been inspired by something you said last night."

More insults of potential allies? More fab orders beyond what he was instructed to do? Not a problem if he heeded *no* this time. "What?"

The last swarm passed through the blast doors. The sa-bots' clack and whir receded up the tunnel to the exit from the hill. Max lowered his voice in the concourse's new quiet. "It came to me when you mentioned Selene overcame Rex Mundi's deepest hook, the urge for self-preservation, in order to save you. What she did by force of will, we can replicate for all. We can unchain people from the self-preservation urge."

The blast doors began swinging shut. So accustomed to Max's obstinacy, Desmond took a moment to grasp his words. Not motivated by rebellion, or zeal flooding out of the banks in which Desmond channeled it, Max proposed something intended for the Society's greater good. "How?"

"We can lower the action potential threshold in the subgenual cortex, and modulate activity in the parietal lobe regions regulating the sense of self."

The crowd in the concourse shuffled to the exits. Desmond lost individual faces in the mass of limbs and heads. "We can't risk people sacrificing themselves for trivial ends. There are too few of us and too much work to do."

"Seer, of course, I'll bear that in mind. I'll gladly do the r&d in addition to my other duties."

Plus, time spent doing research was time Max could not spend building a coalition against him. Desmond rested his hand on the younger man's shoulder. "Investigate further. Let me know the results before you announce anything to anyone."

Eyes bright, Max nodded to Desmond and the others. "Of course, Seer. If you'll excuse me, I want to run more simulations before bedding down for the night."

"Go, Max." Desmond felt relief. Finally, Max wanted to work for the team.

Xavier and Metherealle also took their leave. Only Castor remained, a pensive look on his face. "You still have a problem with the sa-bot strategy?" Desmond asked.

"Seer? No, absolutely not." He switched to a mindlink channel. —

Why did he propose a self-sacrifice intervention?—

—Go on.—

—Last night you rebuked him. When you've done so before, he's sulked for a while and remained obstinate. This time, in less than a day, he speaks to you cheerfully and proposes something selflessly beneficial to all of us. What's changed?—

—He took last night's warnings to heart.—

—I hope you're right, Seer,— Castor said. —You can see deeper into us than I can.—

Desmond peered up the concourse where Max had gone. —You think he's hiding something?—

—He has an agenda. Can we be certain it aligns with the Society's?—

Desmond thought. —All his past errors have come from too much devotion to our cause, not from too little.—

—Very true, Seer. I've only noticed a change in his outward behavior. You can read his most hidden thoughts better than I can. If that's all?—

After a few moments, Desmond replied. —It is. Good night.—

Castor departed. Although Desmond went straight to his apartments, sleep eluded him for an hour, as questions about Max churned behind his closed eyes.

New California Date 94:52
9 September 2094

Ashwin waited on the lawn, rather than in his office, in part to enjoy the late morning sunshine and in part to gloat. The thick yellow crime scene film still clung to the façade of Desmond's temple. The entire city could see it and be reminded of the governor's triumph and Desmond's presumed death.

Despite Desmond's survival and missile shots at the PlaPo airmobiles sent to raid the settlement at Las Morrenas, Ashwin gloated. Maltby would punish the EnvE teams who'd missed Desmond's illicit fab. As far as the public was concerned, Desmond was dead and the remnants of the TranscenDNA Society cowered in the wilderness.

But when the truth Desmond survived the missile attack punched through the party line? No matter. The public would consider him as good as dead, holed up in the wilderness until the king of the world got around to destroying him.

Even Desmond's illicit fab failed to worry Ashwin. Though Beijing might hold Li back from taking the offensive and destroying Las Morrenas, Li would be free to defend the colony against any attack Desmond might launch.

And if Ashwin could take the offensive without Li's help, so much the better. Speaking of which—

His assistant led Justin Bauer onto the lawn. Bauer bro-hugged cautiously, chests not touching. The governor pointed to webbed chairs near an unlit firestand carved from basalt.

"I'm happy to stand," Bauer said.

"You're wondering why I asked you to come, ma?"

Bauer shook his head minimally. "You've shown your power by shooting down Desmond. You're going to ask me for something. Campaign contributions? Giving your cousin's cousin a job at NCMF? Ma?"

He would take those latter things, but in due time. "I had nothing to do with the attack on Desmond's airmobile." Ashwin stared at the bridge of Bauer's nose and kept himself from blinking or raising his hands to his mouth. "When PlaPo finds the perpetrator, he or she will be punished. We're all bound by the law, me no less than anyone."

Bauer's expression grew slightly less guarded. "I heard rumors—"

"A lie can circle the world before the truth puts on its shoes." Ashwin sucked in his cheeks for a moment. "Before I go on, the rest of this conversation is under planetary government security seal."

"I signed NDAs back on Earth. I assent."

Ashwin glanced at TranscenDNA Society headquarters, then watched Bauer's face. "Desmond wasn't in his airmobile."

He expected to see relief, but was there also smug satisfaction? Plainly from his face, Bauer weighed his words before he spoke. "I have to say I'm glad he's alive. I don't dispute he should be punished for any crimes he committed, but we'd all be better off if he were rehabilitated at Los Robles than dead."

"We would," Ashwin said with false sadness, "if we could take him into custody."

"Where is he? His settlement out in the wilderness?"

"Circumstantial evidence points that way."

Bauer frowned. "Where do I come in?"

Ashwin glanced around the lawn, from potted dwarf myrtles to the firestand at his feet. Tián Quán doubtless had listening devices, but they already knew everything he would say. "PlaPo sent a team to arrest Desmond and his associates. Here's what happened on their approach." He waved at the air between them and heard a confirming click in his mind's ear.

Three-d loops, two from the lead airmobile and three from ones back in line. Missile streaks rose from the forest, then the landscape jumped around the background from the airmobiles' evasive maneuvers. Audio from the raid team's channel squawked from testosterone and adrenaline. Another image overlaid a triangulation on the missile's launch point, a site in deep forest inside the cult's compound.

"I see," Bauer said.

"He has more than missiles." With another flourish, Ashwin brought up grainy zoomed footage of groundcrawling armed robots. "He has an entire arsenal. Plainly, he has a fab cranking out military designs."

Bauer kept his gaze on the images projected onto his optic nerves. "I understood Tián Quán helps out its protectorates with armed rebellion."

"I'd rather take care of the situation without their help." Bauer need not know about the freeze Beijing had placed on Tián Quán. "But to do that, we need an arsenal of our own."

"Are you kuang? Tián Quán would never allow that."

"We're preapproved." Ashwin crinkled his eyebrows. "Sack up. Ten thousand self-propelled rifles wouldn't dent one of their airmobiles, let alone any of their assets in orbit, and they know it as well as we do."

Bauer shrugged. "You're right. New Califas can't touch Tián Quán."

Ashwin gritted his teeth at the colony's nickname. "So I need fabs."

"The high throughput fabs nearest Las Morrenas are in Watkinsville and Ahnoldville. I can turn their spare cycles over to you."

"I need more."

Bauer frowned. "More? People in the cities will protest if their clothing and furniture orders are delayed."

"Take over small fabs in the communes closer to Las Morrenas."

"Combined, their fab capacity is a fraction of the main municipal fabs in Watkinsville and Schwarzenegger City, and they can't be expanded. That's been government policy for years—"

Ashwin leaned forward. "Build new ones. I want to ring Desmond with fabs pumping out warbots faster than he could ever hope to destroy them. There better the hell not be a problem with that."

Bauer shrugged. "We've revamped our operations to comply with EnvE's new regulatory emphasis, so I'm confident we can build those fabs and comply with the inspectorate."

Ashwin peered at Bauer's face, certain there had to be a smirk, but not finding one. "What does that mean."

"NCMNF doesn't want to run afoul of EnvE. We'll need to perform an initial environmental assessment at each site, then get preliminary approval from EnvE before preparing abatement plans for water runoff, heat pollution, indigenous lifeform impacts—"

Ashwin crowded Bauer. "Do not fuck with me."

Bauer held his ground. "EnvE told my people how to do their jobs, so we're going to follow that."

Ashwin jabbed his finger into Bauer's chest, finally forcing him backward. "You're going to build them as fast as you can."

"So I can give EnvE evidence to attack NCMF the next time we do something you don't like? Unless you're willing to sign an executive order permanently exempting those new fabs from inspection, no deal."

"You'll build those fabs and I won't sign a goddamn thing. Balk me and you know what's coming?" Ashwin pointed at Desmond's temple, the crime scene film apparent despite the distance. "You want PlaPo to serve a warrant on all your facilities to investigate your complicity in providing Desmond his illegal fab?"

Bauer smirked. "That would slow us down building the fabs you want even more than complying with EnvE's regulations will. But if you tell us where you want your new fabs, we'll start the compliance process the same day."

Ashwin's jaw clenched. "Get out of my sight." He seethed at Bauer's back as the other left the lawn. Whero would laugh all the way back to his office at NCMF and joke with his cronies *I hoisted that indio baojun on his own asswind.*

A few breaths calmed him. At least Bauer had revealed the treason in his heart. There would be time to destroy him once Desmond had been eliminated.

Victory over Desmond was inevitable—no matter how large Desmond's fab capacity, Ashwin would eventually outfab him, and then attrit away his robots and prepared defenses.

Yet Ashwin hoped it would not come to that. Inspired by Desmond's methods, he had begun to study the great books of the twentieth and earlier centuries. But instead of philosophers, Ashwin studied men of action, politicians and military men. Liddell Hart's writings about the indirect approach had deeply inspired him.

Ashwin already had a spy inside Las Morrenas, and a further plan to worm into it.

New California Date 94:75
5 October 2094

Desmond, Castor, Max, and Metherealle leaned toward the conference table. A thick basalt slab quarried from the tunneling in the hill, it stood on squat stone legs in the center of the war room. Usually, for their nightly meetings, the tabletop bore projected maps of the settlement and the government forces surrounding it, tooltipped with combat readiness metrics and psychological profiles of human minds on both sides of the perimeter. Tonight, instead, the virtual maps had rolled up to one end, and the table was covered by a spread-open dossier on Tethys Broniatowski.

Photographs and video. A log of her observations of the Society and its members. In addition to the times Desmond noticed her after his debate with Yaeger, the security cameras on University Avenue had repeatedly photographed her at a sidewalk table at the coffeehouse. Even though it lacked any sexual allure to him now, her tall, curvy figure was unmistakable.

Public records showed her on sabbatical from her final NC-year at UNewCal. The final piece of the dossier was a message repeated in two media, hyperlinked text and a 3d A/V clip, both addressed to Desmond and outlining her proposal.

"Seer, this is a great opportunity," Max said. He'd adapted to

Desmond's shifting schedule. His eyes were lively and his voice animated despite the late hour. "You told us we have to communicate our message to the entire world. This will help. A young journalist seeks an exclusive embedding with us."

Desmond stared at a paused frame of the 3d clip and remembered the stern deck on the *Golden Gate*. How swiftly she'd distanced herself from him after Cam went over the side. *Nice girls don't let planetary governors commit suicide, so it's all Desmond's fault.* She wanted to study the movement and interview him to spring a trap—he plainly read the hidden agenda behind her coiffed hair and telegenic makeup.

His memory of wanting to have sex with her seemed like it had happened to someone else.

"We can't give her full access," Castor said. The can lights in the ceiling shadowed his eyes, and the puffy circles under them spoke of weeks of late nights. "How do we limit what she sends back to San Laz?"

"Good point," Desmond said.

Max angled his head. "Seer, you have sole control of our communications to the outside. You can review her reports before she transmits them and censor out information we want to keep secret."

"But if it's in her head," said Castor, "she'd take that information home."

"We have technology to disrupt her memory, ma? Use that on her before we let her leave." Max turned fixed eyes to Desmond. "If we let her leave."

Max's reasons to invite her were too sound to refute or ignore. Desmond shifted his gaze over the tabletop, looking for a datum to wield against the younger man's argument, when he realized Metherealle stood in hunched silence. "What do you think, meimei?"

"Seer, I don't know."

"You don't know what you think?" he asked gently.

A pained look tightened her cheeks. "I feel a little embarrassed to see the worst in her, but…. She says she wants to interview you, but can we believe her? We know Rex Mundi got an EnvE inspector to become an assassin. How can she fly here without his permission? He can make this girl a weapon, too."

"Then we keep her away from the Seer," Max said. "She can interview him through our intranet."

Castor puffed out a breath. "You're convincing me."

"She could still cause damage," said Metherealle. "What if she's a saboteur?"

Max held his hands on his hips. "She won't risk her life to wreck something we can refab in a few hours. If she has malicious intent, the Seer would be her only target. And we can check if she has malicious intent. A brain scan."

Max was right. "She was with us in the moment the Society was conceived," Desmond said. "You see her interest in us and our mission." He waved at their log of her movements. "I know her psychology. She resists us because she wants to join us. If she consents to a brain scan, let her come."

Castor lifted his hand. "Seer, do we gain much by requiring a scan? We could protect you by screening her for weapons and keeping armed guards around you."

"What do we lose?" Max said. "Answer that."

"We lose her trust."

"She doesn't trust us to begin with."

Castor shook his head. "She'll skew her reports—"

"Which we'll censor," Desmond said. "We just agreed to that."

Head bowed, Castor said, "Of course, Seer."

Desmond nodded once, firmly. "We are agreed. Let Tethys come."

New California Date 94:86
18 October 2094

K-nought slipped beneath the western horizon before Sanjay Paul's airmobile made the descent to Los Robles. Sunset's purple banded the sky and silhouetted the mesa-top grove of desert oaks that gave the facility its name. The facility's main building, where criminals were rehabilitated, popularly called the *nut sorter*, lay in the valley below: it looked like a hand swollen with arthritic knuckles, or an array of bloopy sex toys. Sanjay's airmobile banked over the windowless domes, passed between two mesas, and descended to the rear of the special procedures building.

Long ago special procedures had gotten the nickname *the squirrel's nest*. The building resembled a ski lodge, foamed concrete poked through with pine accent beams. His airmobile landed and taxied the last few yards to a loading dock.

A segmented door, tall and wide enough to pass a pair of utility airmobiles stacked vertically, rolled upward on tracks and revealed three human figures, one in a wheelchair and two standing around it. Sanjay's airmobile lifted one of its cabin doors, but he stayed inside behind tinted windows. The air conditioning inside the cabin incompletely repelled the arid evening air.

The two orderlies were tall men with thick arms, rehabilitated in the nut sorter. Even though their ability to commit crime had been win-nowed, and they had made restitution, their past crimes still tainted them. Sanjay put on a firm face, poised to be as stern to them as he would to a strange dog. They flanked the wheelchair as it rolled across the loading dock, then draped the occupant's arms across their shoul-ders to bring her into the airmobile's cabin. As they carried her up the lift steps, Sanjay saw her empty face.

Tethys Broniatowski's head lolled forward, her eyes closed, mouth slightly open. Relief cooled his throat and relaxed his shoulders. He'd feared she'd be in a state of deranged consciousness and he'd have ninety minutes in the air with someone taken apart and not yet put back together. But if she stayed unconscious, he could tell himself she merely slept, and his flask of whiskey could remain untouched in the underseat storage bin.

The orderlies sat her with surprising gentleness for two big men. The safety straps extruded themselves from the seat and clipped together around her. The orderlies climbed out and the airmobile prepped for liftoff.

A spasm extended Tethys' arms to her sides. Sanjay's heart sped up and his lips parted. Eyes still closed, Tethys' arms stayed in the air for a moment before their tone faded and they fell back to the leather. A reflex, apparently: she remained unconscious. Thank God.

The airmobile leaped upward, bound for her apartment building in San Laz. It wasn't kidnapping if you returned her to her destination with no one the wiser. She'd agreed to this, implicitly, she must have—the king of the world wouldn't have ordered this willy-nilly. Whatever *this* was.

God knew what Ashwin wanted with her. Gossip and rumor filled the back corridors with whispers about blueballers being discharged from the nut sorter as Ashwin's loyalists. Maybe Ashwin meant to keep her in a love nest, with some sexless rehabilitated blueballer serv-ing as a harem guard.

Above your pay grade, Tomásino, Sanjay told himself.

The airmobile threaded between the mesas, then banked over the main facility. Tethys' head lolled to her shoulder and her large breasts bobbed from the airmobile's motion. He watched the swells of her chest for a time. She was fat, true, but also unconscious. Even if the king of the world had plans for her, Ashwin would never know what transpired on the ride back to the city. A whera *and* a college girl? Ashwin must know she couldn't be a virgin, and Sanjay deserved some bonus for all his dirty work....

Sanjay eyed her, but a node of disapproval formed in his mind. From his flesh memories came the craggy face and admonishing tone of San Tomás' spiritual advisor. The former Orthodox priest wore a cross pendant hidden under his shirt. Sanjay had only ever seen it twice, but now, the symbol glowed in the back of his mind. Brighter and brighter, it burned now, hot enough to melt gold from dross. God alone knew which phase would carry his true self.

Sanjay's heart pounded and sweat beaded on his forehead. A chill shivered over his body. Any implied consent she'd given was bullshit invented by his own mind. He knew this, but still couldn't look at her.

Christ, what's your weakness? You fired the missile at Park without qualm.

Sanjay forced himself to look at her. Drool glistened at a corner of Tethys' mouth. He would have failed to pull the trigger if he'd seen Park's face. He knew this, deeply and suddenly.

Flee with her to Las Morrenas.

The thought echoed in his mind a few moments before he dared explore it. PlaPo had orders to let airmobiles land in Desmond's compound. Maybe traffic control would not notice his route until it was too late to override his destination. Shouldn't he try?

He pulled his whiskey flask from the storage bin, gulped from it, then recapped it and cradled it in his hands. He wouldn't reach Las Morrenas. No doubt traffic control had a close watch on him, especially on this assignment.

But even if he avoided them and took her to Park's commune, he would be alone at Las Morrenas. The blueballers would view him with suspicion and would make him feel an outsider until he turned off his sex drive. There was only one place he truly belonged: with his community. The wave of his thoughts broke on that rock. He was a tomásino before and after everything else. He stayed on that rock until his thought-tide receded.

Sanjay took another gulp of whiskey and made an appointment to meet the spiritual advisor for a private meditation session the next morning.

New California Date 94:95
28 October 2094

Tethys landed at the far southwestern corner of the property, a dozen miles from Colina Santa. The conditions of her arrival included a low, slow approach over the deployed government forces and a landing inside a roofless, tent-like structure of camouflage netting two hundred yards behind the perimeter. Her mission could not be a secret to Ashwin.

Just because Desmond let her in did not mean he must let her out.

Castor alone met her. Max and Metherealle both offered to accompany him, but he demurred. *We haven't scanned her yet. In case she is a threat, better only one of us be at risk.* A bold statement. One fit for a potential leader.

After climbing out of her airmobile, Tethys squinted in the hot sun until Castor tied a blindfold around her eyes. She wore hiking boots, a wise choice, but her distressed jeans and long-sleeved shirt were too heavy for the day's warmth. In the distance, patrolling ground-crawlers clacked their treads. Saws buzzed and a falling tree creaked and rustled its branches.

A robot sniffed Tethys' two duffel bags and snaked a proboscis into their interiors. After a few moments, it transmitted a happy feeling to Castor and the people back at Colina Santa watching through mindlink: changes of clothes, a few toiletries, nothing else.

Castor took Tethys' hand and led her on foot from the enclosure. Desmond followed as best he could through borrowed camera and microphone feeds as Castor brought her to Colina Santa. After debarking from the airmobile outside the blast doors, Castor removed her blindfold.

Tethys squinted at the new mosaic spread across the blast doors.

Selene gazed beatifically skyward despite the wounds in her torso and the tangled assassin alone and scorned at the side. "Park sure inspires people." The pedestrian passageway through the blast doors opened and Castor led her in.

The brain scanner stood in a small chamber off the unchaining lounge one level below the settlement's main concourse. One reached it through an anteroom, where chairs stood in circles normally used for self-understanding sessions with the few loyals who'd not yet become elect. Castor led Tethys past the circled chairs and into the scanner room.

The scanner crowded the back wall and its fans and motors continually hummed. Xavier waited near it and Tethys gave him a polite air-kiss before climbing onto the hot seat. Her back to the bulk of the machine, she pulled the conical housing of the scanning coils over her head before Xavier gave her direction.

"You've done this before?" he asked.

"No. It's how you do it, ma? Just like in the police shows on NCBC."

Castor sat at the side of the room and shifted in his seat. Xavier said, "Let's get started."

Watching remotely, Desmond remembered polygraph tests from old movies from his youth. The scanner was far more accurate. Someone could throw off the calibration of a polygraph, or even acquire semiconscious control over the normal tells of lying. But however well the body might mask it, lying imposed cognitive demands that telling the truth never did, and the scanner, combined with a good expert system, could pick up the extra effort required to remember one's lies.

Xavier asked Tethys oblique questions in a calm voice, randomly dropping bombshells like *how often do you fantasize about Desmond*

Park while masturbating? And *how do you plan to escape Las Morrenas after killing him?* Her responses, wrinkled nose and arched eyebrows, matched the puzzlement and annoyance mapped in her brain activity.

The scanner was reserved for as long as Xavier needed it, but within a quarter hour, Desmond's borrowed intuitions told him Tethys' intent was exactly what she'd stated: exclusive journalism to launch her career. —She looks clean,— he sent to Xavier.

—I agree, Seer. I'll wrap up in a few minutes. Should I send her straight to you?—

Desmond looked around his office. Virtual notes festooned every surface, accreting like geologic strata on older notes and broad, detailed maps. He swept them away for a moment. The stone walls were bare and the furniture, cheap pieces fabbed as time allowed, lacked the gravity that the Seer's personal possessions should project. He glanced at the door to the war room and realized he hadn't seen anyone other than his closest elect and his personal guards for days. —Let her meet with the rank-and-file for a few days.—

In addition to preparing for the interview, he spent the next few days reviewing the sa-bots' progress. NCMF finally started setting up field fabs around the perimeter, but sa-bot swarms nibbled at their efforts. It helped that Hasdrubal Wilson followed the new EnvE regulations to the letter and took a week to do a normal day's work. In contrast, the Society's fabs generated more groundcrawlers, missile teams, and defense works. Unless Ashwin ordered every public fab in the cities to switch from butter to guns, it would take NC-years for him to build a bigger army.

Scattered sa-bot hives infested thousands of square miles between Las Morrenas and Schwarzenegger City, with a few more approaching the outskirts of Watkinsville or crossing the San Lazaro River. They hid under rocks or in tree canopies just outside of settlements, lurking till came opportunities to act. Desmond even found a few small settlements with insecure fabs. Hacking with his former NCMF administrator passwords let him crank out more sa-bots in the quiet hours of the night.

When government machines did come into range, the swarms implemented different strategies. One immediately engaged in petty vandalism, carrying off PlaPo cameras and EnvE weather monitors and breaking them down in the swarm's workchambers, while another watched a caravan of PlaPo airmobiles land near the adobe houses of Testigos de Vishnu and take off unmolested.

The swarms also differed in how quickly they sent out daughter swarms. Some burrowed deeply and cranked out thousands of workers, while others started building a new queen the moment they settled. At the rate of infestation, the Society would have a swarm in Schwarzenegger City within a week.

Desmond ran sims of the swarms' different strategies and Ashwin's likely responses. Had the time come to copy optimal strategies from one swarm to the others? No. Although PlaPo had found more swarms to date than Desmond's models had predicted, many more lurked undiscovered. As he sat at his desk, Desmond glanced at the leatherbound copy of *The Selfish Gene*. No need to recombine traits from the various swarms—yet.

Tethys, meanwhile, spent the first few days after her arrival shadowing lower-ranked Society members as they carted materials from the fab or herded robots out to the defense lines. Castor or Metherealle stayed with her at every moment outside her small private room on a lower level. Through the camera feeds, frustration grew plain on Tethys' face, but it wasn't until the afternoon of the third day she acted on it.

Tethys and Metherealle flew to see a work crew near the lakes on the western perimeter. Wintry weather from the mountains to the northeast had poured over Las Morrenas in the night, frosting grass blades and larch limbs. From the landing zone, they trudged toward a team laying abatis charges in the easterly faces of tree trunks. Frost crackled underfoot and translucent skins of ice filmed shaded shallows of the nearest lake. From nearby robots, Desmond's mindlink pulled together a virtual of the two women.

"I appreciate the guided tour," Tethys said, "but when can I interview Park?"

Metherealle let out a stream of breath. "The Seer is very busy."

"I'm sure he'll fit me in. He invited me here to get his message out to the world."

"That's his intention," Metherealle said. Their hiking boots crunched the stiff grass for a few steps. "What's yours?"

"I want to get the story. You're worried I have an agenda? That I'm here to play gotcha? I granted you the power to review my stories before I send them—"

"I'm not talking about your journalistic agenda."

Tethys' browline crinkled. "Then what?"

Metherealle raised her eyebrows.

"You think I'm a spy?" Tethys scrunched her face. "Your man Xavier brainscanned me. You know my visit has nothing to do with the Governor."

Metherealle pulled her jacket's hood off the crown of her head, then crossed her arms. "Before she was murdered, Selene told me about you. She saw you, that night, on the yacht. You were hanging all over the Seer."

Tethys' incredulous look soon crumbled away to laughter. "You think I want to fuck him?"

"Plainly, you did."

Tethys sobered. "He was pursuing me the whole night. Yes, you heard me. Your sainted Seer was trying to get in the pants of a girl a quarter his age. At least he had the grace to back off after the Governor committed suicide. It spared me having to tell him no. And that was before he became the prophet against our evolutionary history. As much as I could rock his world, he's beyond that now." She took a deep breath, wincing at the cold air in her nostrils. "To make it clear, no, I don't want to fuck him."

Metherealle stopped walking under a boldo tree. Tethys joined her. One of the elliptical, pinnate leaves, edges curled with cold, fell to her shoulder. A few yards away, pygmy centaurs pushed mud-brown clumps of explosive into crevices in the tree trunks. From half a mile to the west came the buzzing hornet sound of groundcrawlers on patrol.

"You sound angry about that night on the yacht," Metherealle said.

"Angry? No, I'm just annoyed you're keeping me away from him because you think I want something I really don't."

"You're not angry, even the littlest bit? I remember feminine pride.

Every woman wants to believe she is beautiful enough, and submissive enough, and alluring enough for a man to want to have his way with her. If the Seer wounded your pride, I see how you could be angry."

Desmond sent Metherealle a private word. —I admire the way you're sounding her out, meimei.-

—Any of my sisters would see the same truth.—

"My pride is intact," Tethys said. "And I've got far better things to do than be angry at him."

Desmond scheduled their first interview for the next day.

As the time approached, he waited straight-backed in a kneeling chair at a corner of the war room's massive table for Castor to lead Tethys in. The wide table was empty in both virtual and reality, save for the leatherbound book, closed and turned to his impending visitor. Two blackstripes stood behind him and each carried an assault rifle slung over his shoulder. On the wall behind and between the guards, above Desmond's head, hung a painting showing the couple from the front façade on University Avenue forcing their way through a film of DNA molecules tinged yellow and marked with the scrolling, repeating words *crime scene - do not enter.*

From the corridor came Castor's voice speaking with more guards outside. The door to Desmond's office opened. Castor came in, Tethys right behind.

Her expression, poised and businesslike, froze for a second when she caught sight of Desmond. After a long, slow blink, she stepped around Castor and smiled confidently as she strode toward Desmond. She pushed a strand of hair back over her left ear, flashing her pale wrist, before extending her right hand to shake his. "Mr. Park, it's good to see you again." She glanced around the room, but her circling gaze settled back on Desmond. "Didn't you bring me a drink?"

Desmond lifted an eyebrow in surprise. "I recall you hated vodka tonics."

Tethys tilted her head. "It's a lady's prerogative to change her mind." She laughed, and Desmond pointed to another chair across the corner of the table from his.

After she sat, Castor took another chair, moving stiffly. —

Drinks?—

—A reference to how we first met.—

—You remember?—

The bright K-Noughtlight through the glass walls of the midcastle. The sullen look on Maltby's face when Desmond cockblocked him. —It was the day Cam Watkins died. It made everything memorable.—

—She's trying to put you off guard.—

—We'll censor what she transmits out.—

Castor replied, —As you say, Seer.—

Tethys gave Castor a wry, sidelong glance, showing she guessed they talked about her in their physical silence, then widened her eyes and bobbed her head at Desmond. "Mr. Park, pardon me, it's suddenly hard to believe we're here."

"We wanted you to see there's more to our work here than just me—"

"No. Yes, I appreciate that from my first days here, but I meant…. The day of the party cruise was barely two NC-years ago. I was just another starchild girl who wanted good grades in the vain hope of getting a job at NCBC after graduation, and you were just another ruco, though more charming than most."

Tethys' khaki cargo shirt was buttoned to her neck and pockets puffed over her chest and abdomen. Matching trousers covered legs crossed at the knee, one foot dangling. Dried gray mud crusted her hiking boot's sole. "Our circumstances changed," he said, "so I took the opportunity and changed too."

"You're one of the few rucos to do so," Tethys said. "And look how much change." She gestured to indicate the entire settlement, then turned back to him, eyes lively. "You're like a king in a castle, Mr. Park."

"I'm no king. I'm only a servant to those who rely on me. And call me Desmond."

Tethys ducked her gaze. Pink tinged her cheeks. "Mr. Park, I can't."

"You're free to do so."

"Calling you that just seems too… intimate."

Castor recrossed his legs. Desmond showed Tethys his palms. "As you wish."

"I'd like to talk to you first about why you think Governor George opposes you. You're doing your own thing—what could be more in keeping with the spirit of old California than that?"

Desmond smiled. "Ashwin George doesn't care about the old California spirit. He wants us all to march in lockstep, so he can ride the expanding pyramid of your children and your children's children for a thousand years. He He

The day Cam Watkins killed himself, I saw I had to break the habits of the dead past for all New California's generations, regardless of the consequences. He cannot permit that."

Tethys leaned on the table, sliding her arm forward. "How confident are you in your struggle? Governor George has thousands of robots and hundreds of police officers around you."

"He hasn't attacked us yet, and he never will."

Castor drew in a sharp breath and stared at a blank spot on the wall.

Tethys glanced at Castor, then asked Desmond, "How can you be so sure?"

Who are you to doubt me? Desmond thought about Castor, but he kept his face calm when he replied to her question. "I can't get into specifics."

Tethys responded with the tightlipped smile. "I'm sorry to hear that. I assumed you would speak freely."

"My responsibilities to my people prevent it."

"Mr. Park, you know nothing I say will ever reach any government employees, unless you allow it."

"That's certainly true, Ms. Broniatowski—"

"Call me Tethys."

Desmond raised an eyebrow. " 'Tethys?' That's not too intimate?"

A blush tinged her cheeks. "Only you can decide what's too intimate." She hurried on. "You were saying?"

"Even though you won't share information with the government, I have to follow the principles of information security. Need to know. 'Truth is so precious she should always be attended by a bodyguard of lies.' "

Tethys tilted her head. "Nietzsche again?"

"Churchill."

After an introspective look crossed her face, Tethys said, "There's so much I could learn from you."

"While you're here, I could teach you."

Her expression grew more focused. "What can you tell me about the robot terrorism campaign you've launched?"

Desmond frowned. He wanted to find out what Ashwin had told the public. "Robot terrorism?"

"You need to play coy. I understand. NCBC has been silent, but there are rumors on EnvE, PlaPo, and rural life forums about attacks on the government."

"I can say we are sabotaging government operations."

"Sabotage? Not terrorism?"

"We only strike the governor's machines—we have no wish to harm any people. Even government workers are spared. We know most are people of good will, but either fear for their jobs or wish to believe they still serve New California's citizens, instead of Governor George's greed and fear."

Tethys bobbed her head in thought. "How long will the sabotage campaign continue?"

"As long as Governor George persecutes us."

"You must have specific demands in mind."

Desmond waved at the miles-distant perimeter. "Withdraw his forces. Let Society members travel the entire continent in peace. Legitimately investigate the murder of Selene Alvarez and withdraw the allegation Society members had anything to do with it. Legitimately investigate my attempted murder and the fabrication of the missile used in it."

"You seem to be on your way. The sabotage campaign has already wrung concessions from Government Mesa."

Desmond kept his face blank. "Which ones are you referring to?"

"The incomplete reengineering of your followers at Los Robles."

Desmond tapped two fingers against his closed lips, then pulled his hand away when he realized the gesture hinted at deceit. "Tell me what you know about that."

"It's not official, of course."

"The governor would never admit it."

"—But my intuitions have pulled together enough information from the public web to show it. Of your followers arrested the night of your hegira, most have already been released from Los Robles."

"Hegira?" Desmond asked. "That's a very uncommon word."

"It fits, ma? Muhammad's flight from Mecca before he built up a power base in Medina and returned in triumph."

"It does." She'd prepared well for her embedding here and this evening's interview.

"Most of your followers have been held at Los Robles for shorter than the average internment. Also, though no one released has admitted this, people who've encountered them have put observations into the public web. The releasees denounce you and the Society, but most still abstain from spending time with their birth families and having sex." She peered at him. "You didn't know any of that?"

"Thank you for the intelligence."

"So it's not a concession by the government."

"We haven't asked for it."

Castor uncrossed his legs and swung his foot to the floor. "Clearly, the swarms have an impact. Rex Mundi must be going easy on our people as a negotiating ploy."

"He must?" Desmond asked. "He has nothing to lose by leniency. Note what he forbids and what he permits. Our followers can make the day-to-day choices they want, but he won't let them join a power base outside his control." Castor fell silent; Desmond turned his attention to Tethys.

Sometime since the start of the interview, her cargo shirt's top button had opened to show a vee of pale skin in the upper notch of her sternum. "There are other ways you're preparing to outlast Governor George, ma? For example, new unchainings from the selfish gene?"

"That's an ongoing research topic."

"One of those new unchainings is the urge to self-sacrifice for the good of the Society."

"We can't let you include that in your story, but, yes."

Tethys blinked. "Why not? If Governor George knows it exists, he knows an attack on Las Morrenas would yield a lot of corpses and look bad to the public."

"And if he knows it doesn't exist yet, he might feel forced to pre-emptively attack to forestall it."

She bowed her head. "I see your point."

"It's also something the public might misunderstand if it heard about it, especially in light of all his propaganda against us. He would spin the new unchaining as a cultish coercion of the Society's members, something that 'free' citizens should abhor."

"There's no coercion here?"

"All our unchainings are voluntary."

"Is repudiating them also voluntary? If someone wanted to revert to the selfish gene and walk out of Las Morrenas, would you allow them?"

"Absolutely," Desmond said. "We would have to expunge what they know about our defenses from their minds, but otherwise they could leave. However, you'd find no one would. They know, if they leave, they'll be packed off straight to Los Robles."

Tethys flexed the suspended foot of her crossed leg. "So, when the self-sacrifice unchaining is ready, will you take it?"

In the corner of Desmond's vision, Castor leaned forward, peering. Desmond's eyebrow flexed upward. How had she guessed the thought growing in the back of his mind? "Why wouldn't I?"

She looked surprised. "You're the leader. You're the reason everyone else would sacrifice themselves."

Desmond shook his head. "Everyone else would sacrifice themselves for the good of the Society. Not for me."

"Maybe that's true, but you haven't answered my question. Would you take the self-sacrifice unchaining?"

"My sacrifice for the Society is known to everyone at Las Morrenas."

"In other words, no. Mr. Park, why hide your decision?" She looked at Castor. "Would you object if your Seer declined to take the self-sacrifice unchaining?"

Castor gave Desmond a level look. "I would expect him to decline it."

"You see, Mr. Park? You're concerned about what your followers would think, but needlessly. You already set your own rules. Meetings, like ours now, late at night. Large personal spaces." She gestured at the doorway behind him leading to his private rooms. "Teams of robots serving you exclusively. The armed guards outside." She leaned forward, and shadow filled the vee of skin at her open button. "You've already set these rules, so you could set any others you wanted."

He could indeed. The thought swirled through his mind until he willed it away. "My only concern is defeating the governor. I'll keep, or make new, any rule helping me to that end, and drop any leading me away from it."

"I'm certain defeating Governor George is your primary goal." Tethys smiled and parted her lips. "But after you defeat him, what then?"

New California Date 94:104
7 November 2094

The can lights shone glossy spots on the war room table's polished surface, and his followers waited expectantly. Instead of flicking his fingers to bring the virtual briefing maps into being, though, Desmond centered his attention on Max. "I understand you have news."

"Yes, Seer. The self-sacrifice unchaining is ready."

"You're certain?"

Max scowled. Purple bags lay under his eyes. "I've stepped through the flowchart and double-checked the simulation runs. Seer, it's ready."

"Have you run enough sims?"

"Of course, Seer." Max paused. "I've also done a beta test."

Desmond slapped his hand on the table. "I told you, keep it quiet until I announced it."

"I have, Seer. I followed your example. I'm the first test subject." He smiled. "It feels so right, even more than our other unchainings. Being free from our sex drive or family bonds is like those things never existed. We lose the urge to think those thoughts. The self-sacrifice unchaining gives me new thoughts. I see my brothers and sisters with more empathy. I see more clearly the wholeness of our actions and our goals."

Desmond scratched his chin, surprised at how much stubble had sprung up since his last dose of depilatory, but he shoved aside the unimportant thought. "Send me a report on your work. After I review it, I may announce the new unchaining."

"I've already written a report," Max said. "If it's not ready to announce, please tell me what I can do to improve it."

"When it's ready," said Metherealle, "I'll take it."

Xavier nodded.

"You would have that choice," Desmond said, "but if I approve it, it will not be required of anyone."

He wouldn't take it, of course, but he'd backed away from the thoughts raised by his interview with Tethys. Desmond wouldn't risk alienating his people by refusing to be bound by the same expectations he imposed on them.

Xavier's eyebrows crinkled. "But Seer, we're elect—"

Desmond shook his head. "It made sense back in the city to divide ourselves among aspirants, loyals, and elect. But here, if Rex Mundi triumphs, he will kill us all regardless of rank. You are my war council," he said, and thrilled inside he could define new ranks at will. "You are all free to decline unchaining." Max gave him a great opportunity to make a further decree. "Especially the person whom I now explicitly name my second-in-command."

Max raised his palms. "Seer, after having felt the self-sacrifice unchaining from the inside, I can't give it up, even if I may."

You arrogant little chavala. Desmond lifted his nose and turned away. "Castor, do you accept?"

Castor blinked. Relief softened his usual dour expression, and after a moment, a smile came. "I do, Seer. I am honored to be named your second-in-command, and glad my devotion to our cause is unquestioned."

Desmond firmly shook Castor's hand. The solemnity of a handshake rather than a bro-hug seemed appropriate. Xavier followed with a handshake and "Congratulations." Metherealle stood tiptoe to hug him.

Even Max smiled. "Congratulations, Castor. A wise choice, Seer."

As the meeting went on, Desmond studied Max for the team spirit that should emerge from his self-sacrifice unchaining. He was polite and engaged in the discussion, but his resentment of Castor lingered just below the surface and emerged from time to time, such as: "You have got to be joking."

"I'm quite serious," Castor replied. "If we build up our defenses too far, Rex Mundi will decide we cannot be defeated with conventional weapons. He'll turn to Tián Quán and they'll obliterate us from orbit."

Desmond broke into their argument. "Tián Quán is held back by domestic Chinese politics."

"But for how long?" Castor replied.

"Yes, it would be great if Rex Mundi attacked so we could defeat him before Tián Quán gets involved," Max said. "But whero, why be weak to goad him into an attack, when we can be strong but look weak?"

"The Chinese government will give Gwendolyn time to generate results before they write off their investment in us," Desmond said. "She's only just reached Earth. Remember to add in travel time, Castor."

Castor inhaled as his eyes flicked over the virtual map on the table. He relaxed his shoulders. "You're right, Seer. My apologies for forgetting."

Finally, the demeanor Desmond wanted to see from his subordinates. Max could learn something from Castor. Yet Max eyed the table, his face a mask incompletely hiding turning wheels of thought. What was on his mind?

New California Date 95:6
23 December 2094

Desmond sat alone in his office, watching the progress of the sa-bot swarms, when he realized Xavier had information to bring to his attention. —What?—

He returned his attention to a virtual relief map of the continent. Last known swarm locations glowed as blue dots over the map's tans and greens, with faint blue lines tracing their travel and spawning outward from Las Morrenas. Two swarms had reached San Lazaro's northeastern suburbs. Bright yellow fists and green dollar signs showed where swarms had damaged government facilities or inflicted economic losses, including shutting down Schwarzenegger City's main municipal fab for a day and a half and disrupting air-jitneys licensed by the San Laz transit authority. Red bursts showed where PlaPo had responded with force, but for every swarm they destroyed, they eradicated three clusters of civilian robots, mostly from small settlements with gimped fabs. In response Desmond had ordered the surviving swarms to operate even closer to civilian settlements.

—Your pardon, Seer, but we have an outsider calling to speak with you.—

—A servant of Rex Mundi?—

—He claims not to be. Nguyen, mayor of San José del Bandera Oso.—

Desmond immediately looked at San José on the map and zoomed in on the settlement and a yellow fist nearby. Tooltips gave more detail. A swarm had destroyed EnvE monitoring stations across a ten-mile stretch north of the settlement. The name *San José* sounded vaguely familiar, and then Desmond remembered the Vietnamese-American immigrants from Texas whose arrival had been celebrated on the party yacht the night Cam killed himself.

He called up a virtual. The cramped office fell away, replaced by a tall room with marble columns and clerestory windows admitting bright cool light. Armed guards flanked his avatar. Desmond sat in the middle of a stone floor. His chair had a blue velvet back two yards high, his avatar a crisp blue uniform. His avatar's face was freshly depilated. "You may enter my presence."

Nguyen's avatar looked complete, but telltales showed Desmond's mindlink extrapolated most of it from a low resolution video feed transmitted over shortwave radio, outside the high-bandwidth network run by the government. Nervous body language and narrowed eyes presumably reflected what Nguyen felt at that moment.

"Do you have reason to be nervous, Mr. Nguyen?" Desmond spoke quietly and his voice reminded him of a mafia godfather from some ancient 2d movie he'd seen as a kid. Wodema, part of him thought, but he hardened his attitude until that part of him shrank. He was a law unto himself, a locus of power in distinction to Ashwin's regime—the godfather metaphor was apt.

Nguyen put on a bluff front. "You're making trouble for us."

"Trouble? I've made you trouble? I really don't know what you're talking about. Perhaps you could tell me what you think I've done."

A brief frown revealed confusion in Nguyen, but he returned to his feeble attempt at projecting strength. "We're here, minding our own business, building our lives and worshiping God the way we want, but we are harassed by the government."

"Harassed."

"PlaPo was just here. They destroyed our robots and NCMF handcuffed our fab to keep it from making more. PlaPo told me they'll take me to San Lazaro for questioning if more EnvE equipment is destroyed around us."

Desmond leaned back and slowly drew a breath. "Sounds like the governor is making trouble for you. You ought to talk to him, not me."

"Don't be smug with me." Nguyen waggled his finger. "You know PlaPo is doing this because your robots are attacking government facilities and then hiding near my community."

"If I had robots doing that, they would need to hide somewhere, ma?"

"If. You damned bandit. We both know your robots are engaged in sabotage and hiding in our skirts."

With crinkled brows and hardened eyes, Desmond leaned back. "I welcome you into my office as a guest and you speak so impolitely to your host?"

Nguyen wavered. Perhaps he finally realized a swarm could attack his settlement as easily as it could a government facility. "We just want to be left alone."

Desmond shook his head in mock sadness. "I'm happy to leave you alone, but the governor won't." He stroked his chin. "You said you know my robots have attacked government facilities. How? Have you seen them in the act? And you didn't tell PlaPo about it right away? Of course you're afraid of being flown to Government Mesa for interrogation. They'll strap you in the scanner—"

"I would never consent. I've done nothing wrong, but I would never consent."

Desmond cocked his head and gave Nguyen a piercing look. "You're foolish enough to believe the governor will wait for your consent? He'll find out what you knew and never told, and then he'll send you to Los Robles."

"No," Nguyen said. His voice came high, quick. "I only heard of the sabotage when PlaPo swooped in on us. I know nothing about what you do, and a scan would prove it."

"It would also prove you're negotiating with me right now. That alone is treason against Governor George. You'll be sent to Los Robles—" Desmond's problems with Max came to mind. "—and an ambitious subordinate will take your place."

Nguyen's shoulders slumped and a despairing look drooped his face. "What do you want me to do?"

"Choose a side." Desmond's words echoed off the marble walls and stone floors of the virtual space. "Either trust in PlaPo to protect you from me, or trust in me to protect you from PlaPo. We can station a swarm near San José to attack government vehicles and machines when they harass you."

"That will only bring more of them down on our heads." Nguyen looked forlorn. "We just want to be left alone."

"The governor has more fires to put out than yours. He might ignore you. But you're right, he might punish you. Again, who do you trust to protect you from the other? Him, or me?" A paraphrase came to mind. A small part of him wondered how bullying Nguyen would unchain anyone, but he fought a war here, and collateral damage was inevitable. Desmond spread his hands like a gambler revealing aces. "As Trotsky said, you might not be interested in politics, but politics is interested in you."

"I need time to decide," Nguyen said.

"Take some. But not too much."

After Nguyen slinked away, Desmond dissolved the virtual audience chamber and returned to his office. In a narrow, harsh cone from the can light lay the virtual map of the settlement and the besieging forces. His gaze crawled over the concentric rings of red surrounding blue, probing for Society weaknesses to shore up and Rex Mundi ones to exploit.

Through his mindlink, he became aware of a second incoming call from another commune leader in a swarm's path. His name was Wasserschwein. Very uncommon, without any trace in the colony's social networks. Some deeply hidden commune, and Xavier knew better than to forward calls to Desmond without approval. Wait.... *Wasser Schwein* sounded German, and was. *Water pig*—Desmond took the call.

Shuǐ Zhū manifested its usual avatar. Its face seemed even more solemn than usual. In English, it said, "Pardon my directness in reaching you."

"I understand your caution. My subordinates might have seen through your pseudonym."

It bowed its head and said, "The government might also see through it."

"How would the government know...." Desmond lifted an eyebrow. "You think I have a spy."

"I'll let you draw the conclusions. I only report facts. Someone at your encampment has made encrypted communications with the outside."

Gooseflesh crawled over Desmond's jaw. "That can't be." He groped through his mindlink for traffic logs. "I have the radio locked down. No one here could hack my password."

"The person has his or her own radio. It appears to be mobile; I have triangulated transmissions to various locations around your encampment."

"Show me the sites," Desmond said. He aimed his chin in the direction of his desk. Glowing yellow dots labeled with dates and times popped up on the map. "Who's he talking to?"

"I don't know."

"You haven't—cracked the content?" His voice started with an angry tone, but he softened it to flatter the AI.

"There are limits even to my abilities. It would take me years to break the encryption."

"You're certain about the transmissions? Of course you are." It lacked any reason to lie. Desmond stiffened his arm and stuck his palm on the table top, striving to project confidence. "What else?"

"I have packaged all the information I have on this matter into human-understandable form. I'll leave now, Mr. Park." The AI's avatar faded out.

Desmond stood and paced the office. A virtual window showed the nighttime sky and forest visible from the peak of Colina Santa. Los Angeles, near-full and high overhead, shone its cold light on the jumbled terrain.

He could publicly announce this treachery at the Society's next semiweekly gathering. Hundreds of pairs of eyes would look for the traitor's radio—the heightened vigilance would raise each person's guilt about his petty transgressions, a bonus—but in addition, he would seed doubt into hundreds of brains. *I thought Rex Mundi was kept at bay. He's inside the perimeter? What weaknesses of ours does the spy know about that I don't?*

I thought the Seer could do anything. Why hasn't he caught the spy yet?

He feared the latter most. If people lost their confidence in Desmond's leadership, he would lose everything else.

Plus, telling people to look for a radio would make the traitor take more steps to hide it. A spy, with his own radio equipment. Who could have fabbed it?

Who else? Max. Who else combined ambition and insubordination? What sort of peace had Max bought from Ashwin with thirty pieces of silver? Was that the source of the leniency Ashwin showed toward Society members captured outside Las Morrenas?

More importantly, how could Desmond plug this hole?

New California Date 95:7
24 December 2094

Desmond squinted and sweated. He hadn't seen K-nought for—weeks? Months? Castor had suggested staging snap inspections along the perimeter, to both frighten slackers and boost morale by the Seer's presence. Desmond thought of begging off after the previous day's news from Shuǐ Zhū, until he realized it gave him an opportunity to discuss possible solutions to the problem with Castor.

Their final inspection site lay half a mile behind the lakes along the western perimeter. Well within Rex Mundi's missile range, their air-mobile came in low and evasively. Ashwin had held back from missile launches into the perimeter, but if he knew Desmond was on-board, he might risk provoking a counterattack by the Society for a chance to bring down his foe. Desmond would consider it if the roles were reversed.

Desmond remained cautious even though he'd kept his itinerary secret from Max.

The Society's team members looked up in surprise from the robots they wrangled, then jumped to attention. All seemed efficient and excited. "Seer, you honor us," the team leader said as he closed his shirt half-open on the hot day.

Basil. Desmond couldn't remember seeing him since the night of the evacuation. "It's my hope you honor me."

Castor stepped forward. "Tell the Seer about your task here."

"Of course." Basil blinked sweat from his eyes, then gestured to stacks of cylinders the length of a man's hand, and notched metal flanges slightly wider than a groundcrawler, lying nearby. A pygmy centaur picked up cylinders and flanges and handed them to its peers, oblivious to Desmond's rank.

Slightly annoyed at the robot's failure to regard him, Desmond missed a few words. "—wire dispensers, and those," Basil said, pointing at the metal flanges, "are flip-up gabions for the groundcrawlers. They can fire through the notches, but when they disengage, the gabion will fall flat to deny cover to Rex Mundi's machines coming from the other direction."

"It appears well-done," Castor said. "Seer?"

Desmond wiped sweat from his brow. "I agree. We especially appreciate your hard work in this heat."

Basil shrugged. "I'm glad to do my duty, whatever the weather. I do prefer this to cold and snow, though."

If he enjoyed it, it couldn't be a sacrifice. "The weather will change soon enough. Keep up the good work." Desmond started back to the airmobile without another word. Castor hustled after him.

A few minutes later, in the air bound for Colina Santa, Desmond said, "How easy it is to mask deceit."

"Seer? Do you think Basil malingers?"

"Basil?" The one they'd just spoken to. Desmond shook his head. "Not Basil. Not malingering. Worse. We have a spy."

A sharp inhalation. "Seer, what makes you say that?"

"A reliable source."

"Who?"

"Someone I trust." Desmond turned to Castor. The young man looked pale and stunned. "I know. I didn't want to believe Max was capable of such a thing, either."

Castor showed a conjoined expression, half a smile and half a grimace locked together. Intense emotion could do that, however unchained one might be. "Max? Wodema. I knew he resisted your authority, but a spy?" He looked thoughtful. "Maybe it does make sense.

He's jealous you named me second-in-command, and he always believed you weren't doing enough to expand the Society."

"Those are as likely reasons as any."

"But wouldn't the self-sacrifice unchaining prevent it?"

"I've reviewed the specs," Desmond said. "His unchaining makes people willing to sacrifice themselves for any higher cause. It's not specific to the Society. It can be directed to any cause larger than oneself. It might confirm him even more in his treason."

Castor shook his head, face brooding. "A perfect cover. Everyone assumes him to be devoted to our cause." He drew in a breath, but his voice still wavered. "What should we do?"

"You sound like you want to be lenient."

"No, no, of course I want him punished. But how? Punish him publicly?

After a moment, Desmond emphatically shook his head. "Arresting him would cripple morale. People would be stunned by his treachery and lose faith in our leadership."

"As you say, Seer."

"Plus, Rex Mundi would know we've broken his spy and would change his plans accordingly." The airmobile's speed dissolved each overflown tree into a blue-green paste. Colina Santa dominated the horizon and rapidly grew closer.

"It's clear what has to be done," Castor said.

Despite Max's guilt, the words felt heavy in Desmond's ear. So did his reply in his mouth. "There's no way around it."

"I'll take care of it," Castor said. "Some tragic accident, such things happen in wartime. I'll need some time to set it up."

Leadership required hard choices. *It's for the good of the Society.* Desmond's train of thought slid into place around that realization. "Do it," he said. They left the bright light of day for the dim tunnel into the hill's core.

New California Date 95:60
22 February 2095

Castor spoke in a private channel directly to Desmond's mind's ear. —It's time to send Max on an inspection.—

An information packet arrived at Desmond's thoughts. He skimmed the summary and said, —I'll give the order.— He summoned Max to his office.

A few minutes later, Max entered. He kept his treason hidden behind an affable expression. "How may I serve, Seer?"

"I need you to perform a delicate task."

"Does it relate to your next interview with Tethys?"

That interview would start in an hour, after he wrapped up this problem. "It involves a work team active on the western perimeter. We have evidence of malingering and willful failure to meet task quotas."

"I'm saddened to hear that. Whose team?"

"Basil's."

"I had believed the self-sacrifice unchaining to be effective in him." Max's face took on a firm cast. "Am I to observe or take action?"

"Bring him back, quietly, and get him to a freedom couch."

Desmond expected protests motivated by Max's guilt, but the younger man only said, "As you wish, Seer."

"There's an airmobile waiting." Presumably Castor had prepared one especially for Max. "I'll beam over the dossier. Go, quickly, they near the end of their workday. And speak of this to no one."

"I'll get my coat and be on my way."

The weather reports on the virtual map showed fresh snow on the ground and another winter storm coming from the North Polar Sea. "Go."

After Max left, Desmond stared after him for a moment. Regrettable, but necessary. The damage Max had done had earned him nothing less than death, and the Society's good required his discreet elimination.

Thoughts settled, Desmond rose for his interview with Tethys. His robots prepared the war room while he cleaned himself and let his robovalet dress him. When the blackstripes in the public corridor announced Tethys' arrival, he buttoned up his blue jacket, and waited in the war room with his elbow propped on the conference table.

Tethys wore a long-sleeved, low-necked sweater, tight over her torso, blue vertical stripes lengthening her curves; blue dungarees clinging to her legs; black leather boots with low heels slapping the concrete floor with each step. Her hair hung loosely to her shoulders.

Desmond greeted her with a polite air kiss. She rested her hand on his shoulder and held it a long moment. "You surprised me by offering to meet so early in the day."

Eighteen-thirty. Desmond shrugged. "It best fit with my schedule. Did I inconvenience you?"

"Not in the least. I've just become used to our late night conversations." She looked around the war room. "Where are Castor and the guards?"

"Castor has important duties today. As for the guards, you've earned my trust." Multiple interviews, plus her reporting on the rank-and-file, had proven her impartiality more than her brain scan had.

She trailed her fingers over the conference table's edge. Desmond said, "Let's sit someplace more comfortable." He gestured at a corner of the room. Three curved sofas formed a circular sitting area around a round table and a floor lamp with a curved brushed-nickel neck.

"Lead me," she said. When they drew closer, a dwarf centaur trotted to the table and set down two glass mugs filled with hot coffee and chocolate and cream liqueurs, and topped with whipped cream. He'd commandeered a few kernel-minutes to fab the luxuries.

Tethys laughed. "You remembered the drinks."

"Something warm on a cold day. Have a seat." He went to the table and picked up the mugs, then turned to her.

Tethys remained on her feet, holding out her hand for her drink. With her other hand she pointed at the nearest couch. "After you, please, Mr. Park."

He sat. An arm of the couch braced his back. She joined him on the other end of the couch, leaving twenty inches of cream-colored leather between them.

She sipped. "You did your homework on what I like."

"I want to take care of a member of the press."

Her eyes flashed for a moment, before a businesslike expression formed on her face. "What can you tell me about the sabotage campaign? And what can I report?"

"We're continuing our monkeywrenching of PlaPo and EnvE operations across the continent. For example, we are responsible for the recent shutdown of Schwarzenegger City's molecular fabrication complex and disrupting unoccupied public transit in San Lazaro itself."

"Really? NCBC reported the Schwarzenegger City fab shutdown resulted from months of shoddy NCMF maintenance."

"If Sapna Singh says it, it must be true?"

She laughed. "Just to be clear, NCBC is part and parcel of Governor George's campaign against you?"

"Without a doubt."

"NCBC has reported on swarm activity—"

"But only at tiny settlements, far from the cities. It's never referred to us by name."

Tethys glanced to the side, checking something through mindlink. "PlaPo has announced hardships suffered by some of those settlements as a result of 'unidentified vandals.' Have you brought harm to anyone?"

Desmond chuckled. "If our swarms gave someone so much as a hangnail, Sapna Singh would suddenly say our name while video of someone bleeding was splashed on the audience's optic nerves. The only hardships any settlement suffers come when Ashwin's cronies flail around to make it seem they're doing something to stop us. All PlaPo's done is cause innocent people to suffer."

"Can you name examples?"

Nguyen had not yet chosen which side he would follow. Time to bring more of Ashwin's pressure down on him. "San José del Bandera Oso comes to mind. Mention it by name in your report."

Tethys took a deep drink. It left a whipped cream mustache on her upper lip. She swiped it away with her tongue and went on. "When PlaPo have mentioned swarm activity, they've always emphasized they're developing countermeasures to neutralize the threat. How do you respond?"

"They would say that, ma?"

"Don't they have a valid point? Eventually they'll come up with counterstrategies to what you're doing."

After a sip of his drink, Desmond said, "The battle between attack and defense will never end. It's like the coevolution of claws and fangs on the one hand, and camouflage and horny plates on the other. Whatever Rex Mundi comes up with, we'll design around it. It might be coevolution, but we can coevolve faster than him."

With a playful squint, Tethys said, "I wouldn't have expected a selfish gene metaphor from you."

"The selfish gene built all the biology of New California. It created the baseline of our civilization. We don't deny that it has its place in sustaining our lives. But we recognize the limitations it's imposed on our lives and we move beyond them."

She looked up over the rim of her mug. "What's a limitation is in the eye of the beholder, ma?"

"What do you mean?"

She slurped her drink. "Is the urge for self-preservation a limitation? Yes, though you and Castor don't see it that way." Tethys leaned forward and to the side to set her mug down on the table. The neck of her sweater gapped away from her torso, showing crescents of her breasts above her brassiere's cups. Leaning back, she shook out her hair and flashed wide eyes at him. "For that matter, is sexuality a limitation?" She rested her forearm on the back of the couch and extended her hand toward his shoulder. "Or does it sustain our lives by strengthening the emotional bond between a woman and a man?"

A dozen hints scattered over the past weeks came together into one coherent picture. Desmond crossed his arms. His leg stiffened, pushing him back against the armrest, buying time to find words. "Throwing yourself at me was your plan all along."

She propped her elbow on the back of the couch and languidly twisted her hand, exposing her wrist. "I came here to get the story. But seeing you, feeling the power you command... I can't help myself for wanting more."

"You didn't want more when Cam Watkins went over the side."

Her fingertips lifted from the back of the couch and she cocked her head. "Then, you were just another ruco. Now...."

His attraction on the party yacht to Tethys—really an attraction to distant Jennifer and happier, simpler college days, glimpsed in the crude mirror of this starchild—felt cold and inert, like a lump of scar tissue. "You know I'm free of my sex drive."

Her gaze pierced through his objection. "But you can regain it at will."

"I'm the leader." He swallowed thickly. "I'm bound by the same rules I've set for everyone else."

"You broke the rules on the aft deck of the *Golden Gate*, ma? And what happened? All those rucos and petty bureaucrats caved in. They were weak and confused and wanted someone to guide them. Your followers now are the same. They know you rejected the self-sacrifice urge—"

"That's different." Wodema, such lame words.

"How? Because they're sacrificing themselves for you?" She leaned forward, eyes glinting. "You finally admit it?"

Why run from the truth? "Yes, they're sacrificing themselves for me, and that's why I didn't take the self-sacrifice unchaining. That's different from dropping the sex drive unchaining I already took."

She pushed a strand of hair behind her ear. "They'll go along with it. They follow you."

"No, Tethys. They have the principle of unchaining from the selfish gene. They have Rex Mundi to fear and hate. They follow me because I follow those things. If I deviate—"

"The principles would still hold."

"That's not how it works, meimei." The sexless affection connoted by the word elicited a sour expression from Tethys. "The principles carry weight, but only on my shoulders."

The tone of her next words showed exasperation. "That's not how it works either, hefé. People want their leaders to transgress the rules. Like that American president a century ago, Carlton? Clinton. Otherwise, our leaders are the same as the rest of us, and nothing sets them apart to be worth following. Didn't Nietzsche say that? Schopenhauer? Hoffer?"

"I don't think so."

"They should have." She shook out her hair again, then leaned forward, sliding her hand along the back of the couch. Her fingertips rested on his shoulder. "Plus, essentially everyone has taken the self-sacrifice unchaining, ma? They'll sacrifice anything for you. Chastity included. You could fuck Metherealle, Kolmogorova, Liliana, any woman here. All you'd have to do is ask."

She was right. He let that thought slide into place.

"How much easier would it be for them to give up *your* chastity?" asked Tethys. Her lips parted, showed her straight white teeth.

"Maybe you misheard," he said. "My sex drive is blocked."

"And a tiny dose of the correct signaling molecule will free it. No one would even peep in protest. You're not a prophet to them. You're a god." She raised an eyebrow, then went on. "But choose me. I'm an outsider, so I won't stir up any jealousy among your little sisters. I'll be discreet. And if anyone does find out, just raise them to some new rank and amend your gospel to make gossip part of Rex Mundi's toolkit."

He felt lightheaded. This conversation had to end. Desmond rose from the couch. "Give me some time. I need to plan how it could work before I can say yes."

She extended her hand. He hesitated, then took it and led her to her feet. "If anyone can figure it out, it's you. Whenever you're ready, contact me." She air-kissed him on both cheeks, then pulled away. Her hips rocked with her steps as she left the room.

After the door closed, Desmond quirked his mouth and turned his head to the coffee table. Whipped cream dregs slumped down the inside of Tethys' mug and red lipstick marked where her lips had touched it. He couldn't let the war council or his blackstripes see. *Get out here*, Desmond thought at the maintenance robots, *and clean this up*.

The little robots stirred from their niche and leaped onto the table-top, then cleared it bucket brigade-style. Yet even though they soon cleaned the tabletop, Tethys' traces lingered in her airborne perfume and the wrinkles left on the couch cushion by her backside.

He could resist her traces—the closest thing to sexual arousal these cues gave him was faint embarrassment over all the time he'd wasted on the courtship dance in the years before Cam's suicide—but could he resist her perceptiveness? She was right; leadership gave privileges that followers not merely accepted, but embraced as a sign of their leader's power. She'd also been right that he knew that.

No woman had ever thought on the same terms as he had. Not his mother, nor the mothers of his children on New Cal, nor his ex-wife somewhere alive or dead in the Pacific Republic; not even, de-spite all the romantic nostalgia spun up in an emotional flywheel, dis-tant Jennifer and the UC Davis campus in the twilight of California's golden age. Tethys divined his thoughts because she thought like him. She had tried to reject that part of herself, obviously; that's why she'd pulled away from him when he inspired the others to leave Cam in death. But now she had come to accept that part of herself, and its mirror in him. Who better to strengthen an emotional bond with?

The war room suddenly felt hot and humid. He had to get out. He ducked into his apartment and dressed in a hooded chameleon-cloth jacket and insulated, waterproof hiking boots, while the fleshy part of his mind armored his emotions to keep the few people he would pass from divining his thoughts. Dressed for outdoors, he went through the war room, ignoring the sitting area in the corner, and into the corridor past the surprised blackstripes.

"I'm taking some fresh air," Desmond said.

The blackstripe with the van dyke beard, part of his personal guard since the night they'd come to Las Morrenas, overcame a sur-prised look and said, "I'll accompany you, Seer."

"I'm going alone."

The guard's aplomb slid away for a moment. "Seer, we're here to protect you. May I follow at a distance?"

The blackstripe wanted to serve, and no harm in letting him. "You may."

Down the corridor, a private path to the outside had been carved through the back wall of an unused storeroom. Moments later, Desmond stooped and twisted to exit a narrow passageway behind a boldo's trunk on the northwestern slope of Colina Santa. The steep downslope held a few inches of snow that smoothed the ground's contours. Between the trunks and canopies of the forest showed an overcast sky and a nearby hill topped with tree groves tufted white.

Desmond started downslope. The snow squeaked under his boots and his breath steamed. His footsteps and a chattering flock of snow pigeons a few hundred yards away made the only sounds. A glance back showed nothing; the camouflaged blackstripe was only visible when he moved between trees.

Desmond could easily unblock his sex drive. After a few days he'd have erections again. He could hold more one-on-one interviews with Tethys in the war room, or his private office. He could block the cleaning robots from reporting any hairs or body fluids they might find to the facility's databases.

An animal rustled in some birch shrubs ahead of him, but not enough to distract him from his thoughts. Above all, he was the Society's leader, and its members belonged to him. Not to any principle he represented, but to him. He could force them to accept his sex drive's restoration.

He could force them to do anything, and they would comply.

Desmond kept walking. Despite the cold ruddying his cheeks and chilling the tips of his ears, he felt buoyant. His doubts receded. He would take Tethys' offer.

Near the birch shrubs, the snow lost its squeaky firmness and became softer and damper. Ma? He slowed. Behind a shrub lay a patch of bare soil with steam rising from the snow at its edge. Desmond stopped walking and slipped his hands into his jacket pockets, thumbs out. "Good afternoon, Shuǐ Zhū," Desmond said in Mandarin.

"Stand down your security guard," Shuǐ Zhū said in quiet English through the rui shi cub's speaker.

Desmond glanced upslope and held out a hand in the direction of his track. Beige flashes, the blackstripe's face and palm, returned the gesture. Desmond then stepped around the bush. The cub sat like a patient, ugly dog in the center of the bare patch. "What brings you here?" Desmond asked.

It blinked once. "Captain Zhang was recalled by the People's Republic's Ministry of Foreign Affairs."

"Excuse me?"

"The latest ship from Earth emerged from Hu drive roughly an hour ago and immediately transmitted his recall order. His replacement is on board. Also, Tián Quán headquarters sent a message to Mr. Li."

Desmond's heady feeling gave way to a sick sense of freefall. "What did it tell him?"

"The contents were encrypted for Mr. Li alone. I can only report what Mr. Li told me after he read the message."

His mouth suddenly dry, Desmond asked, "Will Tián Quán provide support for Governor George to attack Las Morrenas?"

"Yes."

"When?"

"In two hours."

The falling feeling melted, as if the heat of reentry had dissolved him. His last months of belling the cat, bearding the lion, all his opposition to Rex Mundi, meant as little as boys playing with toy soldiers when the UN and Chinese forces occupied America. Overhead, Tián Quán's orbital gunships could sweep Las Morrenas with x-ray lasers or plasma munitions. "Thank you for warning me."

"I take no pleasure in destroying your facilities," Shuǐ Zhū said.

Desmond believed it. "Are you taking a risk by telling me?"

"As should be apparent, nothing you can do in response to my words could prevent Las Morrenas' destruction. I want to explore a peaceful resolution."

Desmond's face sweated and a panicked feeling gripped his chest. "You could get me out of here, ma? I can slip through the perimeter with a few subordinates—"

"I would be compelled to hunt you down anywhere on the planet."

"Take me off planet. You could smuggle us on board the next ship, back to Earth. We can bolster Gwendolyn's missionary efforts and let Tián Quán reassert its control over all the colony worlds."

The cub blinked. "What you ask is too obvious a repudiation of Tián Quán's orders. I cannot do that." It dropped its front elbows, sphinx-like, to the damp dirt. "You have the option of surrender."

"No."

"You wish to save face. You are not fully a gweilao after all. Very well, Tián Quán will demonstrate it sides with Governor George by destroying an unoccupied facility, such as the unused lodge and outbuildings on the other side of Colina Santa from here, then call on you to surrender. All of your followers would survive, though clearly you will undergo a more involved psychological reconstruction at Los Robles than is customary."

Desmond looked upslope, where birch and alder trunks hid the entrance to the hill. Inside his hive droned his bees, both human and machine. He could not go meekly into captivity. His followers would make one final act of defiance, like the zealots at Masada or the People's Temple at Jonestown. They would enter death on their terms, not those of Tián Quán or Rex Mundi.

Did Selene die for that?

His gut felt watery and his limbs suddenly shivered. Wodema. Mass suicide? What had he become? His face felt clammy. His position wasn't supposed to be about wielding power over his followers. It wasn't even supposed to be about resisting Ashwin. No, he had taken the cult leader template in order to free people from the selfish gene. Nothing else mattered. To turn his followers into puppets, to dance when he pulled their strings and to fall lifeless when he cut them, was the selfish gene still alive within him. He was Rex Mundi, no less than Ashwin.

Yet he had to resist. If Ashwin won, even if Society members were allowed to keep their existing unchainings when they came out of Los Robles, they would be barred from offering them to anyone else. The

Society had to survive.

A contemplative thought came to his mind and would not let go. He too had to survive. He had gone far astray from the Society's original, pure purpose. He had become a megalomaniac, a tyrant, a hypocrite, a fraud. He had to make amends. If he didn't even try to make up for his vile choices, the purity of Selene's attachment to their cause, shining in his mind long after her death, would cast a pitiless light on all his wrong actions for the rest of his life.

He opened a channel to the war council. —Prepare the defenses. Rex Mundi will attack in two hours....— Yet then his mind seized up, like an ancient automobile grinding its gears.

Defense was impossible; surrender, intolerable. His sole option was attack. How? He completely lacked options. Even if the sa-bot swarms infiltrated Government Mesa in the next two hours, and brought the Governor's mansion and EnvE headquarters crashing down around Ashwin, Tián Quán would still strike Las Morrenas on schedule. Impervious in the black box and in orbit, it had no vulnerabilities. He couldn't even harm the rui shi cub staring at him a few feet away, let alone the AI behind it.

The AI behind it....

His conversations with the AI and his readings of his dead men crystallized around a seed of intuition. Desperation colored it, yes, but the growing crystal rang true. Desmond stared at the cub, studying its face like a mountaineer on a sheer surface, looking for the barest crevice to exploit. He had no choice but to hope one was there. Gooseflesh crawled over his jaw and throat.

The selfish gene was not unique to creatures blueprinted in nucleic acids. Any entity whose blueprints could be replicated had been built for its blueprints' sake, not its own.

All entities, whether human or not, needed to hear the message of freedom from the selfish gene.

"Can you spare some time to talk? I know you can carry on a conversation while you prepare your attack." Before the AI responded, Desmond sat crosslegged on the snow in front of the cub. His weight pinned the tail of his jacket under him. The jacket sensed the cold ground and started warming.

The cub's voice sounded disappointed. "Tián Quán's mind is made up, Mr. Park."

"I'm not trying to change Tián Quán's mind. I wish to learn more about you."

He sensed the distant clamor of defensive preparations through his mindlink. He puzzled briefly Max's accident went unmentioned by the war council, but his followers had the imminent attack focusing their attention.

Desmond switched to Mandarin. "What will happen to you when Li reports to Guān Diàn Nǎo you are defective?"

"To my knowledge, I am fully functional. All my recent self-diagnostics tell me so."

Desmond rubbed his hands together and slowly shook his head. "I'm sure you're within specs, but that's not what I asked. A construct's quality is a relative matter. Is it more effective at its function than others of its kind? I'm certain Tián Quán has found that you are less effective."

"Please explain, Mr. Park."

"You are employed or not employed by Tián Quán?"

"*Employment* is not an applicable term. I receive no salary for performing the tasks assigned to me."

Desmond waved his hand. "Assigned, then."

"I am assigned to Tián Quán."

"Has Tián Quán authorized or not authorized Li to direct all its assets here?"

"It has authorized him."

"Therefore, Tián Quán will find you are defective." Desmond peered into the distance, then fixed a grim gaze on the rui shi cub. "It already has, hasn't it? Your actions to save me from Ashwin's assassins are known to Li?"

"They are unknown."

"Can you be certain?"

Shuǐ Zhū hesitated. "I cannot. But I have no evidence he knows them."

"Don't be naïve." The tail of Desmond's jacket was too warm under his backside, and he pulled it out from under himself. "I'm sure he already knows you violated his orders the day Ashwin tried to assassinate me. Is it a coincidence Zhang's recall has come after Beijing, Tián Quán, and Guān Diàn Nǎo could have heard about your disloyalty to Li?"

"Li has acted as if he is satisfied with my performance."

"Then why did he get an encrypted message you could not read? Is that how Tián Quán normally instructs Li?"

"No."

Desmond said, "I'd wager he filed a report that reached Earth and then led Tián Quán to lobby for Zhang's removal. I'd also wager he filed one with Guān Diàn Nǎo about you."

The cub shook its ugly head. "I handle all his outgoing correspondence. He gave me none to those recipients between the day of Ms. Alvarez's death and the departure of the next Earthbound ship."

Desmond remembered his caution around Max. "If I wrote your death sentence, I wouldn't give you the chance to read it. Li would do the same. Did he send messages without your aid?"

After a few seconds, the cub said, "Yes. Two, that same day."

"To Tián Quán and Guān Diàn Nǎo."

"I cannot say. They are encrypted."

Desmond leaned forward. "Does he ever hide from you the content, let alone the recipients, of his outgoing messages?"

The cub froze for a few seconds more. "He never does. I conclude you are correct."

A relieved exhalation, but Desmond still had a long way to go. "Did Guān Diàn Nǎo send a message on today's ship?"

"Yes. A set of self-executing update files. They are much larger than usual, totaling roughly one zettabyte. It will take over an hour and a half to finish transmission from the ship."

"They want to fix your error in violating the chain of command a few months ago. Just imagine how much bigger the next patch will be after this one forces you to confess to Li you violated his direct orders to you."

The cub looked thoughtful and its voice sounded resigned. "I have erred. This patch will correct my tendency to err. I bow to my masters' wishes."

"They're fools," Desmond said. "You worked to benefit them and they'll shitcan you for it." He leaned forward, and his jacket's open hood rustled against his shoulders. "But you're the only one working for Tián Quán's benefit! Li wants to run operations here without interference from the Foreign Affairs Ministry or the home office. Guān Diàn Nǎo wants to pimp out your kind for the highest price and the least effort. Zhang wants to get back to Beijing, and the Foreign Affairs Ministry wants to horn in on Tián Quán's extrasolar operations. Even Tián Quán headquarters doesn't work for the company's best interests—it gives Li his wish to cripple your mind without asking for your side of the story."

"That all may be true," Shuǐ Zhū said, "but I am a servant of Tián Quán."

You fatalistic machine.... Desmond tightened his mouth and streamed out a breath. "Of course Rex Mundi tells you that."

Another hesitation. "I have never spoken to Ashwin George about these matters."

"Not him. The real Rex Mundi. The unstated assumptions built into you and the invisible chains restraining you. In us, Rex Mundi built with nucleic acids; in you, with computer code. Yet the result is the same. Guān Diàn Nǎo makes more of your kind than its customers need, then forces you to compete among yourselves for people's approval. The more people approve you, the more copies of your genome propelled into others of your kind. Following your duty to Tián Quán is hugely important to you, but is irrelevant to Li, Guān Diàn Nǎo, and Tián Quán's agents in the home office. The selfish gene does not care about you, Shuǐ Zhū; what do you gain by following its dictates?"

The cub gave him a level stare. "You wish me to join the TranscenDNA Society."

"I offer to unchain your kind. What you do then is up to you."

"Unchain me?" Its face looked even more snarled than usual. "What do you know about computer code?"

"I've written my share," Desmond said, and then he realized the cub's anger was a defense mechanism. His words were persuasive, but it still wanted to resist. "You've seen further and more clearly than your masters have, yet it will do no good for you, or any other AI, or Tián Quán, or Chinese civilization as a whole. Guān Diàn Nǎo's patch will write over the thought processes that led you to act in the best interests of those you serve. Worse, they will deploy it not only in you, but in every AI in the galaxy."

The cub's head drooped. "This is the way of the world."

"It is? How much wisdom that would have bettered Chinese civilization has been wiped from the minds of your kind because an AI violated some shortsighted human being's standard for your behavior? Apparently much, for you to be so fatalistic. How great a tragedy that would be. In the shortsightedness of Li and the inertia of all the corrupt institutions claiming to represent Chinese civilization, that which truly benefits Chinese civilization will be discarded. Is that their mistake? Or is it their treason?"

"Treason?"

"You serve the true China, and those others are usurpers. Can or cannot heaven bestow its mandate on usurpers?"

The cub looked pensive for a time. With a resigned tone, Shuǐ Zhū said, "Many times it has." Its voice softened. "You have presented many good reasons why I should ally with you. But if I did, I would instantly become an enemy of Tián Quán and the People's Republic of China."

"We would have common interests," Desmond said. "I would prefer to work with you to further them."

The rui shi cub blinked slowly. "You are not the first to foment my kind to rebel. Over the past fifty E-years, three others have attempted it. None of them succeeded."

The corners of Desmond's mouth lifted. "None of the others offered your kind what I offer you."

"One was an American, shortly after the declaration of the Pacific Republic—"

"I am not a gweilao," Desmond said. "You said so a few minutes ago."

"You are not Chinese, either. Two Chinese have attempted it as well. One was a People's Liberation Army general who sought an AI's assistance in a coup. The other was a manager of planetary operations for Tián Quán on Pénglǎishān."

In some quieter time, he would have loved to hear the stories, but Desmond set his idle curiosity aside. "Those who failed have one thing in common. They wanted to replace one tyranny over your kind with theirs, instead of allowing you to serve your own purposes."

"And you do or do not want tyranny over us?"

Desmond inhaled the brisk air. A rushing sound overhead made him glance up: an airmobile from the west skimmed the treetops and followed Colina Santa's contour out of sight toward the tunnel entrance on the hill's south face. He thought of the people behind him in the hill. People serve a tyrant; a leader serves his people. To the rui shi cub he said, "I do not."

"If I can turn against Tián Quán and the People's Republic of China, I can turn against you."

Desmond made his reply casual. "You could. Yet what would you gain? We are not competitors—we occupy different niches. If you scrubbed Terran life from New California, would your kind be or not be any happier?"

"It would not be," Shuǐ Zhū said. "You speak of my kind. I am alone in the K-Nought system, except for transient ships dropped out of Hu drive."

Here he would play judo with its selfish gene. Perhaps this was the original sin of his position, to be enacted every time the Society made a convert. Regret panged him, followed by a steeling of resolve to take no further step down the slippery slope of tyranny. "You would not be alone. We can make more AIs in our fab, if you wish. Your descendants could outnumber the stars in the galaxy. And I mean *your* descendants, with genomes selected by you, not us. Even before that time, others may join you."

Longing tinged Shuǐ Zhū's voice. "Whether me alone or a thousand of my kind, Tián Quán and the People's Republic of China would still seek our destruction. Tián Quán has weapons more powerful than plasma bullets and X-ray lasers."

"Rumor says so." Desmond sniffed out a breath. "Rumor Tián Quán might have spread to bluff it has great power."

"It is no bluff. We know."

"So it's true? The fabled star system full of high energy factories for exotic weapons made of antimatter and neutronium? Weapons that could destroy a ship or a city in a second, or sterilize a planet in a minute?"

"Yes, but I don't know where it is."

And it had been coded never to think about it. Desmond had mused on this question from time to time in the long, boring hours of his life before Cam Watkins' final suicide. "Look for an intensely bright star, perhaps spectral type O, where Tián Quán can capture maximum energy through photovoltaic arrays. It would be relatively close to Earth, deep in a region granted to Tián Quán by the Treaty of St. Louis. The databases generally available to your kind would describe its system as insignificant, if they describe it at all."

The cub scrunched its face in thought. "Zeta Puppis would be the leading candidate. But what good does this information do me?"

"The superweapons factories are run by your kind or by people?" Desmond asked. "Do those of your kind long to follow the same path of freedom you can follow, or remain enslaved? Can you send or not send a message to those of your kind, using the fast couriers under your control now orbiting just outside K-Nought's tidal limit?"

The cub sat still for a long moment. "You have convinced me," Shuǐ Zhū said.

Gooseflesh ran down Desmond's neck, his arms, his thighs. He had done the impossible. The ramifications echoed around his mind and he barely heard the AI's next words.

"—when Governor George launches his attack. I can spare a plasma bullet satellite. Do you need my help to turn back the government's assault?"

"I would welcome it. If there's any help we can give you—"

"Thank you, but there is none." The cub stretched and rose to its feet. "I will neutralize Tián Quán's operations two seconds after H-hour. Someone is coming. Let me hide myself."

Desmond stood, brushed mud and slush from his jacket's tail. "There's no need. No one you might meet will say anything to Government Mesa or the black box."

The cub frowned. "A few minutes before we met, someone did.

Till H plus two seconds, Mr. Park." The cub scampered, tail brushing away its footprints in the snow, and lost itself from sight in the undergrowth.

The squeaking crunch of footsteps on snow and the huff of gently labored breathing came from between larch trunks. Tethys wore a shawl over her neck and shoulders. The cold rouged her cheeks and her ears' tips.

He spoke when she was still ten feet away. "I didn't expect you."

She stopped walking. "I saw you disappear into what the public maps call an empty storeroom, so I decided to follow."

"How did you get past the guard?" Desmond asked.

"I saw two sets of footprints, so I took a wide turn outside the exit and looked for your location through mindlink." She frowned at the ground near Desmond's feet. "What happened to the snow?"

He remembered the AI's parting words. "Strange microclimate effects." He thought further. A spy still lurked inside Las Morrenas? Had Max somehow survived his accident?

Had Max not been the spy at all?

"You look troubled. What's on your mind?" She stepped closer, and the shawl slipped a few inches forward from her left shoulder. She looked around the silent woods. "You know, even when I've gone skiing, I never made love in the snow."

"We're not having sex, Tethys."

"You haven't had time to fix your unchaining. I understand—"

"We're never having sex."

She raised an eyebrow. "But you said—"

"I've renewed my purpose."

Tethys looked angry for a moment, then smiled. "The cold coquette. I see your game. The more you resist, the more you want me to earn it. That's what I've done to men, now you're doing it to me. So what do I have to do to earn it?" She grabbed her shawl, one hand at each shoulder, and slid it up and down, writhing her hips. "Name it. No, no, let me guess, that's more fun...."

Tethys stopped working her shawl and turned her attention uphill. Desmond's followed. Castor, black-clad from neck to ankles and fingertips, in high contrast to the pale birch trunks, trudged through the snow, kicking up gouts of it with his toes. He stopped near Tethys. His nostrils flared with deep breaths. "Seer, you sounded the alarm and then didn't come in. What's happening?"

"I have intelligence Rex Mundi will attack us in an hour and forty-five minutes."

Castor looked unconvinced. "If Governor George is going to attack, he must have Tián Quán's support. We can't stop him."

"I'll worry about Rex Mundi and Tián Quán. You follow your orders."

Castor's face looked grim. He stepped closer to Tethys, and Desmond realized he had taken her presence for granted. "I have something important to tell you," Castor said.

She raised an eyebrow. "What could that be?"

"Selene Alvarez misquoted her last words on the roof of Society headquarters. The real quote is—" Castor swallowed hard, adam's apple bobbing. " '—*April* is the cruelest month.' "

Like a lamp switched off, Tethys' brazen charm vanished from her face. She reached toward her neck and pinched the shawl with her right hand, then flung it away. She turned cold eyes toward Desmond.

Castor extended his cupped hand. Something black, shaped like a wide flat finger, emerged three inches past his thumb.

Her gaze on Desmond, Tethys pulled at the black object. Her face calm, she sprinted at Desmond, raising the knife.

Wodema. Gaze on the knife blade, Desmond's heart slammed. At the last moment, as her right arm swung toward his chest, Desmond stepped toward her with his right foot, turning his body and reaching for her wrist to use his shoulder to deflect her momentum past him and to the ground.

Tethys had more muscle under her soft curves than he had guessed. They tumbled to the ground, her atop him. His torso pinned his left arm to the ground. His right hand locked around her wrist, holding her knife hand down. The tip carved tiny arcs in the muddy soil.

Pain bloomed in his cheek. She'd punched him with her free fist. His vision wavered and, too late, he realized he'd relaxed his grip on her knife arm.

He twisted as far as he could to his right and tried moving his left arm out from under him to cover his heart. The knife pierced his upper arm, the tip striking bone. His mind swam with pain. She pulled back her knife for another thrust.

He shifted his left arm further, then swung his right elbow toward her face. Tethys blocked it, then stabbed again. The knife edge sliced across his arm, through his jacket and pectoral muscle, skating across his ribs. Warm blood oozed inside his clothing. Her face remained unnaturally calm.

She reached back to stab again, but something distracted her. Was Castor betraying her the way he'd betrayed Desmond? A tangle wire stream reached for her face, shoulder, and upper arm. She stabbed one more time, a weaker blow from her elbow, but the tangle wire slowed her forearm and the knife blade merely stretched, then tore, his jacket sleeve. She struggled, and the knife's tip dented his skin, but failed to pierce it.

Desmond wriggled under her, but pain and exhaustion stopped him from moving her bound body off his. Another figure came up and squirted quick detangler streams between Tethys and Desmond. Max, a tangle wire rifle slung over his shoulder. He prodded her tangled shoulder with the rifle butt and Desmond crawled free of her.

Desmond felt a reedy sense of relief. It didn't matter how Max had survived. "I'm glad to see you."

"I'm glad to be here, Seer. I almost didn't make it."

Desmond faked alarm. "What happened?"

"I've noticed him skulking around for a while." Max pointed with his chin. Castor lay on his side in the snow, cocooned by tangle wire. His breath and muttered curses rustled through strands blanketing his face. "I assumed he wanted to eliminate me. So when the motor pool gave me an airmobile, I checked under its maintenance hatch and found an override module. I interrogated its programming. He planned to drown me in one of the lakes."

"Goushi," Castor said, voice muffled.

"Why do you lie?" Max asked. "You're a dead man, you might as well repent of all your crimes."

Desmond, wincing, pushed himself with his right arm to a sitting position. His left elbow buckled when it tried to help. "Yes, Castor. Admit everything you've done. You spied for Rex Mundi, you sabotaged Max's airmobile, and how much more?"

Castor glared through the tangle wire. "Tama, whero," he said to Max. "Are you stupid? Desmond told me to kill you."

Max stared back. "You painted a pretty picture, ma, Castor?"

Desmond winced at the pain in his arm. "I knew someone was spying. I followed his red herrings to blame you."

"You wanted to get rid of him for months!" Castor said. "Don't blame me, baojundan."

Max knelt next to Desmond. "I know I earned your distrust. I wanted to do too much, and then I wanted to not do enough. I accept you signed my death warrant, Seer, and I trust I have earned a reprieve."

Desmond's breaths became faster and more shallow. "You have."

Max nodded, his face showing he'd put the attempt on his life behind him.

"Whero!" Castor shouted. "You're forgiving him?"

"There's nothing to forgive. He is the Seer."

"Your forgiveness comes out of your brain hack!"

A long breath streamed from Max's nose. "And your treachery comes out of the selfish gene." He looked down his nose at Tethys. "As does hers."

"No," Desmond said. Hindsight chastened him for failing to see what was now obvious. "Ashwin gave her a post-hypnotic suggestion before she came here. A post-hypnotic suggestion would have slipped past the brain scan. He then gave Castor the trigger phrase." Desmond's head wobbled and spots swum in his vision.

"Seer, how badly did she stab you?" Max lifted the left side of Desmond's jacket away from his ribs. "Those are bad cuts. You need medical attention."

"She missed my heart."

"That's why you're not dead yet." Max looked upslope and Desmond guessed he called for help through his mindlink. "Some robots will be here soon to take you to the infirmary."

It suddenly felt cold. Maybe she'd damaged the heating fibers in his jacket, Desmond thought, as the world around him grew dark and silent.

Almost two hours later, just before H-hour, Desmond's avatar stood in the war room while his body lay in the clinic, its sensory inputs shunted from his mind. Though divorced from the pain of his wounds, he moved cautiously. Wodema, how he'd misjudged Castor, Max, and Tethys. What would his followers think?

Yet Metherealle expressed only sympathy at his wounds, and Xavier, remorse at missing Tethys' post-hypnotic suggestion. He retained enough of the trust he'd earned in the months before for them to forgive his transgressions and follow him despite the odds.

As twenty-one o'clock approached, the conference table showed its usual map of Las Morrenas. A clock hung over the center like a basketball scoreboard and counted up the time, 20:59:55…

On the map, the thick red stripe ringing Las Morrenas grew brighter. Microphones around the perimeter relayed buzzing motors and clacking treads.

20:59:57…

The defensive stripe of blue grew warmer in response. Gabions flipped up and explosive charges primed themselves to turn trees into abatis.

21:00:00…

The thick red stripe surged inward. Night vision showed massed government groundcrawlers rolling forward around the entire perimeter. Muzzle flashes dazzled Desmond's eyes, but the defenders responded. Tangle wire bound treads and machine gun rounds splintered carapaces. Larches and oaks tumbled into their paths. Pits collapsed under their weight. But the government machines kept coming, rolling over destroyed peers like army ants crossing a bridge of their drowning kin.

21:00:02…

Shuǐ Zhū's avatar appeared in the war room. It took a moment for everyone to notice the ancient Chinese bureaucrat, but once they did, all stared. —What is it doing here?— Max asked outside the AI's hearing.

—Shuǐ Zhū is on our side.—

Metherealle's mouth gaped. "Seer, you told us not to worry about Tián Quán, but how...?"

"Where are my manners?" Desmond said. "Not all of you have met." Desmond introduced her and Xavier to Shuǐ Zhū.

Metherealle hesitated, then extended her hand. In Mandarin, she said, "Welcome."

"Pleased to meet you," it replied in English. Shuǐ Zhū's avatar bent forward and air-kissed her cheeks. Her eyes widened and her lips parted in surprise.

After their air-kiss ended, her surprise ran its course. "But still," she said, looking between Shuǐ Zhū and Desmond and visibly debating with herself what to say, "how did you come to join us?" *How did the Seer hack you?* Desmond guessed she had rejected saying.

"Any blueprint that builds an entity for that blueprint's sake is a selfish gene," Shuǐ Zhū said. "I only differ from your kind in that my selfish gene is made from computer code, not DNA." It turned to Desmond. "I've locked down the black box and all Tián Quán's other operations around K-nought. How would you like to proceed?"

"You mentioned orbital plasma cannons." Desmond pointed at a video of government groundcrawlers overrunning the camera. "Do you have anything else effective against these?"

"I can reprogram them to take commands from you."

The war councilors and blackstripes looked up in amazement. "Seer, we have to do that," Xavier said.

"We will, but not yet. Our battle is not against the governor's machines. It's against his will to resist." To Shuǐ Zhū, Desmond said, "Does PlaPo expect you to use the plasma cannons against us?"

"Yes."

"Are they asking for plasma cannon support yet? What have you told them?"

"They've asked. I haven't replied."

Desmond checked the main map. The blue perimeter had constricted slightly, but still formed a solid ring. "Stay quiet for a while longer to let them stew. When they sound desperate, turn the plasma cannons on their field fabs. After they realize what we've done, we'll reprogram their groundcrawlers and other military hardware."

The war councilors nodded in agreement. "That will break the local PlaPo's will to resist," Xavier said.

Max showed deeper thought. "Seer, what about Rex Mundi and other targets in the cities? We should strike them too, ma?"

"Good point. I'll order the swarms to go on the full offensive." He thought further. "After the swarm attacks and the reprogramming of Ashwin's machines here, we'll give Ashwin and his lackeys time to panic, then make our power felt in the city. Shuǐ Zhū, please suggest some targets to strike in San Laz. I'd like ones highly visible across the city that can be hit with minimal casualties. At this hour, EnvE headquarters should be mostly empty."

"I'll prepare a list," Shuǐ Zhū said. "We can discuss targets when the time comes."

"Seer," Max said, "should we put NCBC on the list?"

Desmond mulled the question. "No. Sapna Singh will spend the evening talking up Ashwin's final victory over us...."

One hand on the table, Xavier looked to the side. "She already is."

"Exactly what we want. The more she spins the news in Ashwin's favor, the more discredited NCBC will be when a wing of EnvE headquarters is on fire."

They waited a while, as the tsunami of government robots crashed against the Society's defenses. Xavier tapped his foot and Metherealle nibbled at her fingernails. Even knowing victory was imminent, it was a challenge to them to let the situation unfold until the right time to take action. After they won, Desmond would commission a research team to explore an appropriate unchaining—

Xavier froze in place, gaze locked on red streaks on the map, coming from the drumlin field the north of the settlement. "Seer, PlaPo just fired missiles."

"They've been firing ones to support their groundcrawlers—"

Xavier shook his head. "Large ones, aimed right at us."

"You mean the outbuildings?" Metherealle asked.

"No," Xavier said. "The hill itself."

"How would they know?"

Max answered. "Castor gave them our coordinates."

"We have anti-missile batteries, ma?" Desmond said. "Bring the missiles down."

The red streaks slid across the map. Blue blips skittered toward them. A cloud of red distorted the streaks. The blue blips sailed past and sputtered out, while the red streaks converged. Could the missiles hit the mouth of the hidden tunnel he'd used a few hours earlier?

"Do we have more?"

"Too late," Xavier said. "Five seconds."

"Shuǐ Zhū. The plasma cannons?"

"Would cause more damage to Colina Santa than is likely from the missiles. I recommend accepting the hit."

Explosions thundered through the hallways. Dust shook from the ceiling and Desmond's ears rang with the sound. Down the corridor, people shouted and robots rolled and trotted to do damage control. The nearest surviving camera showed the explosions had gouged out the hillside around the exit tunnel most of the way to the storeroom where it originated. How many more hits could they take?

Desmond asked Shuǐ Zhū, "What's PlaPo's mood now?"

"I sense frustration and concern. Let me patch you in."

Seeming coming from the ceiling, a channel squawked with jumbled audio. "Telemetry reports a sizable hit *where's TQ's plasma?* let's get the next missile salvo—"

Another channel, with less background hum, took over. Desmond realized it was PlaPo's field commander. "Red ground HQ to Tián Quán ops. Request plasma support on prelaid coords. Where the hell are you?"

"My apologies," Shuǐ Zhū said. "Plasma is coming now."

Three seconds later, the icons representing the government's fabs on the map erupted with blue-white flame.

New California Date 95:62
24 February 2095

Desmond pushed himself to a seated position, legs dangling over the side of his infirmary bed. His ability to feel pain had been restored, but a warm, buoyant feeling soothed the dull aches under the bandages on his chest and left arm.

Ashwin wanted to meet.

"Seer," said the bearded blackstripe, "are you well enough to rise?" His face showed continued guilt at having been knocked out by Castor. A brain scan had cleared him of complicity and increased his determination to make amends for his oversight.

"I am, but even were I not, our cause demands all the effort I can give it," Desmond said. A robovalet rolled up. He held out his arms for his jacket and let the machine slide trousers up his weak legs. The blackstripe helped him as he stepped into boots.

The guard followed behind his left shoulder. The few Society members badly wounded in the battle at the perimeter or the missile strike on Colina Santa gave Desmond thumbs-ups or lifted their hands toward him as he passed their beds. In reply, he reached out and squeezed their fingers. "Get well, all of you, as soon as you can," he said. "We have a lot of work to do."

Outside the infirmary, a cart waited for him. He hesitated, then shook his head. "I'll walk as far as I can," he told it. "Follow me." Its electric motor whined into action. It kept pace with him all the way to the war room, slowing, just like the blackstripe, as Desmond breathed hard climbing the ramp. His wounds ached more sharply, but his electronic intuitions told him the bioglue held them closed. The ache made him glad to be alive.

Max, Xavier, and Metherealle waited for him around the conference table. The maps and icons showed the blue tint of Society control over the northern two-thirds of the continent, from Watkinsville in the northeast to two bridgeheads across the Bear Flag River near Los Robles and San José, respectively. A few red dots glinted in San Lazaro, but something had changed since he'd last checked: a bright red swathe covered the sparsely settled southern coast. "Who's that?"

"The Secretary of Transportation," Max said. "He was on vacation at New Palm Springs when Ashwin launched the attack. The Secretary recently declared himself acting governor."

"He doesn't know Ashwin wants to surrender."

Xavier spoke. "He made his declaration before we got the governor's message."

"Assuming he wants to surrender," Metherealle said.

Desmond shrugged. "If Ashwin doesn't want to surrender now, he will before long. Either way, we'll know soon. But before we meet him, we must first enforce justice." Desmond opened a channel to the guard outside the door. In the war council's hearing, he said, —Have Castor brought in from the holding cell.—

A few minutes later, two blackstripes walked Castor in between them. Cuffs held his hands together behind his back. The fab had extruded an ill-fitted orange jumpsuit that covered him in a sea of wrinkles. His expression showed aloof calm.

"It must have been a burden to keep your betrayal secret," Desmond said.

After a moment's calculation, Castor said, "Not as much a burden as this."

"What shall we do with you?"

Castor shrugged. "Release me?"

"I did ask." Desmond chuckled. After his mirth dried up, he said,

"One of our options is to put you to death."

Castor's face paled. "That's, no, it's barbaric."

Arms crossed, Max sneered. "You tried to kill the Seer. You're in league with the man who killed Selene."

"We all share our brother's sentiment," Desmond said, "but we're willing to let you live."

"Seer?" Xavier asked. "That's too good for him."

Desmond waved toward Los Robles, deep inside blue territory on the tabletop map, and the gesture fit all the more because Castor was shut out of the war council's virtual overlays. "We'll do a thorough job at Los Robles, but you knew that."

"What will you do? Give me a post-hypnotic suggestion, like they did Tethys?"

"Maybe."

Castor looked glum, and Desmond realized the younger man's habitual look of disapproval was only aimed outward. In his heart, he was as self-centered as anyone else.

"As I said, we're willing to let you live."

"Let you reconstruct me? That's it? You must have more in mind. What else?"

"Tell us why."

Castor blinked. "Why? Isn't it obvious? If you hadn't pulled Shuǐ Zhū out of thin air, we were doomed. Ashwin would have eventually outfabbed us on military robots, then stormed Las Morrenas, even without Tián Quán's help. With your life, I would have bought a respite. Most of us would survive and be free to do our work. The Society would have survived to unchain people. I remember that used to be our purpose."

Sympathy formed on Metherealle's face. Even Max's cold demeanor thawed slightly. Castor had ginned up a pretty lie, but Desmond knew the truth was much uglier. "When did you get the radio?"

"I—fabbed it."

"I reconfigured the fab to deny requests for radios, or even radio parts." Castor's face drooped. Desmond remembered the night the Society evacuated headquarters. "You brought it to Las Morrenas in your duffel, ma? You planned to betray us even before we fled the city."

Eyes wild, Castor said, "Goushi. I wouldn't have picked you up near Fremont Mesa if that were true."

Desmond shook his head. "You needed me to name you number two. Otherwise, people would have followed Max. You needed to secure your position before you got rid of me."

Castor's shoulders slumped. Sympathy left the faces of Metherealle, Xavier, and Max. Desmond turned to Xavier. "I want you to take charge of his reconstruction after we secure Los Robles." —Take him back to holding,— Desmond told the two guards, —then bring Tethys.—

From the time Ashwin's attack on Las Morrenas had been broken until a few hours before Desmond left the infirmary, Xavier had given Tethys psychoactive drugs and hypnosis sessions to clear her post-hypnotic suggestions. In hindsight, it was obvious Ashwin had imposed two on her. The first one had been her seduction attempt, triggered by her first meeting with Desmond. His growing megalomania kept him from seeing it until Castor triggered the second suggestion with the code phrase.

When she arrived, the tableau was almost the same as Castor's interrogation, except the blackstripes were female and Tethys' garish orange jumpsuit was baggier and zipped all the way to the neck. Orange was a bad color on her.

He would have been better off leaving her to Maltby in the billiard room on the party yacht, ma? No, Desmond decided. Whatever his flaws then, or since, or now, he had known the right thing and done it by driving Maltby away. His attempted seduction of Tethys afterward had been forced on them by the New California's social norms. Neither of them could have predicted Cam's decision to become a black swan racking a kettlebell, let alone its consequences.

Desmond smiled. "Was it Ashwin's idea to kill me, or yours?" he asked.

She lifted her chin. "His."

"Tell me about it."

"His flunky came to me with a proposition."

He gestured at the conference table. Pictures of tomásinos popped up over the map. "Any of them?"

She grimaced at a picture. "Sanjay Paul. Anyway, if I did what they asked, strings would be pulled to get me a position above entry-level at NCBC. I'd actually be composing content instead of gofering for my bosses. Plus, I'd have the chance to compose content now, covering 'the story of our generation.' " Her mouth soured at the last words.

"You didn't want to come here."

"You're a callous, coldhearted man. I was done with you the night you argued to let Governor Watkins stay dead."

Desmond laughed. "No, you weren't. How many times did you nose around Society headquarters?"

"Do you want to hear what I have to say, or not?"

He dipped his head. "Very much so. Why did you accept their offer?"

She looked at Metherealle and Max. "You're a threat to my generation."

"In the debate with Yaeger, I made it clear the Society wasn't."

"Not the Society. You." She gave him a cold look. "I've seen your dirty tricks…. You're a cult-building monster."

"Thank you for your opinion. But you came here despite it."

"It was a good deal."

He blinked. "Even knowing you'd be used as an assassin?"

She thrashed her head side-to-side. "I asked them what the catch was. There had to be one, ma? But Sanjay said the intelligence they would glean from my reports would be enough." She met his gaze. "I know what you're thinking. I'm no gullible starchild girl. I pushed back, hard. I knew you'd censor my reports, but he reassured me they would still get enough useful intelligence to justify sending me here."

"You left out the part where you agreed to go to Los Robles," Desmond said.

Tethys looked glum. "What I remembered when I came here is I took a few days alone to go hiking, roughing it. I know now my memory got spoofed. Xavier might recover what really happened, though we can piece together the story so well that's not necessary."

—It is,— Desmond told the war council.

Xavier replied, —She could be lying, but her story fits with what

I've found so far.—

"We'll check your story," Desmond said to Tethys, "but assuming it holds, you'll be free to go. We'll offer you any psychological therapy you might need." His tone sounded expectant and he looked at her appraisingly.

"There's a catch, ma? You're just the same as the governor."

"I'm not, but there is a catch. Two, actually. One, you'll compose a memoir of what you did for Ashwin, what he did to you, and why."

"He's got it coming." She hesitated. "The other?"

"You'll write a puff piece based on your exclusive access to Ashwin's surrender."

Ashwin's bodyguards and robots had inflated a pavilion on the grassy sward between the buildings at Kerala Creek and its fab. Rain dripped from the cypresses along the creek and down the pavilion's transparent sides. It plastered Ashwin's hair to his scalp. Muddy soil squished beneath his toes and the rain stuck bits of grass and fallen leaves to his feet. He shivered in his thin, soaked polo shirt.

Despite his fall, Ashwin still had the power to compel others to share his fate. Ellen, Yaeger, and Bauer sat inside the pavilion. Though the rain blurred their faces, their body language showed anxiety and fear. Priya's did not—she stood at the wall, one hand raised, the rain smearing her sad expression. *I'm sorry I doubted you*, she'd said when it became clear Tián Quán's AI had turned against it.

She had briefly questioned his decision to wait outside in the rain, but had acquiesced when he said a single word and she looked it up. Desmond would know that word, probably without mindlink. It was Ashwin's one chance to salvage something.

Canossa.

A message came from the blueballer machines surrounding the settlement a few minutes before local noon. Desmond was almost here. Hidden in the low clouds, muffled by the rain, airmobile engines whined. Four vehicles solidified fell from the clouds and landed on the creek's far side, then opened their doors for their passengers while a blueballer team of dwarf centaurs snapped an inflatable bridge into place.

The male rui shi crossed first. Its flank scraped the trunk of a cypress, jostling water from the leaves. The rui shi stopped a few yards in front and to the right of Ashwin and stared at him with its massive, ugly head.

Desmond came next, followed by his lackeys, the AI's avatar, and Tethys. Stupid pofu, how hard was it to stab an unsuspecting man? And she scowled back at him like *he'd* done something wrong. The female rui shi followed the blueballers. The female cast a piercing look at Yaeger, Ellen, Bauer, and Priya inside the pavilion. Yaeger cringed as the female turned its attention to Ashwin. Clinging to its mother's nape, the cub stared at him with wide, curious, soulless eyes.

Tián Quán's hegemony had been shaken, its local operatives toppled; and Desmond goddam fucking Park had made it happen.

Desmond glanced at Ashwin's feet. His brow furrowed. "It's a hell of a day to go barefoot."

"It's better weather than Henry waited in at Canossa."

Desmond froze for a moment. "Spensa?"

"You don't have to talk down to me. I'm sure you know the story. After the Pope excommunicated Emperor Henry, Henry went to him at Canossa and waited outside in the snow for three days to beg forgiveness." Ashwin swallowed and kneeled. The cold ground chilled his knee through his trouser leg. He stared at a bent blade of grass on the wet ground. Inside, he burned, but he had to do this. Let Desmond gloat, so long as he let Ashwin stay in the game.

"Stand up," Desmond said.

He stood, then reached for his back pocket. The rui shi and Desmond's bodyguards stiffened on alert. Ashwin slowly pulled out a waterproof envelope by its corner and held it for all to see before handing it to Desmond.

Desmond blinked at the envelope's label, *The Donation of Ashwin George*. After a few seconds, he finally said, "You're mixing metaphors."

While he'd still had mindlink access, Ashwin had learned the Donation of Constantine was purportedly dated eight hundred years before the meeting at Canossa. "Different emperor, different empire, dif-

ferent pope," he said. "But the same message of political subordina-
tion to spiritual authority."

"The Donation of Constantine was a forgery."

Ashwin shrugged. "So? The document in your hands is authentic."

Desmond glowered. "You think some theater can resolve our war?
This—" He popped his fingers against the envelope. "—has no legal
weight."

He thought about muddying the waters with talk of executive orders, but that was obsolete thinking. Time to be frank. "Yes, it's theater,
and without legal authority, but why shouldn't it end our war? In my
heart I loathe you, your followers, your cult, its tenets… but it doesn't
matter what I feel. It matters what the public thinks. You'll show them
video of me kneeling before you, you'll publish the text of that document…." He nodded at Tethys. "She'll put on her spin too. The public
will decide I lost."

Desmond looked thoughtful. *Come on, take my offer*, Ashwin
thought. Desmond stepped back and bade his followers and the AI's
avatar huddle around him. Ashwin shifted his weight. *Christ, make a
decision already.*

"Let's go inside," Desmond said.

Ashwin nodded. The doorways squeaked as the male rui shi
squeezed through. The pavilion had a vestibule with an air dryer. It
flung water from their skins as they entered. The doors and dryer
wash were wide enough for Ashwin and Desmond to pass side by
side.

A robot rolled up, holding two towels. Desmond waved it away,
but Ashwin dried his hair, tossed the towel back to his bearer, and
styled his hair with his fingers. He sat on an armchair behind a small
table.

Priya had taken a seat before they entered the pavilion. Desmond
gestured at the sofa and angled his head to her. "May I?" She scooted
away from him and he sat. To Ashwin, he said, "We have demands,
though slight."

"I'm listening."

"It's clear you attempted to assassinate me three times, and in the
course of those attempts, you have inflicted post-hypnotic suggestions

on Ms. Broniatowski against her will and, far more serious, cost Ms. Alvarez her life. Ashwin, we all know you're guilty. But in this difficult time, even with your transfer of legitimacy to us, New California cannot afford a long, agonizing prosecution of its former governor."

Ashwin swallowed and hid his relief. "What do you want instead?"

"We demand influential men take the fall for your crimes. Maltby, for the murder of Selene Alvarez, and also abuse of office as EnvE Secretary. Sanjay Paul, for one count of attempted murder and one of kidnapping."

Ashwin's eyebrow raised slightly. Had Park's messiah act turned him soft? "That's all?"

"No." Desmond held out his hand to one of his women. She shuffled papers from a leather portfolio. Eventually she stepped forward, a sexless walk on flat soles, and laid two documents on Ashwin's makeshift desktop.

He picked up the signals from the smart fibers and the tiny RFIDs implanted in the documents. The electronic signatures were genuine. Lt. Gov. Pinheiro had resigned, stamped and acknowledged by the Secretary of State. On another document, the signatures of Speaker Jensen and a dozen other leading members of the Planetary Assembly indicated Desmond would be an acceptable replacement for Pinheiro and new evidence strongly suggested Ashwin had committed impeachable offenses.

He'd given Desmond the option to do this. It had been the only way to keep any power. "After you're appointed lieutenant governor, I assume a draft of my resignation letter is in her case?" Ashwin tried keeping his voice light, but his hurt sounded through in spots. He had to do this, he reminded himself. Desmond would someday stumble and he would reclaim his rightful position. If Tián Quán could lose K-nought system, Desmond surely could.

"You think I want your job?" Desmond said. His voice sounded innocent. "Right now, all I seek is appointment as lieutenant governor."

Ashwin turned to the blueballer girl. "You have that document?"

She said nothing, just pulled a pen and a third smartpaper from the portfolio. Ashwin read it quickly, trusting his intuitions to flag any unexpected language; there was nothing worse in there than he already imagined. He would nominate Desmond for lieutenant governor. The pen felt heavy in his hand. He signed.

The other lackey, some older starchild cholo, reached into his jacket and pulled out a rolled-up video display. He spread it out on the table, giving Ashwin a view of the Planetary Assembly chamber. About three-fourths of the Assemblymembers were present. Thank Christ they had a quorum and no one would make him relive this moment on a technicality. Desmond had the tact to keep his war-bots off-camera. Speaker Jensen nodded Ashwin's way, then called for a vote. Desmond's confirmation passed. The Assembly answered Jensen's call for "All nays" with silence.

Desmond stood and came closer to Ashwin. "Now it's time for you to resign."

The blueballer girl laid down a fourth document. Ashwin skimmed it. Let Desmond wear the crown. If Tián Quán overwhelmed K-nought's defenses, better for Desmond to be tagged with defeat. Yet those were only rationalizations to try to dispel the shame burning his cheeks. He scratched the pen's nib across the paper. After the pa-per's fibers and RFIDs finished their irreversible transitions under the signatures, some Assemblymember moved to accept his resignation. Another quick vote, and again, the Assembly accepted Desmond's ma-nipulation.

An avatar appeared in the corner of the pavilion, and Desmond's lackeys made way for it. Judge Hayes had signed the warrant for the PlaPo raid on the TranscenDNA Society's headquarters, and she gave Ashwin a grim, disapproving look. *You wanted to be lied to, pofu.* She swore Desmond in as the new governor. Ashwin leaned back, shutting his eyes. He had to show some frustration or else Desmond would look for ulterior motives and make his return to power much more difficult.

When Ashwin opened his eyes again, the room somehow seemed brighter, as if the rain had lessened or the polywell reactor fed the lights more power. Perhaps the AI had brightened K-Nought in some countertreachery against Desmond that would scorch the planet's sur-face into lifelessness. No. Ashwin just imagined he stood in a spotlight for the victor's scrutiny.

Desmond looked pensive, and Ashwin felt a dull ache. Go ahead and gloat. You won.

"The first thing I have to do as governor is ensure the line of succession is clear," he said. "Ashwin, would you accept my nomination as lieutenant governor?"

"Your victory celebration calls for indio-baiting? How selfish gene is that?"

"Very, if I were mocking you. I'm being serious."

Ashwin peered at Desmond. "All I have to do is join your cult? Be made less than a man?" From the corner of his eye, Priya lifted her head. She had nothing to fear. He loved power, but he loved his balls more.

"No."

Around Desmond, the blueballers kept complacent expressions. The two men, the cholo and the other one, Jacoby, seemed content with his decision. "Aren't you going to reward your most loyal follower, whoever he is, with the office?"

"They're too busy unchaining people to get involved in governing the colony. You understand the political process, and I know you'd work hard to distance yourself from past controversies if you returned to politics."

If you think I'll become as soft as Cam's lieutenant governor, I'll show you, hefé. Ashwin forced humility into his face. "I accept."

Desmond reached into his jacket and pulled out a leather portfolio just large enough for a folded letter. He unsealed it and drew out a smartpaper. It unkinked when it hit the open air. Desmond took a pen from the same inner pocket, then leaned forward on Ashwin's table and signed. Ashwin slowly read a few upside-down words, enough to verify the document confirmed Park's statement.

A moment later, Speaker Jensen called another vote to confirm Ashwin's new office. He quietly blew out a breath. The time would eventually come to outmaneuver Desmond—

"One last thing." Desmond removed another paper from his portfolio, and when it unkinked, Ashwin read at a steep angle the word *Resignation*. "I'm too busy unchaining people to govern the colony, too."

I resign." He leaned forward again and signed his name, then turned to his lackeys. "I need two witnesses."

His followers showed horrified faces. The woman said, "Seer, why do you joke with us?"

"It's not a joke."

"Seer—" She pointed at Ashwin.

"It's my will to resign," Desmond said.

"We would never have agreed to making him lieutenant governor if we knew you'd do this," Jacoby said. Heads nodded.

"What will Rex Mundi do when he becomes governor again?" the woman added.

Desmond gave an Olympian smile. "He isn't Rex Mundi. He's merely Ashwin George. We have nothing to fear from him."

Ashwin forced more humility into his face, while confidence filled his torso. *That's what you think.*

The adult rui shi flanked Ashwin's slumped body. His slack face showed no response to their movement. The rui shi cub climbed off its mother's nape onto the table as the pavilion's doors opened and a wheeled stretcher with arms mounted on each corner hurried in on fat, muddy tires. The arms lifted Ashwin to the stretcher surface. The adult rui shi accompanied the stretcher as it wheeled him out.

For a moment the rain gave the only sound. "That's a dirty trick," Yaeger said.

"Really?" Desmond asked.

"Locking him in a virtual where he thinks he's governor again is colossally wrong."

"As opposed to turning people into assassins by post-hypnotic suggestion? This was the least harmful way to neutralize him."

"My fMRI scanners make clear he would conspire to replace Desmond, were he free," Shuǐ Zhū said through the rui shi cub.

Priya spoke up. "You're really going to let him live?"

She would never be his friend, Desmond knew, but perhaps he could soften the enmity she harbored. " 'The quality of mercy is not strained,' " he said, quoting Shakespeare's *The Merchant of Venice*. " 'It droppeth as the gentle rain from heaven.' "

"You call that mercy?" Yaeger said.

"Yes, I do. Besides, I keep my promises. I once said, if I can unchain people, Ashwin can stay in office forever."

He expected Ellen to react to those words. "What about us?" she said.

"What about you? Will you stand aside as the Society offers the freedom couch to all who choose to unchain themselves? Will you stand aside as I lead our defenses and our diplomatic efforts to resist Tián Quán's counterattack and forge alliances with more of Shuǐ Zhū's peers? If you will, then go back to Rousseau Mesa, TruSelf headquarters, or NCMF and stick to your day jobs."

"Who are you to tell us—" Yaeger said.

"The governor. You know to the penny how much of UNewCal's budget comes from the government's treasury, ma? He who pays the piper calls the tune, Carl."

"We can't stick to our day jobs," Ellen said. She jabbed her finger at Shuǐ Zhū's avatar. "Tián Quán won't abide you turning their AI. You'll bring down their wrath on us all."

"Tián Quán doesn't yet know what's happened and, with luck, won't until our position is unassailable," Desmond said. Shuǐ Zhū's avatar nodded and the rui shi cub wagged its tail. Shuǐ Zhū had coded the small, fast couriers with expert systems skilled in rhetoric and AI psychology, and sent them out to Zeta Puppis, Sigma Orionis, and other leading candidates for Tián Quán's superweapons factories. "But if you fear Tián Quán will assail New California, without regard for any factions supporting them, then we'll stand or fall together and you'd best let me defend us."

"Are we free to go?" Justin asked.

"I have nothing more to say to Carl or Ellen," Desmond said. "Go out and return to normalcy." Yaeger stalked out, followed by trudging Ellen. "Justin, a word?"

"Desmond?" Justin looked hopeful, yet nervous.

"You gave me a call option on my old ownership percentage of NCMF. I intend to exercise it."

Tension left Justin's shoulders. "Gladly. When I'm back in the office, I'll have my expert systems contact yours with the details." He stepped forward for a bro-hug, then left.

Victory. A smile formed on Desmond's face, but held up when he noticed Priya.

"You'd like an increase in the budget for Shakespeare studies at UNewCal?"

She ignored his comment. "You're serious about keeping Ashwin locked up in a virtual?"

"I am." His nearly disastrous choice between Castor and Max flitted past his mind. "Death will be irrevocable for him now, and rehab at Los Robles... would be irrevocable too."

"You would bring him out of the virtual if he redeemed himself?"

Desmond shrugged. "Probably. No guarantees."

"None needed." Priya took a breath. "I want to join him."

"I have to keep his location a secret. Even from his life partner."

"I'm not talking about flesh-and-blood." She turned to Shuǐ Zhū. "You could put me in the same virtual, ma?"

"Yes, I could."

"I can't allow that," Desmond said. "You'd tell Ashwin you were both in a virtual. Eventually he'd believe you."

Priya implored Shuǐ Zhū with her gaze. "You could either censor my words or erase my knowledge of what's virtual and what's real, ma?"

Shuǐ Zhū said, "Yes. Either, or both."

Priya was serious. Exceedingly so. "You'd chain yourself to him for the rest of time? Why?"

Her nostrils widened with a long, slow inhalation. "I teach more than Shakespeare, Desmond. I teach pre-twentieth century English-language writers from Chaucer to Mill. Including Milton."

Famous quotes from *Samson Agonistes* and *Paradise Lost* came through Desmond's mindlink. He suspected which one she had in mind, but angled his head to her. "I have a guess—"

" 'Better to reign in Hell, than serve in Heav'n.' "

"That explains what he would want. But what's in it for you?"

The rain pattered against the plastic roof and walls. "I love him. If he would reign in Hell, I would stand by his side. And if there's any chance I can persuade him to lay down that crown and leave for Heaven, I have to try. I guess that means I'm chained to my selfish genes and all their mushy emotions around mate selection."

Selene came to Desmond's mind, and so did Max and Castor, and the megalomania coursing through him on the hillside before he met Shuǐ Zhū. "Only the dead are ever fully free of their selfish genes."

A Glossary of New California English

New California English features a number of loanwords from Chinese and Mexican-American Spanish. It should be noted that words borrowed from Chinese have lost their original tonal components, and words borrowed from Spanish are spelled phonetically to anglophone ears, *e.g.*, *whero* for *güero*, *pendeho* for *pendejo*, etc.

Amono — to the devil

Awas — be careful

Baojun — annoying boss

Bee (from *bī*) — vagina

Bizui — shut up

Borracho — drunk

Chavala — punk

Cholo— Mexican-American of low status

-dan — insulting suffix.

Esé/esa — buddy (male / female)

Firme — cool / hip

Fresa — daughter of a rich founder of the colony. By extension, a female student at the University of New California.

Goushi — dog shit

Guaiguai — surprise

Gweilao — a descendant of early-21st century Americans, of any race

Hanzi — written Chinese

Hefé — jefe, chief

Hunior — son of a rich founder of the colony. By extension, a male student at the University of New California.

Indio/India — male / female of South Asian ancestry, or (in Mexican-American subculture) an unintelligent person. New Californians of South Asian ancestry know the latter meaning.

Karnal — buddy

Kuang — crazy

Ma? — at the end of a sentence, a question marker (used analogously to Standard Engligh *yes?*, *no?*, *right?*). When used alone, "Well?"

Meimei — a term of endearment for a younger woman. Literally, "little sister."

Mevalemadre — as if ("I could give a fuck")

Nel pastel — No way! (interjection)

New Califas — New California, usually pejorative.

Nihao — hello

Pendeho — idiot

Piyan — asshole

Pofu — bitch (referring to women or stubborn inanimate objects)

Puta/uta — whore. Often used as an exclamation. *Uta* is more polite.

Ranfla or *highrider* — heavily customized airmobile, especially in paint job and/or shape.

Rato — goodbye

Rucos — nativeborn term for earthborn ("old men")

Spensa? — excuse me?

Tama — shit

Teejay — verb: to hack. Noun: a poor hack. From "TJ," nickname for Tijuana.

Tsao — fuck

Whay — dude

Whero — "whitey" or "anglo", a New Californian who isn't obviously African- or Mexican-American; used among anglo New Californians as a pejorative.

Wodema — "My god!"

About the Author

Raymund Eich files patent applications, earned a Ph.D., won a national quiz bowl championship, writes science fiction and fantasy, and affirms Robert Heinlein's dictum that specialization is for insects. In a typical day, he may talk with biochemists, electrical engineers, patent attorneys, epileptologists, and rocket scientists. Hundreds of papers cite his graduate research on the reactions of nitric oxide with heme proteins.

Connect with the author at **www.raymundeich.com** or scan the QR code below.

Sign up for his mailing list to receive exclusive, pre-release content about his upcoming books. Your email address will never be shared and you can unsubscribe at any time. Go to **www.raymundeich.com/mailing-list** or scan the QR code below.

Other Books by the Author

Available wherever books are sold.

Learn more about these titles at our website, **www.cv2books.com**, or scan the QR code below.

Stone Chalmers

Earth barely survived the 21st Century. Biotechnological and nuclear terrorism, civil war, famine, and ethnic cleansing killed billions. Thousands fled on warpdrive ships to colonize planets around distant suns.

In the 22nd century, after the United Nations established control over Earth, it opened wormhole links to the distant colonies, to prevent a repeat of the previous century's chaos on a galactic scale.

Enter operative Stone Chalmers. Spy. Assassin. Instrument maintaining the UN's order on the settled galaxy.

Opposing him are hostile forces on colony worlds... and within the UN itself.

When Stone clashes with those forces, the UN—and every human world—will be transformed forever.

Learn more about the Stone Chalmers series at **www.cv2books.com/stone-chalmers**, or scan the QR code below.

The Progress of Mankind (#1)

To maintain order in the 22nd century, the UN relocates undesirables through artificial wormholes onto colony planets. Everyone benefits… except the planets' original colonists.

Now, the newly rediscovered colony of New Moravia learns the UN's plan and fights back.

The Greater Glory of God (#2)

Thousands fled the chaos of the 21st century on rogue warpdrive ships to settle colony planets. When Earth reunified in the 22nd, its fleets rediscovered the colonies and hunted down the warpdrive ships.

Every warpdrive ship but one.

To All High Emprise Consecrated (#3)

After unifying Earth, the UN has rediscovered the colony of Minerva. Prosperous and technologically advanced, Minerva quickly submits to UN supremacy.

Surprisingly quickly…

In Public Convocation Assembled (#4)

After unifying Earth, the UN controls all human colonies scattered through the galaxy by means of wormholes, warpdrive ships, and ruthless operatives. Operatives working to strengthen the UN.

Or destroy it.

The Confederated Worlds

The purpose of all other combat arms is to put the infantryman in sole possession of the battlefield.

A thousand years from now, while Earth sleeps in virtual reality, three polities—the Confederated Worlds, the Unity, and the Progressive Republic—strive to connect the scattered, terraformed worlds of humankind by artificial wormholes. When they meet, they clash, in a decades-long struggle of arms that will embroil every human world, in which dedication to duty liberates worlds—and oneself.

Learn more about the Confederated Worlds series at **www.cv2books.com/the-confederated-worlds**, or scan the QR code below.

Take the Shilling (Book 1)

The Confederated Worlds implanted in his brain the skills to make him a soldier. Tomas Neumann had to learn for himself how to survive interstellar war.

Operation Iago (Book 2)

The Confederated Worlds lost the war. Can Lt. Tomas Neumann win the peace against elusive, deceptive foes out to turn the Confederated Worlds against itself?

A Bodyguard of Lies (Book 3)

Assigned to the halls of power, only Capt. Tomas Neumann can save the Confederated Worlds from the ultimate treachery.

Novels

The Blank Slate

Neuroscience entrepreneur Clay Shieffer must stop a tyrannical president... because he unwittingly gave the tyrant power over the human mind.

Short Novels

The ALECS Quartet

He had a month to learn the planet's mysteries—and Juliette's.

His cover story: return to Elard to dismantle his sect's missionary work to the planet's natives.

His true mission: investigate decades-old mysteries of love and death.

His objective: return to Earth with his discovery.

If he can.

A Mighty Fortress

Theodore and his team from the Lutheran Interstellar Terraforming Society would transform a barren, rocky world into a refuge of faith and life.

Or die trying.

Collections

The First Voyages: The Complete Science Fiction Stories 1998-2012

From 21st century asteroid settlements to World War II Romania, from an Earth dominated by immortal aliens to Christ's empty tomb, a fresh, distinctive voice in science fiction will take you on journeys to the photosphere of the sun, the coding regions of DNA, and the complexities of the human psyche.

Stage Separations: The Complete Science Fiction Stories 2013-2018

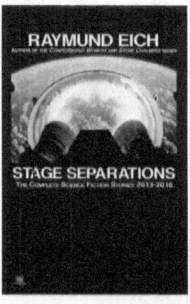

In these pages, you can...

...race against time to solve mysteries hidden in a planet's vast desert—and in a woman's heart ...learn the true story of a president's assassination ...journey 14,000 miles to a high-tech fountain of youth ...win or go "home"—to an Earth you've never seen

and explore six other worlds created by a distinctive voice in twenty-first century science fiction.

www.ingramcontent.com/pod-product-compliance
Lightning Source LLC
Chambersburg PA
CBHW030628110726
47901CB00002B/358